A tough Soviet Black Beret commits the most outrageous act of terrorism the world has ever seen.

Two American SEALs plunge into someone else's war in order to save their country.

An American admiral rises from his wheel-chair to lead a fleet.

The Caribbean and Central America are about to explode.

CHOKE POINT

"Taylor writes with a thorough knowledge of sea power!"

—*Seattle Times*

Charles D. Taylor

CHOKE POINT

JOVE BOOKS, NEW YORK

This book is dedicated to two people who have been long on
encouragement for more than forty years—my aunt, Margaret
Lewis, and my uncle, Don Hunter.

CHOKE POINT

A Jove Book / published by arrangement with
the author

PRINTING HISTORY
Charter edition / February 1986
Jove edition / March 1988

ISBN: 0-515-09866-3

Jove Books are published by The Berkley Publishing Group,
200 Madison Avenue, New York, New York 10016.
The name "JOVE" and the "J" logo
are trademarks belonging to Jove Publications, Inc.
PRINTED IN THE UNITED STATES OF AMERICA

10   9   8   7   6   5   4   3   2   1

ACKNOWLEDGMENTS

While plots and characters emerge from the imagination, ships and weapons systems, geography, history, and politics are acquired by research. There were two extremely valuable sources in learning more about the setting for this book: *The Path Between the Seas—The Creation of the Panama Canal 1870–1914* by David McCullough (Simon and Schuster 1977), and *Inevitable Revolutions—The United States in Central America* by Walter LaFeber (Norton, 1983). The United States Naval Institute remains my most valuable source for technical details. The expert panel at their 1985 annual meeting offered valuable insight into U.S. strategic interests. The articles, professional notes, and supplementary materials from their monthly *Proceedings* provide thorough and rapid access to naval subjects around the world. Two of their recent reference books by Norman Polmar, *The Ships and Aircraft of the U.S. Fleet* (thirteenth ed.) and *Guide to the Soviet Navy* (third ed.), have proven invaluable. *Armed Forces Journal International* provides up-to-date information on a variety of military topics.

Shipmates manage to stick together over the years and two of them have been especially helpful—Bill McDonald, a former commanding officer, remains a fine friend, and Dan Mundy can pack more solid criticism into a lunch without forgetting the latest joke. On the business side, Dominick Abel continues to provide a steadying influence, and Mel Parker's detailed suggestions are incomparable. Gordon Levine offered an excellent detailed technical review. Alice Loomis understands my concept of a simple map to visualize where the action is taking place for the reader, and Candy Bergquist continues to type each of my manuscripts to meet my erratic schedules.

No book can be written without the support of a family, and mine deserves an award for endurance. My wife, Georgie, keeps smiling and remains under the same roof with me, even though that involves giving up a great deal. My sons, Jack and Ben, display remarkable understanding. I know of no other way to let as many people as possible know about the three of them as through these words.

"Deterrence is the set of beliefs in the minds of the Soviet Leaders, given their own values and attitudes, about our capabilities and our will. It requires us to determine, as best we can, what would deter them from considering aggression, even in a crisis—not to determine what would deter us."

—Scowcroft Commission

"If history is any teacher . . . it teaches that when you become indifferent and lose the will to fight, some other son-of-a-bitch who has the will to fight will take you over."

—Col. Arthur D. "Bull" Simons,
United States Army

Havana, Cuba
Naval Headquarters

Victor Khasan brushed at a languid fly, taking his eyes off Commodore Navarro's face for only a moment. The Cuban's immediate reaction had been just what he'd predicted it would be—that of a tired man. Navarro listened to what others said, sorting out what he wanted to retain, cataloging it in his orderly mind. But he no longer offered any expression of approval or disapproval. It wasn't so much that he was controlling his emotions any better. Quite simply, he was tired. The intervening time since 1960 evolved gradually from years of challenge and excitement to years of hard work in creating modern Cuban society. Though tired, he still had never lost sight of his premier's ultimate goal—to bring the United States to her knees.

"Of course," Khasan continued, "American intelligence will be fully aware of the approximate date your combat brigade will return from Africa. It's just that there will be no indication of where we will land them. Here . . . Guyana . . ." He shrugged, then smiled. "Maybe even Key West . . ."

Navarro looked back at him evenly, holding the Russian admiral's stare. He neither acknowledged the statement about American intelligence nor offered his own opinion about the returning troops. It really wasn't his decision. He opened his humidor, selected a cigar, then slid the box across to Khasan.

The Russian loved them almost as much as Navarro. The Commodore produced a long wooden match, lighting it before offering the box to Khasan. Both men remained silent as they held the cigars above the flames, twisting them slowly for an even burn.

Navarro stuck the cigar in his mouth, sucking deeply to insure it was properly lit. Then he puffed slowly for a moment, enjoying the aroma. A smile spread over his face as he studied the Russian. "This thrust is something I have been looking forward to for more than twenty-five years," he said to the other man. "We Latins are impatient . . . passionate . . . . It hasn't been easy to wait." He rolled the cigar between his lips, watching the smoke rise to the ceiling. "You are sure," he queried in a higher voice, "that the Americans will not be able to reinforce so quickly . . . that your submarines can hold their own until the surface forces are ready? You know as well as I do that they have all your submarines well tracked. You can't surprise them. . . ."

"The object is not surprise," the Russian said. "Secrecy isn't necessarily the greatest power of a submarine. Just knowing that they are present is enough to make the most aggressive commander take heed. That," he emphasized, poking the air with an index finger, "is the implied threat." Khasan studied Navarro's features closely, as he had done so many times. It seemed that the Russian had been an advisor in Cuba forever. The two men had known each other for years, been as close to being friends as the Commodore would allow any outsider to be.

It occurred to Khasan that there was more gray in the Cuban's always neatly trimmed hair. And the hairline was definitely receding faster now, no doubt about that. The face seemed puffy, perhaps indicative of declining health, and the circles under the tired eyes were darker. Each telltale indication of approaching age reinforced the decision in Moscow to proceed now, to bait the American eagle in its own backyard. This Cuban, the commander of their little navy, was tired, anxious, and fanatic to a fault to challenge the Americans, just like his leader. Castro, Khasan knew, wanted to be the linchpin, the pebble that started the avalanche, the single most important factor in humiliating the Americans, forcing them back within the borders of their own country. And Moscow knew that now was the time to take advantage of Castro, and of Navarro, to utilize these men they had been so patient in grooming for more than twenty-five years . . . now that they were tired and seemed increasingly worried that the Russians might not support them in this final effort.

The Commodore stroked his chin thoughtfully. Frankly, he had no concern about the problems he often voiced to Khasan—and none whatsoever about the Americans. He had long ago discarded any worries he might have had about American reactions. In his opinion, the Cubans had the Soviets in their back pocket, and as long as they were committed to this venture into the Caribbean, he regarded the Americans with disdain. Although Khasan had often reminded him of the Soviet Premier's statement—"Cuba is our aircraft carrier in the Caribbean"—eventually, Navarro realized, Cuba would be more than that, much, much more . . . and so would he.

Navarro looked back to Khasan. "Victor, I'm tired. You may not believe it, but I truly am."

Now, there was no expression on the Russian's face, no acknowledgment of what he knew to be true.

"I have waited for so long. The years have taken their toll." He sighed almost to himself, puffing contentedly on his cigar. "Would you be surprised if I told you I would like to step down after it is all over? Or that Fidel has said the same thing?"

The Russian nodded slowly, almost as if he were agreeing with his friend about a change in the weather.

"I'd like to spend more free time . . . watching baseball games," Navarro added wistfully. "Maybe after we're finished, Fidel will insist the Americans establish a baseball team in Havana. . . ."

25,000 Feet Above the Caribbean

Bernie Ryng drifted in that pleasant state between sleep and consciousness. It had been induced by a hand on his shoulder —soft, persistent, perfume heightening the sensation—and a lightly accented voice calling his name. Smiling inwardly, he was convinced that in the recesses of his mind it was the lovely girl across the aisle, the one who had only nodded at his efforts in conversation, offering an occasional yes or no until he had drifted off to a restless sleep over the hum of the jet engines.

"Mr. Ryng . . . Mr. Ryng . . ." The hand was shaking him more persistently now. The voice, no longer as soft, became insistent. "Mr. Ryng, we're thirty minutes out of Panama."

Ryng gazed up at the stewardess leaning over him and smiled automatically. She was cute, but she wasn't smiling— just doing her job. "Thank you. Hope I didn't cause you too much trouble." He sat up, stretching his arms in front of him.

"No trouble, sir." She smiled pertly, then turned to the woman across the aisle, speaking to her in rapid Spanish. Ryng had been slightly jealous that the stewardess was friendlier with the other passenger. Then he'd overheard them talking about her taking this flight often.

Ryng smiled across the aisle, nodding at the woman as he ran a hand through his hair. Her features were classic—high

cheekbones, deep, brown eyes, glossy, long black hair. Regal
Spanish, he thought to himself, noting her long neck and
graceful hands. Quite a bit younger than me, he decided—
probably not more than thirty. But it was tough to tell with
women like her. Back in his twenties, more years ago than he
cared to remember, they used to call the aura that eminated
from women like her "class." It was the only way to define
that certain something, a combination of clothes, jewelry, hair
style, the way she held herself . . . the way she'd sipped her
drink earlier in the flight.

Ryng was still an attractive man. Only his thinning hair gave
any indication that he was in his mid-forties. When he was a
kid, it turned white every summer, bleached by the sun. One
year, he'd forgotten which year, it never turned back to its
original sandy hue, so he kept it short. He was average in
height, but his rugged body and ruddy complexion made up
for his hair color, and his expressionless blue eyes belied any
definite age.

He slid over to the window seat to gaze down on the Caribbean. Just beneath the wing he thought he could see land interrupting the smooth blue of the water below. The thought of
what awaited him wasn't appealing. He'd much rather the
flight continued on, past Panama, over the equator . . . maybe
on down to Rio. Glancing across the aisle again, he thought
perhaps that would give him enough time to crack that shell
she'd created. She'd talk with him, he reasoned, if the flight
continued, if cocktails and dinner were next . . . just to pass
the time before they reached Rio.

But they weren't going to Rio. They were landing in
Panama and he would go to work the minute his feet hit the
ground. On the horizon the mountain clouds were puffy,
becoming thicker inland. Ryng had asked to be awakened
specifically to see the isthmus from the air as the plane swept
in. He wondered, as they approached, whether he might see
out of the numerous little skirmishes that occurred every day
in those mountains. But he knew that they would never give a
passenger flight clearance near anything that might hazard it.
It was wise to avoid those black-uniformed revolutionaries,
the PRA—People's Revolutionary Army.

The flight from Miami was, in fact, almost a straight shot

south, except for the diversion around Cuba. Panama was just a bit east of Miami and only twelve hundred miles away, a short distance to be sent for such a bitter war . . . and just about on our doorstep, Ryng thought.

The northern coast of Panama came up quickly, almost too fast to pick out the landmarks his boss, Admiral Pratt, had shown him in Pratt's office. But once he picked out Gatun Lake, he could identify everything else. He couldn't see the north coastal city of Colón or the Gatun Locks. They were on the other side of the plane. But he saw where the lake narrowed down into the canal proper, then the raw, brown sides of the Gaillard Cut sloping down to the narrow waterway. As the plane banked first to the west, then back east, he could pick out the Pedro Miguel Locks, then follow the canal down, past the Miraflores Locks to the capital city itself, gracefully overlooking the Bahia de Panama.

The city came up at them white and shiny, sparkling wet in the sun, following an afternoon shower. He could see puddles on the runway, then the fine mists as the wheels raced through the water.

Ryng looked across the aisle and smiled. "Welcome to Panama," he said, this time using his Spanish.

"Thank you most kindly," she returned, finally smiling back in a pleasant manner. She stretched her arms casually, inspecting her fingernails absentmindedly as she touched the seat in front of her. Then she arched her chest forward, pulling her shoulders back like a cat, and smiled again, white teeth flashing. "You should have used Spanish before," she grinned. "I was tired of English after a week in Washington." She was slim, Ryng noted, but well-shaped too.

"I apologize, señorita," he said, noticing again that she wore no wedding ring. "Spanish is a difficult language for me when it's been so many years." He sighed to himself, realizing it was now too late to establish anything in the short taxi to the gate.

But he never had the opportunity to continue the conversation, for something caught his eye as the craft pivoted to bring a view of the terminal to his side of the plane.

The broad glass windows in the building were bulging out toward him, as was one supporting wall. That first impression lasted only a millisecond as the explosion hurled the side of the terminal toward the plane. The motorized gateway that had been inching out toward the approaching craft had been blown from the building, and as it began to pitch sideways and topple, Ryng saw a man leap outward. At the same time, even before gravity took over, the man appeared to rise up higher. But the jerking of the body also meant that another force was affecting it—bullets. Dropping his eyes, Ryng saw someone below in that familiar black uniform he'd noted in Pratt's photos, an automatic rifle shuddering in his grasp as he finished off the running man.

With the horror outside firmly recorded on his mind, Ryng could now recognize the ear-splitting chatter of the Soviet AK-74s overwhelming that of the jet engines. Other sights registered as split images. Ricocheting bullets were tracing a pattern up the whitewashed wall toward the control tower. The baggage tractor that had been snaking its way toward the plane was now riderless, or so Ryng thought. But as he watched, the vehicle turned rapidly to one side, tipping over as it did. It was then he saw the arm linked through the steering wheel. The driver slid into view just before the machine rolled on top of him.

Another sound came to him now, high-pitched, frantic, urgent. It rose from the other passengers, and the sound was fear, the fear of violent death. Ryng remembered Admiral Pratt's words just a few days before. "They've limited their attacks to military and purely industrial targets so far. But there's been an increase in terrorism there lately. Don't be surprised by anything." So it was only the instant of recognition that surprised him. Bullets ripped into the forward section of the fuselage, and he accepted that fact. It was only logical they should get the cockpit, the crew.

As Ryng reached for his seat belt, an explosion blew back the door from the cockpit. The cries of pain from passengers wounded by the blast were added to the terrified screaming up front. Bazookas, or maybe rockets, decided Ryng. A second blast rocked the forward section, and he saw one of the crew, blood pulsing from his chest, stagger from the cockpit and collapse across two of the passengers.

A third explosion ripped open a section of the passenger

compartment over the wing. This was followed by a pattern of machine gun bullets ripping through the thin fuselage. By now he was free of the seat belt and onto his knees in the aisle.

More explosions rocked the plane. Then, as he searched out the sign over the emergency door, something else attracted his attention, sending a chill down his spine. First a flickering light, then a bubbling sound, then the flames themselves licking into the cabin through first one, then another, then another hole blown through the fuselage. Fire! Jet fuel!

Rising onto his toes, still squatting, grasping the seats on either side, his fingers brushed against flesh. Then a hand was grasping his. He looked up into the terrified eyes of the woman he had been conversing with not more than thirty seconds before. Her mouth was open as if voicing a question, but no sound emerged, at least it couldn't be heard above the screams within the craft and the steady roar of flames and the weapons outside.

Her grip was like a vise. With his other hand he pulled her's away, at the same time grasping and opening her seat belt. Before she could stand fully erect one of his arms went around her waist and yanked her backward off her feet. In three steps he was by the emergency exit, releasing her momentarily to kick open the hatch.

It flew back, opening into space above the runway, the escape slide shooting down. In the same moment that he glanced over his shoulder at the flames engulfing the cabin, he pushed her roughly out the hatch. As she tumbled head first down the slide, Ryng launched himself away from the flames, landing partially on top of her. Together they careened toward the cement below.

A cry of pain was the first sound to escape her lips since the attack had begun. She hit the runway with her shoulder, the impact intensified by the dead weight of the man on top of her.

Ryng, unmoving, peered cautiously over his shoulder. Even a novice could identify distinct teams involved in the attack. Those concentrating on the plane with automatic weapons and bazookas were racing away from the craft as fire engulfed the entire fuselage. It would explode any moment.

"We have to get up," Ryng shouted above the din, still

lying partially on top of her. Her skirt had been pulled up to her waist. "We only have seconds," he added. Rolling away, he was at once lifting and half dragging her as he began to move away from the plane. A tractor and baggage trailer were about thirty or forty yards from them. It was the only protection he could see, and all that would save them from the blast. "Run," he roared, and they sprinted together toward the tractor, Ryng frantically pulling, dragging, coaxing as they went.

The five or six seconds that elapsed before reaching safety seemed an eternity. Then, with Ryng pulling her head down as they ducked behind the vehicle, the aircraft erupted into a huge fireball. The flash and the intense heat preceded the blast by only an instant, followed by shards of metal, seats, glass . . . flying bodies. In less than a minute the plane that had been their home for almost three hours ceased to exist, bursting around them in a fury.

Ryng huddled with the girl facedown on the runway, the abandoned tractor their only protection. Oily, black, suffocating smoke settled over them briefly, forcing them to burrow their faces into their clothing. A thought drifted briefly through Ryng's mind—that perhaps this smoke would discourage anyone who might have seen them escape from the plane.

No sooner had he made his decision to stay there, than the wind came up, a gust pushing the smoke away from them. Cautiously, he peered over the hood of the vehicle. The terminal building was now ablaze. The runway was strewn with bodies. Twice he identified sporadic efforts to return fire on the attackers. Each time, automatic weapons fire stifled it. He could hear the wail of sirens growing louder in the background.

Noticing out of the corner of his eye that the girl had raised herself onto an elbow, Ryng dropped to his knees beside her. He saw that her blouse had been torn from one shoulder, the exposed flesh raw and bleeding. Her eyes watched him questioningly, following his every movement, seemingly oblivious to the chaos around them. Bringing his head down to hers, he pointed to the wound and shouted, trying to make himself heard above the din.

She looked down at the blood, then back up at him, her face still devoid of expression. Ryng took out a handkerchief, folded it, then pressed it to her shoulder. Her eyes looked down at the hand covering her shoulder, but there was no reaction until he gently placed her other hand on the handkerchief so that he was once again free to move about.

There was a strange aura about this girl that Ryng couldn't put his finger on. He had expected hysteria, tears, anything but the silence that greeted him. There was no doubt that her control was largely based on shock, the horror of what was taking place around them, the jolt from being pushed from the plane, followed by his landing on top of her. But there was still an element of toughness in her that fascinated him. Somewhere she must have learned a form of self-control that seemed well beyond the average person.

The sirens were closer now. Ryng watched scattered, black-clothed groups join together to become fire teams of one bazooka and half a dozen automatic rifles. A truck came around a corner of the terminal building on two wheels. It screeched to a stop on the runway as the driver recognized a bazooka aimed directly at his vehicle. The driver dove from the door an instant before a direct hit blew the cab into shreds. From the back of the truck soldiers appeared, firing wildly as they scurried for cover.

Fascinated, Ryng watched a second truck appear. More soldiers joined the action. The rebels in their black outfits were superbly trained. They could draw fire without injury until another team would position themselves. When the second team drew fire, the first would be repositioned. They moved too quickly for the arriving soldiers, who had no idea what to expect. They were unprepared to fight the well-trained teams they faced.

It seemed a standoff until two armored vehicles arrived, their large-caliber cannon pumping shells at the bazooka teams. The balance was beginning to shift to the soldiers whom Ryng assumed were Guardia troops, the National Guard of Panama.

He became aware of a hand on his arm, gentle at first, then more insistent. Turning, he saw her gesturing behind them. Three large, black helicopters, accompanied by two smaller ones, were swooping in low over the airfield, traveling at high speed. The roar of their engines and the wash from their rotors altered the scene of battle. Dust and smoke swirled together to form a cloud that cut vision perceptibly.

The two smaller helos were gunships. They moved ahead of the larger ones to neutralize the armored vehicles. The three big helicopters touched down not fifty yards from where Ryng and the girl huddled. One by one each team raced for one of the helos, the gunships covering their withdrawal. In less time than Ryng could imagine, all five of the helos were airborne and racing toward the inland mountains.

Gently, Bernie Ryng slipped his hands under the girl's arms and lifted her to her feet. Her head nestled just under his chin, and there were tears in her eyes before she was silent again. Together they surveyed the wreckage of the Torrijos International Airport. Another jet plane had also been blown apart. The front of the terminal building was open to the field, and numerous fires burned inside. One of the troop trucks was burning in exactly the spot where the driver had stopped in terror as he came face-to-face with that bazooka. Both armored vehicles had been ripped by the gunships. Bodies, civilian and military, were strewn across the field. But, Ryng noted, there were very few bodies of the black-uniformed rebels. The attack had been well planned, carried out with exceptional military efficiency, and the withdrawal had been effected with a minimum of fuss. The weapons and helos were definitely Soviet.

As Admiral Pratt had told him only a few days before, during the briefing in Washington, these were not awkward peasants from the hills. They were highly trained and well armed. Their methods were much too sophisticated. This sort of thing could only come from Havana or Moscow—more likely both.

Ryng was brought back to reality by a soldier advancing across the runway, gun slung at his hip, finger on the trigger. He was obviously frightened and Ryng had no intention of making him any more nervous. Ryng remained in the same position, his arm around the girl, and waited until the soldier was close enough to speak to him.

Ryng attempted to answer in Spanish, but his accent seemed

only to make the man more nervous. Gesturing with his gun, he motioned for them to move away from the tractor. At this point the girl turned, her confidence renewed, and spoke rapidly. Ryng watched in amazement as the soldier's frightened features softened. His finger slowly relaxed on the trigger and he allowed the weapon to swing easily from his shoulder. Whatever she had said seemed to satisfy any doubt Ryng may have posed. The soldier gestured for her to follow. She took Ryng's hand, looking up at him. "It's all right. Come with me." There was even a slight trace of a smile at the corners of her mouth. Whoever she was, Ryng thought, she continued to fascinate him.

The Airport Visitors' Lounge
Panama

The first soldier had called one of his officers as soon as the girl identified herself. In rapid succession more senior officers had appeared, until a colonel insisted they come with him.

It was evident to Ryng that all the attention was for the girl. The first doctor to appear at the airport ministered to her scraped shoulder before tending to the victims outside. While the girl had introduced herself as Kitty Alvarez, she was referred to deferentially by the military as Miss Alvarez. The colonel did ask Ryng if he recognized any of the hardware the rebel forces had been using. Without a second thought Ryng explained that he was familiar with their Russian-made AK-74s, and he named both types of helos involved.

The girl had just appeared from the women's lounge, where she'd found a fresh blouse. "What did you say you did for a living, Mr. Ryng?" she asked him after she walked in. Her expression displayed both curiosity and amusement as he answered the colonel's questions. She seemed on a very friendly basis with the interrogators.

"Please . . . call me Bernie," he began. "I'm in investments . . . finance . . . mostly on an international level."

"I'd say so," she mused. "That must be some company you

work for . . . I mean to develop a working knowledge of all that weaponry."

Ryng managed a sheepish expression. "It's just a hobby."

She smiled politely, unconvinced.

"But how about yourself? I've certainly enjoyed the reception in Panama since we were brought into this lounge. I'd say the only person in the Guardia who didn't seem to know you personally was that first soldier we met . . . but he certainly knew your name!"

"Kitty is short for Katarina. I also have three other family names to go along with Katarina, but it's the Alvarez they recognized. I'm with the National Bank of Panama . . . international finance also." She grinned. "But I couldn't identify any weapons these rebels used today." She looked at him coyly. "Perhaps there's something lacking in my training program."

Considering what she'd just gone through, she seemed perfectly under control. He was fascinated. "I'll explain it to you sometime." Ryng pursed his lips thoughtfully. "This is a hell of a way to meet, and I don't suppose you're susceptible to another pass . . . but I think we'd enjoy getting to know each other under better circumstances. I suppose tonight isn't exactly the right time, after everything that happened today, but—"

"Mr. Ryng—"

"Bernie . . . please."

"Bernie, how could I say no after what you've done for me? Besides, I'd love to know more about you and this company you work for." She smiled curiously. "And I can't see anything wrong with tonight either. As a matter of fact, I think I'd like to be with someone this evening. I'd prefer not to be by myself."

"What about your family . . . after all this special treatment?"

"My mother is dead, for many years. And my father's in Havana giving a seminar. I really am all alone . . . so I'd love to have dinner with you tonight." This time her expression was warm, no longer amused. "I do owe you something for what you've done for me, so I'll be your guide while you're in Panama."

Ryng wasn't quite sure how to respond. But before he could, the colonel appeared. "Miss Alvarez, we have a car for you outside."

"Come on," she said as she stood up, holding her hand out to him. "I'll have you dropped off at your hotel."

The long black limousine left him at his hotel only after he'd been fitted for new clothes by Mr. Alvarez's personal tailor. A new suit would be delivered by six that evening. The chauffeur would return for him at seven thirty.

Havana, Cuba

Esteban Alvarez squinted against the bright sunlight and the reflection from the cream-colored buildings in the central square of Havana. He walked slowly toward the harbor, pondering his meeting earlier in the day with the Premier himself, Fidel Castro. It had been more than satisfactory. The only aspect causing him even the slightest concern was the presence for a short time of the Russian, Khasan. But Castro had caught Alvarez's antipathy toward the other man, and had sent him out. Alvarez had sensed, rather than been assured, that Castro bore identical feelings toward the Russians. Yet, was he right? Did the Cubans suffer the Russians simply for their aid, as Alvarez had promised the others back in Panama?

A fresh breeze skittering across the harbor ruffled his hair. He pushed the wisps back from his forehead, then smoothed them down to the side with his palm. The only element of vanity Alvarez had ever possessed was concern for his baldness. He was not an atypical university professor—no beard, goatee, or mustache, nor did he display affectations such as earrings, wild clothing, or dark glasses in the class room. He appeared more a business executive. Alvarez wore neat, tailored suits, mostly dark or dark pinstripe, and his white shirts and conservative ties never fit in with the dress on campus. He was a reasonably well-known economist, and he looked the part. No taller than his daughter, the tailored suits looked well on him because his body was trim. Many felt he worked hard to appear so fit; Kitty Alvarez said it was nerves. Nothing anyone ever said about him was cause for concern, except for the baldness. His hair was long on the sides and embarrassingly subject to the deviltry of the breezes. He was constantly patting it into place.

The clean, fresh scent of salt air came to him. A cooling breeze from the harbor brought the additional aromas of fish, paint, and diesel fuel. Alvarez often wandered down to the docks to clear his mind, because these visits to Havana were mentally demanding. The financial burden of funding the guerilla forces rested on his shoulders. Esteban Alvarez, a respected senior professor at Panama's national university, was the conduit for the money that supported the People's Revolutionary Army. He also coordinated the arms shipments that made their way into the rebels' hands, and arranged for their officers to be sent to Cuba for training.

Fidel Castro was first a soldier. But he respected men such as Alvarez because revolutions in the 1980s were so much different than the 1950s, when Fidel and Raul and their band had come out of the Sierra Maestres to crush Batista. The Premier knew that glory still annointed the soldiers, but he went out of his way to work with the administrators, like Alvarez, who were the true leaders. And, although he no longer believed it himself, Castro took the time to convince men like Alvarez that the Russians simply wanted to assist in *Peoples' Revolutions*. Once accomplished, Moscow wanted only to assist the new governments in getting started.

That's what concerned Alvarez more than anything else at this stage, for he considered himself a true patriot—a Panamanian first and foremost, not a communist or Marxist/Leninist in the true sense of the terms. The current government in Panama City was a sham. It could not—should not—survive as it existed. Alvarez was firmly convinced that a socialist system that was part of a unified front, as envisioned by Fidel Castro, was the only form that would benefit Panama. The other countries in Central America were more advanced in this regard. Nicaragua had been first; El Salvador and Guatemala were close behind; the Americans were prolonging the inevitable in Honduras. Only Costa Rica would be a problem, but Castro felt that the little country would fall without a struggle, for they attempted to survive without an army. Such naivete meant simply that it would be a relatively bloodless coup.

Alvarez sat on a park bench overlooking the harbor and lit the cigar that Castro, himself, had given him. Alvarez often came to this very spot, even to this same bench, whenever he had the time, mostly to relax his mind and watch the young women pass. But today there seemed to be more Russians than anyone else. Sailors, mostly Soviet, were in evidence, though there were also a few of their black-uniformed marines. They came from the big warships tugging gently at their anchors in the harbor. Today there were two cruisers, bristling with guns and missiles. He had never seen more than one before. There were also destroyers, new ones that dwarfed the smaller Cuban frigates. And then there were the ones that troubled him most—the sleek, black submarines, so lethal with only their sails and a bit of their hulls above the surface. Again, there were more than he had ever seen before in the harbor.

So often he had heard the promise, so much that he feared it was a meaningless, dreary litany—the Russians came in peace to assist the peoples of the Third World, and they would return to their homeland as soon as their job was done. But would they? Would the harbor once again contain only Cuban ships? Would the sailors who strolled the wharves, eying the girls just as he did, be only Cuban? Alvarez had been promised so often that this would be the case that he truly wanted to believe it. He believed strongly that what he was doing was right, and this was his only doubt. He tried to push it from his mind, but sometimes it kept him awake at night.

Victor Khasan jogged happily in the hard sand along the beach, occasionally diverting to the water's edge to cool his feet. This was superb duty! he thought. His stomach had flattened in the last few months; his muscle tone was improved, which was fully in keeping with his high regard for himself. He had been raised by a well-off family according to Russian standards, well fed, trained in the proper sports since he was a child, and sent to the right schools, which led to admission to the military academies. Khasan benefitted by his upbringing —his teeth were white and healthy and he had retained them all, he had grown faster than most boys, and diet and physical training had left him tall and well proportioned. The result was a handsome, aristocratic-looking naval officer, now graying slightly at the temples but striking in full-dress uniform.

He actually had a tan, and he wrote ecstatically about it to his friends back home. Unless they were lucky and received Mediterranean or Black Sea assignments, few of them could remember what a tan was from year to year. Even his wife had remarked on the new Victor. Lydia, fully aware of Victor's roving eye, had actually shed some pounds herself, once she found that the Cuban women were generally slender.

Khasan had not undertaken this personal improvement program solely for Lydia. There was Chita, his current Cuban lover, and there had been others during his long stay in Havana. Although his comrades back in Russia would write to explain that his extensions for duty in Cuba were ruining his chances for future promotion, they were unable to understand. A man like Victor needed duty in Moscow, and one more major command, for he had been considered as having potential to climb near the top.

Now he could no longer bring himself to worry about such mundane things. Moscow was far away, the winters there were long and cold, and Lydia was as pleased as he to remain in Havana—pleased enough to even look the other way and shrug if the few other Russian wives mentioned seeing Victor at such-and-such a restaurant. Life was good here. After the firm base his predecessors had established over so many years—long, hard years in remote mountains and jungles, forming peoples' revolutionary armies and militias—it was all coming to fruition. And Victor Khasan was reaping the benefits as one Caribbean government after another tottered and then crumbled, right in the American's backyard.

He turned toward the blue water and ran directly out, his knees high until he tumbled forward and stroked easily out toward the deeper water. Floating on his back, he considered the Panamanian who had been in Castro's office earlier in the day. Alvarez was just one more of those banana republic patriots who thought a revolution could be financed without charging interest, that the country providing the brains and money would just fold its tent and wander off into the sun like a knight searching for one more dragon to slay. They never seemed to understand.

Khasan rolled onto his stomach, arched his body, and dove to the bottom. With short powerful strokes, he swam just above the sand until his lungs ached, then shot to the surface, breaking the water with a gasp. It was a good feeling to exert his body once again. He felt younger than he had in years, and he was anxious now to complete the Panamanian deal. Russian patience, coupled with proper timing, would be rewarded. The new government would be as strong as Castro's, the Gulf of Mexico would be a useless lake rather than a great source of power and trade for the Americans, and best of all, such success would make up for his lack of duty in Moscow.

As he turned toward the beach, he saw Lydia strolling down to meet him, looking fabulous in her bikini. If she hadn't been his wife, he might have had designs on her that afternoon. Cuban life had done so much for her that she would no longer be recognized if they returned home. But she would have to wait. He had explained to Lydia that he had to meet with Commodore Navarro, the head of the Cuban navy, for a long dinner—though in fact, tonight was really Chita's night.

The instructor had noticed twice now that Corazon was paying little attention to the lecture. The others were most attentive, some taking notes, others following along in the Soviet manual that had been poorly translated in Spanish. The RPG-7 rocket launcher was not effective at a distance, but it was superb for close-in work, and these students would generally operate that way back in Panama.

"Corazon!" he finally shouted in dismay. He was sure that he had seen the man's eyes closing. How could that happen, knowing they would have demonstration firings that afternoon? "Firing the 'seven' is just one of the things you have to know. You must also know how to dismantle and repair . . . even during a firefight. You can't learn that sleeping, Corazon. Stand up!''

Henry Cobb leaped to attention beside his chair. It was true. He had been dozing. Cobb knew better, but he also knew more about the RPG-7 than the instructor would ever know. He had probably used it more too, in firefights, ambushes . . . he had taken one apart once in the dark when they had been pinned down, and jury-rigged it so they had knocked out a tank when it was within thirty yards of them.

He stood at attention as he addressed the instructor in Spanish. "I apologize, sir. My eyes were closed against the heat, but I was listening. . . .''

The instructor reeled off a series of questions—the muzzle velocity, the weight of a single round, maximum effective range, steps to take after misfire—and as he asked each one, Henry Cobb responded immediately and accurately. His appearance was that of a man who could have been named Corazon. Cobb was of medium height and build. His brown hair had been allowed to grow longer for this mission. It even curled around his ears. Cobb didn't like that at all, but Admiral Pratt had insisted it was an essential part of his cover, and Henry Cobb understood the value of cover more than any other man. The mustache did not appeal to Cobb either, and even his wife, Verra, had found it increasingly distasteful as it drooped over the corners of his mouth.

There had actually been a man named Corazon. He was a lieutenant in the Costa Rican police—even though this was a military organization, they were designated *police* because the government boasted there was no need for an army in their democracy. Sitting back in his chair in his Pentagon office a week earlier, Admiral Pratt had explained to Henry Cobb that Costa Rica had been selected because that country rarely sent people to the school in Havana, and hardly a soul in Cuba knew anything about the junior officers from that tiny country. Pratt never said how he acquired the list of students in that Cuban school, or how he'd determined that it was the logical place for Cobb to infiltrate. On the other hand, Cobb never questioned Pratt's methods or reasons. They were always sound.

When Pratt showed Cobb the photo of Corazon, taken only a few days previously, the similarity of their facial and physical characteristics was remarkable. There was also no purpose in asking about the photo or the orders this Corazon had received. Admiral Pratt's network was that efficient.

The original Lieutenant Corazon was now very dead. Henry Cobb had seen to that, immediately after the young man had been feted by his friends for the promotion which must surely come soon after he finished the school in Havana. As Corazon stumbled back to his quarters, Cobb stopped him. Perhaps even in his drunken stupor the young Costa Rican had noticed the strong resemblance between the two of them. If he had, the recognition was limited. His dispatch was very humane and painless, because Cobb wanted to study the younger man's features to cover anything that hadn't been clear in the photographs. As a result, that night Cobb darkened his hair slightly, added a bit more stain to his skin, and happily trimmed his mustache a bit. Afterward, he made sure there would never be a body found. Corazon's life was cut off much too early because an admiral in Washington had seen his photo and arranged for orders that the young man had been so thankful for; he actually had thought he was one of the lucky few.

When the plane left the capital city of Costa Rica the following day for Havana, Corazon's friends had no doubt that it was their friend, quiet because he was so badly hungover, who boarded the aircraft with a solemn wave in their direction. Both his friends and his senior officers would have been astounded at the brilliance of their associate during his brief stay at the school in Havana.

The answers from the sleepy Costa Rican surprised the instructor. Students like Corazon were unusual in Havana. Mostly they were either uneducated peasants eager to strike back at the landowners or idealistic upper class students more interested in experimenting with communism than in facing the dangers common to a guerilla fighter. This Corazon responded like a professional.

Henry Cobb was a professional, as professional as they came. Trained as a Navy SEAL, he was able to function effectively underwater, on the surface, as a paratroop, an in-

fantryman, a guerilla—just about anything Pratt concocted
for him. Cobb was also a linguist. Within days after his
meeting with Pratt, he had resurrected the regional Spanish
dialect he had once mastered.

There was a mystique surrounding Pratt. Among those who
knew him well, it was accepted purely as an accomplished professional trait. Outside of the intelligence network he was
regarded with awe. But Admiral Pratt never stuck his nose in
too far until he was absolutely sure of his purpose. He felt the
only way he could fully comprehend the methods of what he
saw as a final "liberation" of Panama was to insert one of his
own in the guerilla training programs, and those took place in
Cuba. Since the CIA couldn't tell who was in charge of the
programs or what their ultimate goal was, there was no alternative way of quickly getting to the source of the problem.
The Cubans were intent on changing the face of the Caribbean. Initially, violence was the vehicle—as long as violence,
or even the threat, existed, the Americans could not hope to
sustain any illusion of progress. The Russians were hovering in
the background, and it was apparent to Pratt that Henry Cobb
was the logical operative to get to the source. While Congress
urged the White House not to interfere with their neighbors to
the south, Pratt knew there was no choice. It was no longer a
matter of politics. Closing one's eyes never made a problem
disappear.

Pratt had created a multi-phase plan. He knew that Henry
would know when it was time to leave Havana. He would
disappear just as easily as he had assimilated himself into their
school. And when Henry Cobb was once again on his own, he
would undertake the second phase of his mission—join forces
with Bernie Ryng. They worked well together.

Panama City

In the weeks following their arrival at the airport in Panama
City, Kitty Alvarez and Bernie Ryng became inseparable.
Pratt's only suggestion to Ryng while he was in the field was

that a strong contact in the financial community in a developing country was the key to high government officials. After all, the root problem in Central America—economics—had been fully addressed by the Marxist theoreticians. The success of any future democratic movement would therefore have to be economic renewal, and that would be based on American trade, aid and investment. It would seem sheer coincidence to Ryng until it was too late, that Kitty Alvarez was the perfect answer.

For her part, she had agreed weeks before to once again become involved, only because she, too, could see the creeping influence of outsiders in her country. She had made a clean break years before from the promoters of a socialist paradise. It had been a college fantasy originally to work with the Americans. They had educated her and she would always feel a debt to them, but undercover work had quickly become distasteful. Her country had a much greater need for her. The totally unexpected offer had been accepted weeks earlier, only because she could satisfy both countries. She knew there would be undercover people in Panama, but never once did she hear Ryng's name mentioned.

Neither Kitty Alvarez nor Bernie Ryng had been looking for each other. There was no reason. Both were satisfied with their lives. Complications were part and parcel with relationships. Only one affair, in her college days before she transferred to the States, had ever affected her; after that, she became the initiator with any men who attracted her. Adventure had been Ryng's mistress from his earliest days in the service, and no woman had ever come along to change his mind. Pratt felt a deep sense of security surrounding himself with people like Ryng.

Neither Kitty nor Bernie considered the fact that physical attraction to each other could go any further than drinks, dinner, and a good-night kiss. Yet they never missed an evening together from that first day. The kisses grew longer, quiet moments more intimate, and parting at the end of the evening more difficult. The realization that there was much more between them came quite suddenly, after weeks of overlooking the obvious. The shock was so abrupt, so overwhelming, that neither realized that their dinner had grown cold. It was too important to discuss what had happened to them, then to do something about it.

Bernie Ryng's eyes opened slowly, blinking two or three times as he tried to remember where he was. A ray of sun filtered around the edge of the shade, outlining a clock radio on the bedside table. Lifting his head to avoid the sun's reflection on the clock's face, he saw it was six thirty.

It was morning, and he was in the apartment Kitty had found for him in Panama City. Though it was expensive and supposed to be fully furnished, the air conditioner wasn't working. That's what had awakened him—the sultry, sticky heat so early in the morning. His hotel room had been maintained at a constant temperature the previous weeks, and he'd always needed the alarm. But this morning was different. It was hot, and the stickiness of the day had drawn him from sleep.

But it was more than that. He rolled backward just a bit, and Kitty murmured in her sleep. That's what had really pulled him back to consciousness—the fact that someone else was in bed with him.

Ryng sank back into the pillow, memories of the previous night flooding back. But it wasn't just the sex. It was her, Kitty, the woman he'd only met a few weeks ago. He'd known a lot of women over the years, but Kitty Alvarez was exceptional. This morning it seemed to Ryng that they'd lived together for years. It seemed so natural to be waking up next to her. Yet up till just the week before, it had only been a good-night kiss outside her door or a casual nuzzle on the dance floor at the hotel.

Ryng rolled over slowly. She was lying on her side, legs drawn up. The sheet was down to her waist, but with her arms folded in front of her, there was little of her body visible. He reached out gently and touched her shoulder, then ran his hand down her side to rest on her hip.

Kitty's eyes opened slowly. There was never any doubt in her mind where she was. Her mouth opened slightly as she smiled, her eyes crinkling at the corners. She touched two fingers to her lips then brushed them on Ryng's. "Good morning," she said softly.

"Good morning, yourself." He moved his head toward her's, kissing her on the tip of her nose. "I assume you know where you are this grand morning."

She nodded. "In bed with you, sir. And very pleased with myself I might add . . . and with you, of course."

His hand ran up her back, gently pulling her toward him. "Why thank you, Miss Alvarez. The compliment should be returned." He raised himself onto an elbow.

"Perhaps this evening . . . if I'm lucky." Kitty kissed him quickly and leaped out of bed, padding off toward the bathroom. Looking back over her shoulder, she added, "Nothing to do with you, but look at that clock. I'm already late. I'm a working girl. Remember that eight o'clock appointment I told you about last night?" The bathroom door shut behind her.

Ryng rolled onto his back, hands behind his head. Yes, he remembered an appointment. He recalled that and a number of other things, though he preferred to forget the appointment. The morning seemed to be starting out so well. . . .

His eyes traveled around the bedroom, familiarizing himself with his new home. It was only yesterday afternoon he'd moved in. Kitty had located it not too far from her own place.

The first weeks in Panama were a blur, and the thing with Kitty was welcome, though unexpected. No woman had so enchanted him that his world would revolve around her own. Yet everything he now thought about included her.

Their first dinner together, the night he arrived in Panama, had been pleasant enough, perhaps with too much to drink after the events at the airport. He learned enough about Kitty Alvarez that first evening to feel that this might already be the source he was looking for. What were the odds against something like that? A hundred to one? A thousand to one? A million to one? She apparently had the contacts he would need.

It seemed impossible that it could happen so easily, that she was likely the person he'd come to Panama to meet. She wasn't just a senior employee of the National Bank. In many ways she was the bank. Major projects developed in Panama by outside sources, whether private or government, were her responsibility to evalute financially. Kitty had been educated in the United States and took a master's degree in business at

Berkeley. Her concentration had been international banking.

Her interest in finance was a natural one. An only child, her mother died when Kitty was in her early teens. Her father, a university professor, had influenced much of his brilliant daughter's thinking even before her mother died. Unlike her father, who likely was a millionaire, Kitty had been interested in business to help her country. She'd been in the local university when the students were marching against the U.S. possession of the Canal, and her father had allowed her to march with them. But she had no communist or socialist leanings. Her education had been exacting enough for her to learn that poor countries became rich countries by attracting wealth if they couldn't generate it. Panama was a poor country with little to fund industry or major agriculture, but money for those things was available.

Kitty Alvarez became well known and respected very quickly when she returned to her country and went to work with the National Bank. Her success attracted attention in both business and government circles, and with the military as well, since the military and the government were hand-in-hand in Panama.

In a few short years she became a powerful individual in the little country. The respect directed to Kitty Alvarez was genuine. There were also many men attracted to her because of her beauty, wit, and charm, yet no man was successful that anyone was aware of. Her life seemed to be her work. She was often out of the country and had little time for social affairs.

She was captivated by Bernie Ryng from that first day, for reasons she failed to understand at first. Ryng noticed the admiring glances wherever they went. He was amazed when he realized how many people looked at him with awe because he was with Señorita Alvarez. Of even more curiosity to Ryng was why she was attracted to him. It had to be obvious, what with her contacts in America, that he was more than he claimed. His credentials were real enough, and he could speak their business language as well as anyone. But she also had to know that in their world a man doesn't just drop into another country with no prior contacts and explain that he'd like to spend a little money. As he lay in bed considering the fact, it became more preposterous. Perhaps it was true that women with class were attracted to men without it!

The bathroom door opened and Kitty stepped out, one towel wrapped around her head to keep her hair dry while she rubbed her back with the other. "I'll have to remember a shower cap." She winked at him. "I believe the saying is 'a penny for your thoughts'."

"You are an extremely beautiful woman . . . a glorious creature, and I have been trying to figure out why I'm so attracted to you." He gestured at her dripping body. "Now I think I'm getting an idea."

"You can save your ideas until tonight, my dear. It's business during the day." She crossed over to a bureau, pulling open one of the drawers. Searching through the contents, she extracted a fresh change of clothes, laying the garments neatly on the bed.

"Where in the hell did those come from?"

"I brought them over here yesterday, before you moved your own things here. I don't like to go to the bank in dirty clothes."

"You mean . . . you expected to wake up here this morning?"

"I have enough clothes so that I wouldn't miss them if I didn't stay here!" She bent over and kissed him on the forehead, then scurried away before he could touch her. "But I believe in looking ahead and being organized." She dressed quickly. Ryng noticed how little makeup she used, just enough to highlight her eyes, and some lipstick to set off her dark, clear complexion. And she was ready to go.

"That was quick. I guess we'll just have to wait for the weekends to sleep in."

"I don't know," she teased, sitting on the end of the bed, her eyebrows raised quizzically. "I've always been an early riser."

"Go on then, off to work."

She rose to go. "Don't forget. Noon, at the Palacio restaurant. I'll have Tomas Cornejo with me when I get there." And she was out the door.

"Tomas Cornejo," he murmured softly to himself. What luck! he thought, and so early in the game. Cornejo was a friend of Kitty's and an economic advisor to President Ramos.

He was a man that she insisted Ryng should meet—which stopped him for a second. He wondered why she thought he should be introduced to Cornejo if he hadn't really explained why he was in Panama. He'd hinted only briefly a couple of evenings before of the Cuban influence.

There was no point in going back to sleep, Ryng realized. His mind was now too active for that. Ryng did his best thinking in the shower, and there was now much to think about. His first problem was one of Dave Pratt's agents, a man who had come to him the day before at his hotel. The agent—Moran, he called himself—either spent time with the rebel forces or was in direct contact with someone who did. He knew all their movements and had come with information he considered vital, something that could tie in with Ryng's mission.

There was to be a raid two nights later on the port of Colón, a vital city at the northern entrance to the Canal. Colón was the gateway to the Caribbean, to the U.S., to Europe. There was no doubt about the purpose, a twofold and well-thought-out approach. President Ramos must be convinced of the power of the rebel forces, that they could immobilize a major city as well as an airport. The second, and possibly more important aspect, was to convince an undecided populace that neither the military nor the government in the Presidential Palace was in control. The intent was not to simply hit-and-run as in the past, but to hold off government forces as well. If they could hold the police station and city hall for twelve hours, the people would know. The instruments of accountability understood by the people—President Ramos' government, the Guardia, even the judicial system—were helpless before a revolutionary movement capable of threatening, and then successfully carrying out, violence at any moment and in any place in their country.

The Pentagon

It had all begun more than a month before, in a little office in the Pentagon. . . .

Admiral Pratt chuckled to himself as he looked at the

Potomac from his office window across the highway. Imagine
Bernie Ryng as a financial analyst! The famous Bernie Ryng
. . . well, maybe not so famous. As a matter of fact, there were
few Americans who were aware of what Bernie did for a living. Pratt realized there were probably more Russians, NVA
Regulars, Libyans, and who-cared-how-many-more who knew
about Ryng. And it was primarily by rumor, since those who
had met Ryng head-on were mostly dead.

While Henry Cobb was the smooth infiltrator who could insert himself into the enemy's most secure areas, Bernie Ryng
was the type who charged in and took them apart. Regular
Navy duty hadn't satisfied him, so he became a Frogman. But
UDT wasn't enough either. Ryng became a SEAL and was
soon a team leader. A loner, he preferred the company of his
own kind. While he could put on an effective show in civilized
company, the real world to Bernie Ryng was the world of action. And no matter what happened on a mission, no matter
how bad the losses, Ryng always came back. In a word, he was
a survivor.

Pratt knew Bernie would never consider knocking—he'd
just barge right in. As Pratt looked out at the river, the first indication that Ryng had arrived was the hand on his shoulder.
Ryng had simply barged in! Dave Pratt turned his wheelchair
around, still chuckling to himself. "Bernie, it's great to see
you!" He extended his hand. "I was just thinking about
you."

"Hi, Dave. You're looking good, even riding that thing."
He gestured at the wheelchair.

"Only a matter of time, Bernie . . . then I'll be up and out of
it." He told the others the same thing—it would just be a matter of time until he was back on his own feet. The doctors did
say anything was possible, especially with someone as tough as
Pratt, but the odds weren't strongly in his favor.

None of the men really close to him, like Cobb and Ryng,
ever brought the subject up. They were simply quite thankful
that Dave Pratt was alive. Those around him, those who knew
the real Pratt, knew the Admiral could survive without the use
of his legs. Any man who could command people with the
facility that Pratt did, would never have to leave the Pentagon. The power structure might be leery of sending him back

to sea again, only for his own protection, but they would never let him leave the Navy.

Admiral David Pratt had been the brains behind the strategy that defeated the Russians during the Battle of the Mediterranean two years before. That time, it had been against NATO, a major Soviet effort to expand their borders, to acquire as much of Europe as they could bully away from their neighbors. It had been a sea battle on a grand scale that strategists said would never occur again—but it had, and Pratt foresaw almost every step of the Soviet plan. It was more than just a sea battle, and it took place in locations other than the Mediterranean; but there were few who understood the covert operations that failed to make the papers, operations that had really been the turning point. The President, based on the advice of those who knew Pratt by his less public reputation, gave the Admiral carte blanche to create the means to stop the Soviet machine.

The Russians had intended to send their powerful Northern Fleet submarine force from the Kola Peninsula, around Norway's North Cape, and down through the Greenland/Iceland/United Kingdom gap to destroy shipping in the American resupply routes to Europe. The Americans had established a secret antisubmarine minefield to deny access to the North Atlantic. Intelligence indicated that the Russians had developed a plan to penetrate the barrier. Dave Pratt sent Bernie Ryng and his specially trained SEAL team to the Arctic island of Spitzbergen, where the Russians had established a base of operations to neutralize the American barrier. Bernie Ryng's team had been successful—they had destroyed the Russian threat completely. Their success was devastating to the Soviet plan. The impossible had been achieved by a small group of men, though the public was never aware of it. Nor did many people know that Bernie Ryng was the only member of that SEAL team to come out of it alive. It was a story that was told late at night when Naval Special Warfare Units gathered. Ryng was a legend.

Dave Pratt also sensed that there would never be a clearer threat of nuclear war than during the Battle of the Mediterranean. The only method he could conceive of to avoid it was to remove the key to the Soviet nuclear power structure—the head of their Strategic Rocket Forces. It was a bold plan, so farfetched even in their own minds that it never passed beyond Pratt's small group. Henry Cobb was sent into the Soviet Crimea completely alone with orders to kidnap that one critical individual, right from under the noses of the Soviet hierarchy. He accomplished just what he planned, and with the Soviet military often within an inch of stopping him, delivered the Russian general at the last possible moment. It helped to turn the tide, to alleviate nuclear blackmail.

It was Admiral David Pratt who commanded the task force that sailed directly into the Russian fleet, audaciously halting their drive through the Mediterranean before they could land troops in southern Europe. Pratt had led the battle from the carrier *John F. Kennedy* until she was destroyed. He then shifted his command to the Aegis cruiser *Yorktown* and stayed with her until she was literally blown out from under him. It was then that he had been grievously injured, dragged from the Mediterranean more dead than alive and flown back to the States in a coma.

Pratt's close friends had gathered at the hospital to support his wife. They had come from around the world, many of them survivors of the Battle of the Mediterranean, to join the vigil until the inevitable became a reality. But Dave Pratt didn't die. He also baffled the doctors by coming out of the coma and recognizing each of the friends who had come to honor his memory. At first he couldn't talk. Yet a couple of months later, he was able to be best man at Henry Cobb's wedding. The bride pushed him down the aisle in his wheelchair. And at the party afterward, he had toasted the new couple in his halting, slurred speech.

Throughout Pratt's long recovery, there was another element in the Navy equally concerned about him. He was a god to those close to him and a symbol to the men in the fleet. He was what was called a "sailor's admiral," that strange breed that the men would follow anywhere, and his reputation had grown over the years. The fact that he personally led the Battle of the Mediterranean, transferring his flag from the sinking carrier to another ship that could direct the battle (even though it was the primary target of the Russian fleet), did not escape the sailors' notice. Bernie Ryng insured that ALNAV messages on Pratt's condition were directed to the fleet until he was out of danger. He continued to serve because command is an ethereal notion, a will on the part of the leader and a belief among those who are led. The fact that he led from a wheelchair was overlooked. His intuitive mind, his ability to foresee danger and coordinate the strategy to remove it, was a talent to be respected and encouraged.

It was a long morning, but Bernie Ryng sat in rapt attention as the Admiral spoke. Dave Pratt had a great deal to talk about. He had been frustrated by the CIA. They spent so much time causing trouble, he said, they didn't know how to do some good digging. But Pratt did. He knew something was brewing. The Russians wouldn't allow the extraction of an entire Cuban brigade from Africa just to return them home—not unless they planned something big in the Caribbean. And the military buildup in Cuba was obviously the first step.

At first, the Russians tried to hide what they were doing. Now, the Kremlin was as brazen as could be. They, or the Cubans, still attempted to cover the hardware they were moving into other parts of Central America, but it was almost as if they wanted the Americans to see the Cuban buildup—including the new submarines. Headquarters in Norfolk was hollering that they were going to run out of destroyers to shadow all those Soviet subs.

There was a lot more going on in other regions. Puerto Cabezas, on the Nicaraguan coast, was turning into a naval stronghold. There weren't that many ships there yet, but the heavy construction indicated that it was intended to be at least as big as Cienfuegos in Cuba. To Admiral Pratt, it offered every indication that the Russians planned to stay there when it was finished. There were no navies from any of the Caribbean nations that had anywhere near the tonnage to use facilities like that. And it definitely wasn't designed for tourist ships—not with those missile installations. And at Bluefields, 150 miles south of Puerto Cabezas, Soviet fighters had found a new home. The success of each of these new bases made one simple point clear to anyone in Washington who was open minded enough to listen—the consequence was an erosion of confidence and any belief in democracy that may once have existed in the minds of the people.

Finally, there were too many rumors coming back through Pratt's personal grapevine, especially about Panama. The modern weapons the PRA was using there as they moved out of the mountains were cocktail party conversation in Washington. But the stuff that never made the circuit concerned their National Guard. The Guardia was a combined police/military force in Panama, and they were supposed to be working for the government. But the stories he'd heard about their officers disturbed him. The PRA was getting through to them. It sounded to Pratt as if the Guardia was joining the revolution, or that they would whenever the PRA wanted to move in. If the Cubans succeeded in turning the Panamanian National Guard against their own government, there was no longer a reason for a U.S. presence there, more or less any thought of utilizing the Canal.

"I need you to go in there, Bernie. I need someone to worm their way up into the Presidential Palace . . . to find out what's really happening . . . to get our point across."

"That's Cobb's type of work."

"Henry's going to school."

"School?"

"He's learning how to become a guerilla."

Ryng blinked his eyes stupidly. He couldn't remember the last time he was caught with nothing to say. "Guerilla school . . ." He blinked again. "Where?"

"Havana. I had to send him to the source, Bernie. After that, he'll catch up with you. Meanwhile, you have a few weeks to learn everything you need to know about finance and international trade. Then it's off to Panama. Bring in Russian bodies . . . hardware . . . I don't care—whatever it takes."

Bernie Ryng remembered that he had just kept blinking, though he also remembered nodding when Dave Pratt went on to explain just how he was going to pull it all off.

Panama City

Ryng arrived at the Palacio restaurant first and the head waiter escorted him to a secluded table to await Kitty and her guest. At a moment past noon he jealously watched Kitty enter the room. The eyes of the predominantly male diners turned also. She and Cornejo made an attractive couple, for the presidential advisor was as tall and handsome as Kitty was beautiful. She held his arm possessively as they approached the table. Ryng was amused at his subtle feelings of anxiety, though the previous evening, still vivid in his mind, would have calmed the average man.

He stood as they approached the table. To his surprise Kitty extended her hand in formal greeting, saying as she did so, "Mr. Ryng, I'd like you to meet a very close friend of mine, Tomas Cornejo."

"I'm pleased to meet you after learning so much about you, Mr. Ryng." Cornejo's English was as impeccable as his dress. "Your reputation has preceded even the kind things Miss Alvarez has said about you." The man's handshake was firm, his expression sincere, and his eyes held Ryng's as he spoke.

The small talk over lunch was pleasant and polite, allowing the two men to gauge each other independently. There was never an indication on Kitty's part that her relationship with Ryng was more than formal.

Cornejo seemed the type of man to accept statements at face value. When Kitty excused herself after dessert, Ryng welcomed the chance to approach him directly. "Mr. Cornejo, I'm aware you occupy your responsible position because you are a hard man to fool. My purpose in Panama is a great deal more than purely business transactions."

"I'm aware of that." The response was matter-of-fact, as if Ryng had just commented on the attractive flowers on the table. Then he added, "Even nations as backward as Panama have intelligence services."

Ryng smiled in embarrassment. Henry Cobb would have been able to respond to a remark like that. "A good deal of my interest is in your so-called people's revolution," he said.

"My country feels that you underestimate what these rebels are capable of accomplishing."

Cornejo smiled almost condescendingly. "I see," he sighed. "We have ambassadors for this sort of thing you know, and—"

"That's already been tried."

"Your country has a rather poor record of analyzing and interfering in hemispheric problems, Mr. Ryng. Is it any wonder that your statesmen haven't been well received in their attempts to explain our revolutionary problems to us?"

"I'm not about to teach you about your own country. I know President Ramos is friendly with Havana. If you will give me some time, I think I can show that not only is that ally of yours actually contributing to sophisticated management of the rebels, but that they are directed from Moscow."

"I've heard enough about that so I doubt it's worth either of our time."

"Would you give me half an hour? I don't care to discuss this in front of Miss Alvarez." Both of them rose as Kitty returned to the table.

"I can never refuse a business proposition, Mr. Ryng. Why don't you come back to my office with me."

The Presidential Palace in Panama City was an impressive building. It radiated power, as such structures were meant to do. The military guard outside, which had been tripled since the successful attack at the airport, was brisk and efficient. What appeared from the street to be the entrance to the main building, was actually the entrance to a well-fortified wall which then opened on to a courtyard. The actual palace was toward the rear. Ryng could see by the placement of statues situated on wide bases that there were definite fields of fire for defense against any assault on the building.

Additional soldiers occupied the Palace's interior, and there was little difficulty in identifying the President's suite, from the number of guards outside it. Cornejo's office was adjacent to that of President Ramos. That told Ryng a great deal about the relationship of his host to the leader of the government.

"Mr. Ryng, I'm sure there is no need to explain to you that I am a very busy man and don't have a great deal of time for foreigners, regardless of their good intentions. But I'm not a stupid man either. You are no more a businessman than I am a peasant farmer. If you will be kind enough to tell me who sent you here and the reason for approaching me in this manner, perhaps we can start out with more mutual respect." Cornejo stopped, cocking his head slightly to one side, his hands spread before him as if to say in a gesture, let's not waste each other's time, okay?

Ryng liked this man—he was direct, forthright. There was no need in attempting to deceive a man who couldn't be easily fooled. "Right from the start, just so we're honest with each other, I don't represent the White House or the CIA or any other organization that may be at the top of your President's shit list. I am in the Navy. I represent a branch of Naval Intelligence." He went on to explain why Dave Pratt was so concerned. He emphasized the anticipated return of the Cuban combat brigade, the expansion of Soviet naval forces in Cuba and the Caribbean, and the ominous increase in Soviet naval units in areas contiguous to the Caribbean.

Cornejo's features never altered. He maintained a disinterested, rather than a bored, expression. Finally he interrupted. "Mr. Ryng, we do have an intelligence apparatus in Panama and I am aware of many, though not all, of the things you've mentioned. What I'm much more interested in is how this is going to affect us here in Panama."

"Do you think you are involved in merely a peasant's revolt?"

Again Cornejo's head cocked to one side. "You know my country better than me?"

A direct response seemed the best answer to a direct man. "It's not love of Panama that has me involved. It's the long-range effect on my own country. We are the real targets of the Soviets, not Panama. You're just a means to an end. We're the prize. Your canal may not have the military implications it had fifty years ago, but it still means a great deal. It means we might not be able to support Europe or the Middle East with any of our Pacific forces, and it also means that we can't resupply the Pacific, if necessary, from two-thirds of our ports. Do I really need to explain what Soviet control would mean to your country over the long run?''

Cornejo simply shook his head. "No. There are too many other factors to worry about that could influence the future. I'm more interested in the present . . . and you've been saving that for last, haven't you, Mr. Ryng?"

"The most important factor to you and to President Ramos, I would think, is that the middle-ranking officers, your captains and majors who have been trained in Cuba, are behind a great deal of this."

Cornejo's eyes narrowed slightly, but it was the only hint that what Ryng had said was having any effect.

"As you are aware, I saw a good deal of that attack at the airport four weeks ago. Understanding things like that is my business. Those were no peasants with hunting rifles. They were well-trained guerillas, commandos, rangers . . . whatever you want to call them. And the weapons they were using came directly from the Soviet Union. I saw one of the captured automatic rifles and you can be damn sure they weren't hand-me-downs from Fidel's grand days in the hills twenty-five years ago. And those helos weren't flown by country boys. If those pilots weren't Soviet, I'm willing to bet they were Cuban. Their intervention is always surreptitious. And, Mr. Cornejo, the reason a lot of this news isn't coming back to this palace is that your army is waiting for the right time to support them. Your generals are fat and happy and haven't the vaguest idea what their lower ranks are doing. And what your young officer corps doesn't realize is that they're a front for Moscow via Havana."

Ryng stopped. He realized that Cornejo had not interrupted him once. The man sat quietly behind his desk, only his eyes occasionally indicating that he was taking in what the American was saying. Ryng folded his arms and waited. He'd said enough, maybe too much, for the time being.

Cornejo took a deep breath, his eyes again holding Ryng's. "I've heard rumors of this from time to time, from different sources." And then his eyes lit up a bit, a smile breaking his set jaw. "But I've never heard it put so succinctly in, ah . . ." he looked at his watch. ". . . about twelve minutes. You have a way of being direct."

Ryng said nothing. He had to force Cornejo to question him.

"All right, what is their next step?"

"Colón. A raid on Colón. If they can just once impress President Ramos enough so that he's willing to talk to them, that's exactly the strategy. I can predict what they'll say. They don't want to take over the country. They want to effect some social changes. Then a couple of generals will be retired early. Pretty soon those captains and majors are all generals and all President Ramos's generals are retired. And those freshly minted generals will place combat trained Cuban troops from top command down to company level. Havana bureaucrats will appear as advisors in every level of your governments. Not too long after, Cuban teachers with Marxist views will be volunteered to assist in combatting illiteracy outside the city. And you'll find that Tomas Cornejo has a new job somewhere else, and pretty soon President Ramos will decide that the life of a retired president can be most attractive."

Cornejo's expression remained impassive. "You make it sound so easy . . . so logical."

"The Russians are patient. They're friendly—there'll be no violence. It's a gradual process. First it's anti-imperialist, then progressive, then socialist. The final step is Marxist/Leninist. That's why it's called the patient approach." Ryng leaned forward. "Then do you know who's going to start appearing on the streets? Cuban soldiers . . . a few Soviet advisors . . . at first. And do you know who's going to be running the Canal?"

"And how is the United States going to prevent all this?"

"No one would be happy with my suggestions. And Ramos isn't going to invite us unless some of his trusted advisors convince him that our assistance is the best thing for Panama."

"We will never be the best of friends with your country."

"Mr. Cornejo, I'm not your best friend either. We don't have to sleep together."

Cornejo smiled. "I like that approach. You'll never make it in the foreign service, Mr. Ryng, but I like it."

"Will you talk with President Ramos?"

"Yes. By all means. But I doubt it will make much of an impression on him. There's really no love lost between him and

America." Cornejo paused for a second. "But I have an even better idea. If he won't commit more troops to Colón, I'll go along with you. There might be something that can convince him," the advisor added. "Perhaps we could bring back some Soviet souvenirs."

It was too nice a day to accept the proffered ride back to his hotel from the palace. Bernie Ryng preferred to walk. Strolling along at his own pace, thinking, was like his morning shower. The mind could organize and catalog, making preparations for the next steps as new events took place. It was a process that Dave Pratt had taught him many years before.

Ryng's first introduction to Pratt came in the jungles of Vietnam when the older man commanded a riverboat squadron, leading patrols that were often trips with Lady Luck. The shorelines remained impenetrably green and peaceful, the muddy waters lapping gently at roots and overhanging branches, though the soft green mantle could explode with death at any moment. Dave Pratt was one of the few whose sixth sense kept more of his men alive and more boats intact. Late at night, drinking warm beer with the ever-present insects bombarding them, Pratt would patiently explain his methods of analyzing all of the intelligence reports, charting enemy movements, anticipating the goals of the opposition—he would go on and on and Bernie Ryng would absorb every bit of new information. It was an education in survival and leadership. It was also proof beyond doubt to Ryng that Pratt was a man to remain close to. There were few like him, with the innate talent to succeed so naturally.

As he now wandered the city streets, taking in the new sights and sounds and smells, Bernie Ryng understood how valuable a key Tomas Cornejo could be. Ryng no longer wondered at his luck in finding a man like that so quickly. He accepted it as a logical conclusion to his efforts, just as Dave Pratt would have.

Havana

Perhaps I am paranoid about the Russians, Esteban Alvarez reflected to himself. So what? I've every reason to feel that way. This is my part of the world. To those Russians we are just an extension of their policy against the Americans.

Admiral Khasan had just passed him in the corridor on the same floor as Premier Castro's office. He could be wrong, but Alvarez was sure the man had been with Castro again. When they passed in the hallway, there had been no exchange between them, just a nod of heads, an acknowledgment that the other existed.

But Esteban Alvarez was sure that Khasan was penetrating even more deeply into the Cuban government, and he was determined to prove the man was unreliable. The Russian may have created a power structure for himself in Havana, but Alvarez retained connections underground. That was part of being in the forefront of a popular revolt. He had given orders to his own people to have Khasan followed. The Russian would never recognize any shadow near him more than once, but he would never be alone either. If that meant he was paranoid, so be it! But he would never allow the Russians to set up shop in Panama like they had in Cuba.

Another individual who continued to intrude on Alvarez's thoughts was President Ramos. The man was in a no-win situation. The President had spent a day in Havana recently, mostly with Castro, though he'd taken some time to talk with Alvarez. Somehow their meeting lacked the flavor of the past. Once, years ago, the two young men had seemed inseparable, bound in the close spirit of an awakening Central America. Now, Ramos talked increasingly of concern about the PRA, of its infiltrating the Guardia, of his officers spending too much time training in Cuba.

Alvarez had nothing but respect for Ramos. His intentions had never been other than to gradually coax the President over to the side of reason. In his wildest dreams he never considered deposing Ramos, though the military leaders assumed that would occur. Alvarez envisioned a peaceful change, or as peaceful as it could be once Ramos and the old guard understood that it was really the will of the people. Uncomfortable with Ramos's increasing concern over the Russians, he wanted to guarantee they would not become a factor in Panamanian life—but that would have given him away. Instead, he thought it his responsibility, here and now, to insure that the Russians and the Cubans assisted them in altering Panamanian government and in seeing the Americans out the door. But, once accomplished, he also wanted to make sure they went their own way, as friends, as trading partners, as part of a peaceful buttress against American interference, but never on the same level as existed in Havana today. He was comfortably unaware that others in the leadership back home not only considered him paranoid, but worried about his ties to Ramos. Only his financial management of the PRA kept him alive.

Finally, Esteban Alvarez worried about his daughter, Kitty. She was the one human being in his lonely existence who meant more than life itself. Her achievements, even though they involved business with the Americans, added to his supreme joy in her. He could not admit that she was making life harder for the PRA by her success, so he argued that it was her very success that would insure American respect for their people in the future. He was sure she would never forsake her country. Perhaps, he thought, she might even provide the link that would keep the United States and its money available for business expansion in the future, though that argument alone engendered rumors that he was just plain crazy rather than paranoid.

Alvarez had gotten word through his grapevine that Kitty had been aboard the plane blown up at Torrijos Airport, and he had been enraged—to the point that he sent back word to execute the officer responsible. The first rule in the guerilla warfare that Alvarez had demanded, was insuring that the PRA avoided endangering anyone of value to the country. Just one life taken in one of their attacks could sway the public against them. It was hard enough to fathom that they had almost killed his daughter.

His informant also delicately indicated that Señorita Alvarez was often in the company of an American who had been on the plane with her, a man who had saved her life and now seemed to be a constant companion. Just the thought of an American courting her left a sour taste in his mouth. Though she was old enough to lead her own life, a father was always a father, and she would always appear in his dreams as his little girl. With her mother gone for so long, Esteban Alvarez thought about her now, wondered where she was and what she was doing, and with whom. . . .

Henry Cobb jumped back in the shadows, squeezing against the side of the building until stucco dug into his back in a thousand tiny places. As he waited for the man to pass by, Cobb wondered what it was that alerted him to the man's approach. The guard was a whistler, giving away his path a hundred yards before he could be seen. But for some unknown reason his casual music had either ceased or Henry Cobb's concentration had gotten the better of him.

When he arrived in Havana, Cobb knew he must learn the location of his prime sources as quickly as possible. There was no telling how long he had in Havana before someone figured he was an impostor. So he'd gone about his job the best way he knew—locating the offices of Commodore Navarro and his staff and calmly breaking into each one. The Cubans had not learned the lessons of security practiced in most other nations, Cobb assumed, simply because the threat of compromise was so limited in their little country. But ease of access meant little to him, since there was little of value to be found in the offices he entered.

That's when it became evident to him that this really would be a Soviet operation, just as Pratt anticipated. The Cubans were exactly what they had been for the past twenty-five years—a front for the Kremlin. What he was after would be under the Russians' control, and it was likely not shared with the Cubans at this stage in planning.

The guard passed by, outlined in the glare of a light across the way. But that guard wasn't the whistler, Cobb realized, as he checked his watch. It was after midnight. So that was it. They'd just changed guards, and the Russians patrolled their own areas after midnight! It made little difference to him, but it would change his approach inside. None of the Cuban offices were guarded at night, but you could be damn sure if the

Russians were in charge, they would be much more concerned with security.

He inched away from the corner of the building, moving from shadow to shadow to the side door. He felt up and down the frame with his fingers. Two locks. One was just like the others he'd opened. They were original with the doors and easy to jimmy with the same plastic strip. He snapped on the tiny pen light he carried on each of his evening forays to examine the other one and laughed silently to himself. The Russians had shipped some of their most sophisticated electronic gear to Cuba, but no one in the Kremlin had ever anticipated the need for modern locks or sophisticated security devices. The second lock must have come from a store in downtown Havana, purchased by a frustrated Russian who hoped it would discourage drunks or curiosity seekers. The third key he tried responded with a satisfactory click, and he slipped it open and crept inside.

Silently, Cobb covered the hallway on the first floor a step at a time. Barely breathing, he would pause each time, listening for any sign of life. But there was nothing—not a lighted office, no sign of anyone patrolling the corridors. It was empty and much like the other buildings he'd broken into. Though the Russians had taken the trouble to install additional locks, life in Havana had lulled these people into the casual lifestyle of the natives. He was surprised at the obvious lapse in security.

He moved quickly to the next floor. Admiral Khasan's chief of staff's office was located there. The pen light revealed one more simple lock. He was almost fooled by another sound as he worked the key into the lock, waiting for the telltale click. There had been no initial warning, but the sound he heard was much more than a single click. The sound of the dog's claws on the wooden floor ceased, and Cobb understood exactly what was happening as the German shepherd leaped through the air toward him.

As he rolled to the side, shoulder turned against the impact, arms tucked under him away from those jaws, the dog allowed that first fearsome snarl. With the impact as they both crashed to the floor, came the smell of the animal and the deep gurgling sound as it instinctively dug with its teeth for a grip. But

Cobb was still rolling. The dog had no better opportunity to see him as their bodies met and for a moment all was motion, Cobb protecting himself, the animal lunging, snapping, attempting to grip and tear.

With his feet out and kicking, Cobb felt a heel make contact with the dog's huge, solid head. A yelp escaped from its mouth as it momentarily halted its attack. Cobb knew there was only a split second. It was merely instinct as the beast recovered its senses. But it was enough time for Cobb to make his move. Intuition governed his movements. Getting to his feet would be just as foolish as trying to run. There was more advantage remaining on the dog's level.

He knew where the head was and what the dog's next move would be. Lunging forward and to the side to meet the charge, Cobb heard the deep growl almost at the same time his forearm made contact with its chest. He could feel the animal's muscles ripple as the force of its leap snapped his arm back. Then he was heaving his arm in the opposite direction, first halting the beast in midair—his own muscle and weight opposing the thrust of the charge—then the dog's body was coming back toward him, its feet kicking frantically for a toehold, claws ripping at his clothes. Cobb thrust a leg across the dog's spine, still pulling his arm back with every ounce of strength he had. It was not the first time he had done this, and he knew the animal would now attempt to twist frantically out of his grasp as its head came backward. But Cobb had the advantage of experience. The dog had never before run into this situation.

A high-pitched snarl of rage escaped the animal's jaws as its neck snapped. Both bodies slumped to the floor, Cobb underneath, his face muffled by a huge shoulder. Though he was gasping for air, his body shaking with the sudden effort, there was no time to rest. That last cry of rage and agony from the beast would have been heard outside. He heaved the body away and rose to his knees.

At that instant he remembered that the guards seemed to follow set paths on their rounds, and he had memorized them as he hid in the shadows. Where would the closest one be? How long had he been inside? There was no time to slip into one of the offices and go through a back window. It had to be at either end of the corridor. He made his choice and raced to one end, unlocking and raising a window. With a quick look to either side, Cobb balanced briefly on the windowsill before jumping just far enough to clear the stairs at the door below. Landing softly, he could hear shouts from the far end of the building.

There would be more of them soon, but he had anticipated their moves correctly. It was simply a matter of melting into the shadows. In a few short minutes Cobb managed to work his way back to his own living quarters and creep through the window he had left less than an hour before. Once again he became lieutenant Corazon, a student at the guerilla school who seemed strangely brighter than his compatriots.

Panama City

Kitty chewed on an ice cube after taking the last sip of her drink. Ryng's arm encircled her shoulders. Bending his head closer, he playfully nipped her ear. "Let's go up to the apartment. We can't do it right here on the sofa." They were in a very pleasant, almost deserted lounge in the hotel nearby. The lights were low and soft music played quietly in the background.

She rested her head on his shoulder. "Who says we're going to do anything? Maybe last night was a fluke. Maybe I drank too much and you took advantage of me." She giggled coyly when he lifted her head and kissed her. "Besides, that air conditioning is still broken. We might stick together."

"On the contrary, Kitty. I think we'll have to worry about sliding apart."

"You sure you wouldn't like just one more drink before we go into that hothouse?"

"Can't," he said, shaking his head in mock seriousness. "I'm going to be busy tomorrow and tomorrow night. Sobriety has to be the word."

"Perhaps abstention would be a good idea too. I could go back to my own air-conditioned place." But when she looked up at him, her sardonic expression softened. "I wouldn't do that, honestly. Air conditioning or no air conditioning, it doesn't make any difference to me as long as I'm with you."

"Okay, then it's settled. Let's trip on up to the Ryng hothouse." He tossed some money on the table, then waited until she checked how much he'd left. She'd learned he was one of those Americans who could never understand the value of another country's money. Twice he'd left too much, and twice a waiter had come running after them because he hadn't paid the entire bill.

"You're generous tonight, but not overly so. Let him keep that oversized tip. I'm so ready to get up there that I don't want to wait for your change."

They strolled through the warm streets arm in arm, occasionally slowing or stopping to kiss briefly, anticipation of the night ahead enough to make words unnecessary. As the elevator carried them up to his floor, he pulled her into his arms in a long, deep kiss. The automatic door had opened and was already closing when he realized they'd stopped at his floor.

"We have a choice," he whispered, searching for the 'open door' button on the elevator panel. "We can do it here and ride up and down all night, or we can get off and go into my apartment."

She rubbed against him. "I'm ready to go anywhere with you, but the bed in there will be softer, my love." The door reopened for the third time as the warning buzzer sounded, and they stepped reluctantly out and down the hall.

After opening the door, he backed in, one arm again around Kitty as he fumbled for the wall switch. She wiggled out of his grasp. "First one to get their clothes off wins . . ." She stopped in mid-sentence as she tripped over an object in the dark.

As she fell, Ryng snapped on the lights. Her scream was an echo to the brilliance that flooded the room, almost as if the sudden light had frightened her. Even before Kitty's scream faded, the light illuminated the object she'd tripped over. Red, sticky blood reflected on her hands, for she had touched what once had been a man's face. It was now a hideous, barely identifiable mass. The features were so battered that a stranger would never have been able to speculate what the man once looked like.

Revolted by the bloody mess, she fell against the couch, where she buried her face in her hands, whimpering with fright.

Ryng knelt beside her, pulling her head onto his chest and murmuring in her ear. It took a moment for him to identify the body, for the features were horribly distorted. But he could tell that the man was Pratt's agent, Moran, the one who had visited him the day before at the hotel, and warned him about the raid on Colón. Ryng could tell instinctively that the hit had been done very professionally. There was no need to check anything on the body until Kitty was calmed down.

As her whimpering turned into sobs, he spoke more firmly. "Come on, let me take you into the bedroom. I'll help you to your feet, but for God's sake don't look back at him." He half carried her into the bedroom, sitting her on the bed. Wetting a cloth in the bathroom, he washed the blood from her hands and face. He soaked another cloth for a moment in cold water, then brought it back and laid it across her forehead.

She opened her eyes for the first time, her fear still evident. "I'm sorry. I've seen dead people before . . . just weeks ago at the airport. It didn't bother me then. I didn't mean to lose control, honestly I didn't." She wiped more tears from her cheeks. As quickly as her control evaporated, Ryng noted, it was returning—almost as if she could turn it on and off.

"Don't worry. Just relax. It was the shock. That was part of their idea—to scare the hell out of me." He stroked her cheek lightly with his fingers. "After all, it wasn't what you were looking forward to when we walked in."

She half smiled, blinking back the last of her tears. "No . . . no, I guess not. Do you know who he is?"

Ryng nodded. "I met him briefly. I guess it's better if I tell you more about myself . . . if you're still going to want to hang around with me."

"I do."

He used his handkerchief to wipe away the remnants of her tears. After getting her a glass of water, he related more of his reasons for being in Panama, but there were no names mentioned. She listened calmly, never saying a word, nodding occasionally. Much of it she had heard once before.

When he finished, she stated simply, "I hadn't quite expected that, but I knew you were up to something, especially when you wanted so much to meet Tomas." She placed a hand on his. "But please . . . please be careful with Tomas. He's a good friend, a very special one. Will you promise me?"

He nodded. "I promise."

"Thank you." Her eyes widened. "Don't I remember seeing something on the floor, near that man's body? Or maybe it's my imagination. Oh, I don't know." She shook her head. "I could be imagining just about anything at this point."

"I'll go look." In a moment he was back in the bedroom with an envelope in his hands.

"What is it?"

"An airline ticket . . . to Miami. It's in my name and it's for tomorrow's flight."

"That's all?"

"No, not quite, Someone left a short invitation suggesting that I'd join my friend there if I didn't take that flight." He turned the ticket envelope over in his hands and saw something was on the back.

"I saw that too," Kitty said. "What is it?"

"It looks like blood . . . almost like writing." His brows knit as he tried to determine what it said. "Here, I can't make it out. Looks like Spanish."

"Let me see." Kitty was sitting up now and she took it from him, turning it over in her hands. "It is Spanish, but I don't understand."

"What does it say?"

"*By sea* . . . but I don't know what that means . . . just *by sea*."

"He must have scrawled that before he died. I'm sure it has something to do with tomorrow night's raid at Colón."

Havana

Admiral Khasan pushed back from his desk, stretching, inadvertently placing his feet in the midst of the papers on his blotter. It was unlike him, or at least unlike the Victor Khasan he had been before he met Chita. A picture of her had evolved in his mind while he was moving ships about tentatively on his desk chart of the western Atlantic, Caribbean, and Gulf of Mexico. It was a very simple chart with a plastic cover, and the little rubber ships remained in place by friction. He had developed it himself at sea years before for mental exercise.

Because it was work that he loved, it was even more unusual that Chita's vision took possession of his thoughts. On the other hand, recurring visions of the recent night with Chita had blotted the little ship markers from his mind—Chita was a temptress who reveled in exhibiting herself to Khasan. When they were in the privacy of her apartment, she would model lingerie that Victor had never seen before, never imagined in Russia, and at the same time she would provide vodka, frozen in blocks of ice and served in glasses stored in her freezer. In her bedroom there were mirrors. Wherever he looked, whatever they were doing, she made sure he could also watch in one of the many strategically placed mirrors. While he wanted to boast of these delights to someone, it was all something he would be unable to put into words or commit to paper, because it was nothing he, or any man he knew, had ever experienced.

When he pushed farther back from the desk, his eyes tightly shut, his right heel eased a surface action group—the one intended to close off the Galleons Passage between Grenada and the islands of Trinidad and Tobago—on top of Martinique. The left heel transferred the submarines blockading the Yucatan Channel into the Pacific. Looking at the strategic choices his feet had accomplished, he laughed silently to himself and rose to look out the window at the harbor. A new Soviet guided missile cruiser was maneuvering to secure to a buoy, but his mind saw only Chita balancing on her toes at the end of the bed, teasing him to look at each mirror around the room and use his imagination.

Khasan glanced at his watch. The figures 17-29-33 swam up on its digital face—late afternoon but too early to go to Chita's. And there was no way he'd go home, because he'd already told his wife he was spending the entire evening with Navarro. What the hell, he mused, if I go over there now maybe . . . The more he considered surprising her, the more it appealed to him.

He went back to his desk to reorder his papers. Khasan was a military man and it was ingrained since his days as a cadet that one never left a cluttered desk. And considering the content of the materials on his desk, even his wandering mind could not leave such papers floating about for prying eyes.

He paused briefly over the report from his man in Baranquilla, and his own response. It was exactly what Khasan had wanted, and his man had confirmed that the old American destroyer would be perfect for the mission. Another contained the current position reports of the submarines transiting the Atlantic and when they were projected on station. There was more than enough time to jockey them about. With an inward grin, he moved his errant submarines back to the Yucatan Channel and the surface action group to the Galleons Passage.

For just a moment, a very short one with Chita crowding his thoughts, he studied the ship markers he'd been moving about his chart. There were myriad choke points around the West Indian islands of the Caribbean—Windward Passage, Mona Passage, Anegada Passage, Guadeloupe Passage, Martinique Passage, St. Vincent Passage, the seventy-five mile wide Galleons Passage between Grenada and Tobago which would be the most difficult now, and finally the Straits of Florida between Cuba and Key West. That was the real challenge. He was not yet prepared to communicate with Moscow on just how he was going to handle that. Each of the markers in position displayed in grease pencil the name of the choke point he intended to have that ship cover. As he picked them off the chart one by one and placed them back in the box, he noticed the names were smudging. Quickly, while still clear in his mind, he replaced them in their proper position, to memorize later.

He locked the papers in his file drawer. Looking about the room, he wondered where to place the chart. As visions of Chita swam back from his subconscious, he slipped the chart under his desk, knowing there was no way anyone who might utilize or understand it could gain access to this building, let alone his office.

Henry Cobb felt as comfortable in the Cuban uniform as any other he had ever worn. Not only was it cool, but there were so many uniforms evident in the streets of Havana that little attention was paid to any of them. It was superb cover.

As he approached the apartment building, he recognized the outside immediately. Others in his class had pointed it out as the home of a number of ladies who entertained. At that level of society, they were called neither whores nor prostitutes. They "entertained," and to call them anything else was to insult a number of military and government officials of high standing who patronized them.

He found the name listed next to her buzzer in the lobby —Chita Monteria. He pushed the button twice. When she responded, he said in Spanish, "Señorita Monteria, this is Lieutenant Corazon. I have a message from Admiral Khasan for you. May I bring it up?"

She opened the door cautiously, unchaining it without hesitation when she saw that he was in uniform. Cobb immediately appreciated the expensive decor of the apartment as well as the clothes and perfume. Khasan certainly knew what he was doing, Cobb mused, appreciating why the Russian was taking such a chance.

He turned to her, clicking his heels together efficiently. "I believe you have a meeting with Admiral Khasan this evening?"

"I thought that's why you were calling . . . you had a message," she answered. "Of course, he is—" She stopped abruptly. "I don't understand."

"Perhaps, señorita, this will help." Cobb removed an envelope full of cash from his pocket, counting off a large sum. He handed it to her. "Here, this is for you."

She shook her head. "Who are you?"

"I'm a businessman. I'd like to make a deal with you."
Again he extended the money in her direction. "Won't you take this?"

She shrugged. "You know I am seeing someone else tonight."

"It's not for me. I don't want anything from you. This is purely a business deal, like I said. You take the money, we make a deal."

She looked at the cash remaining in the envelope, which was a great deal more than he had offered her. "What do you have in mind for the rest?"

"That's all part of our business deal. Will you take this?"

"Tell me more about your deal."

Again he extended the first sum to her. "This is simply for spending the evening with Admiral Khasan and keeping him occupied. This," he added, dividing the money in the envelope and adding the second sum to the first, "is if you keep him here until at least midnight." He indicated the balance of the money. "This is if you keep him here until two in the morning."

"He likes to get home early because he worries about his wife becoming suspicious. I don't know . . ."

Cobb shrugged. "It's easy money." He peeled off the initial wad and handed it to her. "Look, this is for you anyway, for occupying him as long as you can." She took it tentatively. It was a great deal of money, more than any of her guests had ever thought of offering her. "I'd just as soon give you the rest right now."

"What if I take it and then he doesn't stay until two?"

"You may be sure I'll be back to collect." In the gray eyes that seemed to look right through her, Chita saw he had every intention of collecting if Khasen did not stay until two. "I have heard that you have a fertile imagination," he added.

It was worth it, every cent of it. She had never seen money like this before. "Will this happen again? Am I going to have to worry about you again?"

"If Admiral Khasan stays here until two tonight, I can guarantee that this is the first and last time you will ever see me."

Again those eyes seemed to assure her that this man was absolutely correct in what he was saying, that she would never see him again. And she had no desire to. Never in her life had she seen a Spanish-speaking person with eyes like that. She clasped the money to her breast and nodded agreement.

Again his heels clicked together. "Good evening, Señorita Monteria," he said over his shoulder as he closed the door behind him.

There was a mirror in the elevator and Henry Cobb grinned cockily back at his image as he descended to the lobby of the apartment building. Now that little episode a few minutes ago was more his style—the perfect set-up. From everything he'd learned about Khasan in the man's files in Pratt's office back in the Pentagon, his greatest weakness since arriving in Havana was sex. With enough money for Chita Monteria, he probably could have kept Khasan there for days, or at least until he was too weak to perform!

As the doors opened and Cobb stepped out into the lobby, his bravado changed to a silent acknowledgment of Dave Pratt. He was the one who had developed Henry Cobb into the specialist who passed through the lobby and out onto the street as Lieutenant Corazon. It was Pratt who recognized Cobb's inherent talents and built them into what Cobb was to-day—one of Pratt's most effective operatives.

There is no man quite like Pratt, Cobb mused, as he waited at a crosswalk for the light to change. No one I've ever met. We are his creations, his eyes and ears, now more than ever. As the light changed, Henry Cobb wondered for a moment about the things Pratt never revealed to them. They would often laugh about the challenges they met on each mission that they had been unaware of, and each time they would agree Pratt had been right to keep quiet.

Would that be true this time? he wondered.

A Jungle Camp in Panama

A shaft of sunlight filtered through the treetops, flashing off a dangling mirror. For just an instant James Grambling was blinded by the glare. Then a breeze whispered through the trees. The mirror fluttered, redirecting the ray to the basin of water at his side, and Grambling put out a steadying hand, smearing shaving cream on the glass. It was just one more of the minor inconveniences when he was on a mission.

Grambling finished shaving, splashed some cool water on his face, and toweled off. While other men trotted about the site in the early morning without shirts, he went back into the tent for his. He was their leader and they expected to see him reappear wearing the khaki short-sleeved shirt with his colonel's eagles on the collar.

He smiled down at Maria, still sleeping on the raised platform that served as their bed. They were used to better accommodations, but at least the wooden deck was high enough off the ground to keep snakes, scorpions, spiders, and other things off them as they slept. The netting that served as a door kept mosquitoes and other airborne insects out, if the tent remained darkened at night. As long as Maria was with him, that was all right with Grambling.

Colonel James Grambling was commanding officer of Special Unit Amador. Each special unit of the PRA was named after a revolutionary hero. He wanted to name his group after the Nicaraguan, August Sandino, but the Sandinistas were giving that name a Soviet smell these days. Special Unit Amador had been trained for months in Santiago, Cuba, in the art of high-speed coastal attacks. The unit was now camped in the hills overlooking Portobelo, a Caribbean coastal town about twenty-five miles northeast of Colón.

Grambling's strikingly handsome features were the result of the mixture of bloods beginning with his great-grandfather before the turn of the century. The first James Grambling had come to Panama in 1882 from New Orleans, one of five hundred jobless blacks hired by the French to work on the Canal. In those days white men were the engineers, surveyors, accountants, and paper pushers, and blacks from America's deep south, Jamaica, and other islands, were laborers along with many of the country's Indians.

The French were paying decent wages in the jungles of Panama. The work day was from five-thirty in the morning until six at night, grueling under the hot sun, whenever it shone, and in the oppressive humidity during the eight-month rainy season. There were a multitude of ways to enter the next world before a man's time was up. If the mudslides didn't crush him, he might be bitten by a snake, a scorpion, or a tarantula or attacked by a jaguar. He might also suffer a pain-wracked death as a result of one of the many jungle diseases, though malaria or yellow fever were by far the most common way to go.

Of the five hundred blacks recruited, more than two hundred of them were dead within three months. Another hundred and seventy-five were gone in six months. It seemed obvious to James Grambling that he must be immune to the yellow fever, but he had no idea why he failed to contract malaria, since there was simply no known immunity to it.

His contract with the company expired at the end of twelve months but, unlike most of the others who purchased tickets from the company to sail back to New Orleans, Grambling stayed. He knew a black man could expect little in the way of opportunity in Louisiana, but he could be accepted nearly as an equal in this Central American country. There were so many mixtures that natives could trace black, Spanish, Indian,

English, Portuguese or Mayan blood in their heritage. The tall, handsome American Negro was accepted there, especially with the money he'd doubled in poker games and a desire to stay in their country and develop a business.

He married a girl he'd met in Panama City and a family began within a year. Each child was more handsome than the next. They displayed the high cheek bones and central African warrior features of their father but retained more of the Mayan color of their mother's skin. The combination created a family of tall, beautiful, strong children.

His first son, Frederick, born in 1890, became a superb manager for the small businesses his father developed to accommodate the Americans who came to finish the Canal. The young man concentrated much of his time on financial stability, investing the profits in other companies developing in Panama. As Frederick often pointed out to his son, Martin, there would be businesses going bankrupt as long as men walked the earth, but the Grambling family would survive tough times if their money was spread through the economy of the little country. By the time Martin joined the family business, the Gramblings were a respected force in the country. Members were elected to government positions, they gave generously to charity, and they offered much of their free time to the cultural development of Panama City.

In 1950, Martin's first son was born and he named the boy after his grandfather, James. There was now little evidence of black blood in the Grambling features, though Martin's children still had the high, wide cheekbones of the first James Grambling. By the time little James was fifteen, and no longer finding the title "little" to his liking, he was being compared to pictures of his great grandfather.

But now, over a hundred years later, the great-grandson, James Grambling, had become a natural leader who had developed a hatred for the United States. He could not abide a country that owned a strip through the center of his own, garrisoned a large military force in his country, and as far as he could see, treated his people like dirt. When he was old enough to attend college, he knew the Americans weren't as bad as he claimed they were, but saying so attracted followers he needed if he was going to have a part in Panama's future. He refused to follow in his other brother's footsteps and attend an American college. Instead, he chose to remain in his own country and joined the Guardia after a couple of disappointing years at the local university.

Since the Americans protected the Canal, there was little need for any large native military force in the country. James soon learned that the U.S. preferred it that way, especially since the natives were restless in the 1960s and 1970s. When he was twenty-five he was chosen to attend military school in Havana. He was the leader in his class and returned to his country as a proud officer.

Pride also inspired ambition, and James Grambling found that too many of the senior officers and the politicians in his country were pleased with what they had once the Canal was returned to them by the United States. Yet the people and the countryside beyond the cities were still desperately poor. His dissatisfaction was encouraged by other young men in the military and he became aware of the existence of a group that wanted to improve their country. They thought that only through a new system of government could they achieve their ends. While most rebel organizations fail for lack of money, material, and training, this organization was very much alive because of aid from their Cuban friends. Much of the assistance they received came from men whom James had known during his years in Havana. They wanted to help and claimed that in twenty years the countries on the Caribbean littoral could be united much like the European community, or the Americans to the north who were their enemy.

Grambling rose to become a colonel very rapidly because of his natural leadership instincts. Almost before he was aware of it, he was looked upon as a critical factor in the major drive to gain President Ramos's recognition. To do this they would have to show both the people and President Ramos that they could appear in any part of the country and secure ports, cities or even airports for as long as they desired. Once the people understood their power, Ramos would listen.

The raid on Colón was planned, then, for the benefit of the people. They would see the government of the second largest city in the country in the hands of rebel forces for as long as twelve hours. What the Panamanian military didn't suspect was the naval effort that was planned. The shock effect of an attack from sea would send the army in the opposite direction. This was exactly what Havana planned when they selected James Grambling and a number of his counterparts for special schooling in high-speed boats earlier that year in Santiago.

Grambling strolled to the edge of the clearing and looked down the slopes through the heavy undergrowth to the town of Portobelo. It was a sleepy little place at the end of a harbor that faced to the west, a peninsula to the north protecting Portobelo's anchorage and piers from the damaging Caribbean "northers." Although the morning sun sparkled on sloped metal or red-tile roofs, it was still too early for the streets to be bustling. And since there were no major highways into Portobelo—her major commerce was fishing—the people were left to go their own quiet, poor way.

Only a select few of the natives realized that the nearby jungle, which reached to the water's edge along the harbor, concealed high-speed attack craft. Some were large Soviet-made hydrofoils delivered only a few years ago to the Cubans. Others were conventional guided missile boats, heavily armed and dangerous. Skeleton crews lived aboard them, and today Grambling and his own men would join them for the attack on Colón. Rebel agents had leaked just enough word for the government to expect a land attack. A thrust from the sea would make an unforgettable impression.

"Jaimé . . . Jaimé." Maria was striding toward him. Few people spoke to him by other than his military title. Only those who were very close called him Jaimé. The fact that he bore an American surname was difficult enough for them to accept, but a first name of James was too much. To them he was Jaimé.

He smiled as Maria approached. Somehow she looked attractive even in the khaki military outfit she preferred. I couldn't have done much better, he thought to himself. The only other woman he'd ever cared for was the student he knew when he'd turned twenty, Kitty Alvarez. But she'd run counter to what he believed in and gone to the United States for her education. When she came home, she involved herself in the system he despised, and any relationship they might have had was lost. But he would never shake her memory.

"Jaimé, why didn't you wake me up? I might have slept there all day." But she was smiling as she chided him, and he smiled back.

"No you wouldn't, not today. I'm surprised you weren't awake before me. You're usually the one sounding reveille." Looking about him, he saw the camp following a well-established routine. Special Unit Amador had constructed this simple camp months before, in anticipation of this raid. Sites had been selected by the leaders at the suggestion of their Cuban advisors, and planning was all-important. Logistics demanded an equivalent effort. Successful battles were won by proper, detailed planning and the selection of and replacement of necessary supplies well beforehand. He realized his Cuban friends had likely been taught that by their Soviet mentors. Grambling hated the Russians almost as much as the Americans—but still, they needed the Russians.

"I heard movement around camp," she answered. "And the food." She sniffed the air tentatively, recognizing the odors emanating from the mess tent. "The coffee and bacon are reveille for me."

"Come on," he said, motioning her toward the source of the pleasant aromas. "Let's have some breakfast. It's the last square meal you'll get for a while." He insisted on maintaining a discrete distance from Maria outside of his tent. There was no point in holding over his men's heads the fact that his woman traveled with him while so many were by themselves.

The Pentagon

Dave Pratt stared in fascination at the bird hopping along the branch outside his office window. He grinned to himself when he realized that he'd turned from his desk because some goddamn bird was making a racket outside, ruining his concentration. But what amused him was the fact that the bird was hopping about on that limb quite comfortably on one leg! It was most businesslike in its approach to whatever it was doing, apparently oblivious to the fact that it had only one leg left.

He wheeled himself over to his office door and turned the lock. The Admiral wasn't about to have anyone wandering in at a time like this. Back at the window he searched in vain for his little bird. It was the only audience he would have allowed, now that he had made up his mind. Locking the wheels of the chair, he placed his hands on the arms and pushed up until he was in a standing position. That was something he'd done before for his wife—Alice had encouraged him to take a step, offered her arm, but he was the kind of man who would first have to do it himself. He promised that when he tried, she would be the first to know about it.

He searched the tree for his little friend, for some moral support, but the bird was gone. The muscles tensed in his right leg as he attempted to lift it. Nothing. Very slowly, he slid the foot along the floor . . . two inches . . . four . . . six . . . and placed it firmly. Then he brought the left one along beside it in the same manner. Again he followed the same process, and again it was successful! Not bad, not bad. His legs were weak, no doubt about that. But he wasn't going off on a hike. The next steps brought him to the windowsill, and he leaned against it thankfully.

He relaxed for a while looking out on the Potomac. It had been some time since he'd seen it from this vantage point. It gave one a different perspective. He fervently wished that tough little bird had been around to urge him along. Very slowly, using the sill for balance, he turned and took the same shuffling steps back to the chair. Sitting was something else again. He leaned forward until he had a good grip on the arms, then lowered and twisted his body at the same time until he was once again seated.

It had been exhausting. One more step and I might have been flat on my face, he mused. But my legs are coming back! I told them they would. Alice would be the first one he'd show —that night. Then he might tell a few others, because it was really something big. This would kill any arguments that it was time for Dave Pratt to retire!

He knew, and the doctors concurred, that the problem was

linked to his mind. There was no evidence of permanent physical damage. It had been a sharp blow to the head—a tremendous shock—that had left him that way, and Pratt believed that one day he would overcome his problem. It could be that the injury and the loss of two great ships in one day created a psychological block. There were others who understood, those close to him like Ryng and Cobb, and they each gave him all the time he needed. Dave Pratt was ready to return that faith—in spades!

Pratt had been analyzing the Caribbean situation for days. His intelligence network, with several small contributions from Cobb and Ryng, added to the picture he was developing. But it had been taking time, more time than usual, enough so that Dave Pratt even hesitated at proclaiming his own genius at this sort of thing. Now that his injury forced him to direct strategy from an office rather than from flag plot on a ship, there were days that he did question himself. Yet he had no doubt it could be done. It was just a bit harder in coming to him this time. Over the years Washington had placed so much emphasis on Europe, the Middle East, Japan, three years in Korea, twelve years in Vietnam, that it was hard to take the Caribbean situation as seriously, to accept what Moscow might have had in mind.

Now the charts on his wall took on a new meaning. Once again his mind recognized so much more than the eye. Water surfaces, land masses, and islands were altered into individual revolutions, leaders, followers, religions, cultures, ideologies. . . . Once again he was seeing a world apart from that which most people perceived. Conflict became an integral function of those charts. It knew no institutional boundaries. Straits and passages became choke points. Submarines and surface action groups not yet on station staked out invisible boundaries over the empty blue expanses on his charts.

The puzzle that he had been struggling to piece together for days began to fall into place. There were some parts missing, sectors that he had yet to fully comprehend and fit into those spaces, but in the next few hours he came to understand them. Panama took on a new meaning. He understood why that country and her canal, which no longer carried the strategic importance of the past, became so critical. It was no longer the

same symbol it had been in the first half of the twentieth
century, but it became an integral, symbolic part of a much
greater strategy. With a set of dividers and a pencil, he was
able to see where the obscure meanderings of those Soviet
ships would have new meaning in the days to come—their
weapons and their threat value established a purpose for each
location he projected for them. Those roll on-roll off merchant ships were probably loaded with military supplies.

The significance was frightening, even to Pratt, for it
negated so much that had been accepted as gospel in geo-
politics. The Kremlin was not about to fight over Europe, or
the Middle East, for that matter. They were going to cross the
Atlantic Ocean and establish the system that would gradually
force the U.S. back within her own borders. There would be
no great land battle for Europe, no nuclear exchange that
would threaten the Motherland. Outside of naval engagements, there would be little loss of Soviet life. It would be the
blood of Spanish-speaking people, more than any other, that
would flow.

Dave Pratt understood that neither he nor any other man
could halt those revolutions that were the natural evolution of
government. They were an element of history still to be written
in the Caribbean, and interference would never settle those
disputes that had been ongoing for generations. But he could
influence elements of the Soviet strategy. Their foothold in the
Caribbean could be limited and the Cuban stranglehold could
be minimized. He remembered telling Ryng the last time he
had been in this office, "Save the revolutions for the people,
Bernie."

He worked frantically, almost afraid that the shadow that
had hovered above his puzzle would return. He plotted lines
and positions on his charts, wrote preliminary orders which
would eventually flow from Washington to fleet commanders
to unit commanders, and most importantly, he prepared the
orders that would have to be delivered to Bernie Ryng. He
hoped fervently that Cobb would soon appear in Panama City
to assist Bernie, and he needed any backup from them he
could get to affirm his decisions.

The Palacio, Panama City

In Panama City, Tomas Cornejo invited Bernie Ryng to breakfast in the Presidential Palace. Ryng arrived in a black limousine sent by Cornejo. He was escorted by an army colonel to an exquisitely decorated private dining room.

Cornejo stood up when Ryng was announced, coming around the table to shake hands. His smile was genuine this morning. "Mr. Ryng, I've been looking forward to this opportunity to talk with you again. I've been doing a bit more thinking since our conversation yesterday, and"—he extended his hand toward the empty chair across from where he'd been sitting—"perhaps I owe you somewhat of an apology."

Ryng accepted a cup of coffee from a silver service offered by one of the many servants hovering about the dining room. "I appreciate your saying so, Mr. Cornejo, but I'm not sure anything was ever said that required an apology." From his first impression, Ryng liked Cornejo, but he was also wary of him, especially when Cornejo suggested he might join him in Colón this evening.

"No, really, I'm very serious." Cornejo leaned toward Ryng, elbows on the table, hands folded under his chin. "You see, the automatic reaction, whenever any American chides us about the Cubans or the Russians, is negative. And I can assure you it will be the same wherever you go in this country . . . at least in government circles. It will take years for our countrymen to accept Americans as friends again, believe me."

"I understood that before I ever left the States. That's certainly nothing to apologize about." Ryng decided it was time to get along with whatever needed saying before they went on to Colón. It was nice to be polite and start the day off on the right foot, but deference from a man in Cornejo's position didn't impress him.

Cornejo's hand rose to stop him. "But there is, Mr. Ryng, and it's time for you to listen to me and try to be"—he stopped for a moment to search for the word—"impartial, if you will. That's how I determined I should be when you were in my office yesterday, and that's how I would like you to be for just a few minutes now.

"You see," he continued, "I went to President Ramos's office shortly after you left yesterday. I explained the conversation we had together. I want you to understand that President Ramos is a good man . . . a decent man . . . and he really has his heart in doing what's right for Panama. Every day there are so many events to evaluate, so many decisions to make, so much to take into account in trying to make our poor country a strong country. When I told him of our meeting, at first he became angry. I think he was about to ask me to leave. But he is a very smart man. He stopped right in the middle of a sentence and looked sharply at me. Then he got up from his chair and walked to the window. His lips were moving almost as if he was thinking out loud. Then he turned to me and was actually smiling." At this point Cornejo's face relaxed into a smile as he related the meeting. "He admitted he was tired of Americans telling us how bad our friends are after everything the Americans did to us over the years. But he said he also saw some things that disturbed him during his last trip to Cuba. You see, we expect to see Russians in the streets of Havana. They have done a great deal for Cuba and it's only common sense that they should be there helping. But he said he also saw patrol boats in Havana Harbor with all Soviet crews, though they flew Cuban flags." Cornejo's brows rose to emphasize his point. "At one military base he saw a Soviet infantry company drilling—all Soviet, no Cubans involved whatsoever. He told me of more sights that bothered him. And what he said next frightened me and made me realize what a great man President Ramos really is. He said that when a country accepts help from another, and continues to keep an open palm out, it eventually finds that the other country is in control—because they are feeding it. In that situation, a man would no longer be his own man. The same is true of a country."

Ryng looked up from his plate as Cornejo stopped abruptly, but again the man's hand was up for silence so that he could continue.

"You see, Mr. Ryng, President Ramos is also very proud, as are many of my countrymen. We need help, but we will

never sell ourselves again, if at all possible. We have watched
foreigners run us for too long, and that includes Havana." He
nodded emphatically, holding Ryng's eyes with his own.
"And more importantly, the Soviet Union. We will never
become another Cuba." He paused for an instant. "So President Ramos still doesn't like to hear what you have to say,
partly because you are an American. But he is uneasy about
our Guardia too . . . about the amount of time the junior officers are spending in Cuba . . . and about the influence that
can develop, just as he has seen it in Havana. You see, we
don't want Soviet submarines at our docks, and we don't want
Soviet bombers using Torrijos Airport as their home base."

Ryng took a deep breath. He hadn't expected such a change
in attitude. "Well . . . I'm very pleased to hear all this. It
wasn't quite what I'd expected—"

"No, it isn't. But please don't get me wrong. We want to
look into what you say further. He will not commit more
troops to Colón because those stationed there seem adequate
for what we expect. But he agreed that I join you there—"

"Something happened last night, Mr. Cornejo, something
that may indicate there's more there than either of us
suspect."

But before he could continue, the other man again interrupted. Cornejo was used to running people. "I am aware of
the problem you found at your apartment last night, Mr.
Ryng. And President Ramos is also. You see, there are not too
many Americans like you in Panama, except for that Mr.
Moran, the man whom you found dead in your rooms last
night." Ryng was about to say something, but to his own surprise, decided to keep quiet.

"The Guardia keep us informed of such matters, especially
when they happen around an American in your position . . . or
a charming woman like Miss Alvarez."

Ryng sat back in his chair, studying Cornejo. "I see." It
was Henry Cobb who had told him never to say more than was
necessary. "But Miss Alvarez isn't involved in anything I'm
doing, believe me." That was something that had to be said.

"I do believe you." Cornejo saw a faraway look in Ryng's
eyes and realized it was a dangerous one. "I know her quite
well, Mr. Ryng. But you can be sure that when the two of you

are together and a situation like the one last night arises, it is reported. I assure you that the presence of Miss Alvarez will remain confidential."

"She told me that the two of you are very good friends. Is that the case from your point of view also?"

Cornejo nodded. "I have known Kitty for years. She has done so much for the economy of Panama that I have the highest respect for her." He smiled again, this time a bit wistfully. "I also envy you, Mr. Ryng. She is a fascinating woman." His fingers drummed unconsciously on the table. "If she is as attracted to you as it seems, that is good for you also. You can be sure of that. Your relationship with her will be kept most confidential."

"That's all I could really ask of you." Ryng extended his cup for more coffee. "When will we leave for Colón?"

"Late in the day. Before six. I have a helicopter at my disposal. It's really a very short trip, just over the mountains."

"There was a message left by Moran last night, before he died. I'm not quite sure what it meant."

Cornejo's eyebrows rose in question. "I wasn't aware of that."

"It really didn't concern the Guardia. It was for me. That's why Moran's dead. It simply said 'by sea.' I suppose it was why Moran tried to get to me."

"Well, whatever it meant, we'll find out tonight. I've arranged for us to be off the piers in one of our patrol boats. President Ramos prefers that I not be in the thick of any fighting." He laughed under his breath. "And I must say I agree with him. I like the part of an observer, but I'd hate to be a target."

A PRA Sanctuary near Portobelo, Panama

The path through the jungle was overgrown but passable. In a few weeks no stranger would ever know it had been there, even though Grambling's men cleared it only six weeks before. The jungle reclaimed man's work quickly, especially in a rainy season with three-inch cloudbursts.

Grambling stepped into the clearing. Tree cover had been left overhead so little direct sunlight came through. A passing plane, even a helicopter, wouldn't notice any change in the jungle. It was a supply area complete with ammunition, diesel fuel drums, spare parts, and food. Logistics—that was the key to success. It had been pounded into his head time and again in Cuba, until he accepted it as an eleventh commandment. In the past year he had come to appreciate that education even more. They had never lost a skirmish against government troops.

On the opposite side of the clearing the undergrowth again closed in. Only an experienced eye would note the path that Grambling was headed for, Maria close behind him. For perhaps twenty yards the trail was like a rabbit furrow. Then it opened onto the water. Camouflage had been introduced so that a passing fishing boat would have to approach right to the edge to see the missile boat nestled against the small pier. It reminded him of old photos of PT boat lairs in the Solomons more than forty years ago.

Grambling's eyes followed the boat's clean lines. Some of his men were lounging on the stern while others on the central missile launchers were making minor repairs. Then he caught sight of the man sitting on top of the pilot house, a black beret jauntily cocked over his right eye.

"Who the hell invited you?" Grambling growled loudly enough for some of the men to hear.

"No one, Colonel. I have orders." The Spanish was heavily accented. It was spoken by a man who knew the language well enough to communicate but had little interest in the niceties of perfecting it. "Care to see them, or perhaps you've already received a copy?"

"I haven't received anything," Grambling said, remaining where he'd halted when he saw the Russian.

"Well, the powers that be, back in Havana, decided that an army colonel could use an old sea dog on a mission like this one."

Captain Second Rank Paul Voronov could have been considered technically junior to Colonel Grambling but he never let it enter his mind. He was a career naval officer with service in the Baltic Fleet and the Red Banner Northern Fleet. After graduation from the Frunze Higher Naval School, he was sent to the Baltic for destroyer duty, where he eventually commanded a small escort as a very junior officer. Fascinated with the possibilities of small, high-speed boats, he requested and was granted an unusual transfer to the Northern Fleet and amphibious ships. He cut his teeth with the Naval Infantry, assisting in the development of new tactics. This culminated in his directing landing operations in Angola. For his successes in Africa he was one of the few officers in the entire Soviet Navy allowed to wear the distinctive black beret with the anchor insignia on the left and the red star on the front. Today he also wore the Naval Infantry's black battle fatigues.

"I hope you are aware that I'm senior to you," Grambling said, seething. "This is my mission and I will give the orders." He stared directly back into Voronov's icy blue eyes. The man was of medium height and stocky. His face was Scandinavian and blonde hair peeked out from under the beret. The only distinguishing feature was an aura of brutal hardness.

"No problem, Jaimé, no problem at all. I'm just along for the ride, so to speak. All I am is an advisor . . . as always."

Voronov was more than an advisor and Grambling knew that. These Russian Black Berets had been sent to Cuba almost two years before to teach commando tactics to the Cuban military. His specialty was missions just such as this one. Night attack. Hit from one side with ground troops. Draw the enemy off guard. Then attack with heavy weapons from the rear, in this case the sea. Voronov was so good he could command a Naval Infantry battalion using tanks and artillery in addition to his rifle companies. Yet his knowledge of guided missile and torpedo boats made him even more effective. He was sent to Havana to teach Castro's men how to fight in the islands and Central America. So far he'd done quite well. Two Central American countries were under their control and he'd scared the hell out of a couple of other tiny island nations.

Grambling hated the man. To him, Voronov had no loyalty to anything but the military. When one of the men in Grambling's class asked Voronov if he could adapt to any other country's service, the answer had been shocking. "Certainly. Wherever I was offered the best opportunity to practice my skills. Perhaps if the Americans wanted me and paid enough and offered enough action, I'd go with them." He'd smiled, leaving them to wonder if he really meant it. "But I am unaware of any other country that can provide me with the action that I want. I am happy with my motherland . . . I am happy with you. I'm happy fighting." Colonel Grambling still found that attitude despicable. He could not imagine killing men for other than a patriotic cause.

"I've been waiting for you, Jaimé. It's boring as hell in this jungle, waiting in this heat for something to happen . . . and nobody to talk to. I'm glad you're finally here."

"I'm glad too, Paul. . . ." He rolled the man's name slowly with his tongue. Grambling hated to be called by his first name in front of his men. "I don't need to see your orders. I'm sure they're correct." He looked Voronov square in the eyes. "Of course, I'd be lying if I said I wasn't disappointed that I won't be taking my men in alone."

"Make believe I'm not here. I'll try to keep out of the way. If I see anything that needs doing, I'll help out. Okay?"

"Fine." You son of a bitch, he added to himself. "Let me know if you need anything."

Voronov eyed Maria appreciatively, nodding to her. "Good morning."

"*Anything but her*," Grambling said. "She's with me . . . only me. Understood?"

"Understood . . . Jaimé."

Someday, Grambling thought, I'm going to beat the shit out of him, if someone else doesn't get to him first. It wouldn't be easy. No man wore that black beret without earning it, and anyone outside of the Naval Infantry earned it the hard way.

Havana

Henry Cobb strode purposefully down the wide walkway between the military headquarters buildings. With the palm tree sand flower beds outlined by the evenly spaced lights, it appeared more like a pleasant resort area. The drab sameness of the military-style buildings could not be discerned at this time of night.

Anyone who passed by noted only that the Costa Rican, Lieutenant Corazon, was out for a late evening stroll. Henry Cobb had decided within moments after his run-in with the dog the other night that there was less purpose in sneaking about these security-weak buildings than in simply wandering about as if you belonged. The experience with the dog was something he had no intention of encountering again. His odds, he was sure, would be considerably lower a second time.

The buildings were secured at midnight. That was when the dogs were set loose. Before then, there was usually someone working late, and security was neglible at that point—only the occasional foot patrols by Cuban troops. So Cobb had decided that Lieutenant Corazon was much the wiser choice to be in the building this time.

Admiral Khasan's office was on the top floor. With the exception of a secretary, he was the only occupant. She was never there after six in the evening. If Cobb understood Khasan, and he was sure he could predict what Chita Monteria would do, he could have the run of the Admiral's office as long as he wanted. However, he had every intention of being out of there before the buildings were secured at midnight. He knew exactly what he was looking for and he had managed in the last few nights to narrow it down to Khasan's office. If it wasn't there, then he would have to start over.

A Cuban sentry at the entrance saluted him as he mounted the steps. That was amazing! No one was required to sign in and out after normal working hours—there was no access control! The Russians had been completely acclimatized. No wonder these Soviet instructors boasted how long they had been in Havana. Imagine duty above the Arctic Circle when this was available. And Khasan's weakness had been encouraged this evening to a certainty.

There were stairs at each end of the hall and in the middle of the building. Cobb had studied the few lighted offices from both sides and had already determined his path. Passing through the front entrance, he went straight ahead up the center stairs, turning to his right on the second floor. There he took the flight at the end of the building to the third level. To get to Khasan's office on the floor above, there were only center stairs, and he was forced to pass one occupied office as he moved in that direction. But that meant only one person, other than the guard out front, would be able to report that Lieutenant Corazon had been seen in the building. What the hell, Cobb muttered to himself, after this Corazon would be a dead duck in Havana anyway.

As he ascended the stairs, darkness softly welcomed Corazon/Cobb. He preferred the comfort of virtual invisibility. His night vision, always superb, adapted quickly. The pen light would illuminate details once he was sure he would be alone.

Cobb stood in the middle of the room, slowly turning in a circle, noting the placement of every item. There was always the chance he would be interrupted. It would be foolish to welcome anyone if there was a chance he could hide, or even position himself to gain the advantage over anyone who might enter. Precautions just such as this had saved his neck more times that he could count.

Enough light reflected in from the outside to create vague shadows. Cobb moved about the room, intent on his own shadow's motion. Good men, some of whom he'd worked with, had died because of the flickering movement in a dark room seen by someone on the outside. Never go to work, Cobb learned long ago, until you are absolutely comfortable with yourself.

Senior Russian officers generally were precise, neat in their work almost to a fault. That was partly the party, which left their lives only in sleep, and perhaps a good deal more because of those around them who schemed for power. The mannerisms of efficiency could often be said to be a matter of self-preservation. Such was no longer the case with Admiral Khasan. Cobb was sure of that in less than a minute as he scanned the working area of the Soviet officer. He had grown lax away from the homeland. There was no longer anyone to fear. There were loose papers on his desk and the surrounding tables, though Cobb quickly determined that they were nothing of value to him. The file cabinet was simple to open, a matter of an instrument he always carried. Here he found files containing ships' names, coded call signs, station assignments, weapons inventory, and a variety of data useful to Pratt and his people. These he quickly photographed.

There were other files he photographed instinctively, though there was little time to determine their value now. Pratt's intelligence people could resolve that. But in the back of Cobb's mind lurked the notion that such inattention to security should yield something even more valuable. It would have to be where he least expected it. Carefully, he returned the files to their proper place and locked the file cabinet.

On his hands and knees he carefully began a search from a different aspect. He had long ago learned that what could be observed from one plane looked totally different from another. His pen light illuminated Khasan's office from a wholly new perspective as he slowly crawled about the room. There seemed initially to be nothing—still a Russian, he thought, though now slightly lapsed in discipline.

Cobb was about to give up when the narrow ray from his light flashed briefly on an object under the desk. He crawled closer, moving the chair slightly away for a better look. What he found was that something his instinct had willed him to search out. There, in perfect order, was Khasan's chart, a plastic covering over it so that he could move his ships about and make notes with grease pencil. It covered the entire Caribbean, from Florida to the northern countries of South America, from the Atlantic to all of Central America. This was akin to having a spy in your enemy's flag plot at the height of a battle. Again Cobb's miniature camera was put to work, recording the chart with all its markings section by section. Together with the material discovered in Khasan's files, Pratt would be able to interpret much of the Soviet strategy.

Cobb considered that perhaps more could be found, though he couldn't imagine anything could surpass what he'd already recorded. A glance at his watch convinced him to leave well enough alone. It was almost midnight. That was when the building would be secured and the dogs would be turned loose for the night. No reason to challenge luck further. Very cautiously he recreated his progress through Khasan's office. That was another aspect of his training. Go back the same way you came. You can cover anything you may have overlooked, for your own protection.

He slipped out the door, leaving everything exactly as it had been, and retraced his steps down the same stairways, past the same offices, and toward the front entryway. It was then he heard the sound of the dogs. Cobb looked quickly at his watch —midnight. The Russian sentries were coming to relieve the Cubans.

As he stepped through the doorway into the cool, pleasant night, he saw the Russian guard not thirty feet away, his rifle slung across his shoulder. Two huge shepherds were pulling at their leashes, low growls emerging from their throats as they saw the Cuban guard first, and then Cobb.

The Russian stopped ten feet away, studying Cobb intently. He could tell easily that this man was no Russian, yet he was emerging from a building that housed mostly Soviet officers and Khasan's staff. He made no effort to quiet the straining dogs, instead calling out in rough Spanish, "What are you doing in this building?"

Cobb turned to the Cuban sentry, whose eyes were riveted on the now-snarling animals. "You can explain to him that I had permission to work inside with one of the instructors." It was an order.

The Cuban, eyes still riveted on the dogs, came to a half-hearted attention in response to the authority in Cobb's voice. "Yes, sir."

"Well, tell him," barked Cobb. The Cuban's concentration remained on the dogs.

"Yes, sir." The Cuban came to a full attention. "He had the instructor's permission."

The Russian studied Cobb again, then motioned with his hand for him to pass by. In the background, as he moved as calmly away from the building as possible, Cobb could hear the Russian berating the other sentry for allowing him to stay in the building after all others had left. Cobb looked back for a brief moment. There wasn't a light in the building. He had been the last one out and would not be overlooked tomorrow. It was time to join Ryng.

•   •   •

Commodore Navarro frowned at the empty humidor on his desk. The Panamanian, Alvarez, had taken the last cigar when he departed. If he had realized it was the final one, it was likely that he would have refused politely. Navarro knew the man loved that brand. So he had insisted, taking it out before Alvarez could refuse, insisting that he accept the Commodore's generosity.

Navarro had come out of the Sierra Maestres with Fidel Castro. In those days Raul had been his brother's right hand. It was years after Raul's death before Navarro ascended to the Premier's most trusted advisor. There was no one else to replace; it was simply that Fidel preferred the isolation. Navarro was a colonel by the time they marched into Havana, a very young one whose tactical brilliance had been recognized by the revolutionary leader. It was only natural from Castro's viewpoint that a colonel who had been raised in a fishing village should be responsible for developing the new Cuban Navy. The rundown rusting hulks that Batista had accepted from the United States were quickly disposed of, and the newly named Commodore Navarro began scraping together a coastal defense force from the Russians, begging and coercing, using Castro's bargaining ability, to develop a respectable force.

The Commodore's age was a mystery to those who did not know him well, though now the stress of his responsibilities had tired him. He could have stepped out of an American recruiting poster. His height and weight were average, his hair was brown and closely trimmed, his uniforms tailored, shoes constantly spit polished, and he was unlike many of his colleagues because he avoided both a beard and a mustache. Navarro was very aware of his appearance, and he was equally concerned with the importance of a spotless reputation. He belonged at Castro's right hand.

The Cuban naval leader certainly wasn't feeling generous, and he was tired as usual, but it was a way of masking his anger. Alvarez had not stopped by to pass the time of day. Instead he had arrogantly proffered a series of problems that Navarro really had not wanted to hear. Maybe, on reflection, it wasn't arrogance. There was a childlike enthusiasm on

Alvarez's part that compensated for a half smirk that seemed to say, I told you so.

Admiral Victor Khasan, up to that particular day, had the Commodore's complete trust. As an admiral representing one of the most powerful nations on earth, he had ingratiated himself to the Cuban power structure. Gradually, even Castro had grown to depend on the Russian.

Now, here was Esteban Alvarez coming to him with proof of Khasan's dalliances—with all the women in Havana he could have had, he had Chita Monteria! That was too much, especially when Alvarez had relaxed in the chair opposite the desk and smiled as he placed a copy of his report on Navarro's desk. Chita Monteria! She was the one with the mirrors who delighted in hypnotizing her men with her body. Fidel Castro had once seen pictures of Chita and her talents. They had been all the proof necessary for the executions of one of his generals and a senior government official.

She would ply them with drink, to loosen them up he had been told, though he couldn't understand the necessity. His intelligence people had indicated that some of the recordings made in her apartment contained revelations about the workings of the Cuban military and government that would have been most valuable to any foreign agent, but no one bothered to remove Chita from the picture. There was always the possibility that she could one day be useful to them. And it seemed that whatever she heard, she kept secret. Either she was too stupid or she simply didn't realize that the intelligence she was privy to could bring her more than she would ever earn from her body. What they never understood was that she liked what she was doing!

But there was always a first time, even for the Chita Monterias of the world, and her downfall, Navarro realized, would be Victor Khasan, the Kremlin's number one strategist in the Caribbean. Victor was supposed to be the most dependable man the Kremlin could provide, the most dedicated, the most . . . he couldn't bear to repeat to himself all the fine reports he'd been given on Khasan. Navarro stroked his chin thoughtfully—a dalliance with a woman like Monteria—and shook his head in despair.

Navarro opened the bottom drawer of his desk and removed

a fresh box of cigars. As he lifted them gently out of the box one by one, and placed them carefully in the humidor, he considered the second item that Alvarez laid before him. While Admiral Khasan had been carousing into the early hours with Señorita Monteria, someone had likely been into his office. Once again this had come from one of Alvarez's snoopers. Why was Castro's own intelligence unaware of this subgroup? One of the students from the military school, a Lieutenant Corazon, had been seen leaving the building in the middle of the night. Further investigation indicated that it was likely he'd been in Khasan's office because certain officers had been working late on other floors. They had seen no one enter or leave their areas. Khasan was the only occupant on his floor!

Navarro considered his options. He could appeal to the Soviet Premier. On second thought, why fool himself? As far as the Kremlin was concerned, this was a Soviet operation. Admiral Khasan was the man in charge, even though he would remain in the background while Fidel Castro did the arm waving. No, there was no point in going to them. Besides, things were too far along. They couldn't hope to find someone with Khasan's background at this stage, and there was no firm proof that the man had done anything more than let his dirty mind get the better of him.

Navarro knew at this point that there was more to this operation than met the eye. He knew about the Colombian destroyer. That part Navarro felt he could pull off himself. But all those ships and submarines—those required a tradition in naval thinking, and Navarro had to admit that his strengths were primarily oriented to land operations.

One afternoon, he remembered, Victor Khasan had invited Navarro to his office, where he cataloged the vast amount of firepower that was planned. It was truly fascinating, but afterward Navarro's brain was whirling with missiles, radars, electronic countermeasures and counter-countermeasures, and submarine tactics . . . so much, that he had to trust the specialists and their claims.

It was the big picture Commodore Navarro understood, especially intelligence, deception, and disinformation. And he was no fool when it came to the United States. He would leave the planning, the fine tuning, the changes of strategy and tactics to Khasan. But now he had to keep his eye on the Russian, until it was all over. He did not want to deny the man his Chita, if that's the way his tastes leaned, but the objective was too important to allow Victor to fall victim to his baser instincts. Fidel would be furious.

And now, he thought morosely, there was even the possibility of enemy knowledge of the operation. This Lieutenant Corazon, the one Alvarez said had been recognized near Khasan's office that night, was nowhere to be found. It was strange that one of the most brilliant students they'd ever had in the school had suddenly disappeared. If these suspicions were true, Navarro wondered how much this Corazon, or whoever he was, had taken with him. Were all those sophisticated plans that Khasan had shown him that afternoon now in Corazon's mind? Those submarines and cruisers and missiles and choke points . . . and that old destroyer intended to lull the Americans to sleep?

There was so much thinking to be done, and he was so tired. For a brief moment he reflected on the pleasure he might gain from wandering down to the closest baseball field and maybe join a pickup game, maybe help some youngsters. It was only a few blocks away, and it was what he really wanted to do. . . .

A Government Patrol Boat
Off Colón

The city of Colón is situated on a small peninsula that juts into
Limón Bay on the eastern side of the Panama Canal. The bay
and the city were once subject to fierce northers that rolled out
of the Caribbean and smashed into the exposed town. The bay
was actually more of an indentation on the north coast of
Panama, six miles wide at the mouth and six miles long north
and south. The major reason for Colón's existence was simply
that it served as the northern terminus for the Panama Railroad. It was where ships brought people and goods for
transfer by rail to Panama City and the Pacific. Colón was
also the gateway to the Old World from the Far East. When
the Americans arrived to complete the construction of the
Canal, they built solid breakwaters across Limón Bay. The entrance was wide enough for two ships to pass. The
breakwaters neutralized the might of the northers and created
a sanctuary for ships waiting to transit the Canal. As a result,
Colón became the second largest city in Panama.

There was no moon that night, but it was very clear and the
glow from the lights of the city provided just enough illumina-
tion to silhouette the ships waiting their turn to proceed to the
Gatun locks. Bernie Ryng and Tomas Cornejo sat side-by-side
on the deck of the small patrol boat, the *Balboa*, their legs
tucked under them Indian style. Their eyes were well adjusted

to the dark and they could identify the merchant ships around them. Their patrol boat drifted innocently between two medium-size tankers, rocking gently and quietly. A warm breeze blew in from the north, creating phosphorescent whitecaps that sparkled against the hulls. They had chosen the location to be as inconspicuous as possible, just the other side of the shipping channel from Colón. It was no more than a mile from the docks, where they understood a diversionary thrust would come. Intelligence indicated that bombs would be set off in strategic locations to draw police and fire assistance. The rebels would isolate these two groups. Then they would move to control the town. This would attract the loyal Guardia troops waiting for movement from the south. But how much of this did the rebel forces know? The more he considered each factor, the more Ryng was bothered. There was too much rumor, too little regard for the PRA.

"What time is it?"

"Ten forty-two," Ryng answered, squinting at the luminous dial on his watch. During the flight over the mountains that afternoon, Cornejo and Ryng considered the details time and again. This was Bernie Ryng's specialty, and something just wasn't right. He had planned and led similar raids before, and this one seemed too easy. There should have been more of a trap by the rebels.

"It was supposed to start twelve minutes ago," Cornejo remarked nervously.

"I suppose that's part of their strategy . . . never do what's expected."

"Look, just to the left of the docks," Cornejo said, pointing to a light that flared, seemed to die, then flared again. The sound of the blast echoed across the water to them. Something near the explosion ignited and was rapidly growing into a steady, bright fire. He whispered as though he could be heard across the water, even from that distance.

"Wait . . . just a little longer. Let's see what else happens." Then, as they watched, eyes straining to pierce the blackness around them, a second blast occurred, then a third. "Okay." Ryng nodded, "let's go."

Cornejo called in Spanish into the pilothouse and the captain of the boat tapped his quartermaster on the shoulder. The engines turned over with a deep cough, then sprang to life, the exhaust sputtering into foam at the stern. Ryng felt the thud reverberate through the hull as the gears engaged and the craft's screws bit into the water, dragging the stern down slightly. Then the wheel was over, the bow began to lift, and they surged ahead, banking sharply as the captain brought his craft to the direction of the flames.

Now for their surprise. Along with police and fireman, heavily armed National Guard troops would also appear. This would counteract the rebel's plans of moving out toward the city hall and post office. Ryng held tightly to a hand grip as the boat heeled sharply to one side to pass under the stern of a large ship. Looking up, he could see the freighter's crew gathering on the deck to watch what looked like an interesting evening of firefighting. They listened for the sporadic crack of small-arms fire.

But there was nothing, only the crackling of flames from an old wooden warehouse and the raw smell of burning, creosote-soaked pilings. It was strangely quiet about the piers as *Balboa* idled a few hundred yards off. Ryng imagined the uncertainty of the commander of the Guardia troops, that emptiness that comes to all men when they anticipate combat and are left hanging with sensations of both relief and incompleteness. He knew the feeling, knew that relaxation would follow—that was when a man was most vulnerable. Either the attack had been canceled or the—

Then he heard it! Was it the sound of helicopters? He looked over his shoulder, searching the darkness for the familiar bulky contour of a helo. No, it was a deeper sound, a growling monotone, similar to the engines in their own *Balboa*. Then he saw the wakes. The phosphorescence in the water marked where they had been, like the sound and vapor trail of a jet plane. It took a bit more time in the dark for the eyes to catch up with the boats themselves. The bulky outlines of the Soviet-made Osas were easier to identify. The Turyas he recognized by the gun mount on the stern and their odd approach, with the stern in the water and the bow raised on foils.

They came at full speed out of the night like huge, graceful bats. They had been unexpected and there was no defense prepared for them. Ryng understood, even before their firing intensified, exactly how it would all end. The Guardia would be attracted by the firing down near the docks, likely assuming the rebel forces were finally attacking on the ground. They would get to the piers and then be trapped by the fire of the boats on one side and the rebel troops who would restrain their enthusiasm until the right moment before coming in from behind. It wasn't classic—it was just intelligent strategy, a pincer movement utilizing surprise and maximizing limited forces by using the element of surprise. *By Sea*—it was such a simple, well-considered idea. It definitely was not the product of a peasant, of a backward revolutionary mind!

Ryng looked toward *Balboa*'s captain. Like Tomas Cornejo, he seemed frozen in awe as the squadron bore down on them. But if they did not make a move shortly, none of them would be left to tell about it.

Ryng was at the controls in two quick steps, elbowing the helmsman to one side as he slammed the throttle forward to full power. With a roar that threw the others to the deck, the craft leaped forward directly at the incoming attack boats. He crammed the wheel full left. For an instant the bow followed the direction of the rudder and the boat's hull bit deeply into the water. But as the screw revolutions increased, it also skittered sideways. Now it was literally bouncing across the surface.

There was no question of facing the enemy, not with Cornejo aboard, and not if they had a choice. *Balboa*'s armament —machine gun forward, deck gun aft—was pitiful compared to the firepower bearing down on them. To Ryng, his first choice seemed his only one—get the hell out! He hoped the rebels would concentrate on the piers and their main purpose of gaining control of the town.

The luminesence of their wake was like a signal fire. It stood out just as clearly to the attacking boats as their tracers did to Ryng when they opened fire on the escaping *Balboa*. For a moment he was tempted to continue the flight—but it was a very brief temptation. His mind was made up as he saw tracers approaching his own craft. Zigzagging was not the answer either. The gunners on those boats were well trained, anticipating his moves.

The initial hit came as he was reversing direction. A shell

slammed into the stern, shaking the boat. Thank God it had missed his stern gun, which was still futilely pumping out shells with little effect. Racing back at them was no solution to their main problem of being a target, but an oncoming craft was harder to hit than one running away. If *Balboa* could fire more effectively, the attackers would have to commence their own evasive tactics, and that would limit the effectiveness of their gunners.

The rattle of machine gun bullets sweeping over the deck indicated that at least one enemy gun had adapted quickly to the change in tactics. Ryng watched as his forward gunner was knocked back from his gun and over the side. The helmsman, who had been huddling against the bulkhead since Ryng took the wheel, screamed and grabbed at his throat, blood spraying from between his fingers.

It was not out of a textbook, not even a movie, Ryng thought as he contemplated the tracers whipping by on either side. This was insane! They were closing the enemy without firing a shot. "Tomas!" he shouted at the top of his lungs, "Tomas!" He had no idea where the Panamanian was.

A hand gripped his shoulder. A frightened voice shouted into his ear, "Right behind you my friend!"

Ryng grasped the hand on his shoulder, pulling Cornejo around beside him. "Take the wheel . . . I'm going to man the gun," he shouted, pointing at the weapon on the forward deck. He placed both of Cornejo's hands on the wheel. "Just aim in their direction. When you see me make a hand signal, turn in that direction . . . and don't worry about hitting anything . . . they'll avoid you." If there was any chance, it would be in the midst of those boats, rather than remaining an inviting target.

As they neared the attack boats, it was apparent only one was concentrating on them. The others were occupied off the piers, pouring heavy fire into the surrounded Guardia troops. Ryng found that their forward gunner had hardly fired a round. A nearly full belt was in position for him as he swung it around to bear on his target.

Ryng located the pilothouse of the other boat with his own tracers, twitching the gun just the slightest bit to rake his fire back and forth. Another shell slammed into their side.

Recovering from the impact in seconds, he had the gun back under his control again and resumed firing. Tomas was somehow keeping them on a steady course.

The thud of shells and bullets tearing into *Balboa* reminded Ryng that Cornejo, in fear, was simply aiming them at the other boat. His left arm shot out and he pointed it wildly in that direction. He wanted to pass across the other boat's bow. It would give him a chance to concentrate his fire on their pilothouse. Just possibly, with a little bit of luck, he could knock out their controls. At this stage he couldn't imagine sinking the other. But perhaps they could escape if he disabled the other boat.

Ryng had fought with boats like *Balboa* before. He knew them well, knew how they reacted to any number of problems. And, as he sensed her slowing down, he could also feel the telltale shudder that indicated she was taking on water. It wouldn't be long now.

The other boat had to turn away, running down their side. As it did so, Ryng was surprised to once again hear the sharp cracking sound of the deck gun on their stern. Somehow, someone was still alive who knew how to operate it. He could see shells striking the other boat.

It turned toward them now, and Ryng indicated with his right arm for Cornejo to turn again. He wanted to get closer to the other boat. If he could get near enough, using both guns, perhaps, just perhaps, they might stand a chance. But before chance could become opportunity, they were bracketed by the other boat and shells once again were ripping *Balboa* apart. The engine room was taking water. Ryng could identify the sound of only one engine above the chatter of his own gun.

The rebel craft swung around and began to circle them, oblivious to the shells from the lone stern gun. Then it became obvious why they had maneuvered as they did—*Balboa*'s stern gun and gunner disappeared in a sheet of flame. His little craft was now motionless.

Now comes the end, Ryng pondered, concentrating his fire on the pilot house of the other. But something had happened to prolong their survival. He had no idea when it had occurred, but there was no longer a gun on the forward deck of the other boat. Somehow, *Balboa*'s stern gun must have had one final, very lucky hit. And he could see flames near the other's stern. She had settled back in the water, off her foils.

Balboa was ablaze, sinking, dead in the water. Ryng could smell burning fuel oil and paint as thick black smoke momentarily blinded him. Yet he continued to fire until there was no more ammunition.

Then he dodged back through the smoke and flames to the pilothouse. It was a shambles. Nothing was left of the once polished control panel, no radio or compass, nor any of the other nautical instruments that always gave Ryng that comfortable feeling at sea. Slumped in a corner was Tomas Cornejo. He knew it was Tomas, though it was hard to identify the man through the blood that covered him. Ryng bent down to check for a pulse, anything that would convince him it would make sense to try to take Cornejo with him. But the jagged tear in the man's neck was all that was necessary to know that it was better to let Tomas Cornejo go to the bottom with the boat.

Crawling cautiously from the pilothouse, Ryng saw only burning fuel covering the water. His one choice was to head for the bow again, take a chance of exposing himself to the other boat's fire, then go over the side. As he crept into the open, he was aware of a deadly silence broken only by the crackling of flames.

Aboard Grambling's Boat

James Grambling was entranced by the hydrofoil. Her lines were sleek and smooth and firm, her motion graceful in flight as she lifted out of the water onto her foils. There was no feeling quite like that moment when she soared, for he was transformed to captain of a vessel on the ocean, captain of a plane in flight, captain of the most graceful vehicle man had yet invented. She exuded power as she raced at high speed, darting over the waves, her weapons seeking out anything in her path. It was a humbling experience to have so much sheer power under his command at one time.

His instructor at Santiago, a Russian, had lectured the small group and showed them a film before they were allowed their first ride on one of the hydrofoils. The instructor said he could not explain the hydrofoil as much as he could show what it meant to have one of them under your feet. First there were pictures of a falcon in flight. "Watch now," the instructor had said. "Watch his wings as he soars." The bird had increased altitude with the slightest movement of its body, the wings an airfoil to steady flight. The bird's eyes were on the ground. "He sees something." The falcon decreased its altitude slightly. "Watch the right wing." The wing dipped almost imperceptibly and the bird banked ever so gently to the right. "See if you can tell what he does now." The instructor's voice was almost a shout. Faster than his own eyes could tell, James saw the bird dive. He had no idea what it had done with its body, but he watched in awe as it approached the ground, braking at the last possible moment with its wings, it talons outstretched. Then with a couple of powerful thrusts of its wings, it was airborne again, a mouse hanging forlornly in its grasp. "The flight, the search . . . the attack . . . perfectly executed." There was silence.

"Now I want to show you something else, something equally exciting." The scene switched to a snow-covered mountainside. James had never seen snow like that before, so soft looking, nothing to break its surface. Then a single skier appeared, legs together as if he were on one leg, knees bent and arms slightly outstretched for balance. As he increased speed down the steep slope, a rooster tail of powdery snow formed behind him. The film gradually shifted to slow motion, and James was fascinated by the easy change in direction as the skier seemed to flow first one way then another, effortlessly. The smoothness of the snow was broken only by the geometric pattern of the skier's path back and forth across the fall line. It was fluid, rhythmic, a ballet, and the rooster tail behind him rose or fell in relation to his speed and shifting weight.

"Now, we switch," the instructor shouted to break the stillness. And there was a skier on the screen again, this time clothed like a jet pilot, complete with helmet and form-fitting silver uniform. He vaulted out of a gate between two flags, a

man with a stop watch bellowing something as he passed. It
was a race, but against a mountain rather than another person. The skier was on a hard surface course, no rooster tail
this time, and his movements were no longer soft and easy.
They remained graceful, but represented tremendous concentration as he increased speed and shot back and forth between
poles. At one point he was in a crouch as he rocketed down a
steep dip. Then he was airborne for a moment, his arms outstretched for balance. As his skis regained the surface, his
shoulders jerked to the left and he shot between two poles in a
spray of snow. Even as he was passing between them, his body
was already shifting in the opposite direction and his skis were
aimed between another set of poles. Back and forth he went,
cutting each corner so tightly that poles flew into the air as his
shoulder scraped by them. Then he was in his final descent,
body tucked in a crouch. And he was through the end of his
run, snow flying as he braked to a stop, arms thrown in the air
in victory.

As the lights had flickered on, James remembered people in
the film running across to throw their arms around the racer.
Their instructor was already at the lectern, an arm jabbing
in the air. "Again you saw the flight over the snow, the grace
and pleasure of discovery. And then . . . then the attack . . .
attacking the mountain . . . racing against time. The fastest,
the most aggressive, the man who wants victory the most—
that's the one who will win. It will be no different in your new
boats. . . ."

Grambling would never forget that lesson. Everything else
was simply a means to an end. The challenge . . . victory . . .
his instructor had been so right.

Now he had the opportunity to put into use everything he
had been taught. The steady pounding of guns, the hollow
whoosh of launchers, the shattering explosion of missiles on
the docks, the hypnotic effect of the destruction and flames
against the darkness of the approach from the breakwater just
moments before, all were a narcotic to add to his love of his
boat, *Pegasus*. It was his own name for her. He had been in
charge of her when she arrived in Cuba, and he supervised the
overhaul that transformed her into a high-speed man of war
bristling with new weapons. The Cubans gave her a number

designation, but he had chosen the name *Pegasus*.

James watched the government patrol boat coming toward them, firing bravely with its little, forward deck gun. It was no match for him. He could see their pilothouse was already badly damaged. The flames from shore created a shadowy effect where a gaping hole had been shot in its bow by his own gunners. He flicked the small wheel slightly to the right to open up the target for all of his guns.

He saw by her decreased bow wave that she was losing speed, yet still rushing headlong at him. Again and again it was hit. Grambling became absorbed in the boat's death rattle as it seemed to disintegrate before his eyes. He was about to turn in toward the boat to make his kill when it veered sharply to the left, cutting across his bow. Grambling threw his own craft hard to port, cutting her speed as he did so.

Machine gun bullets from its bow gun pursued him, pausing at his own pilothouse. James found himself momentarily crouched on the deck until the line of fire swept toward the stern. Leaping to his feet, he saw that the other boat's stern gun could now bear on him. He felt the impact of the heavier shells as they exploded into his *Pegasus*, holing the hull systematically, searching for a weakness that might finish him also.

Grambling cut in under the stern of the other boat, increasing speed, determined to come up on the port quarter of the other craft to complete the kill. But it was almost dead in the water. He could see smoke and occasional flames through the jagged holes in her hull. It couldn't be much longer, though her gunners were still firing.

The door to the pilothouse flew open and Paul Voronov stepped inside. Grambling waited, expecting criticism or suggestions, but the Russian remained quiet, grasping for a handhold as Grambling kept the hydrofoil slewing back and forth across the water, offering as difficult a target as possible. "Have you ever been in a fight like this one?" he shouted above the din.

The Russian shook his head. "Not with someone like that," he said, pointing at the craft they were closing. "They die hard."

As Voronov completed his sentence, their forward gun was

blown apart in a hail of metal fragments slamming through
the pilothouse. Grambling was knocked backward by the
blast, sensing at the same time the shards of metal tearing into
his body. But there was no pain.

He raised himself to his knees, searching curiously for blood
that hadn't yet appeared. Voronov was on one elbow, a look
of surprise spreading across his face. Grambling saw a trickle
of blood start down from the man's forehead. He noted more
blood welling out near the Russian's shoulder. Their boat
yawed wildly, and Grambling could feel them settling into the
water, realizing his *Pegasus* was no longer flying.

Grasping the instrument panel, Grambling pulled himself to
his knees. Looking across the water, no more than a hundred
yards away, he saw the other boat, flames now licking out of
the myriad holes in her hull. She was listing heavily to port and
he could see people leaping off into the water. But the one
thing he noticed, the one factor that impressed him more than
anything ever before in his memory, was that their forward
machine gun was still firing. His own men were scrambling for
safety behind what was left of the pilothouse. Some failed in
their attempt as the bullets searched them out in their last dash
for safety.

The gun on the other boat was finally silent, more likely
from lack of ammunition than guts, Grambling thought.
There was an explosion near the stern on the other craft. Then
the remaining fuel caught and flames raced forward across its
deck. Grambling grabbed his binoculars, focusing them on the
bow. Would that gunner get away before the boat blew itself
apart? He located him through the flames and his respect
became surprise. The man wore civilian clothes. He was not
military. With fascination, James watched him first go into
the pilothouse, then return to the deck alone. The man hesitated for a moment, staring back at *Pegasus*. The flames were
almost upon him when he leaped far out from the vessel.
Grambling lost sight of him behind the burning fuel in the
water.

James was now aware that *Pegasus* was heeling sharply to
starboard, toward the boat they'd just sunk. Voronov was on
his feet, his head out of the pilothouse, looking toward the
stern.

"She's finished, Jaimé. Your stern's just about blown right off. She's not going anywhere again." Voronov pulled his head back in, his eyes staring into Grambling's. "You'll have to abandon. There's no choice." The blood was streaming down Voronov's face from his forehead. His shirt was soaked near the shoulder and his arm hung limply at his side.

Grambling said nothing, nodding his assent silently. *Pegasus* hadn't really flown for more than two or three minutes. But it was a beautiful flight, he thought. She flew, she searched . . . she attacked. His missiles had struck home. She'd sunk another boat. She had done her duty.

He followed Voronov out on the steeply sloping deck in search of any survivors before he left *Pegasus* himself. After insuring that one of his men would take care of Voronov, he dove off. *Pegasus*'s stern was already underwater when his head broke the surface.

The Presidential Palace, Panama City

Horacio Ramos had been President of Panama for a little under two years. In that time he faced a number of situations that never would have come to mind before he took office. If he had to predict the most improbable situation of all, it would be the American now sitting on the other side of his desk, relating the facts of a small victory and an overwhelming loss. The victory was pyrrhic, at best. The death of Tomas Cornejo was staggering, a loss to his small nation, a personal tragedy for Ramos.

"I have difficulty selecting the proper words, Mr. Ryng." The voice was steady, but greatly weakened under the strain. His English was accented but well chosen, the result of an American education. "Tomas was . . . like a son to me. Not only did we work together . . . he felt the same about our country as I do. He saw things . . . imagined the future much in the same way. I . . . I don't think I can make myself clear. . . ."

Ryng understood what President Ramos was saying—about a loss that can never be replaced. He longed for that very special courage to say "I understand. Believe me. I can understand more than you'll ever know." But it was something he knew he couldn't do, not anymore. He'd seen so many go that way that he could accept the loss of most of them.

Ramos sighed. "Everything he did seemed to be the proper thing to do." The President shook his head sadly, staring down at his desk for a moment. When he looked up at Ryng, his voice had regained its penetrating sharpness and his black eyes were as piercing as in his photographs. "We will put this little moment aside for our own memories. That is not why you're here."

"No, sir. I'd hoped to meet you before all this happened. You see, I also represent—"

"I know exactly who you represent. That's why you were not admitted to this office before. Beyond the fact that I wanted to learn of Tomas's death from the man who was there with him, General Huertas's preliminary report this morning indicated that I must put aside my personal prejudices for the time being. And . . . I did not know how to thank you for fighting beside Tomas for our country."

"The choice wasn't mine. I was in the wrong place at the wrong time. Neither Tomas nor I expected anything that occurred. With even the slightest indication that we were in danger, we both would have been elsewhere. Mr. President, I don't really want to be fighting with your people, but I do enjoy killing Russians or Cubans whenever they get in my way. And I have no doubt that they, rather than your rebels, were behind that attack. I very much intend to leave Panama alive, and I'm unhappy enough over what's happened to me that I want to get a point across any way I can." He paused, expecting Ramos to ask just what that point was.

"You and Kitty Alvarez have become fast friends." Ramos stared passively at him, his face expressionless, the subject suddenly changed.

Ryng, startled, looked incredulously at President Ramos. The expression on the man's face remained the same. He seemed to be stating a fact rather than rubbing his face in it. He's stalling, thought Ryng. "I hadn't realized that had become public knowledge."

"It is not public knowledge." Ramos's voice had become hard. "If you want the truth, Mr. Ryng, we have to know what's happening every minute of the day whenever someone like you enters our country. Unfortunately, Ms. Alvarez's private life becomes part of that. You may be sure that what the two of you do together doesn't go beyond those who need to know, but she is vitally important to me." His face softened slightly. "What you have done for her and for us so far, Mr. Ryng, strikes me as very un-American, especially considering my regard for many of your countrymen." The corners of his mouth cracked into the tiniest of smiles. "Let me say that so far, I'd be willing to fight for her honor if your name were brought up. Now that we understand each other, what is the point you want to make?"

"Would you also accept some of what I was sent here to explain to you?"

"Listen, yes. Accept . . . perhaps."

"Mr. President, did General Huertas explain the body I pulled out of Limón Bay last night? It was obviously Soviet . . . blond, blue eyes . . . a letter handwritten in Russian in his pocket? Or the officer in Cuban uniform? The General seemed especially surprised. Tomas had hoped that if I was correct, we could bring back a prisoner to prove our point. The dead ones were the best we could do. . . ." His voice drifted off as he watched Ramos's face, waiting for some expression that would lower the man's guard. It wasn't forthcoming.

"I'll accept that. I believe the saying is, 'Dead men tell no lies.' But I have trouble understanding the reasons, Mr. Ryng."

"With all respect, sir, is the trouble in understanding the reasons, or is it in not wanting to understand?"

Ramos's eyes narrowed, not so much in anger, Ryng realized, as with an inner struggle. "I have traveled to Cuba for many years. She has been a good friend to my country. Premier Castro has been close to me at times. . . ." He was searching for the right terminology.

"It is almost like a priest arguing the existence of God with a non-believer. I am not a priest. I don't have a blind faith in Castro or in Cuba. But, Mr. Ryng, if this were my judgment day and I had to choose between Castro, who has been a friend and offered succor these many years, as opposed to you, who have just walked into my life—what would you choose?"

Ryng had not been prepared for the intensity of a man like Ramos, or the moral distress he was forced to face. What Admiral Pratt always considered cut-and-dried when they were in Washington, became problematical in another man's country. Ramos raised his eyebrows, tilting his head to one side in question. Perhaps he'd wait like that all day.

"You are posed with a dilemma, sir," Ryng answered. "I can truthfully say that I'm not. My mission is to convey some vital intelligence to you through means outside normal channels. I was also ordered to explain the long-range effects of what my country saw—from our vantage point, which is a decidedly different one than your own. The Soviet and Cuban interests in your country are not necessarily the best interests of Panama. I've done this. My job seems to be complete. The decision you have to make, logical or moral or however you want to look at it, is your own. I can't imagine that you'd want an American's opinion at this stage anyway."

"You're right!" Ramos was visibly relaxed now. Ryng was unsure of everything he'd said, unsure if he could repeat it to Pratt, but it seemed to have satisfied Ramos. "A man must make his own decisions . . . and I have done so. Your message is accepted, Mr. Ryng."

"I'm pleased. I guess there's no point in my taking any more of your time. I appreciate your seeing me." Ryng rose to shake hands. There was no point in staying. There had to be another way.

"Please . . . please sit down for just a moment, Mr. Ryng. There is one more thing." He gestured toward the chair, his hand outstretched. "You see, you say your responsibility seems to be over. Mine is just starting, and on a tragic note. You say I have problems within my military organization . . . even within my government. I need help in determining just what steps the revolutionaries will take. You say, yourself, that they want to become part of the government rather than destroy it. You say your country, through Admiral Pratt, wants to offer technical and military assistance if I will ask for it. But who am I to work with? Tomas is gone. No one was closer to me."

Ryng waited, saying nothing. He neither welcomed Ramos's next request, which he knew to be forthcoming, nor could he imagine why he should accept. It was what Pratt wanted, to have him work his way into the uppermost strata of the government. Damn it! He wished Henry Cobb would show.

"Mr. President, I appreciate your problems and believe me, I am honored that you would trust me. But I'm not the type of man you're looking for."

"The fact that you're a professional appeals to me. Mr. Ryng, you're still relatively free of suspicion in this country . . . or as much as you or anyone else could be at this point. I'd like you to think it over."

Ryng shook his head, smiling politely. Hold out, he reminded himself, until Cobb shows. "Thank you, but I think I'll have to decline." In response to a button that Ramos had pressed, a door from one of the side rooms opened. Ryng turned. Damn it, he said to himself as he looked first at Ramos, then back at Kitty. She came directly across the room to Ramos, gave him a paternal kiss on the cheek, and took the chair next to Ryng. He knew what was going to happen now.

Ryng explained before he left Ramos's office that he preferred to wander and think sometimes after making decisions contrary to his own best judgment. This was one of those times. Kitty understood.

What bothered Ryng most was what he didn't know. The events since he'd arrived in Panama seemed to follow a logical progression, haphazard yet understandable when considered from afar. There were times—Henry Cobb had mentioned this before—when Dave Pratt kept too much from them. Everything in their business was on a need-to-know basis. They would never hold it against Pratt when the Admiral decided to withhold information, but there was a patina of uncertainty that seemed to cover almost everything he had encountered in

Panama—even the fates that had brought Bernie Ryng and Kitty Alvarez together. She not only opened all the doors that needed to be opened, but more often than not she was also quite comfortable with the individuals beyond those doors. She seemed always to be slightly ahead of the puzzle that he himself was trying to unravel.

What was it, then, that Pratt was keeping from him?

Grambling's Camp

Esteban Alvarez's features had been set in a perpetual scowl well before arriving in the jungle camp. From the moment he'd set foot in Panama, he had listened to one report after another that displeased him—his flow of weapons, which he felt was a perfect system, was occasionally intercepted by government raiders; the younger officers sent to Cuba for training were too cocksure, flaunting their conceit like their Russian instructors; there was an increasingly ominous presence of Soviet military personnel in the streets; the Colón operation had succeeded, but somehow had also been impaired through an evident weakness in security. Nor had his first short meeting with President Ramos gone well at all—too many questions about Castro and Havana and Russians.

And now he was at the jungle camp which he had an especial aversion to. The day was hot and very sticky, the bugs impossible. Alvarez liked James Grambling, wished that he had been more successful with Kitty years before, but he disliked Maria, who seemed always at Jaimé's side. She was a camp follower in Alvarez's opinion, nothing but a slut he had decided months before, certainly not a future leader of the country.

Almost immediately, Grambling and Alvarez were arguing. "There is a security breach somewhere. I haven't the slightest

bit of time to begin to find out where, but there is a leak."
Grambling was as unhappy that day as Alvarez, and he didn't
mind venting his anger to this city type, this intellectual. He
still hurt all over from the shrapnel wounds suffered a few
nights before. The front of *Pegasus*'s pilothouse and the instrument panel had absorbed most of the blast, but there was
enough metal and splinters in his body the next day for a doctor to be called. It had taken more than an hour to dig for the
shards in his body, a very painful hour. And now the heat and
dank steaminess of the jungle augmented his discomfort. Each
movement of his body was accompanied by a sharp stab of
pain from a healing wound.

"I have heard nothing back in the city. . . ." began Alvarez.

Grambling opened his mouth to retort, then thought better
of it. He rose with a groan and stalked angrily outside the tent,
stretching his arms gently to relieve the stiffness. If only those
comfortable officers in Panama City, those well-uniformed,
self-satisfied clowns could have something more to worry
about than the air conditioning in their offices and the politics
of determining who would come out on top! He wheeled
about as Alvarez came outside to join him. "If only those self-
satisfied—" then he halted. There was no reason to rail at
Alvarez, who understood very well the situation on both sides.
Grambling rather liked the older man, and he understood, better than those back in the city, that Alvarez was a critical factor in their success.

Alvarez removed a wrinkled handkerchief from his pocket
and mopped his brow, just as he had done so often that day.
The neatly pressed khaki shirt he made a point of wearing into
the jungle was rumpled, the armpits and back dark with
perspiration. He brushed at the insects circling his head.
"Jaimé, believe me, I do understand. We are developing a
plan to rotate more of them into the jungle, but it takes time.
There are the older officers to think about, the ones still loyal
to President Ramos. They would ask too many questions if
they noticed their junior officers were missing. You know,
they have a great deal of feeling about showing uniforms in
the streets . . . so the citizens will notice and feel protected."
He sighed to himself. The Guardia was both a military and a
police force, and their presence was just as important as insur-

ing that a policeman was at each busy corner to direct traffic or help an old lady across the street.

Grambling turned, grinning at the older man for the first time that day. "I know what you mean. If they were not on the streets, the people would worry about a revolution"—he laughed—"begin to suspect that the revolutionaries might actually be able to come from the hills right into the city."

Even Alvarez was forced to smile in return. But his expression sobered just as quickly. "What I see on the streets that I don't like, Jamié, is the Russians. There are too many of them. You haven't been to Havana for a long time now, but there you see them everywhere. I know they come with the equipment and supplies—that's always part of the deal—but they don't go home. Instead they multiply." He shook his head in disgust. "Just like rabbits!"

"The other night, on our attack at Colón," Grambling said, "one of their officers came with me. I had no choice . . . I had to take him." He shrugged. "It was Voronov. He wasn't in the way. He was just there . . ." Grambling searched for the right words, ". . . a presence . . . one that never seems to go away."

Alvarez paced across the clearing as they spoke, hoping against hope that the insects might find a more suitable landing spot. "I have had the opportunity to talk with Fidel Castro a number of times, Jaimé. I like him . . . always have. He is a Cuban first, and he loves his people and his country. But he told me once, at the end of the day when we both were able to sit back with a cold beer, that he felt if he had one thing to do over again it would be to avoid the Marxist approach. He said it was not for Caribbean people. Perhaps it was fine for Russians who lived in the north, he said, and had nothing to think about during those long, cold winters . . . but it was not for his people, or any others in the Caribbean." He turned to make sure Grambling was listening. The younger man was more than attentive. It always happened when Castro's name was mentioned.

"So," Alvarez continued, "he said he would have patterned something more specific, something that would not appeal to the Russians so much. He said, if you can believe this, that he used to dream of how he could convince them that they were better off back in those cold winters—still willing to provide assistance, but with no strings attached." Alvarez shrugged. "He also said that in twenty-five years he still hasn't come up with an answer. No matter how well he thinks he is doing, he never gets quite around the bend . . . and when he thinks he is close," he shrugged again, "then they push that bend back a little farther. So . . . then they want him to send off more troops, in exchange for whatever Fidel knows he needs."

"Does he really know what's around that bend?"

"No, Jaimé, I don't think so. He's tired . . . very, very tired. Sometimes I think he offers to help us in order to use us."

Grambling stretched his sore body very carefully, and winced. "Use us?"

"I didn't really understand it until I came back this time, perhaps I still don't. But I am beginning to think that maybe Castro hopes the Russians will pay more attention to us, and less to him . . ." He added after a pause, "And more of a chance for us and our neighbors to intimidate the Americans . . . and that makes sense too. The Americans have grown used to Castro, not comfortable with him, but they're no longer so bothered. They're concentrating all their time on our side of the Caribbean. Now," he added, clapping his hands together, "to Castro that makes sense!"

Grambling nodded thoughtfully. That theory wasn't new to him. It was exactly what he had thought of in the past. Castro would like to see the Americans and the Russians pay as little attention to him as possible.

"Come on, Jaimé. We have work to do. We'll talk of such ideas at another time."

The Havana Docks

Lieutenant Corazon was last seen in Havana departing the building that housed Admiral Khasan's office. It would be the last accurate report of his whereabouts. He slipped into the night following a preplanned, circuitous route toward the waterfront. He stopped only once, to retrieve a packsack deposited earlier near the docks, changing into fisherman's attire.

Near the end of a long, dark fishing dock, he slipped into a small boat, also tied up there earlier. With a silent electric motor, he maneuvered alongside the motley, old fishing boats, avoiding any light from the shore. Then he eased along the banks of the harbor, staying within the shadows until he was well past arousing the interest of any sleepy sentries of the civilian Guardia. Facing open water, he switched the boat to its highest speed and aimed the craft due north.

Two hours later, with just the loom of Havana's lights behind him, he killed the engine and drifted. Moments later he recognized the high-speed whine of the gas turbine engine coming in from the east. He knew the sound well for he had ridden that same hydrofoil one evening not so long before. It was one of the boats from Key West following the pattern of its normal patrol along the northern rim of Cuba.

Admiral Pratt had been sure that within a week of commencement of such a patrol, the Cubans manning the coastal radar stations would become familiar with the patrol and would no longer bother to send snoopers out to track the craft. For the past week, becoming a model of consistency for the Cubans, the hydrofoil followed this exact path. This night her captain recognized the winking light he had been waiting for. Pratt had banked on the constancy and monotony of the patrol to cover this departure. Only the exact date had been uncertain.

Even before the light had been identified, the hydrofoil's radar picked up the reflector Cobb had mounted on the bow of the drifting boat. Now, rather than take the chance of raising curiosity with searchlights, they charged to within a hundred yards before cutting back their speed and retracting the foils. They would be stopped for only a moment, long enough for the man in the small boat to insure that his craft would sink as he climbed over the side into the hydrofoil.

Shortly, the American boat was once again foil-borne and racing around the western tip of Cuba, then south through the Yucatan Channel. Sixty miles into the Caribbean she made contact with a trawler that had reached the northernmost

point of her normal fishing pattern and had turned to head
south. Again there was but a brief pause, nothing longer than
any Cuban snoopers would assume it would take for the
hydrofoil to investigate the fisherman. Then the American
naval craft turned north and raced back along the same path
she had just come, following exactly the same pattern she and
the Cubans had become accustomed to.

It was not unusual in that area of the Caribbean for a fishing boat to return directly home if her hold was mostly full.
Fishing had been good the previous week, and the boat
stopped only twice on the return trip to put out her nets, both
times as she neared her home port on the Panamanian coast.
Four days passed from the time she met the hydrofoil until she
was in sight of Panama.

She dawdled off Colón until after midnight. Then a man in
a wet suit slipped over the side, a watertight pack attached
around his back and waist. The swimmer had spent much time
in the pilothouse with the captain, studying the charts, making
certain of the tide and current into the harbor, memorizing the
channel.

He held a device before him with a thumb button that activated an electric motor. The machine, much like a boat motor,
would ease his passage into the harbor. The water was warm
and clear, and he was as accustomed to this element as the fish
that surrounded him. Checking his watch and his compass
with precision, he was able to follow the channel exactly as he
had planned. There was little danger as long as he avoided
fouling the anchor chains on merchant ships waiting above
him to transit the Canal.

He checked the watch three times on his final leg, to insure
that he was still in deep enough water. When the time was
proper, he unscrewed the plug on the side of the motor and released it. Bubbles floated to the surface as the device filled
with water and sank into the mud of the harbor.

The swimmer surfaced. Against the lights from the city of
Colón, he could see that he was less than fifty yards from his
landing spot. Quietly and easily, for he was rested and there
was more than enough time, he swam to the appointed place.
There was a ladder, just as he had expected, and he climbed
cautiously until he could see to either side of the wharf. Wait-

ing without a motion or a sound, just as he had learned so long ago, he insured he was alone. Then he climbed the last few rungs, slithering over the top until he was lying facedown on the old wooden wharf. It reeked of fish and tar and unidentifiable smells worked into its surface over the years. They were sensations he identified with an inherent satisfaction. Sure now that he was by himself, he slipped off the rubber swim fins and darted into a shed directly in front of him.

Just as he had anticipated, the windows were boarded over. But there was a flashlight, a change of clothes, and a briefcase waiting for him. Stripping off the wet suit, he dropped it through the trap door in the floor, weighted with the lead weights that had also been left for that purpose. After memorizing his new credentials, he was ready to move.

Lieutenant Corazon, late of Havana, no longer existed. Henry Cobb had arrived in Panama to catch up with his old friend, Bernie Ryng.

Cobb sincerely hoped that Ryng would be able to answer some questions for him. He had known what he was looking for when he was sent into Havana, but he was unaware of the scope of the plan. Pratt had never explained how big this operation had grown. There had been little time to really appreciate the details of the papers he'd photographed in Admiral Khasan's office, but he quickly comprehended the chart and its grease-pencil notations. Cobb understood Pratt's practice of limited intelligence on a need-to-know basis. But Cobb also worked better when he knew the scope of an operation. Why the hell had Pratt been so close-mouthed this time? In the past he'd always emphasized aspects of an operation that could affect the way a man worked. Henry Cobb was sure he would have moved more quickly had he been aware of the extent of the Soviet incursion. Hopefully Ryng would be able to expand on it. It just wasn't like Dave Pratt to keep them in the dark like this.

The Pentagon

The people in his wing of the Pentagon, both civilian and military, welcomed the sudden change that had come over Dave Pratt. There were so many admirals and generals running around the corridors that most individuals ceased to be impressed with them after the first few weeks at work. But Pratt was cut from a slightly different mold. Not only was there a certain aura about him, but he possessed a reputation that had transformed him into an almost fictional character. Those who didn't know him were in awe of the tales of his exploits. The awe heightened to reverence after the Battle of the Mediterranean. This was, in turn, magnified by the personality of the hardened admiral allowed to move about the corridors in a wheelchair.

The fact that he was once again smiling, actually exchanging the time of day with those he rarely nodded to weeks before, was cracking that facade. The rumors about the change in Pratt were eventually confirmed by a yeoman whose duty it was to stop by his outer office four times a day to pick up the outgoing mail. On that particular day, the first and only one she could remember that the door to the inner office had been left open, there was Admiral Pratt at his desk—in a chair, not the wheelchair everyone had grown accustomed to. And, to the yeoman's surprise, Pratt had actually looked up from his desk, seen the girl collecting the mail, and waved to her with a smile.

By lunchtime it had been confirmed thoughout the vast building—the legendary Admiral Pratt could get out of that wheelchair! No one, not even his secretary, had ever seen him walk. Betty had come in one morning and there he was, sitting at his desk in the regular chair, the wheelchair folded in the far corner. Since he had simply looked up at her, muttered a greeting, and gone back to his work, she never questioned the change. There was no one there to help him. He had obviously wheeled himself to the office—a number of people had seen him going up the corridor—entered the room, closed the door, and somehow had not only walked to his desk on his own, but

had first folded the wheelchair and left it on the other side of
the room.

And that same day, with the wave and the smile to the
yeoman, Admiral David Pratt was back from that distant
world he had encased himself in for so long. Pratt would never
know how his return changed those around him, for he was
totally engrossed in his new operation. The fact that he knew
Henry Cobb was on his way to join Ryng, if he wasn't already
there, excited him even more.

Pratt's own strategy wasn't as clear yet, though he sensed
what had to be done. The first struggle would be to convince
his superiors, and the President, when the time came and decisions would involve not just experimenting with ships and
planes and men on a checkerboard chart, but the lives or
deaths of his own men.

There were moves the Russians made recently that had attracted no curiosity on the part of American intelligence, even
very little from his perspective, until ideas began to fall into
place. Soviet diesel submarines had generally been intended
for coastal protection of the homeland, and little attention
was paid to the fact that more than a dozen of them had tran-
sited the Atlantic the past month. Some received supplies in
Cuba while others were reprovisioned at sea. A few had made
port visits in South America. None of this sparked interest in
the American intelligence community. Their purpose made no
sense until Dave Pratt acknowledged the obvious—no sane
naval commander would waste nuclear submarines in a blockade of narrow passages like the Windward or Mona or Galleons. Those Russian diesel attack boats were throwaways—
all that was required was a sub that could fire torpedoes and
interdict the entrances to the Caribbean!

Perhaps they would use nuclear submarines, in conjunction
with their surface forces, to impede the Florida Straits or the
Yucatan Channel. That made sense. But the primary responsibility of those main forces would be to keep American ships
from entering the fray, to deny access to the Caribbean. They
would jockey with each other in the Atlantic—threat and
counterthreat. That's where the power structure above him
would come in, Pratt knew. That's when the hotline between

Washington and Moscow would be active. And that was why he was sitting in his chair now, constructing what might be a realistic projection. He understood almost everything, and in time he would have enough to be able to explain it to even the most liberal senator, to detail the military freight on those roll on/roll off ships plodding along through the Atlantic, timing their arrival exactly.

Pratt had been analyzing the intelligence returned by the hydrofoil to Key West days before, and realized again how Henry Cobb never missed a beat. This fellow Khasan has a talent for strategy just like me, Pratt thought as he examined the material. Except, Pratt decided, I'd use my heavies a little differently. Considering how effective those diesel submarines should be, I'd move more guided missile ships off the Bahamas. But then again, there may still be something I've missed.

He saw that same pretty yeoman picking up the mail in the outer office, the one who'd been staring at him the day before. He smiled and waved.

Havana

"Get your hands off me!" Lydia yelled, beginning Victor Khasan's day on the wrong step. Normally, that early in the morning, any words out of her mouth were more often a mumble. But that statement had been clear as a bell . . . and vehement. Lydia rolled over in the bed and rose on one elbow. "What's the matter, Victor? Has your whore found someone better . . . or bigger?" She spat with disdain.

She'd caught him off guard. Because it had been a few days since his last evening with Chita Monteria, it seemed only natural to him that he should catch up on his husbandly duties. Not only had Lydia taken off weight—that winter fat the women in Moscow seemed to add to each year, then never get rid of—but she was developing a lovely tan, too. The more he noticed those tan lines, the more entrancing they became. So, after awakening that morning, he'd simply begun to rub her thigh and suddenly she'd whirled around, rising on one elbow. . .

"The least you could do would be to answer me," she responded to his look of uncertainty, which had followed his look of surprise. "There's no need to think up excuses. We're past that, Victor." Coupled with the flare of anger, Khasan found her even more attractive. "No need to get yourself excited. You're not going to have any roll in the hay with me this morning."

He shook his head in wonder. "I don't understand. I don't . . ."

"You picked the wrong whore, Victor. One or two mistakes are possible with any man but no one takes up with something like her without the whole world knowing." Her voice rose shrilly and there was no doubting the look in her eyes. To deny anything at this point would be a mistake. Finally, as if to prove her point, Lydia jumped out of bed to face him. She was totally naked and the tan and the paleness seemed even more attractive to him. "If this doesn't satisfy you, there are a lot of men in Havana who will be quite happy with it. And you can go back to your whore!" She pirouetted on her toes and stalked off to the bathroom, offering an equally appealing picture as he muttered to himself why the day had to start off like that.

A little after ten in the morning, Navarro appeared in Admiral Khasan's office—no announcement, not even a phone call. Leaning against the doorjamb, the stub of the first cigar of the day protruding from his clean-shaven face, Navarro looked more American than ever. Khasan had heard before that the Commodore showed up that way, though not often—mostly when he was unhappy.

"Not very attentive, Admiral. I could have walked in, taken out my pistol, and shot you. Lousy security." Navarro shook his head sadly. "Perhaps the rumors I hear are correct about this office."

"What you hear are exactly what they are—rumors!" Khasan snapped back. He could sense from the moment he noticed the first faint cigar aroma that this was not a courtesy call. And there was no rule he was aware of that said a Soviet Admiral was required to treat a Cuban Commodore with deference when that Cuban should be thanking his lucky stars every morning that there was a Kremlin that still cared . . . especially given the way the Cubans could screw up everything handed to them.

Navarro wandered across the room pulling along the one free chair, and sat down on the opposite side of the desk. Reaching into his a slender briefcase, he extracted a cigar and rolled it across the desk to Khasan. "I'll bet you could use one of these," he said, thinking about the rumor that Khasan's wife was fed up with her husband's infidelity. "Life hasn't been too easy these past few days, has it?" he added.

Khasan rubbed his eyes irritably. "I'm getting my job done, if that's what you mean. No one's going to stop this operation now, you can be sure of that."

The other man's expression remained the same. He nodded. "Perhaps you're right." He took the cigar stub from his mouth, holding a match to it until the tip glowed. Then he puffed at it until he blew out a satisfactory cloud of smoke. "What are you looking for when this operation is over?"

"The same as you—embarrass the Americans . . . get them out of the Caribbean . . . put them on enough of a defensive in their own country so they'll worry less about Europe . . . the Arabs—"

"That's not what I really mean," Navarro replied, leaning across the desk. "What does it matter whether the Panamanians have a successful revolution? How is that poor little country going to serve you? They already cooperate, and they are as unfriendly with the Americans as your own country appears to be. You seem to have what you desire with us." His head tilted slightly to one side and there was an impish grin as he asked, "What is it really that motivates you to bring over such tremendous firepower, when that little country seems already to be sliding our way?"

"What gives you that idea?" Khasan asked. "I've never said that Panama is so critical. Many of those ships are simply to impress your neighbors."

Navarro shrugged. That irritated the Russian even more. It seemed to be a Cuban habit, or maybe just a Spanish one in this part of the world—a gesture of disdain. He sometimes caught himself doing it from time to time. "I never understood that would happen to Cuba," the Commodore answered, "but look around us today—we have Russian ships and submarines, Russian missiles, Russian rifles and machine guns and grenade launchers, Russian troops, Russian advisors . . . Russian everything," he added with a sigh.

Khasan's eyes narrowed slightly. "Would you prefer to be an American possession? Rather than working hand-in-hand with us, would you like an American president to tell you what to do?"

"What I would like, what I had hoped years ago, was to have a Cuba that belonged to herself. What we got was something different." He removed the tiny stub of cigar from his mouth, touched the end to insure it was cold, and threw it into the wastebasket. "I'm not complaining for myself. We're better off. But I would like you to understand that there are many others who would not accept that. Señor Alvarez is a good example—"

"Screw Alvarez. He's an old fool."

Navarro smiled sadly. "Maybe so. We shall see. But, my friend, keep one thing in mind. The Caribbean of today is quite different from that of 1960, when your predecessors first came to Havana. These men like Alvarez are patriots who have no more love for you than they do for the Americans. They want one thing—to be as free of you as possible after it is all over. If they find your ships in their ports, your troops in their streets, your political officers in their government buildings . . . you will not have so easy a time of it."

"That has nothing to do with me. I'm simply a military advisor—"

"Oh, I know you are more than that." Navarro raised his voice and leaned forward so that the other could not interrupt him. "You have been a good friend and an intelligent one in involving me in all your strategy, and I do understand it, more than you think. I couldn't begin to move all those ships around or bring in each of those units in the Atlantic in the right place at the right time. But I think once they are in place, it will not be so easy to send them home." There was the impish grin again. "And I doubt I know all of your plans."

"Just what do you expect me to say?"

"Nothing. Absolutely nothing . . . right now. I just want

you to think about everything I have said." Navarro stood up, reaching across the desk and clapping the Russian on the shoulder. "You have been around Havana for a long time. You have done a great deal for me and I consider you a friend. So . . . one discusses such things with friends. Come on with me." Now the Cuban's voice was booming and he was smiling. "You look like this has been a bad day for you. I have a car downstairs. I'm going out to a baseball game at the university. The Premier said I could use his private box. Join me and we will talk some more . . . maybe drink a few beers. Baseball parks are a good place to relax."

Because he was not ready to consider right then the ideas that Navarro was hinting at, Khasan accepted the invitation. Besides, maybe the outing Navarro suggested would cheer him up.

It was sunny and pleasant in the Premier's box, and they drank beers and smoked cigars and talked. Baseball was not a game Khasan understood when he arrived in Cuba, so Navarro had taken it upon himself in the last year to teach it to the Russian. As the game progressed, Khasan decided perhaps things were looking up. It wasn't such a bad day after all. Then a line drive was hit right at him. The Russian was paralyzed with fear as the ball sped directly at his head. Navarro reached out in front of Khasan at the last moment and grabbed the ball in his bare hands. Shouting with joy, the Commodore threw the ball back to the pitcher.

"What do you think my friend? A little excitement?"

Panama City

Bernie Ryng's day began well before dawn with pounding fists on the door and Kitty shaking him awake. He rose onto his elbows. The dream had faded, the knocking now a steady rapping on the apartment door, followed by a voice.

"Señor Ryng, Señor Ryng, please . . . it is General Huertas's aide."

He climbed from the bed, slipping into his pants and pick-

ing up his pistol in the same motion as he moved to the door.
"Who is it?" he shouted back, easing to the side of the door.

"Colonel Cassis, General Huertas's aide. I have been asked
by the general to pick you up, sir. It is very important."

Ryng had met Cassis once and the voice seemed vaguely
familiar. When he let the door fall open against the chain, he
recognized that it was the colonel and he was alone. It took
only a matter of moments for Cassis to explain that some
Cuban soldiers had been captured in a firefight near Colón.
General Huertas very much would like Señor Ryng to be part
of the interrogation.

Soon after arriving at the Guardia jail, Ryng realized that
Huertas had no comprehension of the term *interrogation*. It
was torture, pure and simple, and the inquisitors seemed to be
quite experienced and comfortable at their tasks.

"We had three of them, Señor Ryng," Huertas reported.
"But that one there," he indicated a corpse with a gesture of
his head, "was too weak. Maybe these Cubans aren't produc-
ing such great soldiers today," he added with a grin.

From what Ryng could determine, there had never been any
time that this particular corpse might have spoken, torture or
not. From the looks of the head wound the man had incurred,
he felt it likely the man had been dead before he was brought
in, perhaps instantly. The second one looked no better. A
bullet wound in his chest was still oozing. The man was obviously unconscious, and there seemed no way he was ever going
to be brought around so that he could then be tortured. But
Huertas's men were preparing him anyway. Ryng sensed that
all was not right with General Huertas.

It seemed to Ryng that this was a phony setup. One dead
prisoner, one beyond caring. "Where's the last one? Head
shot off?" he inquired sarcastically.

Huertas shook his head. "On the contrary. This last one's
wounded, but he's coherent." The general guided the group
into the next room.

There, propped in a chair and held in place by leather
thongs around his ankles, thighs, chest, and wrists, was a
skinny youth in a torn, bloody uniform. A gash across his
forehead ended by an ear that was mostly ripped way. His face
and neck were badly bruised. Ryng looked into the most

frightened eyes he had ever seen. Tears coursed down muddy cheeks. The boy couldn't have been more than fifteen.

Huertas leaned down in front of the youth. "Now, we begin in earnest." He touched a button on the table beside them. The boy jumped as a shock raced through his body. The general tapped the button lightly a couple of times as the eyes grew bigger. "You see how it works?" There was an urgent nod. "All right, we know you are Cuban—"

"No . . . no . . ." the words were wrenched from his mouth as Huertas held his finger tightly on the button.

"We will start with your name and your unit." He waited for a moment as the boy's breath came in long pain-wracked sobs. Then, "Again, your name and your unit."

"I am not Cuban," he hissed through clenched teeth. "I am—" The button was held down firmly until the body ceased to respond, the head slumped on his chest.

"Water," snarled Huertas. He turned to one of the waiting aides. "Bring him around quickly." To Ryng he added out of the corner of his mouth, "These Cubans are not so tough, are they? We will find out soon enough."

"Have you ever considered, General, that perhaps he is not a Cuban?"

"Ridiculous. Look at the uniform—Cuban. He was captured in a firefight." The general shrugged. "That's enough for me. Soon we will find out." Cold water had been poured over the boy's head. Now they were slapping him with wet towels.

"It doesn't strike me that he's a Cuban at all. Look at the uniform. It's much too big for him. A grown man would wear that. He's just a kid. The troops in the Cuban army are older, well-fed, well trained, disciplined. Look for yourself. He's all skin and bones, more like a peasant than a soldier—"

"Señor Ryng, I have been asked by President Ramos to cooperate with you. I do not like the idea of working with Americans, but I follow my orders. I was told that you want to talk to Cubans, so I have a Cuban for you." There was a groan from the chair. "There, he's coming around. You will see."

The head slowly came up from the chest. Spittle ran from the corners of his mouth. The tongue lolled drunkenly as he tried to talk, his eyes staring at a spot on the general's chest. There was no reaction as Huertas's hand moved toward the button on the table. "We know you are Cuban," the general shouted. "Your unit . . . tell me your unit first."

The face looked up at Huertas. "Ama . . . Amador . . . Ama . . ." His head lolled backward.

Huertas looked at the boy. His eyes were slits. "I don't want code names. I want the identification of your battalion . . . the names of your officers. . . ." His hand came down on the button.

There was a gagging sound as the boy's body jerked convulsively and he choked on his tongue. The men watched as the prisoner strained for air, strange sounds emanating from his throat. Instinctively, Ryng grabbed a pencil from the table. Yanking the boy's head back by the hair, he jammed the pencil in his mouth, digging for the tongue. As the eyes bulged out unseeing, Ryng succeeded in halting the choking, but the head fell forward and the body went limp.

"You are wasting your time, Señor Ryng. You are better off to let enemies die."

"He is dead, General." Ryng lifted the chin then let it fall back. "He's very dead. How do you expect to gain any information that way?" He was facing Huertas, his face only inches from the general. "He was probably half dead when he was brought in here. I suspect that someone put that uniform on him, either before he arrived here or"—Ryng's eyebrows rose—"after you already had him in the room. He's no more a Cuban than I am. Probably some poor peasant that figured there'd be something to eat if he joined the rebel forces. I don't know why you brought me here, General Huertas. But I suggest that the next time you do so, you be damn sure you've got someone who is really Cuban. Then I'll talk to him, in my own fashion, and I'll make sure President Ramos understands that's the way I want the job done." Ryng turned on his heel and walked to the door. "I assume there will be a car and driver outside."

The sun was coming up as he returned to his building. Why the hell would they drag me out in the middle of the night, he wondered, for a sham like that? Then he began to feel a gnawing fear in the pit of his stomach. The time it took the elevator to arrive at his floor was as interminable as the wait for it had been in the lobby. He dashed down the corridor, fumbling for his key. But there was no need for one. The lock was gone, a twisted mess of metal where it had once been part of the door.

There was no need to call for Kitty or even to search for her. She was the reason, their main objective. Reducing the apartment to a shambles had been secondary, more likely done by others while Kitty was spirited away.

There had been no need for secrecy or deception. The call by General Huertas was intended to get him out of there. The display of a couple of bodies—it didn't matter where they'd died—and the torture of the young boy were merely a ruse to occupy his time in case Kitty's kidnappers had been delayed. To Ryng it was right out of a grade B movie, and he was the foil, the dummy who had taken the bait!

Once again he wished Henry Cobb were here. Cobb, who was more experienced in this kind of operation, would never have fallen for it. Instead, Ryng thought, he had been drawn into this web—by Tomas Cornejo, by President Ramos, by Huertas . . . even by Kitty, who had convinced him that he should accept Ramos's offer.

Then a startling thought occurred to Ryng: If he followed Kitty's trail backward, would it end up in Dave Pratt's office? It seemed improbable that anything could fit together so well, impossible that she would be allowed to take part in such a dangerous game. There was no doubt in his mind that she really was Katarina Alvarez, that she was a Panamanian who had done much for her country, that her father was on a first-name basis with Castro, but could Dave Pratt have planned something like this . . . even *plan* that Bernie Ryng would turn against his own best judgment and fall in love with her?

Where the hell was Cobb, then? Henry would have some ideas about this. Or did Henry also have all the answers? No. That was impossible. The one man Bernie Ryng trusted implicitly—even more than himself—was Henry Cobb, and Cobb would never let either of them be drawn in like this.

Unconsciously Ryng pushed the sofa against the useless apartment door. If anyone planned to get through here, he would be ready. He stretched out in an easy chair backed against the wall, facing the door, his legs out in front of him.

Then he closed his eyes and relaxed, letting his mind drift, clenching and unclenching his fists.

As his head cleared and his thoughts became ordered, one improbable item occurred to him that he had never considered. Kitty Alvarez flashed back and forth across his mind, and he realized that he *had* really fallen in love with her. Because she had insinuated herself so deeply into his consciousness, bypassing the weekend-long stand or the vacation infatuation that he was familiar with, he had wholly overlooked the emotional attachment. If it had ever become apparent, before it became a dependence, it was more likely he would have packed his bags and moved on. It was neither his desire nor his nature to fall into a relationship of this kind. Nor did he think he was the type that any woman could easily establish an emotional attachment with. Was it that Kitty Alvarez had seen something he was unaware of in his own makeup? If she did, maybe it *was* time to get out of this business—before he ended up dead.

That was it, then; his mind was made up—but no sooner did he rise from the chair and go to the window, than two planes, old-fashioned prop types, military but without markings, swooped over the city, their machine guns firing at nothing in particular. Finally he could see exactly what they had in mind—the firing was only to draw attention to their target. As they closed toward the Presidential Palace, they climbed slightly.

Ryng watched as bombs tumbled into the grounds of the Palace. He could see the puffs of smoke and dust before the muffled explosions came to him. There had been little effort to even aim at the Palace itself. If they had really wanted to, they would more likely have been armed with rockets or missiles. It was simply a show of force, a display of power to the man in the street as he went to work at that early hour. The rebel forces were busy establishing the fact that they could come and go as they pleased, and drop a couple of bombs on the seat of power if they liked, without facing any retaliation. There was no clearer way to eradicate the peoples' wavering confidence in their government.

Such arrogance on their part confirmed for Ryng the idea he had been working on himself. Arrogance was the answer. Why not go to the father of the girl he had been sleeping with? Why not tell Esteban Alvarez the juicy details, followed by the fact that his own people had grabbed his daughter. Ryng knew Alvarez would never order that, never take the chance that she might be hurt. Why not stir up the waters in the rebel camp—use one of their leaders to muddy the waters? Perhaps that was the way to break it all open. Would Alvarez be the man who knew the real plans, knew what the Cubans and Russians really had as their main target? Creating hatred and mistrust within the enemy camp was always a prime tactic.

Off the Northeast Coast of Cuba

Without fanfare the American destroyer *Stump* went quietly to general quarters at first light. It was part drill, but more anticipation that the Soviet submarine would be under way that morning. Reports of Soviet submarine activity had been increasing in the daily messages. For three days *Stump* had been steaming Blue/Gold watches off Punta Munda on Cuba's northeast coast, half the crew at anti-submarine stations while the other half stood easy. She was as ready as a ship could be. Her captain was not the type to take the chance of his crew growing stale through the monotony of anti-submarine warfare (ASW) steaming without a target.

The Soviets cooperated by sending not one, but two submarines out of the Cuban harbor. One turned northwest and submerged as soon as the coastal shelf fell off into deep water. The second cruised about three miles offshore and commenced a series of drills, submerging to periscope depth, surfacing to put crews over the side in rubber rafts, even darting off in a variety of directions at high speed before reversing course. With only one destroyer standing offshore, this seemed the normal way of confusing the Americans.

Stump's captain, Lou Eberhardt, had been trained to expect exactly what the Soviets were attempting. There was no doubt in his mind which submarine he intended to trail. Before either sub ever reached open water his target had been identified. She had emitted signals with radar carried only by the boat headed for the Windward Passage between Cuba and Haiti. The one moving off northwest in a determined fashion was a decoy, an older submarine given to the Cubans years before. *Stump*'s helicopter tracked that one until a frigate fifty miles away arrived to assume contact.

Dave Pratt's initial plan was to place each submarine he knew was destined for passage blockade under surveillance. His orders authorized holding them down, if possible, to teach them some lessons about anti-submarine warfare even before they arrived on station. The data forwarded by Henry Cobb was vital to Pratt's strategy, for he knew that once the Soviet submarines reached station, they would go silent until ordered to interdict their assigned area. Some of the submarines had come to Cuba for replenishment, and they would be easy to track. Others would resupply from tenders at sea. Those would cause more trouble because they could go deep to evade detection. But he intended to make it as difficult as possible. Each Soviet submarine-resupply ship was under constant surveillance by aircraft and frigates. The one advantage he could give his destroyers was the opportunity to watch their target surface for fuel and supplies, then attempt to maintain contact afterward. If only it could be that easy with the nuclear submarines that would stay well away from the many passages into the Caribbean—they were independent, required no resupply, and could stay down until they were damn well ready to show themselves.

Stump remained at general quarters during the submarine's antics. Now that there was a firm target, the one *they* were responsible for, it was valuable for morale to involve the entire crew. *Stump*'s mission was anti-submarine warfare and she was designed and her men trained for exactly that purpose. From this point until the Soviets gave the signal to blockade each of the Caribbean passages, the submarine would make every effort to evade, and *Stump* would attempt to track her quarry. Once submerged, the game would be to hold the submarine down, making any effort to surface for air or snorkel an unpleasant experience. The objective was not only to know where that submarine was at every minute, but to wear down her crew to the point of ineffectiveness. Short of attack, this was the cold war method of achieving their goal.

The Soviet submarine casually worked its way into deeper water. She was a new Tango class, designed for long-range operations, fast on the surface or submerged, and much quieter than her predecessors. There was no great expanse of deep water for a submarine to maneuver in between Cuba and the Great Bahama Bank. The submarine commander, Captain Third Rank G.A. Fitin, expected a tail would be more than likely and was ready to play the game. There was no doubt in his mind that he could not take his men into action exhausted by a hold down. Yet his orders were to use any American destroyers as training aids for his crew, up to a certain point. A signal would be issued by the Soviet Caribbean commander when it was time to dispose of any tails his submarines could not shake.

The submarine dove while on a northwesterly course. Temperature readings of the water remained constant at all levels. There were no sharp temperature gradients that would deflect the powerful U.S. sonar. Within an hour the submarine reversed course, heading southeast toward deeper water and additional maneuvering space.

On the surface, *Stump* remained at general quarters until the submarine steadied on her course toward the Windward Passage. There was an advantage to knowing her quarry's eventual station. Captain Eberhardt was able to switch his watch to Blue/Gold by mid-morning. He intended to exercise both his ASW teams as independent units. This was the perfect time. His ship was fast and efficient at the game she was designed for, and the weather and the water conditions were on his side. It was important to maintain a positive attitude with his crew. He had told no one about the top secret message Admiral Pratt had issued to commanding officers the day before—that intelligence had intercepted Soviet orders indicating their submarines could use lethal means to reach their stations on schedule. Eberhardt would simply have to become so familiar with the sub captain's tactics that he would be able to sense when the other eventually altered his tactics to fire torpedoes.

Stump's captain noted that it was time to prepare the next

of the many situation reports he and each commanding officer
with a submarine contact would send to Pratt every two hours.

The Pentagon

Admiral Pratt leafed through the sheaf of situation reports.
Stump had made first contact, but it was not long after that
the others began to roll in—then it was a fresh report every
two hours. A disturbing element, one that would concern him
even more later on, was the ease with which the Russians
seemed to accept a shadow as they moved toward their blockade area. Originally Pratt had considered the Soviet message
—that a signal would be sent when they were to dispose of the
U.S. ships—as a bold lie. Now he was not so sure of that. The
possibilities this concept opened up were staggering. No commander looked forward to a shoot-first strategy.

But he also smiled inwardly to himself, smacking a fist into
his palm. Much of what he'd projected was now occurring. It
was time to take his next proposal higher up. The first step was
to take it to Admiral Tommy Bechtel, an Assistant Chief of
Naval Operations. He understood Dave Pratt's feelings and
believed in his good judgment.

Pratt pushed back from his desk, using his hands to assist
him as he stood up. Cautiously he walked toward the wheelchair in the corner. Halfway across the room he stopped. An
observer would have seen him stare sightlessly at a point only
he could visualize on the ceiling. Slowly, Pratt extended his
arms upward, rising experimentally on his toes, as if he were
reaching for that imaginary spot. Then he nodded his head in
agreement with some silent promise to himself. Turning
toward the door, he smoothed his uniform blouse, picking at
some invisible pieces of lint as he walked slowly. It was the
first time since he had been wounded that he had passed
through that door on his feet.

His secretary had been with Dave Pratt whenever he had
found himself assigned to shore duty. It was a strange, silent
loyalty, and she maintained a prudent affection for this man,

discreetly setting the myths aside that others created. "Well, Admiral," she began, a warm smile flooding her face, "will you be out of the office long?" She could think of nothing other than this trite question at such a moment.

"No. I doubt it. Just going down to see Tommy Bechtel for a moment."

"Want me to hold your calls, or should I transfer them down there?"

"It won't be long, Betty. Don't bother." Still slightly in awe of his own accomplishment at this stage, he held up his empty hands. He'd left all the situation reports on his desk. He half turned, then thought better of it. "There is something you could do for me, Betty, if you don't mind. I left that pile of sitreps on my desk. Could you get them for me . . . stuff them in an envelope, please?"

When she handed him the envelope moments later, she asked, "Would you like me to go down to Admiral Bechtel's with you . . . to take notes?"

Pratt smiled. He could sense her concern, like that first flight at Kitty Hawk he mused, though her expression never wavered. "I appreciate the offer, Betty. I think I can take care of everything myself." He moved slowly to the door, then turned down the corridor.

She wanted so much to step outside the door, to watch him make the short but momentous trip to Bechtel's office. Yet she knew he would be hurt if for some reason he might look back and see her watching. Instead, she called Admiral Bechtel's secretary and explained that Admiral Pratt was coming down under his own power, and please don't say anything that might embarrass him . . . and please make sure there was nothing he might trip over . . . but she stopped when she was told that the Admiral's shuffling step could already be heard coming down the hall.

Tommy Bechtel never gave an indication of surprise when Pratt stepped cautiously into his office. He was scribbling on a note pad and simply looked up and said, "Grab yourself a chair."

Pratt snorted, "You mean sit down before you fall down?"

Bechtel looked up again, with a hurt expression. "I didn't mean that at all, Dave. It was the best thing I could think to say, considering . . ." He finished whatever he'd been writing and pushed back from his desk, smiling. "I could say how pleased I am to see you wandering in here on your pins, but you already know that. And you know I don't waste time thinking up nice things to say."

Pratt nodded in agreement. "Maybe that's why I picked you for my first visit."

"Looking for sea duty now?" There was a trace of a smile at the corners of Bechtel's lips, a sign that he was joking—people rarely ever saw a trace of any emotion other than anger from him.

"Not right away, Tommy, but I'll think about it." It was good to hear someone suggest the idea, even in jest. "This time I just wanted to ask some advice." He started to get up, then thought better of it. "Normally I'd come around to your side to show you these sitreps, but you won't mind if I ask you to join me here just this once, would you?" He opened the envelope and began to lay out the sitreps from the individual ships. "I am a bit tired from that dash down here."

There were no secrets between the two admirals. They had been friends for years and knew each other like brothers. If Dave Pratt had asked him to go back and get the wheelchair, Bechtel would have done so without hesitation. Now he peered over Pratt's shoulder at the reports.

"I've got most of those subs under wraps that I said I'd find, Tommy. But, hell, they're diesel boats. If they were nuclear, it would be a different game. Now that I see what's going to happen, I don't have the slightest doubt that they'll torpedo our cans just as soon as they're told to." He scratched the back of his neck. "That kind of thing gets a little beyond my responsibility, without going through you or the CNO or God-knows-who . . . maybe the President. I can't just give orders to blast away at those Russians whenever some ship's captain decides it's kill or be killed." He scratched his neck again, looking up at Bechtel. The other nodded silently as he leafed through the reports. "And the Florida Straits . . ."

"What about them? The last time you told me they were a piece of cake. As a matter of fact, I think I can quote you on that."

Pratt's neck reddened slightly. He wasn't known to make

such rash statements, but he remembered saying it in frustration over his legs one day—when he was trying to justify his continued value among all the other admirals who could walk.

"I'm kidding, Dave. I remember the day. None of us were concerned about it."

"Well, I think we've got something more to worry about. I figured blocking the Straits from the north, between West Palm and the Grand Bahama, would take care of it. But you know what it looks like to me now? They're going to fake that and come up from behind, from the Caribbean right through the Yucatan Channel. That gives them a lot more space to maneuver . . . and it puts us in a tight spot."

Bechtel looked up at the chart behind his desk. "Makes sense too. That also means we're going to have to get some hunter killer groups in there pronto. You got the operation plan for that?"

Pratt nodded. "But it goes a little beyond my responsibility now, Tommy. I can't issue any orders yet for something like that . . . unless you could help me out. . . ."

"When you walked in here, I figured that would be coming next." He squeezed Pratt's shoulder affectionately. "Are those legs coming back as fast as you seem to think they are?"

"Not as fast as if it was twenty years ago."

"If you keep improving, you got it," Bechtel said with finality. "I suppose you want to get sea duty next?" There, that was the second time Tommy had mentioned it.

Pratt looked back at his friend evenly. "It wasn't too long ago that walking in here was a dream. Now, getting back on a ship is the next one."

They talked for another fifteen minutes, conjecturing on what the ultimate Soviet goal might be—other than to harass the United States into something rash—before Pratt rose to return to his office. "Want me to wander back with you, Dave?"

"Hell, no."

"Sorry. Lousy idea. Forget that I mentioned it." Bechtel's smile played at the corners of his mouth again, but this time it was warm and sincere.

When Dave Pratt shuffled back into his outer office, his secretary looked up at him with shiny eyes. Tommy Bechtel's

secretary had called her to say that Admiral Pratt was on his
way back up the corridor. It had taken all Betty's determina-
tion not to wait for him by the door.

Grambling's Camp

The black beret was tilted at a jaunty angle over Captain
Voronov's forehead, but it lacked the military demeanor he
intended because of the large bandage above his left eye. His
left arm was still in a sling, but some feeling seemed to be coming back to his fingers as he flexed them experimentally. A
Russian marine was trained to live with such injuries, but it
was all a new experience for Voronov. Never in his career had
he suffered more than cuts or bruises. The shrapnel wounds
incurred that night in the battle off Colón had initially surprised him, but that surprise had quickly turned to anger. The
pain had never concerned him. He knew he could withstand
much more. It was the indignity of being wounded!

Of less concern to him was the evident disdain shown by
James Grambling. That was an attitude that could be altered,
as long as it came from someone he respected, like Grambling.
It was just a matter of time, Voronov reminded himself
calmly, until Jaimé understood the necessity of a Soviet presence and got over the foolishness of his overblown patriotism.
Among many of the peasants in the PRA, simple jealousy induced such an attitude, but with Grambling it was pride.
Voronov understood that intrinsically because he was a
shamefully proud man himself.

"Look at that, Jaimé. See." Voronov opened and closed his
fingers, then attempted a fist. He winced. "It does hurt a bit. I
must admit." He smiled through gritted teeth. "But pain is a
fine teacher. Here, watch this." With great care he held his injured arm to his side, extending his forearm directly in front of
him. With his right hand he gingerly removed the sling.
"See," he claimed proudly, "it works just as before." He
opened and closed his fist, finally spreading his fingers before
him and cocking them one at a time.

Grambling was impressed. He had no intention of complimenting Voronov, nor openly displaying his admiration to the Russian, but he was impressed. Similar injuries had incapacitated him for a much longer time, and he sensed the pain in Voronov's eyes. Yet there was only concentration evident on the man's face. He possessed an intensity that Grambling rarely recognized in any man. There were times when it was hard to dislike Voronov, even knowing that he was a Russian.

A sigh escaped Voronov's lips as he let the arm fall to his side, then slowly lifted it back to waist level. "Still a little tender, Jaimé," he whispered through tight lips. His forehead glistened with sweat. A slight tic danced at the corner of his mouth as he lowered and lifted the arm once again.

"That's enough, Paul," Grambling remarked uneasily. "You're going to open up that hole in your shoulder again." Then he added in a firmer tone, "I don't care to operate with a cripple."

"Don't worry, I don't plan to make myself a cripple. I wouldn't want you to have to go out on an operation by yourself."

The irritation was evident in Grambling's voice. "Can you imagine the number I carried out without you in the past . . . without ever being sunk?"

Voronov closed his fist tightly now. "The other night, with you, was the first time I have ever lost a ship of any kind."

"Neither of you will give the other an inch," Maria interrupted as she walked over to them. "I think you would both sometimes rather die than admit that you have to depend on each other more each day." She had said nothing until then. The verbal sparring between the two men had lapsed into a habit, and until after the incident at Colón she had accepted it. Seeing them injured, however, made it clearer how ridiculous their bantering had become. She knew the one most important thing in her life was to see James Grambling come out of this alive. And if Paul Voronov was the key to his survival, she would see that Jaimé gave up these ridiculous disputes.

Both men reacted with surprise, neither speaking. Grambling was not used to being interrupted by anyone. Voronov had always considered Maria an attractive little camp fol-

lower, an acceptable female companion if anything happened
to Grambling. They did not expect her to become involved in
their discussions, yet both were shocked that she could comprehend the underlying dynamic of their relationship. Both
reveled in the self-satisfaction of their inner strength, their sur-
vivability, their unquestioned ability to instill others to follow
them. Having found another individual with similar characteristics was a challenge to each, regardless of which side he was
on.

They looked at each other without exchanging a word,
unable to cross the gulf they had established between themselves, sure that the first one to speak would be the loser in the
eyes of the other.

"Would either of you have made it back without the other
from Colón?" she asked. "How many more of our people,
even Russians, will die if you don't work together? Have you
considered that? James Grambling, the great patriot . . . Paul
Voronov, the man who never loses a ship, who never is hurt!"
She hurled the last remarks at both of them derisively, too
angered to be concerned with their reaction.

Voronov's face softened slightly. "You will be our go-
between," he said to her. "You are correct and both of us,
equally, are wrong. What must be done now requires both of
us to help each other."

She stepped forward, grasping each of their right hands.
She looked up at Grambling. "Will you start by shaking
hands, Jaimé?" Turning to Voronov, "You too?"

"Yes," Voronov replied as Jaimé nodded, then they
grasped each other's hands.

When Maria left, Voronov said, "I received new orders
from Havana this morning, Jaimé, and . . ." Voronov paused
for an instant before smiling, "I can't fulfill them without
you. They were never intended to be carried out without you. I
suppose," he added, "that Admiral Khasan really never considered that it could be done without both of us."

Grambling beckoned the other to sit with him in one of the
canvas chairs under a makeshift awning. It was close to mid-
day. The heat was oppressive. Though that section of the
camp was quiet, the jungle was alive with a cacophony of

sound blending to a steady hum. He waited for the Russian to speak.

"I would say the final push is no more than four, maybe five days, Jaimé. I received information this morning about the destroyer. I have to move forty-eight hours beforehand to take it over. I must take you with me . . . there's no one else I want to depend on." He did not mention that Khasan insisted on a senior PRA leader aboard the destroyer.

"You know her schedule?"

"She is scheduled to depart Cartegena in two days. She is primarily a training ship now. It's a simple overnight transit for her to Colón. She will anchor off there until she has permission to enter the Canal. The plans are to take the recruits through the Canal and on down to Buenaventura for a port visit, then return the following week. So there should be no suspicion about her. Your authorities expect her to make the transit."

"What if the signal comes on the fifth day, rather than the fourth?"

"There will be an engineering problem that will take about a day to correct."

Grambling's eyebrows narrowed. "I suppose you have men aboard right now."

"Not me. Who ever heard of blond, blue-eyed Colombians?" Voronov assumed an amused expression of innocence. "But the resemblance between Cubans and Colombians can hardly be overlooked. The ship's officers have no idea of who those recruits are, Jaimé. They report aboard, they receive training. The recruits come from different districts. They have no idea who is or isn't supposed to be aboard."

Grambling leaned slightly forward, his elbows on his knees. "It is always Cubans or Russians . . . Russians or Cubans." He looked at the palms of his hands, then back at Voronov. "There are so many of you, and it seems to me there are so few of us. Only moments ago I had just about gotten that out of my mind. And now we're back to the same thing again."

"Jaimé, you do not have people who understand how a destroyer runs. How could they insure there is an engineering casualty, if necessary?" He stood and walked to the corner of the clearing, then turned, opening and closing his left hand, the effort evident on his face. "I have shaken your hand in friendship, as we should have, and I am explaining just how we are going to go about this operation with that destroyer." Voronov continued patiently, as if lecturing a class, "I want to make it clear that the only reason I have not chosen your PRA to go to Cartegena and board that ship right there is that they could not fool enough people. It has nothing to do with Russians or Cubans or Panamanians or anyone else. It is just common, good sense and that is something that has kept me alive for years. As soon as we take over that ship, you and your men will join me in carrying out the last part of the mission. If you prefer, you can be her captain. I will remain in the background and whisper in your ear if that's what you would like." He moved over to stand above Grambling. "Is that the way you would like to do it, Jaimé?" Without waiting for an answer, he added, "I will do it any way you insist."

Grambling understood jungle fighting, guerilla techniques, and small boat operations. He knew nothing about destroyers that had been built when he was an infant, nor did he understand the full impact of the destroyer, or their exact mission. Voronov continued to claim that final orders were still vague. He stood in order to look Voronov in the eye. "You are, of course, correct . . . again." Damn, it was frustrating. He was about to walk away, then thought better of it. His next words were forced. "You *are* correct, Paul. We did shake hands." He paused. "We will work together."

"You will not be sorry, Jaimé." Then, very softly, so quietly that Grambling could barely understand, he added, "I understand what is going through your mind. It won't happen." At that stage Voronov almost hated himself for being such a liar. But his training overcame anything he might have mistaken as emotion.

When he was once again alone, Voronov considered the other part of the message from Admiral Khasan. The problem with Lieutenant Corazon concerned him, more than it obviously did Khasan. Perhaps the Admiral could not be overly concerned with such happenings when he had his women to worry about! To Voronov, who loved being in the field, an incident such as that tripped a warning buzzer. They assumed whoever this Corazon had been had somehow gotten to Panama via a fishing boat. To Paul Voronov that meant only one thing—the American opposition he had been assured would not appear. Perhaps, he thought, Jaimé's contacts in Panama City would be able to help him.

Panama City

The reactions of Alvarez and Ryng as they faced each other, was surprise. A common thought that struck both was the waste created by their being on opposing sides. If questioned, neither would have denied the possibility that the other might have made a worthy ally.

Esteban Alvarez, though he was Kitty's father, was not an old man, Ryng realized, and wondered why he should have assumed that. On the contrary, Ryng found Alvarez youthful and impressive-looking. He was about Kitty's size, smaller than Ryng, but in surprisingly good shape, with just the barest hint of extra weight around his middle. His dark brown hair had receded and thinned, and Alvarez combed it over the bald area. There was no mustache, nor was his skin very dark. In essence, Alvarez looked no different to him than a Washington businessman who weekended at the shore. Moreover Alvarez was polite, though his deference indicated that he was aware of Ryng and his relationship with Kitty.

For Alvarez's part, he found Bernie Ryng anything but intimidating. The man before him was of average height, though his stocky build indicated that he was powerful. Perhaps he had expected an American with a pencil mustache or pinky rings or a heavy gold chain around his neck. On the contrary, Ryng was neatly dressed, clean-shaven, and he projected an aura of confidence, offering the type of handshake other men appreciated. There was also something in the way he returned Alvarez's stare that made the older man realize that Ryng was a formidable man.

As they took stock of each other, they recognized traits they liked. In another time they might even have become friends.

As it was, both men understood they were facing an enemy. Ryng knew that Alvarez was working closely with Castro to insure at least the embarrassment of the U.S. Moreover, he understood, instinctively, one man to another, that their relationships to Kitty might never allow them to fully understand each other. Alvarez, when he first learned of the American who had saved Kitty's life, had run a security check on him. He found that any man so well covered, was in fact, an enemy.

Alvarez gestured toward a chair. "Please sit down Mr. Ryng," he said coolly. "And may I have my maid get you something cool, an ice tea, a beer, perhaps some juice?"

"No thank you, sir." Ryng accepted the seat and waited until Alvarez was comfortable. "From your expression as I came in, I doubt I'd be here long enough to enjoy one."

Alvarez shrugged. "One never knows. I try to be a gentleman in my own home."

Ryng grinned back. He liked Alvarez's forthrightness, the way he had emphasized the word *try* as he raised his eyebrows. "You already know a great deal about me, I suppose."

Alvarez shrugged again. "Yes and no. Any time a man's background is as secure as your's seems to be, then I don't know enough . . . but it is also more than most other men." He leaned forward. "And, Mr. Ryng, I assume you also know at least as much about me as my own mother?"

"Less of what you would like her to know, more of what she is better off not knowing." Ryng was measuring his words, playing at the game just as Alvarez was, trying to assess the other. "You are also not what I expected."

"All right. We're on equal ground. Let's stop analyzing each other. You came to my door." He cocked his head a bit to one side. "Talk to me."

Ryng nodded curtly. "Let's start off by not fooling each other. It's about your daughter, Kitty—Katarina.

Alvarez pursed his lips slightly, but other than that, there was no acknowledgment. He waited expectantly.

"It may make no difference to you one way or the other, but she and I have a great affection for each other." Then he kept quiet. The ball's in the air and it's on his side now, Ryng decided.

After what seemed like minutes, Alvarez responded. It was

a major effort to control his voice, to contain the anger. "If you are trying to shock me, Mr. Ryng, you have a long way to go. My daughter is no longer an impressionable girl. She's old enough to make her own life now." He smiled slightly, but it was an icy smile. "As I said before, talk to me."

"I think your people kidnapped your daughter this morning."

Alvarez's eyes flashed. He was on his feet. "What do you mean, *kidnapped*?"

"She was in my apartment. I was called away in the middle of the night. When I came back early this morning, the place was a shambles. And she was gone. That sounds like kidnapping to me."

The young officers they trained in Cuba were capable of anything! Alvarez thought. They had to be the ones who did it. No one familiar to the city would make such a mistake. "Who could have—"

"I haven't the slightest idea." For some reason Ryng felt his temper rising. He'd intended to pique the other's temper, but now just the thought of what had happened was increasing his anger. "Why can't you just have your heavies go to her office and— Or better yet, why don't you just call her on the phone and ask her to stop by to see you? Why—"

"Mr. Ryng, you're baiting me," Alvarez snapped. "You are looking for trouble. I know nothing of this. Now you tell me," he said evenly, working to control himself, "exactly what happened, in detail." He came over to Ryng's chair and leaned down, his face inches from Ryng's. "I know just enough about you to believe you . . . and also enough to kill you. You still have my attention," he concluded through clenched teeth.

Ryng sensed that he had made the right move. There would have been no reason for Alvarez to have Kitty taken from him in that manner. All was obviously not roses within the PRA, and Alvarez was obviously seething. Ryng explained just how he had been drawn off. The mention of General Huertas's name unlocked a door with Alvarez, as did the phony interrogation. And as he related the situation, Ryng also began to realize that the kidnapping may have had nothing to do with Esteban Alvarez at all. Perhaps it was to let Bernie Ryng know that his cover was worthless, that he could take the next plane out or that they simply enjoyed toying with him before they took him out! Ryng understood as he talked to Alvarez that he possessed the opportunity to slip the bottom card off his deck. The PRA was playing a lousy game of cloak and dagger when they used one of their leaders' daughters as bait!

"I think I can arrange to solve this problem properly, if indeed such a mistake has been made, Mr. Ryng." Alvarez smiled thinly, although this time it was a barely veiled smile of scorn. "You almost had me. I was just about ready to lose my temper when you came in here. But I recover quickly. The only thing I can think of on your behalf right now is that you apparently care enough for Kitty to walk right into my home with your tale." He took a deep breath. "I won't ask you about your interests, either with me or my country, because I have a very good idea what they are at this point. But I am mystified by your words—*your people*. Just who are you referring to? My people are Panamanians."

Now it was Ryng's turn to shrug, as if he failed to understand the question. "I suppose the Russians in your country are behind it then. It seems to me—"

"The Russians tell us nothing!"

"Well, General Huertas—"

"General Huertas is an ass. And if he spends too much time with the Russians, he is a fool also." That was the soft spot Ryng was looking for! No matter whom he talked to, the Russians, always the Russians, were a sore point. Alvarez stood. "I think we've said all that we have to say to each other, Mr. Ryng. While I am always impressed by a man who has the nerve to walk into another man's home and talk as you have, I sincerely hope this is the last time we will meet." He went to the door and held it open.

Ryng stopped and smiled on his way out. "I'm sure Kitty would have preferred we meet under more pleasant circumstances . . . over daiquiris maybe," he added caustically.

Before Ryng was in the elevator, Alvarez was on the phone. First he would insure that the idiots who had grabbed Kitty were punished. Then he would make sure Ryng was taken care of. But one nagging thought had been planted again—those Russians, those goddamned Russians!

Northwest of Windward Passage

Captain G. A. Fitin peered through the periscope at the destroyer. The white hull numbers, 978, stood out boldly. He'd identified her familiar shape as a Spruance class when they departed Punta Munda the previous morning. But he said nothing to his crew. Would they be able to determine exactly what ship type was trailing them? It would be an exercise.

His leading sonarman had spent six months in the finest school in the Soviet Union listening to tapes of every American ship's sounds and characteristics. First he identified the twin screws. The submarine maneuvered, forcing the destroyer to change course and speed a number of times. Then he could tell from the rapid change in screw beat that she was a gas turbine ship. Though this sonarman faithfully followed the process demanded at school, he already knew that the Americans wouldn't have sent one of their Kidd-class anti-air-warfare ships after a diesel submarine. The only other gas turbine ships designed to hunt submarines were the single screw frigates. This had to be a Spruance class!

The electronic countermeasures experts disappeared into their small, dark room as they cruised near the surface and listened to the electronic emissions from the destroyer. Within a few hours they, too, had come to the conclusion that it was a Spruance class.

Captain Fitin had always been proud of this crew. Not only had they been well trained beforehand, but they were superb in putting that training to work. There would be few chances in the future to be positive of a ship's identification before he knew it was tracking him, but this confirmation of what he already knew meant that he had the upper hand. With such knowledge about any ship tracking him, he could look up everything he needed to know about his quarry—speed, capability of sonar and radar, the range of their weapons. He even had a journal outlining the general tactics that had been employed by these ships during training exercises.

Considering his orders and the fact that he would be operating in restricted waters, Fitin experienced a glow of confidence he had not expected. He intended to communicate this to his crew in the days to come, for they would all need it when they realized they would likely have to sink that ship.

The captain was about to announce to the crew over his PA system that the destroyer shadow was a Spruance class destroyer named *Stump*, and to provide some detailed information. Then he realized that the American ship might possibly hear his announcement. The warm Bahama waters conducted sound so well. Instead, he had the word passed through various compartments by his messenger, along with the fact that they were now going to conduct a series of practice torpedo runs on their shadow. First they would maneuver away from the destroyer, drawing it toward them. It would be a cat-and-mouse game for a while, until Fitin was sure he had a torpedo solution. Then they would take it all the way to the actual firing, stopping the exercise only at the last minute. To amuse his crew, he might even announce to *Stump* over the underwater telephone that he'd sunk her during a few practice runs.

Fitin made a run in toward *Stump*, attempting to lose himself directly off her stern, where sonar contact was hardest to maintain. Then he reversed course and increased his speed to sixteen knots while diving to 350 feet. It was easy for his sonar operator to tell when *Stump* reversed course and increased speed. They maintained an accurate track on the destroyer. At a predetermined point Fitin increased his depth and set off perpendicular to his course. As soon as their shadow gave signs of picking up his new course, he headed right back at the destroyer for a few moments, then executed a series of course changes, varying his speeds as the whim struck him. He needed to understand better how *Stump*'s captain reacted.

The destroyer was good. Fitin had to admit that. If he could read minds, he would certainly have said that *Stump* was practicing exactly as he was. It was time to execute the attack run. Closing, Fitin gradually brought his submarine toward the surface. His attack coordinator insisted that the crew follow the attack manual. They would balance it against the computer solution shortly afterward. Now, it was important to develop such skills for a time when the computer might be inoperative.

As he was about to simulate firing, his sonar operator reported a voice message from the destroyer's underwater telephone. Using her Anti-Submarine Rocket (ASROC) launcher, *Stump* had already simulated firing a rocket-propelled torpedo. One of Fitin's sonar operators was trained in English and he was able to explain to Fitin that the American ship thanked him for the fine exercise but requested that they continue evasive tactics for another hour at least. That was the one thing Fitin had hoped to avoid. The word would pass through the submarine quickly. Damn! The objective was to inspire confidence!

On *Stump's* bridge Captain Lou Eberhardt was enjoying his game of oneupsmanship. His Blue Team officer of the deck (OOD) had been tentative about letting the submarine play the game as long as it did. Diesel submarines often participated only until they could find open water—and breathing room, he claimed. "Not to worry," Eberhardt had responded. "There's no open water to run to around here, only comfortable warm water with perfect sonar conditions. Plus, he's taking us with him to his duty station. He can't afford to mess around too long and miss being on station on time. Exercise your team. Go ahead and have some fun with him before I give the Gold a chance."

As always, the captain seemed to be right. The Blue Team experimented with torpedo attacks, the Gold with ASROC situations; next time they would try the other's methods. Eberhardt gave each of them an opportunity to use the Light Airborne Multi-Purpose System (LAMPS) helicopters but he insisted the helo sonars remain passive. There would be a time to use the helos, and he wanted them to be a new experience for this Soviet submarine.

When the time came to show off, Eberhardt couldn't resist. He should have kept his mouth shut, but he just had to rub it in a little. He knew every Soviet sub on duty in this area carried English-speaking sailors. So rubbing it in, he reflected, would give the other guy a bit of a temper—enough so he might just forget I'm able to fly two anti-submarine helos, Eberhardt thought.

Panama City

Ryng knew in an instant that Henry Cobb never would have been caught this way. Ryng was tired, exhausted. It had been the middle of the night when Huertas's aide came pounding on the door, starting a day that seemed to have no end. He should have understood that he had blown any cover he might have retained when he went to see Alvarez.

He took little notice of the man reading a newspaper in the lobby as he came in, and he never saw the one near the elevator. They appeared beside him and they were good—effortless, efficient, silent. One slipped a hand inside Ryng's jacket to remove his gun and the other calmly moved him forward as the elevator doors opened. Perfect timing.

Ryng could neither see nor feel a weapon, yet he knew one was trained on him. As the elevator door opened, he found himself once again swept forward by a calm yet menacing force, and realized it would be foolish to make any move at all. He was sure they would react without a sound and he would either awake in his apartment or, perhaps, never wake again. Though Cobb would never have allowed this to happen, he had also explained to Ryng more than once that this was the type of situation to keep your cool, shut up, and listen—not to mention praying for a miracle, which appeared to be the best possibility with these escorts.

The management had been so efficient, that his lock was not only in place, but he recognized a new door. One of the men inserted a key in the lock, a perfect copy, opening it as easily as Ryng might have done. The apartment was still a shambles. Apparently, management had yet to get to that.

"You may sit right there, Mr. Ryng." He wasn't pushed, yet he found himself propelled into a straight-backed chair. "Hands underneath the seat."

Without thinking, Ryng instinctively moved his hands behind him, reacting to the words without really hearing them, assuming that was the way it would be done. A hand shot out, open palm catching him in the side of the head. His head snapped back from the shock, his ears echoing with the sound.

"Underneath the seat!" the voice repeated with more intensity. Ryng leaned forward and down, his wrists dropping below seat level. The other man was behind him with barely a sound, slipping a pair of handcuffs around his wrists.

This was much better from their point of view. For Ryng's part, there would be no chance of standing up, no pulling his head when another slap came his way. This was more uncomfortable, more undignified. In this position he could not see what was going on around the room. One's complete attention was necessarily riveted on the person who demanded it.

Two more resounding slaps came, one from each side, timed so that his head was involuntarily snapping away from the first as the second caught him from the opposite direction. Then a hand was grasping his hair, lifting his head until a set of very dark, venal eyes were even with his own.

"Have you received my message, Mr. Ryng?"

Ryng heard the voice echoing through his head, saw the face in alternating phases of red. He managed to mumble, "Yes."

"Fine, pain is not necessary. To me it is a last resort. There is not a great deal I want to know from you. On the other hand, what I want may be something you do not really want to relate to me. If that is the case, you do not have my apologies, but you do have my sympathies. I had to learn some of this through experience so that I might better judge how to influence people like yourself." These were totally unlike the PRA types he'd encountered before. They worked for someone else, and they knew their business.

This is what a professional is all about, Ryng's fuzzy mind noted. It was crazy what you thought about at a time like this. Just like a politican—tell them what they need and then tell them how they're going to get it and who's going to give it to them. That's the way to get their attention. He caught his breath and swallowed a couple of times. His throat was dry. "At least, you could tell me who wants to know." The words came out in a rasp. He swallowed again. "You don't plan to send me into the streets after this."

"With unpleasant things like this, who knows. There are always many phone calls first. No one really wants to be implicated. And what does it matter anyway? Better that you have no grudges."

Ryng nodded but said nothing. It was to be expected. He

was sure he could have traced it back to Alvarez. Now came
the interesting part.

"All right, Mr. Ryng, we're always too short of time.
Would you please tell us who you really are and who gives you
orders."

Ryng looked up at the man awkwardly. Not only was looking up an effort in that position, it was almost impossible to
look belligerent or tough or whatever was the right attitude in
this situation. He had never been a prisoner before, had never
found himself in an indefensible position. Bernie Ryng was a
specialist of a different kind, a SEAL team leader—he was
trained to jump out of planes, work underwater, conduct
guerilla warfare, handle any type of weapon a man invented,
do almost anything but play undercover games. Why the hell
had Pratt put him in this position?

He was watching the man's hands, anticipating the next resounding slap, when the initial shot rang out and the man in
front of him was hurtled backward into the wall, his chest
gushing blood as he crumpled to the floor. Instinctively, Ryng
threw his weight to the side, tipping his chair.

The second man was alert, no doubt about that. He was diving toward the sofa before his partner hit the wall, his gun
already out. Searching for a target, he squeezed off one shot
before a slug ripped into his shoulder. His gun flew into the
air, spinning in an arc before it landed in the middle of the
room. The second shot tore into his stomach as he thrashed to
his knees searching frantically for his weapon. Then he died
without a sound.

Ryng wiggled and kicked, trying to see the source of the
shots. But as he scrambled, a voice said, "No need to wear
yourself out, Bernie." Then with that soft laugh, his typical
attempt at humor, Cobb added, "I intended to save you right
from the start, my friend. No need to panic."

Henry Cobb had arrived! His skin was darker, the mustache
was new, but it was Cobb!

The chair was turned upright. Cobb put down the Beretta
with silencer, then went through the pockets of the dead man,
extracting the key for the cuffs, talking softly all the time, explaining that there was no reason for concern. Then he added,

distastefully, "You'd think I would have improved my shooting by now, Bernie. Imagine taking two shots. Look at that mess." He unlocked the cuffs. "I wasn't sure which way you'd fall," he said grinning, "otherwise I would have taken him with one."

"Henry," Ryng was exasperated, "why didn't you take them out when we came in the door? You would have saved me a lot of grief."

"Bernie, if they'd started to cause you too much damage, I would have had no choice but to take them out right away. But it would have been more difficult with you still between them. I wanted to find out the same thing you did—see if we could possibly trace these guys back to the source. Dave Pratt could really use anything at all that we could drag out."

"You've been in touch with Dave?"

"Just this morning." He raised his eyebrows for emphasis. "Boy, was he unhappy that he hadn't heard from either of us."

"For Christ's sake, I think every phone in this city that I could come near is tapped. Wherever I go the last couple of days, I have a tail. How the hell did you manage it? Just pick up the nearest telephone and dial?"

"Not exactly, Bernie. But I have this little device I can use. You see, I can hook it into just about any phone. I guess there's going to be one of those fish companies down by the piers with a large phone bill to Navy Intelligence next month."

Ryng loved it. When others said it couldn't be done, Henry would love it even more. And they worked well together, at least until it had been planned backward like this. "What in the hell did Pratt send me down here for, Henry? This isn't my style."

Cobb looked back at him under his eyebrows, unsmiling. "You were had, Bernie. He didn't tell any of us. But I think he wanted you down here real bad, for whatever comes next— and you know he never tells until he's sure . . . if he's sure. And the other thing is, he probably wanted the PRA down here to think that we weren't really into what's going on." He wasn't looking at Ryng yet. "I don't know what kind of story he gave you, but I understand the idea was to insert someone who was good, but not good enough to scare them."

"You mean if it was you, they might have gotten scared and changed their plans?"

"I didn't say that, Bernie," he teased.

"But that's what you meant."

"Yeah. But I can also tell you what he told me this morning. He's got something big going down here. He's not sure what. But from what I learned, the Cubans or the Russians are going to heist a destroyer and do something none of us are certain about yet. And that's going to be your baby."

Kitty Alvarez had not seen her father for over a month, and the change she recognized in such a short period of time was a shock. She had been released with an overabundance of apologies from numerous government officals who had learned of the "grievous mistake," as they put it. She was whisked to her father's apartment and escorted to the door by two senior officials who could hide their embarrassment neither from her nor her father.

Face-to-face with her father after she had prepared to scream with anger, she could not even bring herself to speak. To a casual friend he might have looked little different, but to Kitty there was a tautness to his features that she hadn't seen before. To her, it was a pathetic transformation—that of a man who suddenly found he had lost confidence in everything he had held dear for a lifetime. She felt sorry for him.

Instead of the prepared speech she simply repeated his name over and over again as she hugged him tightly. She realized her experience had angered more than frightened her. Though she knew there was no conceivable way any government organization in Panama could mistake and detain her, what had disturbed her most had been the officers who had cared little what her name was, only that she dealt with the Americans. There had also been Cuban officers—she could always identify the Cubans. But even more disturbing was the presence of a Russian who seemed quite confident in the orders he was delivering in passable schoolboy Spanish.

The first words between father and daughter expressed the affection of two adults bound by a special relationship that has matured over the years. Though they were worlds apart much of the time, for this brief moment they related to each other as they had when Daddy was a hero and his little daughter could do no wrong. Then Alvarez's eyes shaded over as their conversation quieted awkwardly.

"Your private life is none of my business anymore, Kitty," he stammered, "but that man, Ryng . . ."

As if she had been slapped in the face, she stared at him, her eyes flashing. "What about him, father?" The anger that had developed before she actually came face to face with her father, welled up in her throat.

"That's how I knew what had happened to you. He came to see me this morning." His features had also altered. Once again he was the dominant father, the protector of innocence as he remembered the conversation with Ryng. The words came fast now, with an anger that surprised even Alvarez. "Of course, the two of you seem a lively topic of conversation. I had heard intimations even before I left Havana."

"My private life is no longer your concern," she replied evenly. "Nor is it the concern of your friends here or in Havana or anywhere else. I seem to be able to take care of myself quite adequately."

"Is that how you ended up being dragged off in error by a bunch of thugs?"

"I can't explain that."

"I can," he said more softly. "Perhaps you could use a little advice. Your Mr. Ryng is an American spy of some kind—"

"He is a businessman and he saved my life."

"He saved your life. I am aware of that. That was the first news I heard."

"And he is here to help our country."

"He is here to help the United States and only the United States." The words flowed in renewed anger. "He cares nothing about our country. None of the people he works for care about our country. The only people who care are trying to save it right at this moment. And he is dangerous to us."

"I disagree—"

"And you are sleeping with him like a local alley cat," he interrupted bitterly. "Is that what you call growing up?"

For an instant she was tempted to lash out. But she realized there was nothing to retaliate against. His anguish, so clear in his face when she came through the door, was not so much aimed at her specifically, but at so much more he was unable to speak of. To fight back, to say some meaningless words that might force him to hate her, made no sense. "I would much rather talk to you about my experience today. We are gaining nothing by this hatefulness," she replied softly.

Caught off guard, Alvarez said nothing, nodding his assent as he rubbed his eyes and forehead. Finally, he said, "All right."

She told him of the Cubans and the Russian officer, of the captains and majors in the Guardia who cared little for who or what she was while the older officers and the civilians were so upset over her situation. How, she asked, could two such disparate groups exist within the same military structure? And how could these outsiders fit so comfortably in this framework? "I'm frightened," she finished.

"I am too," Alvarez admitted, reaching out to touch her hand. He was also confused. These changes—they were coming so fast. Had he ordered this Ryng's death because the man was an American spy? Because he was living with Kitty? Or because Estaban Alvarez was as frightened about what was happening as his daughter?

The Pentagon

As the Soviet ships approached their rendezvous points, there was little reaction from official Washington. There wouldn't be until individual units became squadrons, squadrons became battle groups, battle groups became a task force. Then this Russian naval force would be properly recognized.

Pratt had anticipated their method long before. Ever so stealthily, like maverick stallions located one by one and driven until they became part of a fall roundup, they joined the herd. There was a modern guided missile cruiser from Sevastopol, along with two sleek destroyers, though the smaller ships had dispersed after passing Gibraltar. *Kharkov*, a small aircraft carrier, had come up from the South Atlantic after completing exercises in the Indian Ocean and steaming casually around the Cape of Good Hope. On the way she paid a courtesy call at Luanda in Angola, where she joined company with a destroyer. A second destroyer, this one a fast Udaloy-type bristling with missiles, tagged along after a good-will call in Sierra Leone. A third joined the group five hundred miles east of Barbados after a goodwill visit in Brazil.

From their bases at Murmansk and Pechenga on the Kola Peninsula, sleek warships stood out of their harbors, each at a different time, each on a seemingly different mission. A nuclear battle cruiser dawdled about the North Cape of Norway before cruising down that rugged coast, pausing haughtily off certain cities to flaunt her power. At times she would acquire a destroyer or two for exercises with other Soviet units. She would join in tracking long-range bombers simulating cruise missile attacks, or coordinate teams to chase down nuclear attack submarines attempting to penetrate their screens. Eventually she turned southeast to proceed independently.

However, there were other cruisers and destroyers and submarines, each advancing in that same general direction, seemingly unaware of the destination of the others. They were joined by sister ships from the Baltic which had steamed contemptuously past the staid ports of Sweden and Denmark before passing through the Skagerrak into the North Sea. Some of these turned down to the English Channel while others headed north between the Shetland and Orkney Islands to dally with their comrades from the Arctic waters.

None of this would have interested the average observer, and it certainly never piqued the curiosity of the power seekers in Washington. Yet each movement of each ship was carefully plotted in those corner offices of the Pentagon where Dave Pratt and Tommy Bechtel were engineering their response. There was no way either man would take their theory to the Secretary of the Navy, or the Secretary of Defense, or the Secretary of State, or even the President, until they had incontrovertible proof.

They had more than enough help to substantiate their theory. Satellite cameras continued to whir and click, sending a revealing array of photographs back to earth. An agent in Havana had provided more of the details than even Pratt had anticipated. Another in Panama had confirmed growing suspicions about Soviet influence in that country and throughout the Caribbean.

When the evidence was overwhelming, they followed the chain of command, explaining the steps they had already taken to counter this plot.

Panama City

The Presidential Palace now seemed less of a seat of government and more of an armed camp. To Esteban Alvarez, from the moment he entered the front gates until he was before President Ramos's door, it was a secretly pleasing sight. Though no single revolution systematically paralleled a previous one, he could sense from what he had learned over the years that Ramos's government was indeed entering the final stages.

The Guardia seemed to be going through the motions. They were present, in place where they had been ordered, armed, and reasonably alert. But there was now an element in their makeup that had to be obvious even to the most unconscious observer. Their uniforms—those of the Palace Guard were different—were clean, but they lacked the crispness that had once been evident. They came to attention and saluted, but there was none of the élan and pride that once made them exceptional.

Alvarez was exhausted, physically and mentally. Everything was right; everything was wrong. The progress made by the PRA was astounding, beyond belief as it picked up power, an avalanche taking all in its path. Yet there also seemed to be a terrifying loss of control—also common to an avalanche. And Kitty's visit had sapped his moral strength. Was he really sure why he'd come here today?

"Esteban, I'm pleased that you read my mind." Horacio Ramos greeted his friend with a firm handshake and a clap on the shoulder. "There has been so much that has concerned me in the last few days that there was little time to think of whom I might turn to for some relaxing talk. I'm glad you anticipated me."

Alvarez returned the greeting heartily. He liked Horacio Ramos. At one time—many years before, when they were young men—they had been the closest of friends, almost like brothers. But the years, and widening horizons as they married, stood between the affection they once had for each other. Ramos was a steady man, thoughtful and well educated, much of his stability coming from years in American universities. He had been one of the framers of the agreement returning the Canal to his country, but he had also been one of those who urged his people not to turn totally from the United States. He insisted that the Caribbean nations could not exist without the Americans and that a level of coexistence was possible, one that might one day again be friendly. Esteban Alvarez, however, had never agreed with those precepts. He had been the dissenter, preferring to be considered the honorable opposition rather than be associated with a popular revolution. In this manner he had remained a friend of Ramos, offering the opposition a dialectic but never totally espousing it. When Horacio Ramos became President, there was no other man close to the PRA who could claim access at almost any time to the Presidential suite.

Alvarez squeezed his old friend's shoulders with both hands. His affection for the beleagured President had never waned. Perhaps in the quandary he now found himself in, it was Horacio's affection that he had come for today. He sincerely intended to insure that Ramos was out of the country, hopefully to the United States if Kitty could be convinced to assist, before the PRA ever entered the Palace gates. Now Alvarez shook his head from side to side sadly, with understanding. "I know what is bothering you. This killing is futile. Soon our youngest and bravest will be in the cemeteries rather than leading their country." He held Ramos's eyes with his own. "I would like to see our system change . . . no doubt about that, my friend . . . but not by force. You know me well enough that I wish I could be in a position to stop all of this if there were any way I knew how."

Ramos nodded and sighed as he moved slowly to the window overlooking a courtyard below. "If I couldn't believe you, Esteban, who could I believe?"

Over rich, black coffee and fresh croissants they talked of lighter subjects, of days when they courted the proper girls of their own class, then stayed up all night the following evening among the looser women who frequented the clubs on the other side of the city. Each had stood beside the other when they were married, and Horacio Ramos later became Kitty's godfather. It was not until Alvarez's wife died that they saw less of each other. While the godfather was dutiful and insisted on helping with Kitty's upbringing, her father grew more distant from his acquaintances. He maintained his friendship with Ramos but it didn't remain as strong as it had once been. As they grew older, their bond became their disparate opinions on the country's future. Perhaps they understood that their disagreement had evolved from a common base and that both of them might still have something to learn from the other.

"You called me, Esteban. You were the one who wanted to talk about something. I prefer to talk about our youth, but too many things demand my time . . . and this was something urgent, you said."

"You know me too well." Alvarez smiled sadly. "So you also know that I wouldn't attempt to bother you now unless I thought it was something for you to know. You are aware of an American, a Mr. Ryng, who has been seeing Kitty?"

Ramos nodded slightly. His chin rested on his folded hands. He said nothing. There was no change in his expression. Alvarez had hoped for some indication.

"I won't be dishonest with you, Horacio. You know I've just returned from lecturing in Havana, and you know I have many friends there . . . more probably than I have here today," he added with a sigh. "Anyway, I heard about this American . . . and Kitty . . . while I was there. Mr. Ryng is the type of man you would not like to see with your daughter, believe me."

There was still no sign on Ramos's face that he knew where the conversation was leading. It was an art he had mastered years before, a necessary one for a politician. As Alvarez waited for some acknowledgment, Ramos remained mute, finally inclining his head slightly for the other to continue.

"All right, there's no need to play games, Horacio. This Ryng's a spy—an American spy, pure and simple. . . ." Alvarez searched for the proper words. Was this why he was here? Was he really looking for help from Ramos because the PRA's hired killers had failed? Finally he settled on what he thought might impress the other. "He is using Kitty."

Ramos blinked his eyes, moving his hands only far enough from his chin to say, "What, or who, do you think he is spying on?"

It was not the response Alvarez had expected. "Why . . . I think the Americans are likely going to try to regain control of the Canal . . . to use this revolution to take it back."

"I don't consider the internal problems we are having as a revolution, Esteban. I learned that revolutions were fought against tyranny, much like the American revolution against the British . . . the October Revolution against the czar. What we have here is an insurgency that I think your friends in Cuba are paying too much attention to." He removed his hands from his chin and stared firmly across at Alvarez. "Is it an American spy you are worried about, Esteban . . . or do I hear a father concerned for his daughter?"

Alvarez looked back blankly across the space between them, surprise evident on his features. For a brief moment he really wondered if it could be a form of jealousy. Was it the fact that this man, Ryng, was living with Kitty? And that he hadn't the slightest concern about waving that in her father's face? Mentally withdrawing himself from that room in the Presidential Palace for an instant, he considered the suggestion. His confusion expanded with his inability to articulate what he really felt.

"If you are concerned for Kitty, then you are no different from me, Esteban. I have watched her grow just as you have. And many times I cared for her when you were unavailable, especially after her mother died. It is equally difficult for me, like yourself, to see a little girl become a woman . . . but remember that she is over thirty now. She is quite capable of making her own decisions, even those we don't care for—"

"No, that has nothing to do with it," Alvarez interrupted. "I had thought that perhaps you were right for a moment, but that isn't it. This Ryng works for the American government." In his anxiety to press his point, his words came quickly. "He is a spy. He's not here on business, Horacio. I know he is attached to their intelligence system somehow."

Ramos pursed his lips in thought, knitting his brows, then massaging them absentmindedly. "Though you and I are friends, Esteban, and I hope always will be, we have gravitated to opposite political sides over the years. Whom do you see this Mr. Ryng threatening—your side or mine?"

"Why . . . our country. We are both patriots." Alvarez was

startled by the question. Now he stammered. "Why . . . why else would I be here? I . . ." He knew, and he realized Ramos knew, that the real reason was in doubt.

"Aren't you really trying to get rid of this man?" Ramos responded cruelly. "He's conquered your daughter, is that it?" With sorrow, he watched a kaleidoscope of emotions pass over the other man's face, reflected through increasingly tragic eyes. There was something so much deeper in Alvarez's soul that Ramos might never fathom. He moved quickly beside his friend, squeezing his shoulder tightly. "I am sorry, my friend. Please believe that I did not mean it . . . what I said about this Ryng and Kitty. I had to be sure."

Alvarez looked perplexed. "Sure . . . sure of what?"

"Of what really brought you here."

When Esteban Alvarez left President Ramos's office, he was less confident than ever of what had brought him there—hatred, revenge, patriotism. Ramos had concluded their discussion by voicing his concern about the Russian presence in Panama, in the Caribbean, in Havana. Alvarez was in a quandary, no longer sure himself why he had gone to Ramos's office.

The Waters North of Ile de la Tortue

Captain Fitin grimaced as he peered again at *Stump* through his periscope. There was really no purpose. The hull numbers —978—were embedded in his brain, racing through his mind whenever he tried to nap. The American destroyer was transformed into an apparition, a specter, a djinn dancing before his eyes. For three days the submarine and the destroyer had played a game of cat and mouse. Scorekeeping had been initiated by *Stump* when Lou Eberhardt claimed first blood with his simulated ASROC attack. Fitin appreciated the game well enough to claim two dummy hits on the destroyer within hours afterward. Eberhardt acknowledged.

That had been forty-eight hours ago. But there was never an end to the game. Fitin was keeping score because each man in the submarine also was, and he was behind. Not only would he eventually sink that ship, but he would do it after he was ahead in the game. He speculated as to whether the captain above was as consumed by the sheer fantasy of this prelude to the game of death as he was. For Fitin, who had eaten only sparingly since departing Punta Munda, energy was derived from the fact that he would soon fire live torpedoes at *Stump*. One would be aimed forward of the bridge, directly under that ASROC launcher. The next should hit aft of the rear stack, beneath the helicopter deck. Then he would be able to sleep.

Now, looking at the radar, he could see that the American was keeping perfect station two thousand yards on his starboard beam. Forty-five more minutes of this—the necessary time to keep his radio antenna extended for any orders—forty-five more minutes and then the dance would once again commence.

The Gold Team OOD on *Stump*'s bridge called down to the warroom pantry and ordered the captain's breakfast brought to his sea cabin. Then he pushed the buzzer that would sound next to Lou Eberhardt's head. He envied the captain's ability to sleep anywhere, anytime, whether a five minute catnap or a solid two or three hours.

"Captain here," the voice came back to the OOD.

"Good morning, Captain. This is Lieutenant Taron. Our friend is on course 095 at six knots. If he follows his standard procedure, he ought to keep at it for about another forty minutes for any radio messages. Your steward will have your breakfast in your sea cabin in five minutes. I've already called down to radio and they'll have the morning message board up to you shortly. Is there anything else, sir?"

"No . . . no, that sounds fine thanks." Eberhardt yawned. "I'll be on the bridge ten minutes before he dives. Why don't you sound general quarters before that. I'd like to try a couple of new ideas today." Unlike the captain of the submarine, Eberhardt was well rested and calm. He had two ASW teams that he trusted, and he had a sixth sense that told him he would only have to worry each morning after the submarine secured its antenna and dove with whatever orders it had received.

During the night they had passed Windward Passage. Once

he was sure the submarine did not intend to head for that final station, Eberhardt had turned in. Now he estimated they were somewhere north of Haiti's Ile de la Tortue. Closing his eyes for one last time before he arose, he pictured their location on the chart.

That was it! There was a deep trench that opened north of Haiti and ran up between Great Inagua and the Caicos Islands—deep enough for unexpected currents and sudden temperature gradients, and plenty of room for a submarine to maneuver.

Captain Eberhardt called the bridge and asked his OOD to take temperature readings. A sudden change in the temperature of the water could negate sonar conditions instantly, and the first one to know about those changes was generally the submarine. What foolishness it would be to lose him after all this work! When he came to the bridge that morning, the first thing Eberhardt would do would be to reexamine the Soviet captain's habits. Anticipation might be his only weapon if his contact suddenly raced off under the protection of a sharp alteration in water temperature.

Captain Fitin gave his diving officer orders for five hundred feet. Nothing rapid—just ease on down, searching for that sudden change in temperature. If it was discovered, then he would take her down another hundred feet, increase to maximum speed, and see what the American was made of. His orders, the written orders that each of the captains had been issued, called for evasion as a primary responsibility. It was only if a submarine was still under sonar contact within twelve hours before the operation was signaled to commence, that they were to sink the surface ship.

The submarine slipped through the layer at 420 feet. Fitin's sonar operator called it out clearly, his voice echoing through the control room. There was no sensation, no feeling, but to Fitin it was akin to breaking the sound barrier. The water temperature dropped so rapidly that it was like slipping behind an opaque curtain. The sound wave from *Stump*'s sonar would ricochet off that temperature gradient like a bullet off steel.

Fitin gave orders for six hundred feet. Once leveled off, he called for maximum speed and began his maneuvers. He did not intend to reverse course and head directly for the Windward Passage. Any idiot could assume that would be his final plan. The idea now was to give the American a real challenge. Captain Fitin was confident as he moved off rapidly to the north that his own trace of the destroyer would soon show the surface ship going into one of those preplanned search patterns. A copy of that particular U.S. Navy publication had been distributed to each Soviet captain before they ever left port. The English had not been translated, but handwritten notations in his own language had been inserted where appropriate. All he really needed to know was that a search pattern had commenced. That would tell him that *Stump* had not only lost contact, but had no idea where to start looking for him.

The pattern did not immediately become evident, as Fitin had hoped. Instead the American ship was also on a generally northerly course, moving at a higher speed. Eventually the destroyer pulled about six miles ahead of the submarine. At that range it was time to alter course. Fitin gave orders to turn west, confident that the American, though yet to undertake one of those giveaway patterns, was off tracking an imaginary contact.

Lou Eberhardt glanced at his watch. They had been chasing off to the north at least six to eight knots faster than the submarine. "How far astern do you estimate he is now?" he called to Lieutenant Taron, his General Quarters OOD.

"Roughly six miles, Captain."

Eberhardt looked at his watch again—almost half an hour since they'd lost contact with the Russian boat. He'd reviewed both his own notes and the computer printout on the sub captain's habits. Almost every time after diving he moved out at high speed, generally holding course for twenty to thirty minutes, perhaps to insure that everything was operating normally, a nervous habit before commencing evasive tactics. Well, thought Eberhardt, if he followed his basic habits, he should be turning to port right about now. The guy must be lefthanded, he grinned to himself—as predictable as can be. And military, too—always squared his corners. Eberhardt was almost willing to bet that the submarine was headed due west, exactly a ninety degree course change, or close to it.

"Okay," the captain called to Taron, "increase your speed three knots and come around to 230. We'll cut him off at the pass." He indicated an imaginary point on the horizon. Then he pushed the speaker button to talk to his Combat Information Center. "Just in case he fooled me this time, I want you to vector one of those helos out to the east and set up a sonobuoy pattern where we decided a little while ago—he might have had a change of heart. And put the other right off the bow where we figured he'd head."

The captain's plans were simple. He'd moved ahead of the sub. Then, when the Russian turned to the west, Eberhardt turned to the southwest and increased his speed. He intended to complete the long leg of a triangle, intercepting the submarine at the far corner. And if the Russian happened to be faster than he thought or turned south sooner than expected, then he'd probably run into *Stump*'s other helicopter, which would be setting up a sonobuoy pattern to the south.

Stump's sonar remained in passive mode, listening. While Eberhardt knew the submarine could hear him coming from a long way off, he didn't intend to use his sonar until he was just about on top of the Russian. It was kind of childish, he mused, but what the hell! It offered terrific psychological value. That Soviet captain had to be tired. Why not piss him off just a little bit!

Captain Fitin was pleased with himself. The American destroyer had chased off to the north at high speed, even after the submarine headed west. Now the destroyer had altered course and seemed to be headed vaguely back in his direction. No need to turn south right away, Fitin determined. That's what I'd be expected to do. Instead the Russian followed precisely the plan he had established earlier that day. When it was time, he came to a course that would carry him directly back to his preliminary station, which was just off Ile de la Tortue. He was to remain there until orders arrived to formally block the Windward Passage.

Obviously the American destroyer was confused by the temperature gradients, Fitin thought. Her sonar was inactive. She must figure that it will be easier to listen for me than try to detect me, he reasoned. Fitin was deeply satisfied. He massaged his eyes slowly, feeling the tension drain out. In only a few more hours at this speed he would be back on station.

The announcement from his sonar operator cracked through the humid control room like a whip. There was sonar activity directly ahead. A different frequency than the destroyer. There were one . . . two . . . three . . . maybe more, it was hard to tell . . . sources of sound. Before the sonarman had time to feed the signals into the computer for identification, it became obvious to Fitin. Sonobuoys, dropped by a helicopter! He understood too clearly. First, set up a pattern of buoys, properly spaced, then activate them after they are plotted on the operator's chart so any contact can be quickly cross-fixed.

Damn, that American hadn't used the helos earlier! This came as a surprise. But the sonobuoys were as dependent on good water conditions as the sonar on a ship. As long as he remained under the temperature layer, there was no way they could pick him up. But just to be sure, he cut his speed. The temperature layer was like a cloud of dense smoke. He might as well remain under it as long as possible.

Temperature layers, like clouds, were subject to weather patterns and environment. The currents in that area, extending all the way from the tip of Florida in a southeast direction between Cuba and the Bahamas to the tip of the Dominican Republic, were tricky. No computer could predict their variations. There were no absolutes. It seemed all a matter of whim, and Lou Eberhardt accepted that. He was familiar with these waters, having brought *Stump* down to Guantanamo Bay in Cuba for retraining the previous year. It was like being back home to him, but it was a strange and distant place for the captain of that submarine.

Eberhardt anticipated that the temperature gradient would change. It could be in his favor, it could be in the Russian's. But whatever, conditions would not remain the same for long.

He was correct. The sonobuoys detected the submarine sporadically, but that was enough. They were able to gain enough lines of bearing to determine a rough course and speed on the submarine. When *Stump* was only a thousand yards astern, conned into position by the helicopter, Eberhardt gave the order to turn on the sonar, and he made sure it was peaked to the maximum.

The sound echoed through the submarine like a hammer slammed against the outer hull. Though Fitin and his entire crew heard the destroyer approaching, realized it was somewhere above them, they had no idea that *Stump* knew their exact location, no idea that the water above and below them was close to the same temperature and that the conditions were once again perfect for a surface ship to detect a submarine.

Fitin cursed loudly as the first ping literally reverberated through each man like an electric shock. As his voice echoed through the confines of the submarine, a second ping, and then a third, drummed through the tight metal tube. It required every fiber of mental strength for Fitin to keep from slamming his fist into the chart table. The men were watching him closely. His duty was to display, at all times, total confidence. Reflecting later on his thoughts as the destroyer regained contact, he might have sunk *Stump* right then, if his torpedoes had been ready and his computer had a firing solution.

Fitin understood that there were other Soviet skippers going through exactly the same game as he was, though he might never know how each was progressing. Above him, enjoying constant radio contact, Lou Eberhardt was aware of each one. In the vicinity of other island passages—Mona and Martinique and Galleons—the same macabre dance was taking place. In some instances the destroyers were successful and held contact with their submarine. In others, the Soviet captains less dogmatic than Fitin were now, for the time being, on their own.

The Pentagon Helicopter Pad

The pilot peered curiously from his cockpit seat as his passengers came toward his helicopter. His engines were still running, the rotors slowly whacking the air in a loud, pronounced monotone. He had made this flight often, ferrying VIPs from the Pentagon out to ride one of the ships for a day or two, and he was used to them moving as quickly as they could through the wash and dust of the rotors. The important person, the only one he was really watching, walked haltingly across the grass onto the landing pad, never altering his awkward stride, never increasing or slowing his gait.

The pilot had already heard the rumors. Tales like that moved from the corridors of the Pentagon into the fleet rapidly. Within days word had probably traveled to the Seventh Fleet in Japan and to Gonzo Station in the Indian Ocean that Admiral David Pratt was actually walking again!

It really was true. The pilot tapped his co-pilot's shoulder and nodded for him to take the controls. Quickly undoing his safety harness, he moved through the fuselage to the hatch and down the passenger steps.

He wasn't a moment too soon. Pratt was almost there. As the Admiral approached the steps, the pilot snapped to attention with a sharp salute. "Admiral Pratt, it's an honor to have you aboard today."

Pratt registered surprise. He really couldn't discern what the man had said. The wash from the rotors drowned out words, flattening his silver hair as dust rose into his eyes. But he could interpret the pilot's words. With a slow smile he returned the salute just as sharply, then climbed into the helo. He would have been embarrassed if he'd seen the pilot's hand out—just in case the Admiral had trouble climbing up. But Pratt was slow, steady, and cautious, and plopped down happily to strap on the safety harness. The pilot nodded pleasantly as he moved forward. Damn, thought Pratt, what a damn fine feeling it is to be back in the fleet!

The flight was a short one. They ran down the Potomac for a few moments before swinging east, passing over Chesapeake Bay and the Delmarva Penninsula, then out over the Atlantic toward their destination.

Within a few minutes the helo heeled slightly as it banked and began its descent. Pratt saw a wide, white wake flashing in the bright sunlight, but he was in no position to see the ship. A pulse of excitement that he had known so often before ran through his veins. It was an electric feeling and he could never quite determine its source. It could have begun in the heart or the pit of his stomach or between his shoulder blades. Whatever it was, it radiated through his system in an instant, and he could feel his pulse quicken as they dropped toward the fantail of the ship.

USS *Hayler* was the last of the Spruance-class line, commissioned in 1983. She had been diverted from her station in the carrier screen early that morning specifically to take Pratt aboard. *America* and her escort of cruisers and destroyers continued south toward the Bahamas, and *Hayler* would have to catch up as quickly as possible.

Her captain learned only after he had been detached from the screen that he was to take Admiral Pratt aboard. The message had been very brief. This was to be a shakedown cruise for Admiral Pratt. If it didn't work, a helo from Norfolk would pick him up the next day. If everything went well, *Hayler* was to chase after *America* at maximum speed and transfer Admiral Pratt to the carrier as soon as she rejoined the screen.

The helicopter's engines were cut at the moment it thumped solidly onto the tiny, pitching flight deck. As he reached for his safety harness, Pratt could hear the click of guy wires snapping into place to secure the helo to the deck.

The pilot appeared from the cockpit, his helmet in his hand. "Admiral, I'll bet you've never seen a destroyer at sea quite like this one." He was grinning from ear to ear.

Pratt looked up curiously. Smoothing his hair, he put on a baseball cap he'd carried inside his jacket. "What do you mean?"

"I think every crew member not on watch is assembled aft, sir, and they're all in whites." He shook his head. "I never saw that before on a destroyer at sea," he added with wonder.

"Damn it, I told Tommy Bechtel I didn't want any of that," Pratt muttered to himself. The hatch was opened. He blinked at the reflection of the bright sun off the ocean as he stepped out onto *Hayler*'s flight deck. Squinting, he looked first at the water, then aft. The pilot had been right—nothing but sailors in whites.

As Pratt stepped forward to meet the man with *Commanding Officer* stitched on his baseball cap, the ship's PA system clicked on and the familiar and traditional words were passed, "Admiral David Pratt. . . arriving." His job had no title, no magical distinction that was normally used when a flag officer came aboard. But that didn't seem to bother this ship.

"Attention on deck," bellowed a chief at the end of the flight deck. Assembled around the aft missile launcher on the next level and on the fantail around the five-inch gun, every sailor came to attention.

"Hand salute," came the order. Every sailor's white-sleeved arm raised in unison. Pratt returned the salute as quickly as he could. "Two." The arms snapped back to their sides.

"At ease. Now let the Admiral know what you all got gussied up for." The sailors let loose with a raucous cheer, waving their hats to the man on the flight deck.

Pratt waved back. Then he removed his baseball cap and swung it around his head. That electric feeling had returned!

The captain held out his hand. "Welcome aboard, Admiral. We're sure pleased to have you with us." The words were simple and polite, more what Pratt had anticipated than the reception he had just received.

Pratt returned the handshake. "Thanks, Captain. I told Tommy Bechtel I didn't want any of that." He waved his arm toward the noisy sailors. "I just wanted to get back to sea."

"I understood that, sir. This wasn't my idea," he added, extending his hand to include the throng below. "It was their's. You know how rumors race through the fleet. I think that first message about your coming aboard got to most of the crew before I ever saw it." The captain smiled. "The chiefs came to me right after I saw the message board and said the crew wanted to do this. It really was their idea, sir," he insisted. "Even to getting into fresh whites . . . and you know how a destroyer sailor hates to wear his whites, more or less wrinkle them, unless he's headed on liberty."

Pratt nodded. A destroyer sailor and his dungarees were inseparable at sea. "Well, I don't think I know how to thank them." This was not the way he'd planned to take a shot at getting his sea legs back, if they still existed.

"Excuse me, Admiral." It was the same chief who had barked the orders to the crew. "They'd be awfully happy if you'd wear this while you're aboard." He extended a new baseball cap. Across the front was *Admiral David Pratt*—

USS *Hayler*. Even the gold scrambled eggs had been sewn onto the bill. Pratt removed his own cap, handing it to the chief, and fitted the new one on his head. Once again Pratt waved to the crew. "I'll keep it, Chief . . . fits perfectly," he added gruffly.

"May I show you to your cabin, Admiral?" the captain offered as the crew dispersed.

"Hell no, Captain. I came out here for a specific purpose and we might as well get to it. Let's get on up to the bridge and we'll run back after that task force you belong to. I really don't plan to see much of that cabin if I can help it."

Toward the end of that day, with the sun setting in a great, golden splash to starboard, *Hayler*'s captain turned to mention something to Dave Pratt and found the Admiral dozing in his chair. It was understandable, after all the man had been through since he had been injured. The captain could only imagine what it must be like to be crippled for so long and then suddenly determine that it was time to walk again. As far as he could conclude, every story, every rumor that had passed through the fleet about Admiral Pratt must have been true. He would hate to transfer this man to *America*, but carriers were the command posts for men like Pratt.

James Grambling's Camp

Paul Voronov's request had been simple, to the point. He explained to Grambling about the man named Corazon who had mysteriously disappeared from Havana and in an equally mysterious way reportedly surfaced in Panama City. Digging for someone like that was intelligence work; it wasn't Voronov's style. Would Grambling help out with his contacts in the city?

James Grambling was more than willing. This was the opportunity he was looking for to discover what really was happening in the capital. He couldn't dig on his own with the price the loyalists in the Guardia placed on his head. Rather than send one of his men into the city, he chose Maria. There was no one he trusted more, and there were many days he was positive she was a better intelligence expert than those who claimed it as their profession.

There were really two Marias. One was totally in love with Jaimé Grambling and would follow him through the deepest, foulest jungle just to be with him, to be available when he needed her. That Maria could adapt to the jungle—she could be comfortable in fatigues, eat the same food as the troops, remember to shake crawling things out of her clothes in the morning. And if their situation ever became desperate, that Maria could also field strip or fire an AK-74, a mortar, or an anti-tank gun, not to mention her ability to build devices that exploded for any number of reasons. That last was a trick she had learned in her university days.

The other Maria, the one she had put behind her to follow Jaimé Grambling, had been an exemplary student and could converse equally well in English. Jaimé would tease her and call her his "poor little rich girl" because that's exactly what she had been. Maria had come from a wealthy, conservative family. Her parents felt she had gravitated to all the "wrong people" at the university, but Maria, defiant and rebellious, accepted without question the opposite of whatever her parents believed. If there was one benefit to claim from those confusing years, she knew it was Jaimé. And because of him, she could never be comfortable again in the serene world of wealth she had discarded.

There were neither fatigues nor tailored suits for the Maria who arrived in the capital. Rather, she was absorbed by the mixed crowd that frequented the university area. At one time the administrators had intended that students would be the main population, though that was never entirely the case in third world countries. Instead, there was an eclectic mix of radicals, professional students, and quite a few ne'er-do-wells. Not only could one acquire minute details of the most highly classified intelligence at the university, it was also possible to find someone willing to do anything—for a price.

The university was exactly as she remembered in the years before she had slipped into the jungle with Jaimé Grambling. While there were many new faces, within hours she had also managed to locate most of the familiar ones of the past. She garnered many details neither of them had heard before—the bombing of the Presidential Palace, clandestine skirmishes involving Cuban or Russian troops—and she was appalled by new faces in the Guardia which had been mysteriously absent in Havana for many months. None of this intelligence set easily with her. Few of the facts she heard that day seemed to have originated with the PRA. She listened to the same trusted contacts of the past, who sipped the same never-ending cups of thick, black coffee, smoked the same funny-looking cigarettes, and told her how much the Guardia had changed, how many new Soviet and Cuban faces appeared on an almost daily basis.

There were other situations Jaimé would want to know about—especially the relationship between the Alvarez woman and the American who had been seen with President Ramos. Corazon, however, the main purpose for her excursion, drew a blank. There was no one by that name who could be traced by her contacts. But there was one man, an individual unknown to them who had been seen with the American, Ryng, whose description vaguely fit that of Corazon. There was a photograph for her the following day to take back to Voronov.

Usually after Maria returned from these forays, she brought Grambling stories of renewed acquaintances and fascinating and controversial ideas generated around the university. This time she had none of those stories.

"Jaimé, there is a different atmosphere at the university," she said as Grambling studied her face intently, observing a flood of emotions never before evident after one of her visits to the city. She had always returned flushed with excitement. This time it was different, disturbingly so. "It's not just the students, but the hangers-on, the ones you hate so." Grambling despised the non-students. He considered them leeches in a nether world of intellectualism who neither studied nor worked, and spent most of their time trying to incite those who did. None of them would ever have considered joining him in the jungles. He told her they were parasites. "Even the hangers-on are concerned, Jaimé. The ones who hated the Americans so much now see that there are just as many Russians who have replaced them, and more Cubans too. They say the uniforms are different, the theories are new . . . but the end result will be the same—that they will herd us like sheep.''

Grambling concentrated on what she was saying. She spoke of this new, latent Soviet authority as she had once spoken of the Americans, as if their objective was to conquer rather than to assist in establishing a new government. When the left wing of their own country reacted as negatively as she perceived, then there was indeed a reason for concern.

Grambling had begun to feel the same way. He had expressed it before to anyone who would listen, even to Paul Voronov. But his fears had always been rejected. It was claimed that his reasons for being part of the PRA were based on an aberrant patriotism that few of them understood. He was not associated with the new intellectualism of the university nor with the hatred associated with anything American. His was a perverse affection for his country that had been instilled through generations of Gramblings who had shaped their nation. To many, he was neither right nor left.

There were PRA faithful in the city, too, and Maria had been in contact with them. ''They have never felt so strong, Jaimé. And at the same time, they have never felt so weak. I don't know how to put it into words for you,'' she said, wheeling about to face him with tears streaming down her cheeks. She pounded futilely on her chest. ''Something has gone out of here like . . . like a candle has flickered . . . not from me, but those in the city. There is no longer the joy in each new day. It's almost as if the Russians have extinguished that flame. This war . . . this *golpé* . . . is no longer ours. They are taking over our *golpé*, and when they win that''—she paused, sobbing through deep breaths—''they will be here to stay.''

Grambling held Maria gently, rocking her slowly in his arms, stroking the back of her head. There were words, phrases, that he wanted to repeat, but none of them made sense. Each would be intended to soothe, to make everything right again. But it *wouldn't* be right. Maria knew that. Grambling knew that. They were in the vortex of a maelstrom and it seemed there was little difference whether it was the Americans or the Russians whirling about them. Though they struggled to escape, there seemed no limits to the raw power that now surrounded them. Neither right nor wrong existed.

Substance evolved into gray matter—black and white were blended.

Maria's sobbing masked the sound of Paul Voronov's approach. The Russian watched for an instant, was tempted to learn what was wrong, then thought better of it and left. It was almost time to depart for the coast. The Colombian destroyer would be anchoring offshore shortly.

A Colombian Destroyer off Colón

To say that security was lax on the Colombian destroyer would have been a misnomer: it was nonexistent. The purpose of this training cruise was to take raw recruits, who had spent six weeks ashore learning how to march and take orders, and turn them into sailors. There was as yet no effort to identify any talent among the recruits. Rather, for the initial part of the cruise, they learned where their bunks were, when to show up on the mess deck, how to chip paint, and hopefully how to keep themselves and their ship clean enough to discourage cockroaches and rats. Perhaps on the return from Buenaventura they would have the opportunity to learn more about the engines and guns and torpedoes that were their reason for being there.

They were also instructed in how to stand watch, which would be a major responsibility during their years in the navy. Unfortunately, it was a raw-boned, inexperienced pimply recruit from an inland plantation who first saw the flashing light, who had no way to understand the blinking until the realization finally came to him that there was some regularity to it. He pointed that out to the petty officer in his watch. The petty officer could not only understand what that blinking meant, but he had been instructed to inform a certain chief petty officer as soon as it appeared. Both petty officers were Cubans.

The man off duty rushed up to the bridge, made sure there was no one nearby, and quickly flashed a response. The code and its meaning had been determined much earlier in Havana by Admiral Khasan, who had, in turn, passed it on to Paul Voronov. There were more than a dozen men aboard that destroyer, none of them Colombians, who would have understood that flashing light and could have responded with equal facility.

From the moment of response, which the chief checked on his watch, it would be exactly two hours before the Colombian ship was boarded. By that time the radio room would be secured and the bridge under the control of the Cubans aboard. A number of the ship's officers had already taken the whaleboat for a night in Colón. They would be taken care of one at a time, very quietly, before Cubans wearing their uniforms returned to the landing. As Khasan had explained, most of the remaining crew members would be more than willing to cooperate considering the alternatives, and the recruits were necessary—someone had to continue the normal ship's operations, the cleaning and chipping and potato peeling that is part of being in the navy.

Armed with automatic AK-74s and grenades, and with no need for dramatics, Voronov led the boarding party up the ladder that had been placed port side, amidships at the quarterdeck. Signal light had already confirmed it was safe to board the ship. The bridge and the radio room were under control. Resistance had been minor. The only unsecured spaces were gunnery plot and the after engine room. In both cases, loyal officers had retreated to these spaces. Nothing had been done to harass them.

"Welcome aboard, sir," a man in the uniform of a Colombian chief petty officer remarked as he saluted Voronov.

The salute was returned with a smile. "Any casualties?"

"None of us. One Cuban has a bullet in his gut. Ship's company lost two regular officers and six enlisted dead, half a dozen wounded. Two officers are holed up in the plotting room and two in the after engine room. We're not sure yet how many enlisted are with them or how many of those really want to hold out. The captain and six officers are ashore. Three officers are being held in the wardroom . . . scared to death," he added with a smile. "They really expected this to be a sun-and-fun cruise, I guess. The rest of the regular crew are being very cooperative, and the recruits still haven't figured out quite yet what's going on.''

''Very well,'' Voronov said to the petty officer. ''I want the boat unloaded immediately. Separate the concussion grenades. If we can't talk our rebellious friends into surrendering, we'll go in after them.'' To Grambling, he added, ''The computer in plot controls the target solutions for the five-inch guns.''

''You can't fire them without that computer?''

''Oh, we can fire all right—on local control in the mounts. It's just that we have to eyeball the target, and that doesn't work if we're attacked by anything moving very fast.'' Prior to his transfer to the Caribbean, Voronov had made a point of visiting a Greek ship just like this one. Though it had been modified to suit its new owners, the Russian officer, dressed as a tourist, had seen enough of that ship to know his way about.

Voronov could speak Spanish but did not read it. On the bridge he studied the phone box set in the bulkhead, trying to determine which button to select. ''Which one is for the plot room?'' he finally inquired. ''I want to talk first.'' One of the Cubans pointed to the correct button. Voronov pressed it down, bending slightly to speak. ''This is Captain Voronov and I am in command of this ship now. Please give me your names.''

A click could be heard as the corresponding button was depressed at the other end, but there was only silence, followed by some muttering in the background.

''Do you hear me down there?'' he persisted.

Again there was a click. Then, ''Go ahead.''

''You are aware you are outnumbered and trapped. There is no way of escaping. If you agree to surrender, you will be treated as prisoners and allowed to leave the ship when there is an opportunity. You will not be harmed.''

''Where are the other officers?'' The voice, though it was metallic over the speaker, could not mask the hesitancy on that end.

''Those who did not resist are in the wardroom. Call there if you like. You are welcome to speak with them. I will wait on the bridge until you call me back.''

There was no further response, only silence. Voronov preferred to work that way. Men in a dangerous position often weakened if they were allowed to speak with others who were safe. It seemed human nature, he surmised, that men allowed to think after a period of action generally preferred to avoid further danger.

He called the after engine room and went through the same routine with an officer who seemed more cooperative. The chief engineer and one of his junior officers were holed up in that space with a few enlisted men. That meant one of those in plot was the executive officer. He was the least likely to surrender in such a situation. Voronov waited impatiently, pacing from one wing of the bridge to the other while Grambling explored the ancient pilothouse with curiosity. For a man trained in small boats, the destroyer was a fascination.

The men on the bridge, waiting for any sort of response, jumped at the unfamiliar click as the interior communication speaker came to life. It seemed to Grambling that each of them ceased breathing. "We're staying right where we are, all of us," a voice said. Damn, Voronov muttered under his breath, they must have learned there were two spaces holding out when he let them call the wardroom. Mistake number one! He hadn't thought of that. "You can't really go too far on only one shaft," the voice continued, "so we'll just stay in the engine room and in plot."

"Who is this?" Voronov shouted into the speaker. "Who am I speaking with?"

"This is Commander Radón, executive officer. . . ." There was still an air of hesitancy, though a decision had been made. "I . . . I don't know what you intend with this ship, but I can assure you that we can damage plot so that you will have little use of the guns, if that's what you want."

"As you wish, Commander. I'm sure you understand that I wouldn't have taken this ship if there was any intention of my giving it up because of a couple of stubborn men. You have had your one chance."

"Wait a minute—"

"Will you surrender now?" Voronov's voice boomed through the bridge area. There could be no doubting his attitude, even to the men on the other end.

"No . . ." There was that hint of hesitancy again.

"Then I have nothing further." He flipped the switch off. "Come on, Jaimé. I'm going to show you how we handle stubborn people."

On the quarterdeck Voronov wasted little time, and Grambling was surprised to see that there were already Soviet marines present, ominous in the black uniforms he had grown to hate so much. They appeared both efficient and dangerous with their flak vests and automatic weapons. Voronov ordered them to open the hatches to the engine room on either side of the ship. Following a simple plan of attack, smoke grenades were dropped from either side.

James Grambling could sense the engine room was an indefensible position, especially against these men. Four marines slipped down the ladder of the hatch on the opposite side of the ship as the smoke billowed below. Before reaching the bottom each man vaulted off to the side, covering themselves behind machinery. On Voronov's side two more climbed down that ladder. At the halfway mark, protecting themselves just as those on the opposite side, they attracted attention by shouting and banging their weapons. They had yet to fire a shot. They were greeted by just what they anticipated—sporadic pistol fire. Unless Voronov had been mistaken, there had been no time for the engineers to arm themselves with anything better.

The holdouts had given their positions away to the four on the other side, who dropped concussion grenades toward them. As Voronov suspected, it was all relatively simple. The grenades knocked the defenders senseless. Beyond broken glass on some gauges, there was no machinery damage. The concussion had little effect on the Russians hidden behind heavy equipment. In moments it was over, more easily than even Grambling would have expected.

Grambling had never seen Paul Voronov direct an action of his own using his own marines. In the past he had always been the "guest" advisor, but now his assumption of command was evident. The Russian was cool and efficient, his orders crisp. There was no hesitation here. He knew what he wanted, how to get it, and expected it carried out immediately. "Now," he said casually, "the easy part is done. I will give that executive officer one more chance . . . explain to him that the engine room was a simple effort." His eyes twinkled. The man was thoroughly enjoying himself.

The ship's executive officer was in a tight spot. To surrender to a man who could be called nothing more than a pirate would mean the end of his career—if he ever survived. He opted for valor, as misguided as he felt it may have been. Beyond hand weapons, there was no other defense, and he cautioned the ensign with him to hope that their end would be as quick as possible.

Voronov had no intention of frontal assault on armed men when anything as valuable as the computer system for the main battery was involved, so first, he set men to work on the ventilation system. That would be noisy and would carry easily to the plot room, perhaps convincing the two men inside that there were ways to get at them other than through the hatchways. At the same time Voronov kept up a constant one way monologue with the executive officer over the interior communication system. There was no way it could be turned off, and neither the executive officer nor the ensign considered destroying it.

While the pressure to surrender increased for the two in the plot room, men with torches were in the process of cutting two holes, high up, through the bulkheads on either side of the room. It really didn't matter to Voronov which side broke through first. The idea was to avoid losing his own men. As soon as one of the holes was large enough, the concussion grenades were dropped through the hole. Voronov could not be sure whether the explosions were as loud in the plot room or over the speaker he was listening to. Within seconds his men swung open the large metal hatches to find both men unconscious, blood streaming from ears and nose. The computer, set in its old-fashioned heavy metal frame, was undamaged.

The ship now belonged solely to Captain Second Rank Paul Voronov. Though the preliminary plans for this feat had been generated within the walls of the Kremlin, how they were carried out had, as usual, been left to Voronov's guile. Once more Voronov did not disappoint. He had been called worse names than a pirate before.

Aboard the Soviet Carrier *Kharkov*

Commodore Navarro again inched over to the edge of the flight deck on the port side. The carrier was a constant source of amazement to him, as the azure Caribbean sped by, its frothy wake peeling back from the bow to accentuate their speed. *Kharkov* was so huge, its flight deck so high, that his experience aboard an old, moored aircraft carrier on a tour of South America years earlier was feeble by comparison. Not only did this massive ship sprout missile launchers of every kind, but *Kharkov* also was armed with guns and torpedoes. And that was not even her main armament. She also carried a dozen jet fighters and twice as many helicopters bristling with deadly weapons.

"Don't lean over too far, my friend. It's a long way down to the water." Admiral Khasan had known the Commodore long enough to tell when he was impressed. If there was any way to regain the respect lost when his office had been broken into, this was it. Khasan was willing to bet Navarro would dream about this little trip.

Navarro straightened up, pulling at his borrowed flight jacket, knowing he was just like a child peering over the side once too often. Composing himself, he responded, "I have been to sea many times. There is no need to worry. I know how to handle myself aboard a ship, Admiral." But he did not want to appear arrogant. "I must say though that this is certainly an impressive day." He nodded in satisfaction. "Let me thank you again for bringing me out here."

It was a magnificent day. *Kharkov* had altered course to launch, and the wind whipped his hair, making his eyes tear. Navarro had been like a child, insisting on seeing everything the great ship had to offer, peering into spaces deemed unimportant by the ship's company, examining the missile launchers and guns as though he had never seen one before, and finally circling half of the helos and jets down on the immense hangar deck as if each one were different.

"Sometimes you need to get away from your desk, get some fresh air," Khasan said, his hand stretched out to indicate the vacant expanse of water in every direction. "Where else could you find better air to breathe. And the temperature, eh? Not like Havana. You don't have to get too far to sea to enjoy the cool air. I thought you needed a day like this."

No, my friend, that's not the real reason, Navarro thought to himself, though he smiled back at the Russian. "Yes. A good idea. I'm not sure how to repay you. Some good cigars, maybe. I have nothing quite like this to show you, but I think a couple of boxes of those cigars you like so well might be a starter."

"This is a pleasure, believe me. I expect nothing." He beamed. "But I would enjoy some of those cigars you mentioned."

"Now tell me," Navarro said, peering over his shoulder at the sailors on the bridge wings a few decks above them, "what are you planning with this big ship? You obviously didn't bring her all the way here just to show her off to me . . . but to the Americans perhaps?"

"Possibly," Khasan said. "We must let them see a ship of this magnitude near their shores, certainly. And for exercises with your own navy, of course."

Navarro listened vaguely as Khasan offered a litany of reasons for sending this newest of their carriers to the Caribbean, but he was sure the Russian couldn't have repeated them five seconds later. There was more to it than that. He had grown to understand the Russians after all these years, and he knew they never did something without a firm reason. There was much more than Khasan was willing to say. But that was all right too. It was comforting to see a ship like *Kharkov*, to know that your ally could summon such power to support you. But was that the purpose of this display?

The School of the Americas
Panama Canal Zone

The School of the Americas was established by the United States in the Panama Canal Zone to train Latin American military officers. Ostensibly, the intent was that these future leaders should command indigenous armies defending their own countries. Though Washington would control the curriculum, the methods, and the selection of students—the goal being to instill anti-communist policy and techniques—theory and reality were at odds. Because the U.S. could not control the citizens of these Latin American countries nor the power structure that continually turned the people against their governments, the Americans became the enemy. The door was left wide open for the Cubans and the Russians.

To Henry Cobb, who understood the people, the School of the Americas was anything but a proper place to use for a headquarters—but there was no other place that provided both the communication and command facilities and the necessary security. Situated in the Canal Zone, access to the school had always been restricted, a symbol of the power of the United States over the host country. Though Cobb agreed that it would serve for the time being as a command post, it was not the type of place he wanted to brag about.

"This is one of their leaders," Cobb remarked, sliding the glossy photograph across to Ryng. "Trained in small craft operation in Havana, top of the class, one of the most brilliant students they had. Also a superb jungle fighter . . . natural leader. The Russians love this type of guy, yet he hates Russians almost as much as he hates us.''

Ryng studied the picture closely. If he could have compared this photograph to the man driving that hydrofoil off Colón, he would have sworn they were the same person. From what Henry Cobb claimed, this had to be the man who bore down on him that night, the one who sunk him, the one he had also watched go down. ''And the girl, who's she?''

''I'm told she's a camp follower, which makes sense in this type of thing, but that's a lot of crap. Name's Maria. I heard she was in the city in the last day or so inquiring after the two of us. She's got an underground system working out of the university that our CIA could take some lessons from. She's the key to the leader, Grambling, I believe,'' he added pointing to the picture.

Kitty Alvarez looked up startled, at the mention of that name. ''May I see that picture, please.'' Her face softened as she studied the photo, a faint, knowing smile appearing at the corners of her mouth.

''You know him,'' Ryng remarked matter-of-factly.

Kitty rose slowly, wandering aimlessly to stare out the window at nothing in particular, her head tilted to one side as a flood of poignant memories crossed her mind. ''Yes,'' she answered softly. ''I knew James—Jaimé—quite well at one time.'' Now her eyes held Ryng's, and they were moist as she added, ''My first love. I have been told that the first should be the best because you never forget it . . . both the pleasure and the pain.'' A tear coursed down her cheek. ''But there was more pain than anything else. Jaimé carried so much anger within him and he dealt it out in big doses to everyone he came in contact with. He almost convinced me at one time,'' she concluded wistfully.

''Convinced you?'' Cobb asked.

She looked over, expressionless. ''That he was right . . . that his revolution was right . . . that we were all wrong.'' She held the photograph at an angle to the light. ''Still as handsome as ever, and I'll bet still turning on the charm.''

''If he is, he's only charming his followers,'' said Cobb.

"He doesn't come out of the jungle anymore. The girl, Maria, does all his running for him."

Kitty looked at the girl in the photograph. "She's pretty, in a hard sort of way, I guess." She looked back to Ryng. "It makes me jealous, in a way. Can you imagine that?"

Bernie Ryng shook his head, saying nothing. Jealousy was not an emotion he understood, though he had to admit that he felt a twinge of it when she'd said Grambling was her first love.

"When was the last time you saw him?" Cobb asked.

Kitty handed the picture back, shaking her head with a smile. "Too long ago to make any difference now." She shook her head again. "It's been a dozen years, maybe more. It was when we were students at the university. I was studying economics to learn how to help my country grow strong again, and James Grambling was studying political science, but practicing radical politics. He was trying to learn how to tear down everything I wanted to build up. And I was going to save him," she said with finality.

"Obviously your mission failed," Ryng said with amusement.

"Yes . . . yes it did. But his did also. He was trying to radicalize me, to teach me his liberation theology . . . that the masses will become the catalyst for their own freedom. That doesn't mix with economics, and it also tends to shorten love affairs," she concluded, reaching over to touch Ryng's hand.

Cobb was interested. "Is he a purist? One of those who really believes in the people?"

"Henry, he is the purest of the pure—a patriot in every sense of the word."

"Can you imagine what he thinks of the Russians and Cubans running about?"

"If James Grambling is the same now as he was when I knew him—and that's one part I doubt would ever change—what you said a few moments ago about his hating the Russians as much as he hates you Americans hasn't changed."

"That," Cobb turned to Ryng, "may be the weak link."

Kitty changed the subject. "You've got a lot more than that picture, don't you?"

"I love to dig," Cobb said, smiling. "It seems that there is already a contract out for my neck, and probably Bernie's too. That's how I came by that picture. It seems that the girl, Maria, was looking for information about me. But my sources back in Havana have passed the word that it's really a Soviet Black Beret who has orders to track me down. That's why I was curious about this Grambling and the girl. It may not be by choice, and they may not like it, but they're into it in a big way with the Russians," he added casually.

Kitty glared at Cobb uncomprehendingly. "Jaimé, with the Russians . . . that's impossible!"

"I thought that might be the case, but I had to be sure."

"You mean you knew about me and Jaimé beforehand?" Kitty asked, shocked by the anger in her own voice.

"I'm not a trusting soul," Cobb responded. "Ask Bernie. He'll also tell you I meant no harm. Just have to establish my priorities. Now I know where you came in . . . and left. And I know what Grambling's weak point may be." He saw in Kitty's eyes that she failed to understand him. "Again, ask Bernie. You trust him. My type of fighting comes from more than one direction. I've got to know my enemy." His curious gray eyes once again had that faraway look that seemed not to see her before him. "Not only how to beat him head on, but how to take advantage of every weak point if he's as good as I am. Grambling hates Americans, which I thoroughly understand . . . hates Russians, too, which may be our ace-in-the-hole later on. But I'll bet if he reacts to his first love the same way you just did, we might even have a secret weapon."

There was no doubt in Ryng's mind what Cobb was driving at. He wouldn't consider the idea of using Kitty yet, but it made exquisite sense. It was a factor to consider only if the situation deteriorated beyond repair. Ryng could see in Kitty's eyes that she had learned the essence of Cobb. Yet she would have been even more wary if she had known more of Cobb's background—the stories Ryng never told.

A phone call for Cobb interrupted them. The conversation went one way, Cobb responding only with a series of grunts. But Ryng caught the slight raising of eyebrows, followed by tightening lines at the corners of his eyes. He had seldom seen that look, for Henry Cobb rarely altered his facial expression.

He did not speak immediately after hanging up the phone.

Instead, following a habit Ryng had always appreciated, Cobb rose from his chair and walked slowly to the window. If anyone had spoken, he likely would not have heard, or, at least, wouldn't have responded. He stared pensively at the scene outside. Cobb preferred to order his thoughts before he expressed himself to others. Pratt said that it was why Henry Cobb was alive and so many of his other men were no longer with them.

"The Russian's name is Voronov," he finally remarked, turning from the window. "I know of Paul Voronov by reputation. He is a captain second rank in the naval infantry. If I could choose one of them, just one to work with, I would take Paul Voronov," he concluded.

"This is the one you were mentioning a few moments ago that is in the jungle with Grambling?"

"The very same. But they're no longer in the jungle. They were seen leaving Portobelo by boat the other evening."

"I thought the PRA's main push was about to start. Who's going to be running it if they're off somewhere?" asked Kitty.

The corners of Cobb's eyes again reflected deep thought. Ryng waited until the other said, "Much of that call was about intelligence I was after from Havana. There's something else I hadn't figured, something that puts the Russians a lot deeper into Panama than even Dave Pratt suspected."

There was, he explained, a medium-sized force of Soviet warships approaching from the Pacific side. Considering that any overt acts would affect security and close the Panama Canal to them, it seemed odd that they would be approaching so boldly—as if they assumed they would be able to utilize it upon arrival. The Soviet admiral in Havana, Khasan, had apparently issued orders to Voronov concerning the Canal. The content was unknown. The source who attempted to find that information had disappeared. But it was the type of intelligence to build on—Voronov, a covert operations specialist, and the Canal.

"I'm going to see if I can trace that girl," Cobb said. "It's almost time. President Ramos is going to have some surprises soon if you can't get him to establish some type of martial law with Guardia officers he trusts."

Ryng nodded.

"And why don't you spend a bit of time learning some more about security for the Canal. I don't know yet, but it's got to be a key."

Aboard An American Hydrofoil

The hydrofoil, the same one that had retrieved Henry Cobb a few days before, departed Key West at its normal time. Standard operating tests completed, it rose onto its foils, following the same course as usual, a creature of habit. But there was more than a slight difference about the craft this time. To the uneducated observer, even to the Cubans grown bored with its constancy, little could be seen to indicate its new mission. Rails running either side of the main deck about midships to the stern, just in front of the Harpoon missile launchers, had not been visible the previous day. They were close to the deck and had been designed to blend with the hull. Only a low-flying plane might possibly have interpreted their purpose.

The little ship remained foilborne for the long run out, insuring that she followed essentially the same route, radiating the proper electronic equipment at the appropriate time. That would satisfy Cuban electronic intelligence specialists. It was a classic imitation of a standard patrol.

The only deviation from the norm came when she swung in closer to Cabo San Antonio at the farthest tip of western Cuba. There she settled in the water and commenced a slow run southwest, plotting a direct path to Isla Cancun off the Yucatan peninsula of Mexico. It was a distance of approximately 125 miles across the Yucatan Channel and the seeding would take about ten hours hullborne. Because it was a one-shot operation and installation time was limited, the designers of the rails would not guarantee the mines would survive at a greater speed. Much of the minelaying effort would be possible under the cover of darkness, but the last two hours would see the sun rise.

Dave Pratt concocted this strategem after receiving intelligence that Soviet submarines would pass through the

Yucatan Channel from the Caribbean to interdict the Straits of Florida. There had never been the least doubt in his mind that it was an act of war in international waters. But, he reasoned, that's why the Soviets would be sending those submarines into what he considered American territory. A detachment from his office had been sent to Key West to design and install the rails. The mines were experimental. They had been delivered to Key West days before by an innocent enough oceanographic research ship, an integral part of Admiral Pratt's covert fleet.

After the officer in charge of the detachment called to confirm that the job could be done, Dave Pratt explained it to Tommy Bechtel. The senior admiral loved the concept. It then went to the Chief of Naval Operations, who considered the scheme imperative. But the CNO knew enough to wait until he had perfect copies of Pratt's intelligence photos of the Soviet task force forming in the Atlantic Ocean. Then he took Pratt's plan to the Secretary of Defense and the President. Since the final responsibility for approving the minelaying operation was in their hands, they each thanked their lucky stars that Dave Pratt had enough foresight to develop such a unique solution.

The orders, once it seemed probable that no more than forty-eight hours remained, went from Washington to Dave Pratt on *America* to Key West. Such precise planning had allowed the little hydrofoil to follow her appointed path without attracting suspicion.

The minelaying proceeded according to plan through the night.

What hadn't been anticipated, nor could have been, was that the opposition intended to keep an eye on that specific channel. It was critical to them. At sunrise, unknown to the Americans, patrol flights of the Yucatan Channel were initiated from the airfield at San Antonio de los Banos, west of Havana. The patrol planes, old Soviet Mails, were slow and cumbersome, but they served their purpose well.

The hydrofoil was spotted by radar with only about twenty miles left to complete their mine seeding before returning to base. The Soviet pilot was dumbfounded when he spotted the American boat. There was no doubt about which boat it was—the pilot had overflown this hydrofoil near Key West only weeks before—and there was no doubt, as he swooped down to take a look, what she was doing.

The mines were unique, developed by Dave Pratt's engineers to inderdict submarines. The explosive warhead was weak, designed to damage but not terminate the submarine. Rather, the submarine's mission was to be terminated by fear of penetrating such a minefield. Activated only by the submarine's noise signature, the mines would also self-destruct within fourteen days. It was an act of war by the definition of the term, but it was a defensive one, Pratt insisted.

As the plane circled away, obviously preparing to make a torpedo attack, the hydrofoil captain sent four of his men to the 76mm gun on the forward deck. It was their only defense against air attack. With the entire crew involved in minelaying, they had simply not anticipated patrol aircraft. The Soviet plane—designed to conduct anti-submarine warfare, certainly not to sink high-speed surface craft—was a huge, lumbering stork chock full of electronic gear and made to seek out and attack submerged submarines.

The Soviet pilot increased his engine revolutions at the same time he began a zigzag pattern. It was a slow motion dance, one wing raising slowly as the other dipped in concert with the course change, then back again. It was evasive action in its most primitive form, especially against an automatic weapon. Unfortunately for the plane's crew, the torpedoes would be effective only if dropped at low altitudes and reduced speed.

The hydrofoil turned to meet the attack. The minelaying stopped while the boat rose on foils and increased speed—an impossible situation for the lumbering aircraft. A torpedo attack was worthless, yet the plane bore in, its lazy path an easy target as the shells arched up from the speeding hydrofoil into the huge fuselage. There were puffs of smoke as the shells hit and exploded, but it would require a number of hits to sufficiently damage the big plane, still droning on toward the boat.

One of the engines began to smoke, the propeller fluttering lazily. A chunk of the tail broke off, then the tip of a wing, more smoke appearing from the central fuselage. Then, within a few hundred yards of the hydrofoil, the plane exploded in a fireball plummeting end over end into the sea. Though there were no parachutes, there was no doubt in the hydrofoil captain's mind that their operation had already been radioed back to Cuba. It would take little time for Havana, or more likely the Russian advisors there, to resolve Dave Pratt's strategy. It was unequivocally blunt.

East of Antigua

Though there had as yet been no words of anger exchanged between the Soviets or the Americans, the incident in the Yucatan Channel was the precursor of a series of reported individual engagements committed by on-scene commanders.

Just east of the Guadeloupe Passage that separates the islands of Antigua and Grande Terre, the Soviet attack submarine *Leninets* cruised quietly on station. Her commanding officer had seen combat a couple of years before in the Mediterranean. He was one of those Russian officers so affected by the heavy losses that he found difficulty in separating personal revenge from unquestioned authority. In more peaceful times, if more stable and competent officers had survived, he would likely have been replaced by his superiors. *Leninets*, surfaced but with decks awash, had been tracking an American *Knox*-class frigate for the better part of the night. Her captain had exercised his crew in nighttime identification, tracking, and attack procedures, until he was confident they could sink any U.S. surface ship that interfered with their blockade of the passage. The first glimmer of dawn painted the Atlantic sky to the east—the frigate's sharp profile was outlined against an increasingly brilliant purple-orange sky. Even with five miles between them, the air was so pure and clear that the Russian bridge watch could make out through their binoculars every last feature of the frigate, even to the sailors' round, white hats or baseball caps as they came on deck.

The American ship, *Thomas C. Hart*, could see nothing to the west, nor were they able to pick up any contact on sonar as the other cruised on the surface. The dull, black submarine blended perfectly with the still inky background, the sub's captain possessing the instincts of a cat silently tracking a bird. He called down from the bridge to the diving officer to take the boat down another few feet. The water was calm, not a breath of air stirring the surface. Once level, it remained dark enough that he could barely see the water four feet below him.

Life was stirring aboard *Hart*, the Blue Team having been awakened for breakfast prior to relieving the Gold. Sailors now wandered sleepily out to the main deck to stretch and sniff the warm air. Since their ship had spent most of the previous months on patrol in the North Atlantic, the seasonal change was still unique, and some had already written home gleefully bragging of the pleasant weather change. Little had been said to them, however, about the current patrol. Each captain in the squadron had been asked to withhold the details until the final mail helo had departed. This morning they would be told exactly the situation they were in.

Leninets' commanding officer studied the other ship through his binoculars. He could sense his entire body beginning to shake. It was much more a mental than a physical reaction—and a frightening one too! Dropping the glasses for a moment, he made a concerted effort to control himself. He could not. His mind drifted back to that morning in the Mediterranean when the American and Soviet navies had rushed headlong into a battle, one that had escalated to the fringes of nuclear war.

Leninets had been lucky that day. Two homing torpedoes were tracked bearing down on the submarine. Both had been evaded, by how little margin he would never know. When the battle was over and the two forces had limped away to lick their wounds, *Leninets* had been the only boat in her squadron to survive. Remembering those carefree companions he had once caroused with, the shaking now intensified, though he knew his orders were to avoid contact. There was to be no shooting unless precipitated by the Americans, at least not until orders were issued to destroy any ships that interfered with their mission.

On board *Hart*, the age-old customs were being followed—sweepers were manning their brooms, mess decks and living spaces were being cleared. Having spent so many hours steaming Blue/Gold, *Hart* was not nearly as clean as her captain preferred. The word was passed for a short but special field day to make her shipshape before general quarters was sounded. Like centuries of captains before him, his ship would sail into battle clean!

In *Leninets'* control room, the computers were whirring, transmitting target information to the four torpedoes nestled in the forward tubes. Her captain ordered one more exercise, this time to prepare for an attack and carry it to the point of the firing order. He altered course gradually to close the American frigate, but he hesitated to increase his speed a great deal. It was likely that his submarine's screw beats might then be detected, but he didn't want a torpedo run time of more than three minutes!

The blackness above had changed to a deep blue, growing softer as his eyes moved toward the east. It was still dark to his rear. And he had been correct about his crew. Their performance was flawless. The approach was classic. They had yet to be discovered.

At three and a half minutes the doors were opened on the torpedo tubes. Everything was perfect. His shivering was uncontrollable now, but it no longer concerned him. His mind was wholly involved in his objective. This was a superb opportunity!

At three minutes and fifteen seconds he was forced to crouch down, resting the binoculars against the bridge railing to compensate for his shaking. The American ship stood out perfectly, silhouetted against a brilliant dawn, her crew unaware of anything other than the placid, warm waters.

The words came as clearly as if they had been shouted in his ears—"Three minutes." He took a deep breath and answered—"Fire." There was no reassuring shudder under his feet, as should occur as each torpedo left the tubes.

His executive officer called up "Fire?"

"Fire!" the captain bellowed, his voice echoing across the water, but not quite far enough to be heard on the frigate.

Then he felt his boat shudder—once . . . twice . . . three times . . . four!

Lifting his binoculars to his eyes once again, the captain recognized he was no longer shaking. Rather, there was an overwhelming serenity coursing through his system. He overheard the control room reports that all torpedoes were running normally; his luck still held—he was unable to believe that his target was steaming placidly on the same course, oblivious to its doom.

On *Hart*'s bridge, the watchstanders were itchy. The final minutes of the four to eight watch were always irritating, perhaps because it had been twelve full hours since the last meal. The wait to be relieved at that time of day created moodiness, and it would be hard to fault men who were not entirely alert—particularly those as yet unaware of their ship's mission.

A torpedo warning would have been difficult to react to even for a watch anticipating attack. In this case when it came, it was prefaced by disbelief on the part of the sonarman who first recognized the strange sound. He had been trained to identify it but he couldn't believe his own senses when it first came to him. He reached forward to tune his equipment before remembering—the automatic reaction was to hit the torpedo alarm! It wouldn't have made any difference, and there would certainly be no one to criticize him.

To evade a torpedo after the alarm, it was necessary for the bridge to know the direction the torpedoes were coming from. Though danger would register immediately, there was a certain amount of time lost, seconds, when the shock and then the ingrained reaction took over. Turn toward? Turn away? Increase speed? Then there was lost time between human reaction and the time when four thousand tons of ship actually reacted to the human orders. The rudder would sweep over, the screws would bite into the water, and gradually the ship would react.

But it was all too late! The time of day, the sunrise, the placid waters, the darkness to the west, the hungry stomachs, the shaking Soviet captain—all contributed to the horror that followed.

Three torpedoes struck the calmly cruising frigate split seconds apart, one under the forward gun mount, one just aft of the bridge, and one under the hangar deck. The explosion of the magazine under the forward gun mount coincided with the last torpedo blast, and *Hart* lifted out of the water. Her bow opened up to the sea, separating itself from the hull.

Flame gushed skyward from the magazine, sweeping back over the bridge. Scalding, agonizing steam from the boilers engulfed the lower spaces before flames reached the few survivors. Helicopter fuel splashed in a burning pyre over the men still on deck. Then a mightly blast ripped through the hull and *Hart* rolled onto her side.

There had never been time to send a message from *Hart*. In less than thirty seconds she ceased to exist. There were no American ships in the area to detect her end, and there would be no record of her loss other than the confused stories of her few survivors. And those fortunate souls would not be located until search craft were deployed late that day, when *Hart* failed to make a position report.

Leninets dove shortly afterward and proceeded to her patrol area.

Panama City

Kitty propped herself up on an elbow, dabbing with a sheet corner at the perspiration on Ryng's forehead. "You don't take to the heat well, do you?" she sympathized.

"Never have." He rolled over just enough to reach the half full beer bottle on the bedside table. "This has always been the best defense I've found," he said, taking a long swallow. "That's mighty cagy of your friend," he said, indicating the small refrigerator that had been built neatly into the table on Ryng's side of the bed.

"Francisco is a man who has always thought of everything."

Ryng frowned. "How well do you know him?" He had asked the same question before.

"Only as a friend, my love." She wrinkled her nose. "Are you just a little bit jealous?" she inquired, pursing her lips.

"I'm in no position to be, I suppose . . . I came into this a bit late to be a complainer." But his eyes avoided hers just long enough.

Kitty reached over again with the corner of the sheet and

patted at the perspiration above his upper lip. "There." Then she kissed him softly. "You don't have to worry about Francisco. He's a business friend and a casual friend when we meet at parties, but there has never been anything between us, not the slightest." And, as if to reassure him, she concluded, "He's never even suggested anything like that. But you can see what a good friend he really is," she said, her arm sweeping the huge bedroom.

The main room of Casa Rejean was at least twenty-five by thirty feet. Buttressed against the center of one of the longer walls was an imposing king size bed. On the opposite wall was a floor-to-ceiling mirror. The casa was designed for a bachelor. There was also a mini refrigerator on Kitty's side of the bed. An instrument panel built into the headboard above contained controls for the giant TV screen to one side of the mirror and the radio, tape deck, and video recorder. To compliment this sybaritic palace, a huge bathroom, the largest Ryng was sure he'd ever seen, contained two showers, a sauna, and a whirlpool bath. Sliding glass doors from the bedroom led out to a hidden garden and swimming pool, and a door just inside the bathroom went directly to a small combination dressing room and cabana near the pool.

Francisco Rejean was a highly successful banker who lived mostly in a high-rise condominium with a beautiful view of the Pacific. In addition he owned a country estate, and this hideaway within the city, mostly bedroom, that he more often lent to friends. When Kitty Alvarez, who had never before asked a favor of him, called and expressed interest in Casa Rejean, he was pleased to be able to assist her. Such courtesy brought Francisco a long range return that would, he knew, make him even richer. He never asked questions, and it made no difference to him that it was a woman this time who had called. And Rejean was discreet enough never to inquire about the guests or the manner in which his place was used—only that a large tip be left for the cleaning woman who arrived each day at noon.

The pool and garden were so withdrawn, so well hidden by other buildings and specially placed hedges, trees, and outbuildings, that they could be seen only from the air. Even then, one would have to be searching for that particular location because of the natural cover, almost a camouflage effect. As a result, few people knew of Francisco Rejean's casa, and only those trusted few who had used it were aware of the pool. Therefore, in the little guest booklet provided on one of the bedside tables, it was explained that bathing suits were purely a personal decision. As far as Rejean could determine, the people he selected to use his house appreciated it to the extent of never boasting about these facilities, even to their closest friends. Perhaps that was another of the reasons that Rejean's business dealings were never questioned by outsiders.

When Kitty Alvarez called Rejean, she and Ryng likely had no more than eighteen hours left to themselves. Henry Cobb, in a rare moment of enlightenment, suggested they might make the most of that time. The suggestion that two people actually take advantage of some limited time together was something Henry Cobb would not have made a few years before. Ryng had told Kitty the story of how Cobb had fallen in love with a Polish girl, Verra, whom he had rescued during the Battle of the Mediterranean. Prior to that Cobb had always been controlled by the mission, his only constant mistress. But Verra had managed to change all of that. She countered Cobb's hard-headedness with an audacity of her own that penetrated his defenses. Now, Henry Cobb could understand why two people might need those few hours together.

Ryng leaned over to kiss her. "We both are fortunate to have such good friends. I won't say another word about Rejean. I'm not worried about a thing . . . promise," he said, kissing the tip of her nose. Then he reclined on the pillow with his hands cupped behind his head. "Cobb never had the chance for even a few hours like this when he first met Verra. It was another assignment like this, but there was no time. With a man like Henry, it's hard to believe he'd understand."

Kitty rolled over on top of him. "Then we'll call this Cobb's time. We won't tell him all the juicy little details." She giggled. "But we'll tell him he was properly honored for his understanding." Her face hovered above Ryng's. She rubbed noses and kissed him again. "He'd be ashamed if he knew you were wasting time." She held his face in her hands. "The time is now, Mr. Ryng."

He moved his arms around her back, hugging her for a moment, then rubbing them up and down as he returned her kisses gently, whispering in between, "The time is now, Miss Alvarez."

Afterward they dozed for a few moments, but sound sleep was impossible. There would be time for that later. Ryng rolled over and took another beer from the refrigerator at his side. Reaching above his head, he pressed the button for the television set. Immediately, an immense, blurred color picture swam into view. The huge trees and lush undergrowth of jungle became clear as the focus self-adjusted. The familiar whap of helicopter rotors provided dramatic acoustic background for a speaker reporting the news. The camera swung back and forth across the green background, apparently searching for a guerilla camp. Ryng switched from channel to channel. No reason to watch such things now. It would all come too soon. He switched it off.

Next, he punched the button for the tape deck. Even before they'd gone to bed, he made sure to load it with the music he considered appropriate for the occasion. Somehow, the semi-classical sounds didn't sit nearly as well as he'd hoped. They always seemed better beforehand.

"Are you suddenly bored?" Kitty inquired with a grin, propping herself on an elbow again. "Had too much of a good thing?"

Ryng spotted the twinkle in her eyes. "Often happens with older men, my dear. It's just something you'll have to get used to." He grinned back at her, then playfully pushed her elbow from underneath. "There will never be too much of a good thing, but there are times I like to play other games before I get back to my favorite."

"Why don't we go for a swim?" She again patted at the perspiration on his forehead. "You look like you could stand some cooling off."

"I can think of nothing better right now—but where?"

"I always save the special surprises for last." She rose from the bed and moved to what Ryng assumed was simply a window, drawing back the heavy drapes to reveal the outside gardens and swimming pool. "Whatever you desire."

The words simply wouldn't come to him. The pool was

small—just right for two people. At the far end, the top of the
heart, the flowers grew right to poolside, some of them tumbling over the edge to float in the water. It was designed so
that the sun would always be shining through the overhead
growth on a section of the myriad-hued beds of flowers. Ryng
was dazzled by a perfectly designed garden of white and pur-
ple, its geometry remarkable, planned and trimmed exactly to
satisfy the human eye. At the close end of the pool a small ter-
race contained just the barest necessities for two people, soft
couches for sunning, and a glass and wrought iron table for
dining. Ryng spied another of the small refrigerators just inside the opening to the cabana. Perhaps the next session, he
mused, should be dedicated to Francisco Rejean for his exquisite thoughtfulness and taste.

"And I suppose bathing suits, perfectly fitted, are available
for our use?" he questioned, stretching lazily.

"You didn't read Francisco's little booklet. If you had, you
would learn that this little pool is so well-protected that you
may use it with whatever you are wearing." Kitty pirouetted
slowly, raising her arms above her head, blowing soft kisses
across the space between them. "I hope you find my suit acceptable. I've had it for a long time . . . but it fits perfectly, as
you can see." She unlocked the heavy glass door, sliding it
back with an effort. A warm breeze wafted into the room,
heavy with the fragrance of the multi-layered flowerbeds. To
Bernie Ryng this was what dreams were made of—Kitty
Alvarez was what dreams were made of, he silently acknowledged as she moved languorously onto the perfectly raked
white gravel. Then she turned, her feet set wide apart, and
beckoned seductively for him to follow.

Ryng moved outside to the sunlight, watching appreciatively as Kitty poised on the edge, feet together, then rose on her
toes and arched out into the pool. Sunlight danced in the
water. He gazed with admiration as she swam near the bottom, rising to the surface when she reached the other end.

"Come on," she called. "I was right. This is just what we
both needed." She ducked underneath, smoothing her hair
back as she came up shaking her head. Then she reached
backward, resting her arms on the edge of the pool while her
feet gradually drifted to the surface. Her body glistened in the

sunlight. Ryng was mesmerized. Ripples of water magnified
her movement as she kicked her feet rhythmically. On the bottom, her shadow swayed with the motion of the water in a sen-
suous dance.

Ryng remained on the side, staring, committing each second
to memory. He was reminded that too often his dreams had
been easily shattered. The shadow of a lone cloud passed over
the pool as if a thin curtain had been drawn. The picture of
Kitty and the reflection darkened for a moment, and Ryng was
shaken from his reverie. But Kitty was still there, her feet
slowly kicking to hold her place, the come-hither smile still
teasing him. He dove in.

The water was a solvent, cleansing, refreshing his mind and
body. He stroked across the bottom of the pool in the same
manner as Kitty, surfacing beside her. He reached out and ran
his hand up and down her body. "Just checking," he murmured. "Just making sure you're real."

"Does it feel like a dream?"

He shook his head in response, his eyes wandering up and
down her figure. There were no words he could think of that
would be an adequate response for the way he felt. He
desperately hoped, as his eyes moved up to hold hers, that she
could understand.

"I love you," she whispered softly.

Ryng nodded, still unable to break his own silence.

She moved her arms around his neck, letting her body float
down gradually until it was against his, the contrast of the
coolness of the water and the warmth of their bodies making
her skin tingle. The emotion that surged through her core was
a new experience, equally as surprising to her as it had been to
Ryng.

"I love you," she repeated again, almost in a whisper, as
her mouth touched his. Then they were squeezing each other,
both holding on as if the dream would suddenly come to an
end.

Ryng pulled back just enough to whisper with even a softer
voice than her own had been, "I love you, Kitty." They sank
together below the surface momentarily as they kissed.

The explosion that followed a split second later shattered
Casa Rejean. Under the water there was no difference between

the sound and the blast as the shock wave thudded through their bodies. Debris rained down on the surface above them, heavier pieces dropping like rocks.

Kitty jerked away in fear, breathing out in surprise and shock. Instinctively she looked up to the surface, seeking the precious air expelled from her lungs. Ryng went to hold her tighter, struggling against her frantic need to breathe. Now his years of training took effect, forcing him to wait, terrified she would drown, anticipating the possibility of a secondary blast.

Believing she would drown, she clawed at his face in desperation, her body writhing in fear; and finally he released her.

Peering cautiously over the pool edge toward the cottage, he saw only traces of the building they had been using such a short time before. The narrow walls at either end were partially upright. The longer ones facing the pool had disappeared. In the distance Ryng could see the street through the trees lining the long driveway. He considered the fact that the bedroom they had recently vacated no longer existed. There was no sign of the huge bed, or the mirror, or any of the amenities that had seemed a dream only moments before.

Whoever had bombed Casa Rejean was unfamiliar with it. The bomb had been designed for a larger building with many rooms, one that would require excess force to destroy any partition that might protect the inhabitants. They had been unaware that this one had been designed with only comfort in mind. Francisco Rejean was sure there was little need for anything more than a combination drawing room and kitchen, for the large bedroom and its appliances had been intended as the center of activity.

The blast had been so tremendous that the house simply disintegrated, rather than crumbling into the ensuing fire that normally occurred. It had blown the casa into small pieces that shot up and outward in every direction. If either of them had been out of the water at the time, the flying debris would have killed them outright.

Ryng held Kitty close to him as she gasped for air, choking violently on the water that had invaded her lungs.

Was there anyone still out there? Any expert would have had it timed to insure his escape. But Ryng waited cautiously, alert for the slightest indication that there was life where there should have been nothing moving. Satisfied, he lifted himself out of the pool, keeping low. He whispered quietly to Kitty to remain where she was. One wall of the cabana remained perfectly intact, the mirror still in place, a small shelf of toiletries untouched and terry-cloth robes hanging on hooks as if intended only for the two to them.

Ryng remained in position for another moment, crouched near the pool edge. Then he reached down and took Kitty's hand, lifting her gently and quickly from the pool without ever touching the edge. He removed two of the robes from their hooks and helped her into one of them. "It might be a good idea to wrap this around you," he remarked quietly. "I imagine we're going to be overrun by the Guardia in a few minutes." He inhaled deeply, then let his breath out in a long sigh. "I guess this is where the dream ends," he muttered quietly.

Horacio Ramos was not an easily discouraged man. Well before he had ever considered the presidency, he had seen just about everything imaginable in the chaotic, riddled fabric that was Central American government. More than a "school of hard knocks," it was an education in reality in a world where the average family scrimped a living out of a couple hundred dollars or less; where a small select group of families controlled ninety-five percent of the wealth; and where these families ruled, in conjunction with an equally select military educated at the School of the Americas, a government that was merely a mouthpiece for the United States.

A few American companies, with the benign approval of Washington, controlled an economy based on agriculture. These companies dictated the crops, the prices, the ownership of the land, and the methods used to crush any unions. Whenever the people became so fed up with the system that the terror of revolution overcame even basic survival, the aristocracy called in their military and the peasants were then educated, generally through a policy of slaughter and scorched earth, in the realities of life. On rare occasions when the military failed to quickly put down a revolt, the United States generally sent Marines to reinforce the power structure. The Marines departed when the old system was reestablished.

Most liberal leaders, such as Ramos, were either dead or exiled to the mountains and jungles at that stage of maturity when people began to listen to them. But this had never been the case with the current president. His moderation, coupled with an inherent ability to soothe the fanaticism of both right and left, appealed to both the peasants and the emerging middle class as a changing world forced Central America to come to terms with reality. Ramos envisioned a policy whereby moderation would bring together all of the countries of the Americas—which would in turn create a new spirit of cooperation between the United States and Cuba, a spirit of goodwill engendering mutual support by the United States and the Soviet Union for the poor countries of Central America. In a word, he was the ideal leader to emerge at the crucial moment. Unfortunately, he was also naive.

The man who now sat across from him in the President's office, Esteban Alvarez, was the opposite. He was a man ruled by emotion, and Alvarez hid that passion deep within himself. He was not so much a communist as just plain anti-government. If the communists ruled the country, it was quite possible Alvarez would have been working in opposition to them. As it was, the times were ripe for men such as him, men who could offer a respectable front for the PRA. Men of education were still revered, especially academics like Alvarez who became government advisors; eventually many were exalted to an even higher position as they developed international reputations. Alvarez himself became a cult hero of sorts to the generation he helped educate at the university, when he was seen in news photos standing beside Fidel Castro or when he spoke before the Organization of American States relating starvation to imperialism.

Thus President Ramos wasn't surprised when Alvarez announced that the bombing of Casa Rejean had damaged some of his deepest, most fundamental beliefs. It became even more evident to Ramos when Alvarez could not look the other man in the face when he stated earnestly, "We must reach a gentleman's agreement, Horacio." It seemed almost as if he feared the other.

Ramos smiled and nodded, massaging his tired eyes. "I have always been a reasonable person to deal with. Have you suddenly decided I am some kind of an ogre?"

"Please, don't treat me with that overhanded courtesy. We have been friends. And now I am about to violate my own principles." The strain was evident on Alvarez's face as he chose each word. "Only by the grace of some god somewhere is my daughter alive today. You know I am a practical man, Horacio. I don't believe in myths or spirits or gods or saints or anything of that nature. But something saved Kitty today, and luck like that never comes in twos. I want to stop whoever used that bomb before they do it again." The PRA was out of control as far as he was concerned, though the group might have a slim possibility of returning to its original goals if the perpetrators of that bombing were exterminated.

Ramos's eyebrows rose perceptibly. He could not help it. Was Alvarez about to offer some unexpected intelligence? It seemed important to him to remain as bland as possible. "There are very few of us who don't agree with you," he said, realizing he had to avoid saying anything that might change Alvarez's mind.

"Thank you for understanding." Alvarez could sense that Ramos was trying to make it as easy as possible for him and he appreciated it. At times like this it was difficult to assure himself of who the enemy was! Ramos had once been his close friend. Now it was a relationship no longer based so much on friendship as on a mutual respect that often flourished. Why did so many in the PRA, the young colonels in the Guardia, consider this gentle man an enemy—one whose death they openly discussed?

"I have no idea who committed the crime," Alvarez continued, "nor why they would do such a thing." That was the first lie. They knew the American, Ryng, was at the Casa Rejean and they were willing to kill him, regardless of who or what was destroyed in the process. That was the element that must be removed before the PRA took power, for they were the same men who would then revel in disposing of Ramos. "But I think, Horacio, I can provide information about the headquarters where these insane bombers are located." There . . . it was out!

"You are positive?"

"Yes." He was sure of that part of it, though he wasn't sure everyone there was involved in indiscriminate bombing. That was the second lie, but he held it within himself. And that part didn't matter. Those who associated with murderers were equally as guilty. They would be the looters and rapists and murderers in the chaotic aftermath of revolution. "We have talked in the past of our differences, Horacio. You know the government I want to see someday. But you also know I am a man who abhors indiscriminate violence. Today I almost lost the only human being I have left close to me. Kitty is the only one," he added sadly. "The last blood . . ." The words drifted off as he felt a swelling behind his eyes. He stopped because he could not allow himself to display such emotion.

Ramos waited patiently. There was so much to be done, and he was so tired. But he could see the range of emotions crossing the other's face. Finally Alvarez reached for a piece of paper and wrote an address across it in his neat, precise script. He studied it for a moment as if he did not really believe it was correct. Then he slid it silently across the desk. He held Ramos's eyes with his own for the first time. "You must take great care in choosing who receives this address. There are many in the Guardia, majors and colonels, who may not be trusted. Have this carried out by someone close to you . . . someone without the slightest suspicion. . . ."

Alvarez's voice had drifted off as he considered what he had just done. It was more than likely that this would be traced back to him. But it didn't matter now. The PRA was too far advanced at this point. The vicious ones would be caught, but it was too late to stop the PRA from succeeding. Though they might get even with Alvarez, he no longer cared. It was a strange, not altogether unpleasant sensation as he considered what he had just done. His conscious mind was drifting somewhere above, looking down at these two men sitting across a desk from each other, silent, staring self consciously as people sometimes do when they are pleased with each other's company. From that lofty position it seemed that both men were doomed . . . doomed by a force that one man fought and the other supported. Though one had betrayed it, both were doomed by it.

Aboard the Carrier U.S.S. *America*

"Admiral Pratt is on the bridge, sir." The bosun mate of the watch's voice boomed across *America*'s pilothouse. Just the sound of the name *Admiral Pratt* created a sense of excitement among the bridge watch. *America* was like a small city of 5500 men, yet the opportunity to actually see or meet the Admiral was limited. Pratt had already spoken to them over the ship's television. But that wasn't quite the same as seeing him in person. Each man now stood a little taller in Pratt's presence, forced that extra effort for a special sharpness that would distinguish him from another sailor or another watch group. It was all part of being a crew member on a flagship.

Captain Elmendorf, commanding officer of *America*, slid down from his bridge chair and saluted. "Didn't expect to see you up here so early, Admiral." The morning sun was now full in the sky. The heat of the day could be felt in southern waters even at seven in the morning.

"I couldn't resist, Bob. I heard that announcement over the PA concerning flight operations and I had to come up. I know, I know," he added before the other could interrupt. "There are more private places I could go, but there's something about the port bridge wing during flight operations that I'll never get out of my system."

Elmendorf understood. "Something gets into the blood, Admiral. I don't know what it is, but I have the same bug." The feeling had emerged decades before, as far back as men, once pilots, found themselves resting their chins on their arms and watching one plane after another catapult down the flight deck to be committed to the air. Emotionally they were in the cockpit with each pilot, experiencing once again that sudden pressure from the catapult followed by grateful release as the plane was airborne. Behind would be the postage-stamp flight deck outlined against a shimmering sea. Ahead was their destiny. Both Captain Elmendorf and Dave Pratt belonged to that legion of men who understood. . . .

America had reoriented the screen twenty minutes before and was now steaming into the wind at twenty-five knots. Pratt stepped out onto the bridge wing, pulling his baseball cap tighter against the brisk wind sweeping bow to stern. On the flight deck business was well in hand. Destroyers were already in plane guard stations. Helos hovered tentatively. A squadron of Intruders, the Blue Blasters, were in the first launch and were poised at the rear of the flight deck, their pilots tucked in the cockpits, mechanically checking instruments. Men in multi-hued, outfits scurried about the flight deck intent on their missions, each one critical to the success of the next.

It was an experience that, once witnessed, was never forgotten. The immensity of the ship, the sheer power of the system that nurtured and launched these powerful planes, the grace of the aircraft themselves, each step and the entire operation became an awesome exhibition of man's ingenuity. To Dave Pratt, the man responsible, this was a humbling experience. He had witnessed in the Mediterranean the destruction and death his force was capable of, and he once again felt dwarfed by the potential within his grasp.

It was entirely possible, he acknowledged to himself, that some of these men would not return that day. Their mission was such that the Russian ships they were to harass might retaliate. Pratt waved to each pilot as his plane squatted on the catapult. Many saw him, knew who was up there wishing them well, and waved back before the g-forces pounded them into the padded backing as the catapults hurled their planes down the deck. The flight deck crew noticed this familiarity and, looking up at the bridge when they had a spare moment, recognized Pratt and waved a friendly greeting of their own. They experienced that very same feeling their grandfathers had forty years before when they saw Halsey looking down from a carrier bridge somewhere in the Pacific. He remained there until the last pilot was safely aloft.

When the final plane was a disappearing speck, Pratt studied his widely displaced screen of ships for a moment, then moved slowly about the bridge in his jerky gait saying a few words to each sailor. He never mentioned a thing about himself. Instead he talked about the last time U.S. sailors faced the Russians, about ships and planes and submarines and missiles, about heroic crews, about the loss of *America*'s sister ship, *John F. Kennedy*, which he had been aboard, and about what it took to turn back a powerful foe. He was preparing them.

Pratt knew that as soon as this watch was relieved the word would be passed below decks until every sailor on the ship knew what he had said in one form or another. He knew that signalmen would pass it back and forth between ships. He knew that the word would be spread to ships that came alongside for fuel and supplies and movies, and that they, too, would pass it on. Sailors possessed an ability to create and dissemimate a mythology before an actual battle, and that prepared them for the terrible forces thrown against them. In this era they never saw the man that pushed the button, nor the ship or aircraft that launched the missile or torpedo. Instead there was a violent blast caused by an unseen object and it was either over or they were a survivor. The mythology was a necessity of their existence, and Dave Pratt recognized that.

The last man he talked to was Captain Elmendorf, whom he invited down to flag plot after breakfast to participate in the final planning.

Elmendorf paused for an instant as he stepped into flag plot. It was a space he was well acquainted with on his ship. He had seen it managed by other admirals during more exercises than he could remember. Even before Pratt came aboard, he'd visited there briefly to insure that everything was in running order for this new flag staff that had boarded just the night before departing Norfolk. It had been reassuring to see these strangers immediately make themselves at home in their private estate within his ship. Their systems and displays, as different with each staff as each admiral was to the other, were already in place and functioning. But now there was something different. Before Pratt came aboard, before this staff was sure who would be coordinating this task force, they had been efficient and professional. Today Elmendorf sensed an effervescence as he stepped into flag plot.

Wherever one turned, whatever display was considered, not only the name of a ship (rather than just a hull number) appeared, but the commanding officer's name was also there. And whenever possible, the same was true for the Soviet ships and submarines. It was a human element. Instead of insensitive weapons platforms, Dave Pratt intended to establish the identity of ships honored with the names of past heroes, actual places in the United States, and real battles that Americans had fought around the world. And these ships were manned by flesh and blood captains who knew the names of the men serving under them. It was a personal touch that Captain Elmendorf had never before seen, and would never forget. There was a spirit of leadership beyond anything he'd ever encountered.

The session that followed was also unique. Conducted beyond the staid boundaries of naval tradition, it was a non-military meeting. Each man could contribute in his area of expertise with no fear of being overruled simply by seniority.

The strategy employed by Admiral Pratt to bring his task force to this stage was at least as complex as that planned to meet the crisis. Countering force with force was something that could quickly be accomplished in Washington. But developing a peacetime strategy to meet an offensive that was only projected, one that was based on Soviet forces seemingly employed on a variety of unrelated missions, required careful planning by those military leaders selected by Pratt to assist him.

The material compromised by Henry Cobb confirmed everything that Pratt could only surmise. With that he was able to literally go hand-in-hand with Tommy Bechtel from one office to the next, detailing the Soviet plan until access had been gained to the White House. Those operation orders not already in preliminary form were etched in Pratt's memory. They made sense to each person, military or political, in the Washington hierarchy.

No single individual could claim for a certainty every single step the Kremlin would take, but for each action of theirs an equal or stronger one was planned to change their minds. No one could predict exactly what it would take to convince them that the United States was serious. But Pratt's objective was a show of force in reverse. Instead of appearing off another country's shores to establish the might of the U.S. fleet, the Americans would be displaying the same message off their own coast. It would be a stern warning, with teeth bared. And

Pratt intended to strike at the least provocation. There was no intent of giving ground when his ships were already backed up against their own shores.

Elmendorf's only briefing before they sailed indicated to him that this was to be a show of force, an effort to discourage Russian and Cuban military adventurism in the Caribbean area. There was no hint of cold war stridency to Pratt's meeting. Now, Elmendorf found himself listening to men who were preparing for battle. It was a distinct shock for a man who had not expected affairs to deteriorate to that level; but Elmendorf was also a professional military man. He was adaptable—but of even more importance, he was totally impressed by the strategy he was witness to.

There was a distinct picture emerging. The mining of the Yucatan Channel had accomplished two vital functions—the Gulf of Mexico was preserved, for the time being, from Soviet incursion, and the Florida Straits could not be interdicted from the west. Patrol planes from Pensacola and Corpus Christi, along with reserve destroyers and minesweepers, would be responsible for containing any submarines that had entered before the Yucatan Channel was seeded. The passages into the Caribbean, from the Windward between Cuba and Haiti to the Galleons between Grenada and Trinidad/Tobago, were secured for the moment. The loss of the frigate *Hart* was as yet unknown. Though American ships in the Atlantic would face submarine attack if they attempted to enter the Caribbean, the same was essentially true for those Russian surface forces not already there or operating out of Cuba. Most Soviet surface and sub-surface forces approaching or already on station east of the Caribbean had been tracked and identified. Pratt's task force was equal to them on paper.

It looked to be a perfectly anticipated and analyzed sea battle until Admiral Pratt expressed his one major element of uncertainty. He went over to one chart and covered his problem with both hands—Central America! There, under his hands, was essentially the Soviet goal—and what was it that they were planning? Pratt discussed the issues for a few more minutes, occasionally peering at his watch. Finally he rose to his feet, thanked each man for his time and input, and asked his staff communications officer to patch a special frequency, one he had written on a torn sheet of paper. Then he left the meeting. Elmendorf sensed that the solution to Pratt's Central American enigma depended on that special frequency.

Panama City

As evening approached, Henry Cobb sauntered across the wide plaza in front of the university's main administration building. Lights winked on sporadically as the plaza, almost empty for more than an hour, filled with people once again. It was an area occupied mostly by a university group, the ever-present non-students and self-styled intellectuals.

Cobb attached himself to a group sipping wine at an outdoor cafe. It was not difficult. Noticing others pull chairs to the edges of the gathering, Cobb followed suit as if he were one more hanger-on. Three or four students huddled around a single table were involved in a rabid controversy. Those on the fringes attracted no attention.

Henry Cobb might not have been recognized that evening by Ryng. Cobb's hair and eyebrows were now black, his skin had already acquired a brownish hue from the Caribbean sun, a neat, black mustache replaced the droopy brown one, and smoky contact lenses masked the gray eyes. His attire blended easily with those around him.

Unlike their elders, students could discuss and accept casually that which others might call sedition. In other words, an argument concerning the merits of overthrowing the government was a pleasant way to spend the evening. This was certainly the right group to become part of, Cobb realized, as the talk turned to the PRA and then to the underground that operated in its behalf at the university.

He had no intention of participating in the discussion, which could only draw attention to him. Cobb was a good listener, a sorter and absorber of information. His time was limited, and even before he worked his way into the city, he had determined that he would select one person, an individual who either by his words or his silence or respect accorded by the others indicated that he had contacts. Cobb hoped that this person would eventually lead him to Maria if she was still in the city, or to someone who knew where she was. He had to find out where Grambling and Voronov had gone after they were seen leaving Portobelo.

The plaza filled quickly that evening, the hum of voices adding an electric background to the warm night air. Listeners drifted into the group at the cafe, noted the conversation for a time, occasionally offered an opinion, and wandered off. It was all part of the excitement and fear that was an integral part of a country at war with itself.

There was no doubt in Henry Cobb's mind that the PRA had infiltrated the university and that there was solid intelligence to be gathered there. Cobb was expert at sorting out people, dismissing frauds and liars, spotting self-professed experts, and recognizing disguises that were never as expert as his own. When the man who moved across the plaza with a purposeful stride, yet was dressed like a student, joined his group, Cobb concentrated on his appearance. There was too much of the military in this man, Cobb thought. He lacked the looser, youthful mannerisms so common among others in this group. Cobb watched him for an hour, deciding not to make his move until he was absolutely sure that he'd overheard more than one person ask the man specifically about Maria. The answer each time was that he expected to see her that night.

"You're not any more interested in this than I am, are you?" Cobb began in Spanish, sliding his chair over.

The man turned, startled. "I . . . I don't follow you."

"I've been watching you. You're not really listening to them." He indicated the core of the group. "But you've been watching many others—"

"Who the hell are you?" the man interrupted, all pretense of his disguise vanishing.

"My name is Miguel," Cobb replied. "But it really doesn't matter who I am right now. I'm tired of all this shit," he continued, indicating the group of students with a wave of his hand. "I don't want to argue about some goddamn revolution. I want to be part of it."

The man eyed him with a feigned indifference, uncomfortable that he was being approached in this manner. He started to rise. "I don't know what you're talking about."

Cobb held him with a gentle hand on his arm. "I'll bet you do . . . and I can tell you how to improve that silly disguise." The man allowed himself to be pulled back down to his seat. Cobb smiled. "See. I was right. You're no more a student than I am."

"What do you want?"

"I want to join the forces."

"There's nothing difficult about that." The man's brows were knit in curiosity. "What are you really after?" he added after a momentary pause.

Cobb nodded off in another direction, away from the group. "Let's move away from here so we can talk. Like I said, that disguise of yours is bad enough. You don't want to attract any more attention." He sensed he had the advantage now. Nothing can be so damaging to an individual gathering intelligence as to find himself compromised by a total stranger. Cobb was buying time. They eased away.

"Your time is very short," the man told Cobb when they were out of hearing of the others. "Tell me who you really are." He was regaining partial control of the situation.

"I do want to join up," Cobb began. "I don't want to shoot a rifle like a peasant, though. I want to do your kind of work." Then he cautiously added, "It didn't take me long to figure out who you were."

The man moved away, allowing Cobb to tag along behind him as they crossed the plaza. Cobb went on weaving a story about what he had done in the past and why he wanted to become involved with this man, who eventually identified himself as Luis Calderone. At the far end of the plaza Calderone turned up the main street.

"I want to work with people like you," Cobb persisted as he trotted to move alongside.

Calderone waved him away with an irritated gesture.

"Okay, I'll tell you what," Cobb said. "I understand you're looking for assassination teams. If I were willing to do that, would you consider me?"

Calderone stopped suddenly, turning to face Cobb. "Why are you sure I'm the one who can help you?"

There was no doubt in Cobb's mind. He had overheard

Maria's name mentioned in relation to this man, and it was Maria whom he desperately wanted to locate. "I'm sure. That's why I was waiting on the plaza tonight. I was told I'd find someone like you."

Calderone turned and picked up his purposeful stride again, cautiously aware that this person called Miguel who was tagging along behind him might be as aggressive as he claimed. The PRA had recruited men under stranger conditions in the past. And with the climax nearing, according to his superiors, they were in fact preparing assassination teams. He decided to let this Miguel follow along. When they got to headquarters later in the evening, he would turn Miguel over to security. They would determine whether or not he would fit in. "Come on."

After a block Cobb inquired, "Where are we going?"

"I have to see someone before I take you back to headquarters."

"Oh." He had no intention of asking anything that would make Calderone suspicious. Play it by ear for a while.

Calderone paused at each corner, looking up and down for street signs. Finally he asked Cobb, "Do you know this area?"

Cobb nodded. "Pretty well. What street are you looking for?"

"I'm looking for a house. It's supposed to be an old one set back from the street on Dolorosa, a few doors up from San Blas. The woman I'm looking for moves often. This is my first time there."

Cobb pondered for a moment, then decided to take the chance. This woman had to be Maria. "We're close. Just a few more blocks. Turn left at the next corner." Calderone moved off with his long stride, and Cobb, with no real idea of where they were, followed a few paces behind, waiting for the right moment. It must be done properly—no noise, no witnesses.

Another block up, they crossed the street into an unlighted area. Now was the perfect time. Cobb moved with a quickness and efficiency developed by years of experience. With tremendous force and precision, he chopped Calderone in the back of the neck. In a single, fluid motion, he caught the body, dragging it into a side alley. He bent down, feeling with one hand. There wasn't a doubt in the world. Calderone's neck had snapped perfectly. He removed the man's wallet, pocketing it. He would dump the clothes a few blocks away. In the present political situation a naked body found in a dark alley would simply be carted away to the morgue. There would be no way to trace this corpse back to the university plaza.

Cobb trotted out of the alley with the clothes rolled neatly under his arm, disposing of them in a trash barrel a couple of blocks farther on. Then he headed back to the nearest street light. There he extracted a map from the inside of his shirt. To his surprise, he was very close to San Blas and Dolorosa.

He ran the last few blocks, conserving wind as best he could, though a breathless man with a message would be more acceptable. The house, set back from the street, was easy to identify. He went to the door and banged frantically. His response was a muffled shout from inside followed by approaching footsteps. Then the door was eased open carefully.

A man peered out, keeping it ajar. "What do you want?"

"I have to see Maria," Cobb responded breathlessly. "I was told she was here."

"Who told you that?"

"Calderone!"

"Wait out here." The door shut in his face.

Less than a minute passed before the door was opened cautiously once again. The woman he had seen in the picture with Voronov and Grambling peered out. "I don't know you," she remarked softly both to Cobb and the other man who was behind her. She was about to push the door shut.

"No, please. Wait. I have a message for Paul Voronov. I must get to him."

"Voronov is not here," she said matter-of-factly.

"I know that. But I was told you knew where the captain was," he implored breathlessly, "and I must get this message to him immediately. Please, my life is worthless if I don't get it to Voronov," he added pitifully. His subservience was effective. The two people relaxed. They no longer showed concern for this stranger. "I was told you could help me." Cobb's eyes were pleading.

"I am sorry. Captain Voronov—"

The man behind her pushed her gently aside before she could continue. "Listen, we can't help you. You've come to the wrong place." He looked down at his watch. "You've got thirty seconds to get on your way or—"

Cobb never let him finish the sentence. One hand shot out with incredible speed, jerking the man out through the doorway by the collar. The other, rising in anticipation as the person hurtled toward him, flashed down in a crushing blow behind the right ear.

Before the woman could turn away, Cobb grabbed her roughly by the shirt front. Buttons popped as he rudely yanked her forward. The crude material ripped, baring one of her shoulders. Before she could make a sound, Cobb's open palm whipped across her face. She gasped as her head snapped back. The hand came back across her other cheek, knuckles opening the flesh. Before she could utter a sound, he forced her back inside, pushing the door shut behind.

There was no time to ask questions. There could be others in the house. Cobb knocked her to the floor, falling with her, landing on her back, pulling both her arms back in a crude hammerlock. Holding them with his knees, he dug the blade of his knife into the side of her neck. He drew the blade slightly up, and as blood oozed out of the gash he growled, "Ten seconds . . . that's all you've got to live unless you tell me where Voronov is."

"I don't—" Her words were cut short as Cobb forced her face brutally down into the floor. The knife bit deeper into the neck, blood now flowing freely.

"Five seconds." He yanked her head back up by the hair. "I promise I'll make it slow . . . and painful."

As her head was drawn back sharply, the knife shifted down to her throat. There was definite purpose in his movements. She'd seen it in Voronov before! "He went out to that destroyer!" she gasped.

"What destroyer?" He yanked her head back until she was sure her scalp was lifting.

"I don't know . . . just the one offshore . . . that's all I know . . . please." Agony and fear shrouded her voice. People forgot how to lie at that point.

He let her hair go, slamming her head against the floor with
the flat of his hand. She was motionless as he leaped up. There
was the sound of running feet from another side of the house.
Yanking open the door, he leaped over the body slumped in
the doorway and raced out of the circle of light.

Cobb reached the street as the first shot rang out. He darted
to his left before the second one, then to his right before the
third. Without drawing a breath, he was racing down the
street and out of the line of fire. Running as fast as ever in his
life, he darted down a series of alleyways until he was sure no
one could follow him.

But now he knew!

Paul Voronov was on a destroyer somewhere . . . with
James Grambling. They had been seen leaving Portobelo last
night in a small boat; so that destroyer couldn't have been far
offshore. He doubted any Soviet ships were that close to
Panama. But he understood that Paul Voronov had to be involved in a very special operation. Ryng would be back by
sunrise. Together they could put together the puzzle and figure
exactly what it was that Voronov intended to do.

Dave Pratt would, he knew, be waiting anxiously for
anything over the radio . . . anything that would answer the
riddle of Voronov.

The Destroyer off Colón

Paul Voronov leaned out, stretching over the bridge railing of
the destroyer, peering down the starboard side to the stern. He
smiled to himself, pleased that she looked as much like a
school ship as before, maybe more so now that his style of
discipline had been installed.

The sailors on the forecastle were decked out in white summer uniforms. Only the party hauling the anchor and washing
down the chain as it came through the hawse pipe wore work
clothes. Student uniform caps were obvious to anyone paying
attention to the ship. Whether they were worn by Cubans,

Soviet marines, or students who realized that it was better to cooperate than spend this trip below decks, would never show through binoculars.

Voronov was a natural in the captain's uniform. It fit him perfectly, and he rather favored the visored hat with the gold braid. Years before, he commanded a ship of his own in the Black Sea Fleet, but he'd never been senior enough to warrant the gold. He also had to admit to himself that he liked being back on a bridge again. There was something special about command of a ship, something impossible to describe—it was an experience ingrained in one's soul forever, an integral component of the spirit. He moved quickly through the pilothouse to the port wing, again leaning out.

"The chain is up and down, sir," a talker in the pilothouse called out.

"Very well. Rudder amidships. Tell the engine room to stand by for all bells."

"Aye, aye, sir."

A gusty offshore breeze carried a legion of scents from the city of Colón and gradually pushed the bow a few points to starboard. Voronov called out orders to the helm and engine room. The bow came back around toward the entrance to Colón Harbor.

There was never the slightest concern on shore about the destroyer. Official permission had been granted for the transit well before the ship departed homeport, and the formal permission to get under way had come over the radio early that morning. Merchant ships swung at anchor in Limón Bay, waiting their turn to begin the initial passage to the Gatun Locks. Voronov had the students saluting foreign flags with a fervor. To anyone who might be curious, and there were none, his school ship was setting an example for the young cadets.

His ship's appearance was superb. Voronov had inspected the hull from the ship's whaleboat. He insured that any red-lead showing through the gray was covered. She might still show her years, but not the makeup that masked her aged body. It was truly a performance directed by an expert.

In the magazines and loading rooms in the bowels of the ship, Voronov's marines and Cubans were busy cataloging the ammunition for the forward gun mounts. Armor piercing rounds were separated for the hoists. It would not take long to move them up to the mounts, but Voronov was not a man to take any chances. The possibility always existed that one person might get wind of who really controlled the ship; or, there was even the long-shot chance of an engineering casualty before they arrived at the Pedro Miguel Locks; or there could even be an accident within the Canal itself that would keep them from reaching their goal. If so, he intended to be ready with as much firepower as possible. If for some reason they never reached their main target, his alternatives would be equally impressive.

Booted feet echoed on the ladder coming up to the port wing of the bridge. Seeing Grambling's head appear, Voronov called out, "Hey, Jaimé, how do you like this little ship of ours?" He knew Grambling was uncomfortable.

Grambling looked unhappily at the rusted hull of a freighter they were sliding past, then back to Voronov. "I prefer the comfort of my small boats. I can feel the boat under me then. Here," he shrugged irritably, "I feel helpless."

Voronov smiled. "Soon enough, Jaimé, you and your men may be seeing enough action to take your mind off this ship. When will your men have the defensive positions ready?"

"By noon," Grambling finally muttered irritably. "I'd still be better off doing what I do best." He paused, weighing his words carefully. "This is not a hill to be fortified against an attack, or a beachhead, or a mountain pass. It's a run-down, old piece of junk. It wasn't meant to be defended with pistols and rifles and grenades."

Though a ship could never be a jungle, James Grambling was doing his best to turn the ancient destroyer into a command post that could be held against an armed attack until Voronov could carry out his orders. From the main deck to the superstructure Grambling's men, with the help of Voronov's marines, and even some of the students, had converted the ship to something her designers had never imagined. Bulkheads had been cut out to impede passage or, even more valuable, create fields of fire. Steel plates were welded into position to close passageways. Once the ship was immobile in the Pedro Miguel Locks, Voronov anticipated an assault. He'd explained to Grambling that this ship would have to be defended in the same manner they might defend their jungle camp. He and Grambling would be ready in their specially designed fortress—ready to hold the old ship at least as long as Admiral Khasan needed to bargain for the prize.

"You know," Grambling added, "they could just as well bomb us, and everything we've done won't help one damn bit."

"They can try, Jaimé, but I'm willing to bet they won't. It would be their last resort, and I can't imagine they'd sink this and block their own canal." He knew that Grambling was bitter, and he didn't really blame him. But Voronov was also certain that there probably would be an assault of some kind once they were in position, and it could only be accomplished with specially trained units. Since there weren't enough of his marines, his next best option was using James Grambling, because only he could command those PRA fighters in defending anything as ridiculous as this old scow. It was absolutely critical to his marines, who would be wiring the machinery deep inside the locks, to have this ship controlling the battle on the surface.

Grambling stared moodily across Limón Bay, increasingly uneasy with the ever-expanding Soviet presence. Now, more than ever, he feared for his country and for his revolution.

Havana

Not only was Commodore Navarro totally unaware that he was pacing back and forth in his office, but he also failed to realize that his cigar had been unlit for the last ten minutes. Normally he was a man of reasonable disposition, and that was one of the overlying reasons Fidel Castro had chosen him as both a defense minister and commander of the small Cuban Navy. Even when his fleet began to expand—after the Russians indicated a desire to see more than a tiny coastal patrol force—Navarro maintained his calm personality. Soviet gifts of destroyers, frigates, and guided missile boats were a goal within Castro's overall strategy, and the Commodore grew with it. Though he did not understand submarines, he made a point of taking a three-day cruise aboard the first one when Fidel accepted it as a gift in 1979. Finding he was slightly claustrophobic, he politely declined future trips as others joined his fleet.

There came a day when Navarro learned a bit about humility, but that was never evident to anyone around him. That was the day a Soviet aircraft carrier called on Havana, escorted by a guided missile cruiser and an even newer guided missile destroyer. He did pay a courtesy call to each ship and agreed to an informal tour of them, but there was never an outward indication that he was impressed. However, that day changed his mind forever. He did thank the Soviet admiral for the invitation to spend a few days at sea aboard the carrier, but explained that the demands on his time were excessive and he must decline until a future visit to Havana.

It was that same day, after his polite decline of the Soviet offer, that he went to Fidel Castro and explained that the Russians were doing them no favors at all. Rather, they were unloading undesirable hardware on the Cubans as an affront to the United States and a balm to Cuban ego. There was no way, he continued, that the Americans could be impressed with the growth of the Cuban Navy, other than as an irritant to be put up with. The Soviets, as far as he was concerned, were giving away nothing of value.

In retrospect, as Navarro now paced his office, his mind awhirl with a multitude of problems, he realized that was probably as much a day of awakening for Castro as it was for him. It was then that they began to analyze their part in overall Soviet strategy in the Caribbean. When the Americans realigned the government in Grenada, both men realized that an unspoken but obvious part of this Soviet strategy was to have Cuban troops do the dirty work in the Caribbean, in exchange for what Castro and Navarro once felt was a menacing fleet. But because those gifts were all related to economic aid and Cuban troop presence, and the Cuban economy would cease to exist without the Russians, Navarro learned humility, and he was certain that Castro did also, though neither man ever mentioned it.

Today the calm and unruffled Navarro was as nervous as a hen because the harbor was empty. Once again he had been forced to acknowledge the place of the Cuban Navy in the overall strategy, and he also understood his place in the picture. This was unacceptable to Commodore Navarro, and he had voiced his dissatisfaction to Fidel that morning. Perhaps it had been the first time he had ever raised his voice in that manner to his old comrade, and Castro, too, had lost his temper. They shouted at each other. When it was over and Navarro had stomped out of the Premier's office, he was thirty steps down the hall before he heard his friend's voice call him back.

They then drank coffee together and smoked a first cigar of

the day. Castro's words were calming. He insisted that the Russians were there to insure that the United States did not interfere in matters that were not their concern. Yet he failed to refer to the statement the previous day by the American Secretary of State—that Central America was the umbilical cord that united North and South America, and that the Caribbean nurtured the entire hemisphere; furthermore, problems within that area were mutual problems of the countries of that hemisphere, and foreign intervention was totally unacceptable. Navarro pointed out that the language of that statement was as specific as any pronouncement from Washington in the past twenty years. That was why, he was sure, the Russians preferred to utilize the Cuban Navy for the Caribbean expedition in Panama. If it failed, it would be the Cubans who failed, not the Russians, who did not directly interfere. Once again, just as in Grenada, the Cubans would be doing the fighting.

As a favor to Castro he had gone on the Soviet carrier the day before. "Please do it for me. Don't insult them," the Premier had requested. Navarro had not wanted to insult Admiral Khasan, who had grown to be the only Russian he cared to call a friend over the past couple of years. To the commander of a coastal patrol force that day on *Kharkov* had been an experience he would never forget. But, of more importance, he came away understanding the true meaning of power—and its limits, or lack of them.

Now, observing the empty harbor, unable to erase that question concerning the limits of power from his mind, the normally calm, perceptive Navarro was experiencing a roiling in the pit of his stomach and a thumping in his chest that had never been there before. His first duty—was it to Cuba or to his Premier?

The empty harbor loomed large before his eyes. There were a variety of water craft out there, freighters and tankers and fishing boats. But the piers and anchorages where the Cuban and Russian military ships had been were vacant. To Commodore Navarro that meant that Cuba was essentially defenseless!

He halted in midstride, realizing what he was doing—pacing like a caged animal. Navarro had been totally unaware of his reaction to this paradox. It was as if he had just awoken from a bad dream. But it was no dream, and he knew what had brought him back to the world of here and now. It was a pain deep in his gut, and the pounding of his heart. He couldn't tell whether it was real or imaginary. It flowed and ebbed, now intense, now a memory. Was it real? Never before had he experienced any physical reaction to the weight of his responsibilities. Was this what it all came down to? Would something other than his violent profession claim him?

Navarro threw open the window looking out to the harbor and sucked in the fresh air in great gulps. It was similar to slapping himself with a wet cloth. My God, he asked himself out loud, do you realize how your mind was wandering? What you were thinking of one old comrade and one new friend, Castro and Khasan? Or, even more ridiculous, that you thought it was affecting you physically? Another twinge of pain shot through his gut, and he realized there was at least one thing that he had not imagined.

Then he heard a low roar, increasing perceptibly in volume as his mind raced to identify it, coming from the mouth of the harbor. No more than a second or two in real time was required to recognize that it was the sound of jet planes before he saw them, four to be exact, racing down the harbor. They were no more than fifty feet in the air, just above the spars of the freighters, and they came at an incredible speed. It seemed for a moment as if they were going to fly directly into his window. But they banked following the midline of the harbor, increasing their altitude as they passed over the buildings at the edge of the city. There was no problem in identifying them. They were from that new squadron at Cecil Field in Florida. He saw the star on the fuselage just under the cockpit and the word *Navy* was clearly visible as they banked and climbed away, the sound following them with a deafening thunderclap. Then they were gone—American attack planes . . . Hornets! Yet he had seen no missiles under the wings. Somehow they had come at sea level, racing below Cuban radar capabilities . . . apparently unarmed! The message was ominous.

Only a matter of seconds had passed. The jets were gone, invisible now to the naked eye, though the exhaust trail was still visible in the clear sky. Then he was moving, racing down the hall to General Martinez's office. Other doors opened at the same time, familiar faces emerging, heading in the same direction. When Navarro entered, others had arrived before him and were strangely silent. Martinez stood at the window, his back to them, unmoving. His aide circulated slowly among the gathering crowd, whispering, and Navarro could overhear him saying, "Yes . . . American . . . Premier Castro received a direct call from Washington fifteen minutes ago . . . assuring they were unarmed . . . any attack on them would mean immediate retaliation. No, we don't know what it means yet. . . ."

But Navarro knew exactly what it meant. It was a show of force, and he was sure those American planes came in over the water at supersonic speeds to show Castro and Martinez and Navarro and anyone else who was capable of understanding that it could all be over very quickly. This wasn't a Cuban affair, nor was it really Panamanian or Honduran or any other Central American problem. It was much bigger, and this was a warning that the two superpowers were involved.

Navarro again felt that twinge of pain. Power . . . superpower . . . limits of power . . . were there any? He bolted from Martinez's office. He had to see Fidel, had to tell him of what he had been thinking. His little navy was being used, and shortly there would be nothing left of it.

Lydia Khasan also heard the thunder of the four Hornets as they roared down Havana's empty harbor. Frightened, she rolled over hastily, one elbow in the sand, the other shielding her eyes.

She'd awakened that morning to a hot, clear day and realized almost from the moment her eyes opened that all she really cared to do right then was to sun on the beach. After a glass of fresh juice and a few bites of toast, she'd strolled out to the water's edge in her bikini, carrying only a towel and a thermos of coffee.

For a few minutes she soothed her feet in the cool water, occasionally stopping to inspect a seashell. Lifting her sunglasses to study something on the horizon, she became acutely aware that she really was suffering from a hangover. It was a feeling she hadn't experienced in years, and one she was now sure wouldn't happen again for many more.

Because the sensations in her head and her stomach remained so unpleasant, she was forced to consider the previous night. It had been revenge against Victor's dalliances—especially that bitch, Chita Monteria—but it had not been sweet. Somehow, if Victor had been home instead of at sea when she returned last night, she probably would have sent the Cuban officer home. But that was not the way things turned out. She had invited him in and then had been disappointed that the invitation was obviously something he expected. He was as drunk as she was and had no interest in the after dinner drink she offered him. Instead, he was ready to get down to what he had been anticipating since she had introduced herself to him a few days before on the beach.

A clear picture of that meeting flashed through her head. At the time it had seemed the right thing. It was right after her big fight with Victor, and another man—any man—seemed the logical way to strike back at him. The Cuban was very handsome, and she could tell he at least appreciated her looks by the eager way he studied her in her bathing suit. She welcomed the attention. So last night she met him at a downtown restaurant and they had proceeded to get quite drunk.

She didn't find the Cuban especially interesting, but he was physically appealing. And, she concluded now, that's more than likely exactly what he thought of her also, though there was nothing in their lovemaking that greatly appealed to her.

Whatever she felt about it, though, she realized it was not something she intended to do again soon. She shaded her eyes against the brilliance of the day to search for the source of that racket and saw them, four American jet planes, racing out from the city, climbing. She had seen pictures of them before in Victor's books. She couldn't remember what they were called but it made no difference anyway—not as long as you knew they were American and considered them the enemy.

As they roared overhead, passing out to sea in a wink, she became aware of both the increasing headache and the fact that she had completely forgotten the top of her bikini when she rolled over. Looking over her shoulder now, she gazed at the tiny wisp of cloth. She had opened the single button right after she sank on the beach towel, face down, with a groan. Then she looked down at her body. If Victor had been there, she knew he would have been appreciative. The tan lines around her breasts stood out in a bold relief. There was almost nothing to the brief bottoms.

Yes, Lydia Khasan thought, Victor would have been more appreciative. Why the hell did they have to have that fight before he left? Admit it, she murmured silently, you aren't cut out for that sort of thing. Would Victor have wandered like that if you had been different? She didn't know the answer; she had no idea whether it was she or Victor who was weak. But she did know that she would welcome Victor back when he returned from sea.

Lydia buried her head facedown in the towel and wept silently. I hope . . . I hope above everything in the world that those American planes don't mean what I think they do. And if so, she prayed silently, let Victor come back alive. If he did, she would insist they leave Havana . . . go back home where they belonged. They would be happy back home. They would. This wasn't their world, and they didn't belong here.

The Western Atlantic

On that same day there was no warning phone call concerning a flyover to the partially assembled Soviet task force to the east, still not fully assembled. Nor did Admiral Pratt deem it necessary to inform them. There was as yet no state of war, and flyovers frequently occurred in the North Atlantic, the Sea of Japan, the Mediterranean, anywhere U.S. and Soviet forces operated. It was often a test of the opposition's defenses as much as an exercise in penetrating those defenses. Since probes of this nature could come at any time, it was doubly advantageous to senior commanders to learn how their crews operated under these conditions.

Soviet picket ships were the first to paint the low flyers screaming in just a few feet above the ocean surface; occasional unidentified blips on their *radar* screens were enough to sound a warning. The carrier *Kharkov* scrambled Yak Forgers, Vertical Takeoff and Landing (VTOL) aircraft, to intercept the incoming aircraft. So low were the approaching jets, and so fast, that the Soviet radar was still unsure of exactly what they were tracking.

For the Forgers it was a hopeless cause. The speed of the American and Russian jets approaching each other was near Mach 3, almost three times the speed of sound. To locate the low flyers on radar would be one thing, to actually identify them with the naked eye was another; an impossible situation. To even turn and come alongside, the Forgers had to commence their turns a hundred miles before the other jets were on top of them. Then it was a matter of trying to catch a plane passing at double their speed.

The Hornets remained at twenty-five feet above the surface of the Caribbean until they were within thirty seconds of the carrier. Then they climbed to just above bridge level, one passing on each side, two directly down the length of the flight deck. Then they, too, were gone, sweeping out and up with a roar which penetrated to the engine rooms of the carrier.

Similar flyovers occurred with Soviet ships in other areas, but they had the advantage of receiving immediate messages that the American planes were approaching. Yet it was still difficult for even the most advanced radar to consistently locate and track an aircraft flying close to the surface of the water at 1500 miles per hour. Those able to track went through the exercise of alerting missile crews and putting computers through the paces.

There were other Soviet captains who, like the commander of the submarine *Leninets*, had survived the horror of the Battle of the Mediterranean and were more than anxious to even the score. They were not affected by the mental pressure that eventually touches submariners, but they were spoiling for a fight. For two of them the final port of call had been in the Canaries. In a bar in Las Palmas, where they became extremely drunk and mourned for lost comrades, they talked of their orders. Both ships were in the same squadron, or would be, when they once again rendezvoused east of the Bahamas. Together they were to pass through the Northeast (north of Spanish Wells) and Northwest Providence Channels to take station between Freeport and Boca Raton. They would be part of the task group intended to interdict any American ships attempting to use the Florida Straits.

On that morning, they were cruising in company about thirty miles east of Eleuthera. There was every reason to expect that the Americans would be shadowing them. Both captains, therefore, agreed they would exercise their crews at general quarters one hour after first light.

One ship was a Udaloy-class guided missile destroyer. The Russian word *Udaloy* meant "courageous," and the captain and crew of that ship, *Vitse Admiral Kulakov*, intended to uphold the reputation of the WW II hero. Though intended for anti-submarine work, *Kulakov* was armed with surface-to-air missiles and her captain expected his ship to be as dangerous to air as to undersea attack.

The other was an older guided missile ship, a Kashin-class, *Krasnyy Krym*, which had actually sailed through the midst of the missile blitz in the second hour of the Battle of the Mediterranean without damage. Designed to counter air attack, she was a compliment to *Kulakov*'s anti-submarine capabilities. Together they provided a formidable team.

Both ships approached their early morning exercises with a zeal that comes with the realization their weapons could be used at any moment. They began by tracking small private and commercial aircraft using the airstrips at North Eleuthera and Rock Sound. A few of the larger yachts and fishing boats in the area offered low speed surface tracking opportunities. But there was little thrill in feeding a missile computer information on a target that could be tracked by the naked eye.

It was no more than half an hour after their crews were closed up at stations that the initial reports of American jets were intercepted. Cessnas and Otters and cabin cruisers and sport fishermen were forgotten in the excitement of real targets. The announcements over the PAs on both ships created an electric charge in the atmosphere. Goa missile launchers fore and aft on *Krasnyy Krym* spun about on their barbettes, dual missile arms alternately elevating ninety degrees, as if a new missile were slipping onto the launcher arms. Then, launchers whirling about once again, the arms assumed whatever angle the computer ordered.

Aboard *Vitse Admiral Kulakov* the crew responded in the same manner, though there was no old-fashioned missile launcher. Instead, her missiles were embedded in a vertical launcher within the hull. More technically advanced, her exercises were completed by highly trained technicians in sealed compartments, who monitored advanced computers. It was a matter of electronic impulses traveling through a complex system to the devices that would rocket the missiles vertically to a safe distance. They would then alter their own direction to seek out the assigned target.

Both ships also increased their speed to thirty-four knots and commenced evasive maneuvers. Anti-missile defenses were activated and the excitement of the moment negated any fear that might have existed. There was simply no time. American Hornets might be bearing down on them at any moment, closing at supersonic speeds, ready to launch air-to-surface missiles. Time passed without notice.

The older ship's Big Net was the only long range, air search radar. She picked up the first jets at almost a hundred-mile range. They were caught as they dove from their fuel saving altitude down to the surface for their in-run. Even at that distance they would be on top of the two Russian ships in less than five minutes and within missile range before that.

That preliminary information was fed into the computers to assist air search and fire control radars scanning their next projected positions. The exercise was totally realistic. Protective covers over *Vitse Admiral Kulakov*'s vertical missile launchers rolled back to reveal pointed nose cones peeping from their cannisters. *Krasnyy Krym*'s launchers wheeled about. Launcher arms elevated straight up and down over magazines. Sleek, shiny missiles shot onto the rails. Both launchers, fore and aft, wheeled about to the direction of the approaching menace. Their arms lowered to a point above the horizon. Target information flowed into missile computers.

Electronic warfare systems were activated, creating dummy targets or processing signals to jam target acquisition radars on the approaching jets. The Hornets would be armed with smart bombs, whose intent was to create uncertainty for the attackers until the last minute—until a surface ship could put a missile up for defense.

With just a minute to go, the Hornets were reacquired by the radar. Fire control reported lock-on. Electronic circuits transmitted pulses of correct information to the poised missiles. Gunnery reported ready to the captain of *Vitse Admiral Kulakov*, the senior officer.

"Fire!" The order was received instantaneously aboard *Krasnyy Krym*. There was a burst of smoke and flame from one missile on each of her launchers, followed by a deafening roar as two missiles leaped skyward. *Kulakov*'s bow was enveloped in a cloud of smoke. Then a single missile emerged, surging straight up from her vertical launchers. Her captain registered a split-second image of the missile as it curved over almost to the horizontal, disappearing behind its own exhaust cloud.

The Hornet and Intruder missions that morning were to overfly their targets in a visible show of force, to leave no doubt in the minds of military or civilians that the United States was completely prepared to face any challenge. Admiral Pratt acknowledged from the beginning that there was no way that each aircraft could arrive at its assigned target at the same moment as all the others. Word would necessarily be passed by the Russians to all units so that some would be anticipating the American planes.

Vitse Admiral Kulakov and *Krasnyy Krym* probably had more notice than most of the others. Beyond that, there certainly had been no indication of any kind concerning hostilities. But because the U.S. flyovers were provocative and these two Soviet ships were looking for any possible excuse, the Russians fired. Well before the missiles locked on their targets, new ones were poised and ready.

But there was no reason to expend additional weaponry. The Hornet's warning devices did activate; their on-board computers did recognize the threat; decisions were implemented electronically; chaff was fired to decoy the approaching missiles; evasive action orders were transmitted to the controls; and the pilots recognized the threat soon after the computer reacted.

If they had been in an attack mode, there would have been more opportunities generated to survive. At this stage, however, it was already too late. Both Hornets disappeared in a burst of flame and metal shards, their speed tearing apart whatever the missile blasts missed.

The School of the Americas, Panama Canal Zone

Neither Cobb nor Ryng were as yet aware of the hostilities developing in the Atlantic. Their concern was centered on the ship-scheduling list Kitty had just brought in for the Canal that day.

"It doesn't make sense to me. How about you?" Ryng asked.

Cobb looked at the list again. "A school ship?" He was just as confused. "What the hell would Voronov want with something like that?"

"I honestly didn't know any of them were still afloat." Ryng was familiar with the ship. It was an old American Sumner-class destroyer whose keel had been laid during World War II. He'd once spent a year and a half aboard a sister ship, and even back then it had been considered her last days. He looked at the chart on the wall. "What was her berth, before she received permission to transit the Gatun Locks?"

"Stayed well outside the breakwaters off Colón," Kitty answered. "Her captain had asked permission to remain offshore rather than come into the harbor, so that he could put men over the side to scrape and paint—a school ship, you know. Show your best even if you're just passing a bunch of rusty freighters."

"That probably explains the boat they took out of Portobelo," Cobb mused.

"Do you have a ship's roster of officers, Kitty?"

"I've already looked it over. I don't know much about this sort of thing, but there's no reason to doubt the officers . . . if they're still alive."

"Where would she be now?"

Ryng checked his watch, then scratched some figures on a scrap of paper. He moved over to the wall chart of the Canal and stepped off the expected path of advance along the central channel. "Lower part of Gatun Lake." He made a wide circle with a grease pencil. "Right about here if she's moving at normal speed."

"Any idea how long normal speeds can be held?"

"If she's where Bernie estimates, not more than another hour . . . maybe less," answered Kitty. "Once a ship gets near Las Cascadas, it's a matter of getting in line and proceeding according to orders."

Cobb studied the chart from the desk. "I'm going to get some pictures." He called Southern Command (SOCOM), the U.S. military headquarters in Panama, for an intelligence overflight. Then he turned to Kitty, "What would you say is the most vulnerable part of the Canal?"

"From whose point of view?"

"Let's say that I'm the one who commands that destroyer. If I wanted to threaten the Canal itself—not ruin it forever, because I wanted to be able to continue using it—but I wanted to be in a place where no one could stop me, a place where if they came after me I could ruin everything . . . so they'd have to wait to see what I was going to do. . . ."

"The Pedro Miguel Locks are the most critical . . . by far," she offered, running her finger along the line of the Canal. "Miraflores empties into the Bahia, and Miraflores Lake is on the other side . . . but the Pedro Miguel is narrow at both ends, and the steepest drop. But what does it matter? Every lock is critical. Any damage would close the Canal."

"I'll bet access to Miraflores is a lot easier than Pedro Miguel," Ryng answered.

"It's mostly jungle leading to Pedro Miguel, although the road runs all the way along the Canal. You can get there easily enough. That's how the workers get back and forth."

"I'll bet there are perfect spots for machine gun teams where it would take a small army to break through," Cobb replied. "See if you can get some topographic maps of the area . . . something that will be useful to helicopter gunships."

"Why don't we take that ship out right now?" Ryng asked.

"We could be wrong. Imagine what would happen if we not only closed the Canal by sinking a ship in it, but that ship was an innocent from a friendly nation. We can't do that." He sighed. "By the time we really know, she'll probably be in the

Culebra Cut," he pointed, "and close enough to charge right into the northern lock. If we'd figured this out earlier, we might have put them under in Gatun Lake." He looked at Ryng with a bemused expression on his face. "If you remember what you were doing at that time, there wasn't much you could do about that ship—if I recall your wild story correctly, the two of you were skinny dipping—"

Ryng interrupted, mocking Cobb's expression. "This guy Voronov knows what he's doing, and he's been at it a long time—he's what you might call an expert, Kitty. What your friend President Ramos doesn't understand is that these are not peasant revolutionaries now. They're professionals who get paid to do things efficiently. There's almost never any room for luck. They leave bodies behind them." He turned to Cobb. "How would you stop that destroyer?"

"Without ruining the Canal?"

"Correct . . . without ruining the Canal," Ryng echoed.

"Past experience calls for SEALs. I doubt anyone else could—" Cobb interrupted himself, the answer already obvious. "I'm scheduled to talk to Pratt shortly," He glanced at his watch. "I'm going to have him airlift at least one team. Maybe San Diego can provide us with another. You arrange with SOCOM to get them everything they need."

There was a knock at the door and a sailor stuck his head in. "Mr. Cobb, I have that frequency set up now. Anytime . . ." Henry Cobb followed the sailor out of the room without a word.

When he returned, he looked a bit pale. "I was more right than I thought, Kitty. The shooting's already started, a little ahead of schedule . . . but the ones who are doing it are the Russians. We need permission to bring in our teams, and maybe to use military force. You've got to get in to see President Ramos."

Cobb explained over a map of the Caribbean how Pratt expected the scenario to fall into place. Much of what Pratt saw was still theory, but everything leading up to it had actually taken place just as predicted. Satellite photos showed the Soviet warships approaching Panama from the Pacific side and the small force of Cuban naval ships that would arrive on the northern side in the Caribbean before nightfall. If she could convince Ramos to listen, he promised that SOCOM would provide copies of the satellite pictures as soon as they were relayed.

At Sea North of Windward Passage

Captain Lou Eberhardt of the destroyer *Stump* and Captain G. A. Fitin of the Soviet submarine that could not shake her shadow, possessed increasingly divergent pictures of exactly what was developing in the Caribbean conflict. Fitin was following a set of written orders, promulgated before he ever arrived on station. Since departing Punta Munda he had no news of any other part of the operation. He supposed that if there was anything of value to relay to him, it would have been sent during the normal communications period each day when he extended his antenna. On the other hand, Eberhardt was privvy to the entire operation as it unfolded. Not moments before, his radio shack intercepted a message reporting wreckage and survivors. It was followed by a second message indicating that only seven survivors had been located from the frigate *Thomas C. Hart*. All were enlisted; there appeared to be no others.

Lou Eberhardt mumbled something to his Gold Team OOD to the effect that he was going to make a surprise inspection of the ship's watertight integrity. What he really intended to do was find some place aboard the ship where no one could possibly find him and see if he still had the ability to cry. Billy Haggerty had been the CO of *Hart*; Billy Haggerty had also been his closest friend, as close as anyone could be in a career where you often didn't see a friend for two or three years, keeping in touch only by the transfer orders printed in the *Navy Times*.

Eberhardt and Haggerty had been roommates at the Academy. After graduation they'd gone separate directions, one to the Atlantic, one to the Pacific. Somehow they had kept in touch long enough to wangle similar orders to Destroyer School in Newport. After that they were both department heads on destroyers in the same squadron. Their luck held when the squadron deployed to the Mediterranean for the summer and the two bachelors hit the best liberty ports like college boys—Spain, France, Italy, Malta, Greece. But it was the last party. Eventually new orders separated them. The next phase was growing up and marrying. Then it was the Haggerty and the Eberhardt families enjoying life together whenever duty stations brought them close.

Since their early days at Annapolis, everything between them had been a contest—whether it was the choicest orders or the fastest promotion. Part of the fun of being best friends was the competition. But there was never much difference between them. Billy Haggerty had gotten command ahead of Eberhardt, but six months later Lou received orders as CO of a larger ship. Only once since becoming commanding officers had they seen each other. That had been less than a month before, when *Hart* called in Norfolk and the two of them had gotten happily drunk in Lou Eberhardt's living room, recounting stories about classmates spread all over the world.

Now Billy Haggerty was dead.

Back on the stern Eberhardt sat down on a winch and stared back through *Stump*'s white, foamy wake. The tears would not come, but the memories of almost twenty years, from the first day they met as plebes, flooded his mind. Bancroft Hall, the USS *Neversink*, middy cruises, ports in the Orient and the Mediterranean and Scandinavia, older ships with guns before newer ships with missiles, beautiful girls laughing and talking with exotic accents, stormswept seas, cold nights before fireplaces with kids—a lifetime, his and Billy Haggerty's, swept before him. The last picture before his eyes was a snapshot— Billy's wife and three kids.

Then he heard the words boom over the PA, "Captain to the bridge . . . Captain to the bridge . . ." He was on his feet and running before the second phrase had finished. As he burst into the pilothouse, Lieutenant Taron was already issuing orders to his team. "Almost got fooled for a moment there, Captain. The submarine decided to pull the plug and drop down a little deeper . . . fired noisemakers at the same time, and now she's evading, or trying to. We've still got a solid contact but it was touch and go for a moment."

Lou Eberhardt thought about the first message that morning from Admiral Pratt:

Conflict on an individual or combined basis may be anticipated at any time. All units are authorized to take any means to protect themselves. If at any time a unit commander has reason to believe that an attack on his unit is imminent, he may use his own discretion.

Stump's captain no longer had the least doubt that the Soviet submarine he had been tracking for so long was attempting to position itself to fire—just as one must have been when *Hart* was sunk with no warning at all. There was no way to determine when a submarine was about to torpedo you. You just had to assume that when it deterred from its customary habits it was about to send you to kingdom come.

"Range to target?" Eberhardt called out.

"Five five zero zero yards, bearing zero four seven."

"Course and speed?"

"Course is erratic . . . southwest . . . speed nine knots . . . almost a corkscrew course, Captain. Turns toward us, then away. It may be the noisemakers in the water that are confusing us down here," a voice from sonar reported.

"Sound general quarters. Prepare for an ASROC attack."

"Attack, Captain?" asked the startled OOD, as the quartermaster sounded the GQ alarm.

"That is correct. I have every reason to believe that our friend may be preparing to attack." Eberhardt's eyes flashed as he returned Lieutenant Taron's gaze. "It's already happened once today." The GQ alarm echoed through the ship.

"Will you be running the attack from CIC, sir?"

"Negative. The ASW officer can handle it in his sleep." He paused, staring sightlessly toward the horizon. "I want to see that bird fly. Then I want to see it hit the water. I want to hear a rumble . . . and I want to see the water boil out there." His voice was unnatural, brittle. The tone was one that none of the men on the bridge had ever heard from their captain before. It was spoken in a monotone, devoid of expression. "Then I want to steam over there and I want to see oil and wreckage come to the surface." The last words increased in intensity, pronounced one by one with anger. His gaze seemed to pass right through the shocked lieutenant.

"Yes, sir," the OOD responded awkwardly.

Below the surface Captain Fitin rubbed his eyes in exhaustion. He tried to imagine what he *wouldn't* give for just a few hours of uninterrupted sleep. To add to the misery, the air conditioning system in the boat was operating erratically. There were blasts of air, always warm at first as it started up, followed by cool drafts flowing from the vents. Such relief rarely lasted more than a few minutes before the welcome hum of the blowers died and they were once again soaking in the fetid, dank humidity that was the environment of the submarine.

Fitin's eyes ached, sore around the edges from too much nervous rubbing. Salty perspiration only made him more uncomfortable. What he really needed, and what he couldn't have, was a run on the surface—a chance to open the hatches and let in fresh air. What he felt lucky about was his fine crew. They had every reason to complain, but there wasn't a complainer in the lot. They suffered silently with their captain. The only difference between them all at this stage was that the men, even their officers, could relieve each other for periods of time and rest. For Fitin, however, there was no respite; the responsibility was his and his alone. He had accepted it and now he must live under the strain, set an example for his crew. It was becoming more difficult.

Half an hour before, he realized that this could very likely be *that* day, the day orders would come authorizing them to sink their shadows. There was no time like the present, he decided, to attempt to improve his situation. All night they had cruised slowly, reversing course along a line he laid out on the chart near their assigned station. Always, always there was the ever-present ping of the destroyer's sonar intruding on them. Why not lead the destroyer on a merry chase? If he couldn't evade the ship above, he could at least place it at a disadvantage. And it would be an encouragement to his crew. Why not let them hone their skills one more time before . . . before he planted his torpedoes into the hull of 978—one forward of the bridge under the ASROC launcher, the other aft of the stack under the helicopter deck!

There wasn't a great deal of water under the hull, Fitin noticed—maybe seven or eight hundred meters at most. He would not take her below five hundred—though on second thought he could chance six hundred if he could find another one of those temperature gradients. The exercise commenced with his standard procedure—take her down before increasing speed, take the first course change only after they were at ordered speed and fire a noisemaker before making the second course change. Fitin, after all, was dogmatic; he had never been one of the more imaginative submariners, which was why he now commanded a diesel submarine instead of undergoing nuclear training and commanding one of the new-construction attack boats. After four course changes he would be ready to turn back on the destroyer and commence his first attack pattern. . . .

As the submarine commenced the third leg of its pattern, Eberhardt called down to his ASW officer. "He'll make one more course change and try to work his way out on our beam, then turn in for a shot. I don't want him on that final course for more than thirty seconds before you fire that first rocket."

"Aye, aye, sir. I'm going to feed a preliminary solution by hand just to see if he follows that pattern. We'll be ready." The rhythmic ping of the sonar could be heard in the background as the ASW officer's voice came over the intercom. The button had been taped down for instant communication between them, since Eberhardt chose to remain on the bridge.

The day was bright and clear. A hot sun reflected off the water. Eberhardt squinted through his dark glasses at an imaginary point about five thousand yards off his starboard bow. As if his eyes were shut tight, he imagined the outline of a submarine swimming into his vision. As it came toward him, the features grew sharper—the tall sail and conning tower, the bow planes, the blunt nose tapering back slowly. He could almost see inside the double hull where the Russian sailors were poised at their stations, and then there was her captain, intent on culminating his attack. Eberhardt saw the outer doors open to expose evil-looking torpedoes nestled in their tubes. He could see the captain staring intently at his watch, counting off the seconds to fire.

"He's made his turn, Captain, at four six five zero yards. . . ."

"Do you have a solution?" Eberhardt interrupted, his voice high with tension.

"Yes, sir," the voice crackled back over the intercom. "I have a solution."

"Fire!" Lou Eberhardt's eyes had been locked on the launcher directly below and in front of the bridge. Fascinated, he had been watching as the large rectangular box pivoted about jerkily in the target's direction, jockeying about until it settled on the exact angle the computer ordered. Simultaneously, one section of the box elevated to the precise angle for the rocket's flight. All of this had been accomplished in an instant, well before the ASW officer had reported a solution or Eberhardt ordered him to fire.

Now, the men on the bridge gazed in wonder as a rocket-propelled torpedo leaped from the launcher, the roar of the rocket engine coinciding with the flame and smoke emitted from its tail. The rocket sped skyward, reaching its apex in seconds. The engine and airframe broke away. The torpedo poised for an instant, then a white parachute fluttered open as it fell to the sea, a very long, slender messenger from *Stump*.

"Sonar reports torpedo has activated, sir," came the shout over the intercom.

Eberhardt turned to Lieutenant Taron. "Bring that helo," he said, pointing to one of his LAMPS helos circling a few miles from the submarine's location, "in near the contact. Tell him I will limit my ASROC to that one shot for now. I want him to dip his sonar and report back everything he hears over that." Eberhardt pointed at a speaker just inside the pilothouse door. "Have radio patch his circuit in there. I want to hear what happens to that son of a bitch."

"Submarine has decoys in the water, sir . . . they're masking the torpedo's run . . . no, I can hear it again . . . faintly. . . ." A jumble of sound filled the background as the voice reported the sonar "still running . . . wow! . . . listen to those screws.

He's trying to evade, Captain . . . running as fast as he can. . . ."

To the men on the bridge with Eberhardt, it was as if they were watching a movie. The excited voice over the intercom and the background noise from beneath the ocean surface combined to create an image before their eyes as they stared across the placid blue water at a point more than four thousand yards away. There, a few hundred feet below the surface, approximately seventy men were involved in a race for their lives as an acoustic homing torpedo, moving at a much higher speed than they were, was guided by the sound of their own boat's propellers frantically thrashing the water.

Fitin did not hear the splash as the American torpedo entered the water, but there was no doubt throughout the submarine as the sonar operator screamed "Torpedo in the water!" as loudly as he could. He repeated the words again and again, his voice rising in pitch, until there could be no doubt in anyone's mind that they were under attack.

In a voice just as loud Captain Fitin bellowed, "All ahead flank . . . hard right rudder . . ." Should he increase his depth? Or move toward the surface? He mentally scanned all the information he had been fed for years about the operational capabilities of American torpedoes. What would confuse them the most? "More noisemakers," he bellowed. These would be acoustic torpedoes, homing on the sound of his screws—he must create as many sounds as possible. To his diving officer he ordered, "I want a down angle . . . as sharp as you can make it."

"What depth, sir?" the man's eyes were like saucers, and as they held Fitin's, the captain knew that each man aboard the submarine possessed that same fear and carried that same total dependency on him . . . their captain.

"Level off at fifty feet from the bottom . . . your judgment!" he added.

"The rudder is hard right, sir. Do you have a course?" Again, fear, this time in the voice. Fitin's senses were acute as fear came to him in every manner—sight, sound, smell, yes, even smell. He knew someone had lost control, and he sincerely hoped it wasn't him.

"No course . . . tight circle . . ." Was that voice, now calm, no longer shouting, his own? What more could be done? He was in a corkscrew, going down at increasing speed in a tight circle. Nothing more could be done. It was all luck now—and then there was a tremendous explosion. The lights flickered out. As he was thrown off his feet by the blast, Fitin could tell by the sounds around him that the impact was affecting both men and machinery. All was noise and chaos, men screamed in terror. Were they hurt or just frightened? It amazed him during that immeasurable instant that he could still think and rationalize at this stage. Then he hit the deck hard and could feel the submarine sliding off at an angle. The deck was decidedly tilted in a different direction than it had been seconds ago. He could smell electrical smoke. Is this, he thought as he struggled to get to his knees against the wildly careening submarine's downward motion, the way it's going to end?

"We have an explosion!" The deep rumbling could be heard over the intercom along with the cheering from sonar. Never before had these men fired in anger, and now, their first time, they had a hit.

"What bearing? I need a bearing!" Eberhardt shouted back.

"I'd say about zero four five, sir . . . that's the best I can guess. It's all over the scope down here," came from sonar.

"Come to that bearing," Eberhardt ordered Lieutenant Taron. "I want to see oil and I want to see wreckage." His binoculars were fixed on an approximation of that spot as he gave his orders to the OOD. His helo hovered in the same vicinity, the sonar ball descending from its underside.

The seconds passed interminably as Eberhardt waited for some report. Was that the submarine they'd hit or had one of the noisemakers set off the warhead? It seemed unlikely to him. It was a surprise attack—the sub couldn't go too deep. The fish just about entered the water on top of him, the waiting gnawed at him. He could feel his fingers intermittently tighten and then relax around the binoculars, and he couldn't stop them. It was an uncontrolled reflex.

And then he saw the ocean boiling in just about the spot he had anticipated. "What does the helo see?" he called out, and was interrupted by the pilot's voice over the speaker just inside the pilothouse door.

"I'm right over the spot now . . . can't see anything yet . . . wait, maybe that's a little oil . . . nothing else . . . can't pick up anything listening . . . it's a mess down there. . . ."

The men on the surface waited. They were not afraid now. They knew that even if the submarine had survived the blast, it would either be trying to patch itself or take at least preliminary evasion until it could disappear or fight back.

"I've got something, Captain." It was the ASW officer over the intercom. "I think I can hear the screwbeat . . . only one though . . . those boats have three shafts . . . it's very weak and slow. . . ." There was a long pause, then he added, "It doesn't sound right to me. I'd say we hit him . . . but something's still moving down there."

They were just about on top of the spot now. The roiling, bubbling water had now smoothed out to a fine, milky subsistence, the surface flat in comparison to the wind-whipped ripples beyond. Eberhardt strained his eyes for the proof he wanted, but there was nothing to satisfy him beyond a bit of oil that spread out on the surface in various spots. From what he could gather, from what he saw, plus the reports from the helo and sonar, the submarine was hurt. One of the fuel tanks was probably leaking, but it wasn't dead yet. Those oil slicks could even be discharged by the submarine to decoy him.

The *Stump* was now turning in a wide circle about five hundred yards beyond the spot. "Ask the helo if he has contact yet."

The answer came over the speaker. "Affirmative. It's still kind of mixed up down there, but I've got something that seems to be moving . . . must be damn deep . . . probably on or near the bottom . . . but we got him. . . ."

"Is he under way?" boomed Eberhardt.

"That's negative. I think . . . yeah, definitely negative. I heard something like screwbeats before, but now there's nothing . . . kinda mushy. . . ." The sonar operator on the helo was reporting at the same time he was listening. "Wait a minute, Captain . . . there's something else! I never heard that sound before but I'm willing to bet he just bottomed. What's the water depth out here?'' he asked excitedly.

His voice could be heard in CIC as well as on the bridge. The depth reading came off the charts from both a radarman and a quartermaster at the same time—685 feet.

"Mark . . . mark that location," Eberhardt called out from the bridge wing. "Have the helo stand by for a torpedo attack."

As the submarine ground into the bottom, Captain Fitin was once again thrown to the deck. The boat hit nose first, the stern settling quickly, more than twenty degrees lower than the bow. They were on an underwater slope. Fitin had barely regained his feet when the boat rolled to one side. He slipped against the bulkhead, all the gear that had come to rest once again sliding noisily in the opposite direction. Screams of the injured came to him as the submarine finally rested firmly on the sea floor.

As he issued orders automatically to his executive officer, he could overhear the reports coming in from each space. A junior officer was furiously scribbling them on a status board with a grease pencil. The events of the preceding moments flashed through his brain. With the sound of the explosion there had been a series of incidents that occurred instantly— lights out, the sharp tearing sound of metal seams, bursting pipes, screams of terror followed instantly by shouts of agony. All of this was followed by the pain shooting through his own body as he hit the deck. Then the submarine was out of control, careening madly from one side to the other as if a gigantic hand had grasped the bow planes and shaken the boat. There was a struggle to regain his feet, then more pain—it was a tremendous effort to react to each of the emergency steps that had been ingrained in his mind from the day he first entered submarine school.

Then the emergency lights, those that remained undamaged, flickered on. Over the confusion and cries of the injured, Fitin learned that the torpedo had exploded aft, perhaps detonated by one of the noisemakers, far enough away not to be fatal, close enough that his boat was in serious trouble. The bow planes were still operable; two of the three shafts were beyond repair; the third was functioning, but there was damage from the sound of it, probably warped, the chief engineer reported; there was a growing list of flooded compartments, and there were others that seemed hopeless. They would have to be sealed off.

Fitin called for depth readings, but the fathometer had been destroyed. He studied the chart, unsure of where he was. They must be where his index finger rested—if his own depth estimate was correct. It was supposed to be fairly flat and muddy. Better to hide, stay quiet, inventory the casualties, take time to figure the next move. He did not venture his greatest concern to the executive officer—that, with luck, the Americans would believe they had sunk the submarine. If not . . . but he forced himself to concentrate on the here and now.

He sent the executive officer forward to inspect the damage while he moved aft to the engineering spaces. The smell of leaking diesel fuel quite suddenly reminded him of that inescapable proof of *subsunk* that he had read in the compromised American manuals—oil! Oil bubbling to the surface was the universal message from the depths that a submarine was sunk! He ordered slugs of oil to be discharged . . .

"Ready to commence attack." The voice from the helo echoed through the bridge speaker.

Eberhardt spoke to his ASW officer. "You're sure we have a good chance even though he's not on the move?"

"We've got him pinned down, Captain. It's not a chase situation this time. We're not telling a torpedo to go racing after anything that's trying to escape. We're dropping it in right on top of him. That fish will go into a search mode and dive deeper until it picks up sound, then she'll home on that sound. We can still hear a racket coming from that boat, sir. They've got some big troubles. . . ."

"Good enough," Eberhardt replied. He turned to his OOD. "Tell the bird to commence the attack, Mr. Taron."

The men on the bridge of *Stump* watched the helo move into position to launch her torpedo. The long, narrow, menacing fish dropped in a graceful arc, hitting the water with a splash.

"Torpedo is activated," came the report from sonar. "I have her screwbeats."

Eberhardt held the binoculars tightly to his eyes in the direction where the torpedo had entered the waters, but his eyes were closed. He was picturing the torpedo moving ever deeper, circling, searching for that sound that would close the final switch to send it directly at the source of the noise.

Fitin's sonar had also been destroyed. But there were hydrophones that hadn't been damaged and he could not put the constant reports of the American destroyer from his mind. It was above him, circling, searching for proof of a kill, its presence an ominous reminder that life could still be very short.

"Captain!" The voice was hoarse, strangled. "Torpedo . . ." the last syllable faded in a whimper.

"Is it homing on us?" Fitin inquired matter-of-factly, with a calmness that surprised even himself.

"Not yet . . . it's circling." The words were choked, lost. Then the man seemed to find his voice for an instant. "Wait a moment . . . there's a change . . . yes, Captain, it's homing. . . ."

The high-pitched sound came to each of the men encased in the submarine. The sonarman's words had been heard and passed about instantly. There was absolute silence. As the sound increased in intensity, the silence of the crew seemed almost audible.

Captain Fitin wondered about his men . . . then there was a terrific blast. The pressure hull fractured and the bulkheads crashed inward with a roar of sound and water and final darkness. . . .

Lou Eberhardt directed his OOD to within a hundred yards of the spreading diesel fuel, a dirty brown patch flecked with white foam. "Now you can see the difference between an oil slug—like that first he provided—and the real thing. Ease out a little," he added. "That'll be a hell of a mess if you go through it."

The helicopter pilot was reporting debris surfacing in the area and Eberhardt called his gunnery officer to the bridge. "Get out there and collect everything you can. I don't care how many trips you need. There's no telling what you might find."

Before the sun reached its apex that day, Lou Eberhardt had collected exactly what he was looking for, including a remarkable discovery—a relatively undamaged copy of the main American tactical manual for ASW operations, but with appropriate notes provided in Russian. There wasn't a moment to lose by encoding what he had to say. It might save another ship that day! He contacted Admiral Pratt directly over the voice radio net.

Dave Pratt's orders to every ship followed instantly. Forget your standard ASW tactics! Today was the day to use intuition in each situation!

Aboard U.S.S. *America*

For the first time in his life, Dave Pratt was frightened—not for himself, but of the awesome power under his command, and what might take place if he was forced to utilize it completely.

Once before, during the Battle of the Mediterranean, he had to use almost every weapon available to him—everything, that is, except nuclear weapons. But there had never been the concern that he now was experiencing. He freely admitted, as he analyzed his own prudence, that the Europeans were right. Americans preferred to maintain their battlefields across the seas. Unless a war escalated to the unthinkable—when in fact no one would be safe—the United States remained securely bound by oceans to the east and west. The death and destruction would be experienced by countries and cities and people bearing strange-sounding names beyond those protective ocean barriers.

But today it was all different. Today, the Soviet Union had managed to tip the scales. The battlefield *could be* the United States. Russia had successfully crossed those oceans, bringing this conflict to the North American continent. Each step of the way they utilized proxy nations to draw Washington deeper, until there seemed no escape. And only after the Americans made their commitments did the Russians show up. When they appeared, they came by sea. There were still no Soviet divisions marching, no tanks or artillery, nor any elements of modern warfare other than their navy, and, most importantly, these ships and submarines could be withdrawn at any point in time. In that event, the United States could be left in a struggle with their neighbors to the south, looking to all the world like an ugly aggressor, subjugating her impoverished Caribbean neighbors once again.

Or, if all went well for the Soviets, then the threat against the United States had never been greater. The battlefield was no longer "over there." It was much too close to home, and Dave Pratt couldn't have been more frightened at the responsibility weighing on his shoulders. He was no longer prosecuting a war against a faraway enemy, no longer protecting distant allies. He was attempting to halt a tragedy before it began, before his own country was swept into the unavoidable. That's why Pratt was not afraid for himself; he was afraid for his country.

Today the battles at sea were occurring in the Caribbean and the Gulf of Mexico, near familiar islands like Puerto Rico and Jamaica and the Bahamas, and each incident was taking place closer to American borders. The last two carrier aircraft lost could not have been more than two hundred miles from Florida, brought down by an enemy now boldly heading for the Florida Straits to rendezvous with other ships for a blockade of American waters.

Admiral Pratt and his operations officer had spent the past hour poring over their charts, measuring distances, speeds of advance, and time to reach station for both U.S. and Soviet warships. They could see choke points closing, supply routes strangled, free access to seas denied—actions unprecedented in the history of the region.

It was at this stage that the critical piece of the puzzle fell into place. Both the satellite photos relayed to *America* and the facsimile pictures from Cobb coincided with the latter's report from the Canal Zone. There, anchored securely before the Pedro Miguel Locks, was a World War II vintage destroyer. In an age of guided missiles and sophisticated electronic warfare, Pratt recognized that the real key, the one that had eluded them all along, was a relic of the past. With so much emphasis on the PRA in Panama, why hadn't they figured the Russian game beforehand? That the Panama Canal was as good as a hostage! If the Pedro Miguel Locks were destroyed, or even just damaged, Canal use would be denied to everyone, but more importantly, Ramos would fall. There would be no loss to the Russians, who had never controlled the Canal or the government anyway. They would either win or the situation would revert to what it had been previously. In either case, the Soviet Union would be attempting economic piracy. And success in Panama meant control of the Caribbean. They had everything to gain and very little to lose—except a wider war, which would be of their choosing.

Dave Pratt, since arriving aboard *America*, had devised a tally sheet. He understood that all that ever motivated the Russians was what they stood to lose. In this case they had planned well. The destroyer in the Pedro Miguel Locks was Colombian. The troops in Panama, or in transit, were Panamanian rebels, Cubans, and only a few Soviet advisors and Black Beret marines. The small naval force now approaching Colón to reinforce the Panamanian revolution were Cuban. And the great numbers of Russian ships were hovering just beyond the chain of outer islands, the West Indies. They were strategically placed, but they were also waiting. They became a show of force to support the PRA takeover in Panama, and would act only when it was obvious the odds were in their favor. There was no outward sign of aggression, at least none that could motivate a Security Council to condemn them. Once again the Soviets were manipulating proxy forces.

There were only two moves that Pratt could convince himself would work. Somehow that destroyer had to be taken before sufficient damage could be inflicted on the Pedro Miguel Locks; and it was necessary to inflict heavy enough losses on the existing Soviet naval forces to make them think twice.

After finishing his conversation with Henry Cobb, he called a staff meeting. Within an hour the word had been passed to his task force commanders. Dave Pratt had assumed the burden of the aggressor.

Panama City

Exhausted and baffled, Horacio Ramos had very little to say about the photograph Kitty Alvarez had placed before him. Since the Canal opened in 1914, security had been exceptional. For many years, until the advent of the airplane had shown that an attack from above could be successful, there had been a feeling that only nature could damage what engineering genius had constructed. The locks had been placed inland, beyond the range of big naval guns.

But now there was a totally new threat, one that had never been anticipated, especially in the nuclear age. The Panama Canal was literally a prisoner, held hostage by a group of pirates in a rusty, aging hulk. Ramos was appalled.

"What additional proof do you need?" Kitty implored, but Ramos seemed dazed, unable to accept the reality of the situation.

Ramos rose from the chair before his huge desk and wandered over to gaze out of his one window at nothing in particular. Today there was no conceivable answer to Kitty's question. He had seen the report—a Colombian school ship manned primarily by men from that country, some Cubans, some Russians, and apparently at least one of his own countrymen. He had heard of James Grambling before, known that the man was a respected leader in the PRA, but he could not imagine how a fellow Panamanian could possibly allow himself to be part of a plan to victimize the Canal—the heart and soul of his country. Only a traitor . . .

He turned from the window, still unable to believe it. "Just how do your American friends think that old ship is going to penetrate that concrete with those five-inch guns?" Every school child in Panama was taught the history of the Canal, along with the vital statistics of its construction. Just the thickness of the concrete itself, up to fifty feet near the base of the locks would protect the vital machinery that moved the giant gates and controlled the water level. Without waiting for an answer, he continued, "I need more than what you have there to convince me. I have nothing, Kitty," he added in a softer tone, "against those Americans, but all I see here is a bunch of pirates—and a traitor—making threatening motions. I know—you know—that the guns on that ship can't cause enough damage before we are able to stop them." His arms were stretched before him, palms up, as if he were pleading with Kitty to provide him with an answer.

"I don't have all the answers. But look at that photograph!" Her finger jabbed at the various sections of the ship as she repeated what Cobb and Ryng had pointed out. "Look at what they've done since they took it over—you can see doors that have been sealed shut with heavy metal plates . . . that armor right there to protect anyone trying to move forward from the stern. They've cut away ladders . . . there's no telling what's been done inside. But that ship has a specific purpose, and they mean to defend it for as long as they have to. This Russian, Voronov, is supposed to be a genius, and he is commanding the operation. He wouldn't be involved in this unless there was some master plan with the Pedro Miguel Locks. . . ." Her voice drifted off in frustration, afraid she was failing to make her point.

Ramos looked at her, his eyes misty. "Those Pedro Miguel Locks have become the key to our . . . my failure." He pursed his lips. "And now you say, because of the Russians and our canal, I must now do the bidding of a couple of Americans."

"But you asked Bernie Ryng to help you. What we think we need is for you to go on television and radio—let the people know what's really happening—declare a state of emergency . . . and you must—no, we suggest that you send certain loyal units of the Guardia to the Pedro Miguel Locks now to support us."

Ramos nodded, then smiled tiredly. "And . . ."

"They have requested backup support from the United States—SEAL teams they're called—to arrive here within a few hours. They'll be followed by Marines, and the Marines will need tanks and artillery and—"

"And you want me to authorize this . . ." Ramos searched for a word to express himself. ". . . this invasion force?"

"It's not that, but it will look that way without your help. We only want permission for them to land. They'll remain in

the Zone . . . within their bases unless you ask for their
assistance." He was facing her now and she crossed the few
steps between them. "If you don't allow them to at least land,
it will be too late if you learn later that you need them. We're
dealing in hours, not weeks or days." She reached out,
touching his arm lightly. "Please . . . you have been as much a
father to me as my own father. You helped to raise me when
he was gone . . . and you remember as clearly as I do what you
taught me about this country. You don't think I would turn
against her, or you, now?" They were words she never had
planned to use. She had never wanted to use his love in this
manner.

Once again Ramos turned to his window. There were so
many responsibilities, each one weighing more heavily on his
shoulders. He had almost put off her request to meet with
him. Now there was one more—no, two more. To this political or military decision, she had attached a deeply personal request. He was forced to make a choice between the neutrality
he desired and the side she represented. Why did he have to be
the one to ask the Americans to return to defend against . . .
he was not sure what his country would be defended against at
this point.

President Ramos turned from his window. "I cannot tell
you my decision immediately. There are others I must talk to
first. Some are waiting right now," he said, gesturing in the
direction of his outer office. "Please, go through there, and
my secretary will take you down the hall to wait in another
room. I prefer that the people who come next not know who I
have been talking with." He held open a side door for her. She
had waited in that room a week before, when Bernie Ryng had
first met Horacio Ramos. That time she had done Ramos a
favor. "You know where to wait. There is a phone there. I will
call you shortly."

When she had gone, he went to his desk and called to the
outer office for his next visitor—Esteban Alvarez.

The Pedro Miguel Locks

The destroyer was securely anchored now. Paul Voronov had used the engines to set both the bow anchor and one that his men had jury-rigged from the stern. Outside of hurricane force winds, the ship would remain in one position.

James Grambling peered around one of the hastily erected splinter shields on the port bridge wing. The sight of his men on the bluffs above was reassuring. Hours before, the first solid feeling of security he had experienced since boarding the destroyer occurred when he caught sight of one of his guerilla squads. They had secured their designated objectives, and at exactly the appointed time. Their signal to him was simple, yet it answered the one question uppermost in his mind— and Voronov's—who controlled the guard shacks to the approaches to the Pedro Miguel Locks? It was now the PRA, though the technicians controlling the locks remained unaware of the fact.

The main control station was another matter. A decision had been made in the jungle days before to wait until the destroyer actually arrived at the locks. Any preliminary attempt to take control might serve as a warning, or at least offer a reason to be concerned about the Colombian destroyer. Paul Voronov wanted the ship in a secure threat position before its purpose became clear. There were a number of places they might have been stopped—Barro Colorado Island, Las Cascadas, Culebra, anywhere along the Gaillard Cut! No, Voronov had wisely decided. No action was to take place more than an hour before the ship arrived at Pedro Miguel. The guerillas could handle scattered military opposition; the ship's five-inch guns would assist at the control station.

He heard Voronov's voice in the pilothouse before the man stepped through the hatch to the open wing. Grambling dropped the binoculars and turned. "Two minutes, Jaimé, two minutes." He looked around the edge of the shield toward the control station. "One would assume that by now they must realize something is wrong. At least they should have heard something from the guard stations."

"What makes you so sure my men are going to make a mistake? The lines were cut before any of them were near a post. Then, they called in just like the guards." Grambling had been on edge earlier. Now he was angry. Before he realized how tense he had become, the words spilled out. "Those are not Russian soldiers up there. Each one of those men is capable of leading a squad. And you can be damn sure any one of them could probably manage an entire Soviet company."

"My, my, aren't we on edge." Voronov was amused rather than angry. He had rarely seen Grambling lose control like that, but he preferred it happen now, and with him. It would not do when other Russian officers were present, or when they were in the midst of the operation. Let him get it off his chest. "Go ahead, my friend, say what you want now. I am a fine listener, but"—he laughed—"I have only a moment to hear everything you have to say."

There was only silence. The outburst was as much of a surprise to him as it was to the other. Tension had been building since they boarded the destroyer, as Grambling began to feel that he was taking part in an operation that could set his country back for years. And Voronov troubled him more as each moment passed. He talked often with Grambling, asking his advice, explaining each step of the plan over and over again. But that wasn't all of it. It seemed more a courtesy. The Russian actually spent more time with his own men, as if it were exclusively a Soviet operation. As each hour passed, Voronov also seemed to be in continuous contact with the overall commander, Admiral Khasan, who had established his command on the Soviet carrier.

None of this uneasiness was new, Grambling realized. His discontent had been evident for some time, whether he acknowledged it himself or Maria pointed it out to him. It was his country, Panama, that was the battlefield, and mostly his people, the PRA, who would do the dying. If the plan failed, his country would suffer; if it succeeded, the Russians would benefit. Did the Russians make so many of the command decisions because they felt Grambling and his people couldn't make them? And would the Russians leave after the victory was won? The more he considered it, the more he wondered if the Russians would be the real government behind the scenes after it was all over.

And if it wasn't Paul Voronov and people like him, then Grambling was afraid the Cubans would eventually replace the Russians. He had seen exactly that scenario when he was in Cuba. There, in Havana and all the other cities and military bases, the Cubans had learned to live with the Russians in the background. Would James Grambling and his people have to learn to live with Cubans, or would the Russians be there, hovering in the shadows just as they did in Havana?

"Nothing to say for yourself, eh?" Voronov asked. He understood. "Well, it's good to get something like that out of your system, Jaimé." He handed the radio mike to Grambling. "It's time, my friend. It's your game. Tell your men to move."

At the same instant he gave the signal, Grambling felt the deck shudder underneath and the sound of small arms fire shattering the silence. The forward gun mount rumbled around to bear on the control station, and Grambling imagined the shock of the men in the station and the soldiers on duty there. They had no reason to suspect a thing. The destroyer had arrived on schedule, radioing ahead that she would have to stop for no more than an hour to make some minor repairs before she entered the locks. Although it didn't happen often, there were regulations that ships must report any engineering casualty while making a transit, and they must effect repairs before entering the locks. It was all perfectly planned, and it ran smoothly.

Voronov caught sight of a Guardia detachment approaching from a concealed position on the far side of the hill above the locks. In a moment they had a number of Grambling's men pinned down with machine gun fire. Very softly the Russian spoke a couple of words into the ship's intercom. He gestured with his thumb toward the gun director on the level above them and muttered something barely heard about taking care of the problem. Seconds later a deafening explosion burst over the bridge. The left-hand gun of the forward mount belched flame. The shock wave rolled over a startled Grambling, followed by the smoke and heat of the blast.

The shell burst on the hillside above the Guardia soldiers, giving them no time to react, no time to scramble to safety. Then the right-hand gun let loose. Grambling stared through his binoculars as a direct hit flung the detachment through the air like rag dolls. There was little left for Grambling's guerillas to worry about.

A few moments later the guerilla commander on shore declared the area secure. Immediately Voronov ordered the ship's whaleboat cast off from the safety of the other side of the ship. There were six men in the boat—the coxswain, the engineer, and the four men who would be setting the explosives deep in the bowels of the Pedro Miguel Locks. Paul Voronov had no intention of taking chances. He knew that the destroyer could be put out of commission before her five-inch guns caused enough damage. The Soviet engineers in Havana had studied the design of the locks weeks before and come to the conclusion that a combined threat, from the interior and exterior, was the most likely way that the authorities could be convinced that the Pedro Miguel Locks could be immobilized.

Once Voronov confirmed that his explosives experts had entered the locks chambers, he contacted Admiral Khasan aboard *Kharkov*. Now the next step could be taken.

Aboard the Soviet Carrier *Kharkov*

Admiral Khasan was strolling on the bow of *Kharkov* when Voronov's signal arrived. Excited, the captain sent a messenger down. The Admiral turned to the bridge and gave the thumbs-up sign.

Khasan leaned far out over the safety lines. Navarro had the right instincts—there was no better way to experience the true power of this great ship than to marvel first at the graceful white bow wave flung back as they cut through the water; then he slowly turned to survey the expanse of the flight deck to one side before scanning the myriad weapons systems on each level toward the bridge. The scene was awesome.

Breathing in the fresh salt air, Khasan reveled in the sheer excitement of the day. This was freedom as he understood it— freedom of movement, freedom of decision. The day was his. There were no worries out here of Navarro's hesitation or

Lydia's anger or Chita Monteria's hypnotic beauty. Out here sea birds and flying fish were racing *Kharkov*'s bow wave, and within her numerous compartments were efficient Soviet sailors.

As he meandered back toward the main island, he paused to observe the impressive weaponry—the RBU-6000 launchers, the SUW-N-1 launcher, the twin 76.2mm AA gun mount, the SS-N-12 missile tubes, the SA-N-3 launcher, more SS-N-12 missile tubes, the 30mm gatling guns—and that didn't even take into consideration the power of the air group. *Kharkov* was an incredible fighting machine, and Admiral Khasan at that moment was impervious to the Americans. Never before had he felt such supreme confidence.

His staff officers were waiting for him. He had announced a meeting after Voronov's message arrived. Now it was time to issue his orders. He had been waiting for this moment since that horrible hour in the Mediterranean when the Kremlin had finally ordered Soviet forces to cease fire.

When he dismissed his officers, Admiral Khasan's last words were to his staff communicator. "You may issue the order to all units to be on station no later than six hours from now. Blockade all choke points. Local unit commanders may now fire on targets of opportunity." When the explosives were secure and Voronov's second and final report was received, he would contact Moscow.

Panama City

Esteban Alvarez had no idea to whom President Ramos had been speaking moments before. There was a faint trace of perfume in the air, a slightly familiar one, but it never occurred to him to search back through his memory.

Upon entering the office, the words he intended to open his discussion with escaped him. He was momentarily mute as he stared back at Ramos. The President returned his gaze, a slight trace of amusement showing at the corners of his mouth as he waited for Kitty's father to begin.

Ramos had been prepared to speak, because he wanted to explain that he had no time for even an old friend to lecture him once again on political philosophy. But he, too, withheld his comments when he saw the pain in the other's eyes. Alvarez had been hurt and confused his last time in this office—when he had revealed where the PRA demolition team could be found—but now there was anger and confusion evident in his expression. Ramos determined that his best decision would be silence.

"I am sorry, my friend. . . ." Alvarez began haltingly.

"*Sorry*, Esteban?" Ramos tilted his head slightly to one side. "Sorry?"

"I shouldn't be here . . . I mean, I don't want to be here. . . ." He searched for words that remained in the shadows of his mind, almost as if a shield had been erected.

"In that case, I'm very busy. If you just want to talk, Esteban, perhaps this evening before I retire . . . we could have some brandy together—"

"No, now!" he shouted. "Now!" After a deep breath, the words literally flew from his mouth. "You must listen to me, Horacio, and understand. You are in danger. The country is in danger. I have been asked by the PRA to speak to you—"

"I want to hear nothing from the PRA!" Ramos shouted back angrily.

"You have no choice. This is no longer just an irritating little revolution. Right now, right this very moment, there is a destroyer anchored beside the Pedro Miguel locks. Her guns are loaded with armor-piercing shells. She has control of the military guard there and the control house. Demolition experts are now inside the lock's chambers placing bombs where they will do the most damage to the electric motors and bull wheels. The ship's guns are capable of piercing the steel plate over the gates and filling them with water. There is no way to stop them from destroying it all once they start. I know you won't want them to complete—"

"I won't let them! I will destroy them. Right now—"

"Horacio. Don't interrupt me again. Let me finish. I want to help you."

"No!" Ramos roared. "You're a traitor!" His face was

flushed with rage. He had not intended to say such a thing, even in anger.

"No, Horacio, neither of us are traitors. Perhaps you might be considered one if you allow the Canal to be destroyed . . . and I warn you they will do it. Instead, listen to me . . . let me explain." He couldn't let Ramos interrupt him. "I want to insure that no danger comes to you, and the only way we can be sure of that now is for you to agree to leave this country. Perhaps my daughter can arrange for you to go to the United States. But,"—he waved a finger in Ramos's direction, pointing at his chest—"you have to understand. The people who are planning this are in the forefront of the PRA. They want a new government and they do not want you involved in it. If you agree to step down, they will disarm the explosives inside the locks' chambers and the ship will pass on through to the Pacific side."

"Why you, Esteban? Why are you turning against your country?" Momentarily Ramos's anger reverted to sadness. The words he had spoken really hadn't been directed to Alvarez. While he was asking Alvarez the question, he was also directing it to those of his countrymen who could destroy their nation but for the decision of one man. Then he looked up, anger flashing in his eyes. "Why are you the one coming to me, Esteban?"

"Simply because I know you better than any other man."

"I see you, Esteban. And I hear you. But I'm not listening."

"But you must . . . you must or we lose everything!"

"Who loses everything? Are you talking about yourself or our countrymen . . . or is there someone else? Who are the people on that destroyer, Esteban? Who are the people setting the bombs inside the locks? Are these people from your PRA? Are they all Panamanians? Who are they?"

"One of the leaders on the ship . . . one of them is a PRA colonel."

"Who?"

"Grambling . . . James Grambling. You've heard his name certainly."

"Another traitor, Esteban. And how many others are there

on that ship? Can you name another besides Grambling? You want to know who I think is running that?" he continued without waiting for an answer. "There are Russians and Cubans there, and they're using you and others just like you to try to force me to give up my office."

"No . . ." Alvarez faltered for a moment, searching for words. This was what he had avoided for weeks, refusing to accept the reality.

"Come with me." Ramos grabbed his arm firmly, walked him back through the anteroom he'd come from and through a couple of others until they could look down on the main street. "Look down there, Esteban, in the street. Where is your peasant army?"

There was no more than the usual congregation of people in the street, along with occasional Guardia officers. More obvious were the uniforms of Cuban advisors. But here and there, as Alvarez followed the jabbing finger that Ramos used to pick them out, it was evident there were also Russian advisors among them. "You are representing *them* now?" Ramos inquired harshly.

"No . . . not at all. I have been asked by senior members of the PRA, because it is known that I am your friend, to serve as a go-between. . . ." Alvarez's words were stilted and mechanical. Those same words he had memorized and planned to repeat when he first entered Ramos's office now spilled out. "To cause any damage to the Canal is contrary to our beliefs." The format was neat and logical. "Since human hostages often are no longer negotiated for, we have determined that the most viable option is to make the Canal a hostage."

Ramos stared at him in shock.

"We will guarantee no harm will come to you and your family if . . ." Then he looked up at Ramos as if awakening from a dream. "But harm will come, Horacio. There are too many who care little for human life, yours or mine or anyone else's. You must let me arrange through Kitty to escape the country."

"Esteban, I should have you shot right now, out there." He gestured toward the street. "And I may regret later on that I did not follow my own best advice. But I have some idea that if I let you think all of this over for a few hours, knowing full well that I am also thinking about what I should do, then maybe you will still be of some use to me, maybe even to your country. I will leave orders that you not leave the building. But you may be sure I will not forget you are here—"

The sound of low-flying jet planes startled them. Searching the sky outside, they spied two fighter aircraft sweeping low over the city, directly at the Palace. They passed not more than fifty feet above, their Soviet markings standing out boldly. Both men understood that there would be many more flights of that sort before the day was over, and quite possibly those planes would be firing on future sorties.

"Were those PRA planes, Esteban?" When he was certain there would be only silence from the other, Ramos returned to his office. There was much to do, but the first orders he issued were to notify his loyalists that American support had been offered and accepted, and that right now special units were on their way to Panama. They would be landing shortly.

The School of the Americas HQ

Jimmy Wright, the lieutenant in charge of the first SEAL team to arrive, was familiar with the legends surrounding Cobb and Ryng. Those two names would come to the fore in late-night sessions in O clubs and EM clubs in Little Creek and Coronado, and as so often happened, it became difficult to separate fact from fiction. The lieutenant, therefore, found the preposterous idea acceptable that he and his men would soon be in action to capture an ancient destroyer and locks of the Panama Canal. If either Ryng or Cobb were involved, he'd believe anything.

Wright soon understood why the Pedro Miguel Locks were the most logical for the PRA to both take over and defend. It was the least accessible. After passing through twenty-three miles of Gatun Lake from the Caribbean access, a ship traversed nine miles of the narrow Gaillard Cut, which had been blasted and dug out of the Continental Divide. At its southern end was the Pedro Miguel Locks. Beyond and below them was

the artifical Miraflores Lake leading to other locks of the same
name. Any objective could be taken by a well-coordinated action, but Pedro Miguel would be a complex action even with
proper support for professional troops. The only other
method was the one outlined by Ryng and Cobb. Wright
understood intuitively that it was a higher risk mission than
any he'd ever approached.

The tiny village of Pedro Miguel was situated on the east
side of the Canal, which was the same side the railroad and all
support activities occupied, and it was where the rebels had
established their base to protect the destroyer.

Cobb had two sets of photos. One had been taken by photo
reconnaissance aircraft. The second was provided by a two-
man team that paddled up the west bank of Miraflores Lake.
At the far end of the Pedro Miguel Locks, where ships were
lowered into the lake, they penetrated the dense undergrowth
on the west side. There a well-camouflaged site was established to photograph the ship with a telephoto lens.

Bernie Ryng was finally back in his element. He was coordinating the attack on the destroyer. It was well protected—
from the splinter shields erected on the bridge to the defenses
constructed toward the stern. An assault on the ship would
have to come from the most accessible part, and that was the
stern. Ryng's objective was to prevent the forward gun mount
from destroying the control station and damaging the locks'
giant gates. No one could penetrate a sealed, armored mount
with small arms, so it would be a two-step operation. First, cut
power to the mount so any firing would have to be done by
hand; second, capture the handling rooms so that the ammunition couldn't be passed up to the mount. To cut off electrical
power to the mount, two men in the team would be attempting
to cut through the bottom of the hull of the ship in the approximate area of the ship's generators. That was a long process
and would require more time than Ryng thought he had. But if
his attack failed, flooding the hull was his last resort—because
a sunken ship would block the Canal.

Cobb would lead the team into the immense subterranean
caverns of the Pedro Miguel to halt the internal demolition of
the locks. Though he couldn't be sure, he had to assume that

with just four explosives experts, they were concentrating on the northern gates.

The locks were gigantic, each one a thousand feet long and one-hundred-ten-feet wide, and they were built side by side to facilitate ships moving in both directions. More than eighty feet in depth, their walls and base were catacombed with passageways and tunnels providing access to every space within these gigantic vaults. Cobb's plan was to enter on the south side. Then he and his team would descend into the vast chambers and work their way toward the north end, wiping out resistance as they progressed. The most complex part would be to locate and defuse the explosives. He had to assume that if they began to detonate them, anyone inside the chambers was doomed.

"We don't know for sure how many Black Berets Voronov has aboard that ship," Ryng said. "From the pictures we've seen, there must be at least a dozen, maybe more."

"And don't forget Grambling and his men," Kitty Alvarez added. "They're guerilla fighters. There's no telling how they'll handle themselves aboard that ship. Remember, they won't do anything the standard way."

"The best time to hit them is at dusk," Ryng said, then pointed out the team's insertion point above the locks. "The water's muddy here so there's no problem with being seen. The main problems have to do with seeing where you're going in the water. Wright and I will lead the team at about thirty feet. Everyone else will be attached to us on the string. There should be enough wind to rough up the water, so the chance of being spotted is minimal. Helicopter gunships will keep the defense on the hill busy."

Ryng went on to explain just how they intended to board the ship, where the main defenses seemed to be, and how they would work their way forward. The few diagrams they had found of that class of ship were old and yellowed. He pointed out that there would be passageways sealed by the guerillas. They would have to secure the front section of the ship before they could make their way to the forward handling room.

"Please," Kitty interrupted before the briefing ended. "President Ramos would like to have Voronov and Gram-

bling alive, if you can. Grambling could be the key to the PRA
surrendering.''

Havana

The course of the small Cuban task force that had departed
Cienfuegos days before had been ordered by Moscow and laid
out in Havana. The objective was to arrive at the appropriate
time off Colón in support of the PRA movement. If properly
timed, they would appear at the moment the Canal was
threatened. The U.S. would be occupied with trying to contain
the Soviet pincer movement into the Caribbean, they were
told.

As in all operation plans, however, timing was of the essence and the element of surprise was critical. Unfortunately,
Navarro had already recognized that achieving both could be
impossible. From the day the ships weighed anchor, patrol aircraft from Guantanamo and Roosevelt Roads tracked them.
That they were being trailed by air was of little concern, for
Soviet air support had been guaranteed. But now Navarro had
confirmation of submarine sightings in the area, and his own
patrol aircraft identified American surface vessels apparently
converging on a point off Panama's north coast.

"We're toys!" Navarro raged at his premier. "We're being
used as toys!" He had been well educated by the Russians.
Now he was turning against his teachers. The strategy wasn't
unique—Navarro realized once again the Soviets were using
one of their proxies to do the dirty work. If things went badly,
the Russians came out of it with their noses clean.

Fidel Castro searched Navarro's face with tired eyes. He
agreed but found that impossible to admit in front of his
senior naval officer. "I doubt the Americans would attack us
at this stage. They like to threaten and ruffle their feathers,
but they have a fear of upsetting us. . . .''

"I disagree." Navarro knew the Premier hated it when his
senior officers disagreed with him, but it seemed now that it
was a choice of having his navy saved or destroyed. After all,
three of his frigates were in the force, four out of five of his

minesweepers, and half of his small missile patrol boats. If he issued the proper orders now, the submarines would stay out of trouble. If he waited, he would not be able to get the message to them and they would make an effort to defend the surface ships. He knew they were no contest for the Americans.

"There has already been contact," Navarro said, "between the Americans and the Russians, and they shot down that patrol plane of ours in the Yucatan Channel." He stabbed at the huge chart of Atlantic and Caribbean waters that covered one wall of the Premier's office. "The carrier *America* is on station right there. She has a strong screen of missile ships around her, and if my intelligence is correct, she has just launched an air strike against the Russians." He paused, staring back at Castro, then walked to his desk and leaned forward, his palms resting on the edge. "If they will send a strike against Soviet warships, why should our little popgun fleet even rate a second chance? They can sink it in less than half an hour."

The Premier pulled at his beard, now longer than in the past and quite gray. His eyes went from Navarro to the wall chart and back to Navarro again. "I can't order them back just like that," he said, snapping his fingers. "I have to have some reason. Admiral Khasan expects them to be there . . . to do their part—"

"Their part is to be the sacrificial lambs."

"Only if we are unsuccessful."

"Our success, I think, has been based on the idea that the Americans would give in, that they would look at what was happening and decide that they shouldn't get involved. Much of that comes from Moscow. They seem to think that the Americans have no stomach to get involved again after the Mediterranean." Navarro considered going on, explaining that it appeared the Americans weren't as concerned about U.S. aggression in the Caribbean as the Kremlin expected, and that perhaps Washington wasn't quite as frightened about the use of military power as had been hoped. Navarro had expressed these concerns before, and once Admiral Khasan accused him of being afraid to fight. "The Americans seem to have the stomach . . . at least it appears that way with this air strike from *America*. If we wait to see if they will actually attack the Russian task force, it may be too late to call back our own ships."

Castro continued to pull at his beard. "I can't order it. You know who gave us those ships, Commodore."

"The Russians gave us those ships because they were of little use to them. The power out there today"—his arm swept across the wall chart—"is with the Americans and the Russians. We are nothing. What we have sent all the way across the Caribbean is a little old-fashioned coastal defense force in the guise of an invasion fleet." He looked at his watch. "By nightfall they won't exist." He excused himself, turned on his heel, and stalked out of the room.

Castro continued to pull at his beard as he gazed at the chart. He knew that Navarro was correct, that everything the man had said was correct—about the old fashioned ships, that they were ships the Russians didn't want, that they were being used, and that they might not exist by nightfall. But he had no choice. He was totally committed.

Aboard U.S.S. *America*

Admiral Pratt was still in his favorite spot on *America*'s bridge twenty minutes after the last Hornet had disappeared from the flight deck. Elbows resting on the railing, arms folded, he watched the clouds in the distance, soft, billowy, fair-weather clouds that dotted southern waters. This time, he repeated silently to himself for the twentieth time, this time if any of my planes don't come back, it's going to be because a lot of Russian ships aren't going home either. . . .

For Admiral Pratt aboard *America* and Admiral Khasan aboard *Kharkov*, the ensuing hours would determine the course of Caribbean government. The Soviet carrier, never intended to be a match for its American counterpart, was in the Caribbean to display naval power and to provide air support over Panama City. Her short-range Forger aircraft were reinforced by the long distance Fitter, recently based at Bluefields on the east coast of Nicaragua. Khasan's decisions in the next few hours would be determined by the success of Paul Voronov turning the Canal into a hostage long enough for a change of government. If the Russians faced opposition in the air, it would be from American jets based at Howard AFB near Panama City, but they had to be called upon by President Ramos.

David Pratt kept *America* well to the east of the Bahamas in the Atlantic Ocean, out of the range of Soviet surface ships. Soviet doctrine for attacking an aircraft carrier called for cruise missiles launched by both submarine and long range bomber. Pratt's defenses were based on meeting the Russian Blackjack and Backfire bombers beyond missile range, and with luck, during their refueling. Of greater concern, however, were the Soviet submarines. The SOSUS hydrophone system on the ocean floor provided essential intelligence on approaching submarines, but by the time an ASW group could converge on the target, a nuclear submarine would be long gone. Pratt established a long range shield of destroyers, frigates, and their helicopters in a preplanned, moving screen.

Conflict was really only a matter of hours, and once contact was established, just minutes in most cases. Pratt's surface ships were responsible for opening the Caribbean choke points and driving away or sinking the submarines that blockaded them, even though these American ships would be harassed by Soviet surface ships moving into position on schedule. Pratt's carrier aircraft had to protect his ASW force and harass the approaching Soviet ships. All of it was timing, all of it based on percentages and success rates and the personal judgment of men spread over a wide area from the Atlantic Ocean to Panama. It was also a test of whether the Soviet Union could extend its power across the oceans. That was a feat it had never before accomplished. On the other hand, the United States had continuously extended her authority around the world for more than two hundred years. The Russians were willing to gamble on the U.S. having lost touch with her own neighbors, coupled with an anticipated inability to react to a combination of regional terrorism and strategic challenge.

The Caribbean, North of Colón

Commodore Navarro's little task force picked up the air attack on their radar approximately the same time the American planes launched their first missiles. The operators reported contact with a flight of aircraft, followed immediately by a report of incoming missiles.

The anti-radiation missiles homed in directly on the frigates. The range of the little ships' missiles was limited—they were not designed to defend against a coordinated missile attack. They were in a spread formation, but in their inexperience, they had failed to expand the range adequately. There was an attempt to jam the incoming missiles and to create false targets; they even maneuvered as they had been trained. But they were coastal defense ships in an open ocean environment, and superior technology overwhelmed them.

The Standard missile warhead contains over two hundred pounds of conventional explosive. As the lead missile struck the first ship somewhere between bridge and mast, a second impacted just forward of the main deckhouse. Perhaps, one of the observers on a sister ship concluded, it hit the forward gun mount. When the smoke cleared, the force of the explosion had leveled the forward part of the ship to the main deck. Oily, black flames soared more than a hundred feet into the sky as she veered directly across the path of the nearest frigate.

The second ship turned sharply to avoid collision. Passing just fifty yards distant on a parallel course, the burning ship exploded, showering the other with hot metal shards and burning fuel. The third frigate was halted by a Standard missile detonating in her stern. Her after gun mount toppled end over end through the air. The engine room filled with flames. Steering control was lost instantly. The second frigate, bodies spread over her main deck, turned away, her captain fearful of a corresponding blast.

The smaller missile patrol boats darted about like confused water bugs, searching for an enemy they could not see. To the pilots of the American planes, the sight below seemed a pond covered with insects aimlessly skittering about with no apparent purpose.

The one remaining frigate now had contact with the approaching flight. It tried futilely to direct the others toward the attack. But all they could fire back at the high-speed jets swooping down on them were 30mm guns. These small boats were designed for coastal defense against surface shipping. They were never intended to be a match for the diving planes.

Missile and rocket fire concentrated on the Cuban boats. Direct hits by the huge missiles disintegrated the small Osa and Komar craft. Two of them, scurrying aimlessly in search of any possible reprieve from death, collided in their frantic chase over the ocean.

A missile from the lone frigate finally brought down a jet. A second broke off the attack after being hit by gunfire. When their ammunition was exhausted, the American planes left behind two sinking frigates, one badly damaged, and only six missile boats able to operate. The action had taken less than ten minutes, and the remnants of Commodore Navarro's task force—the one that was to stand off Colón in a show of force in support of the PRA—had already turned to the north.

The entire action had been witnessed by a Cuban submarine snorkeling a couple of miles to the rear, and it immediately reported back to Cienfuegos. The massacre of the task force was then passed from Cienfuegos to Havana, where Fidel Castro and Commodore Navarro were already in conference. The Commodore was in the process of explaining to his Premier once again that his ships had been set up by Khasan and that they would have little chance against an air attack.

As they considered the impact of the report, the final stage of the little conflict north of Panama was coming to a close. The captain of the remaining frigate, her fires extinguished, had nursed the ship back to a semblance of order when a horrified report came from her sonar operator. Just as the air attack had been accompanied by missiles in the air, a submarine was now directly on the frigate's beam and at least three torpedoes were in the water. The captain stumbled out on the wing of his bridge and saw that indeed there were three tracks approaching dead on his beam. Too stunned, he gave no orders to the helm. Two of the torpedoes hit at the same instant. A sheet of flame rose into the air, masking the frigate.

The captain of the shadowing Cuban submarine remained

at periscope depth, watching until the flame and smoke became bubbles and steam. To his dismay, the frigate was no longer there. Realizing how open he was to a similar attack, the survival instinct took over and he ordered a crash dive. Hours later he would realize that he had become senior officer present and in command of the remainder of Navarro's first and last task force.

While Fidel Castro debated the realities of what, up to then, had been Navarro's perception of Soviet intentions, it remained for the officer-in-charge of one of the six remaining missile boats to attempt contact with his home base. There was no apparent evidence that anything existed other than the six boats, and he was sure he was the senior of the other five young officers. Someone had to report that what was left of the Cuban task force on the surface of the Caribbean would run out of fuel before they were more than halfway home. They desperately needed someone to refuel them—if they survived the next few hours.

When this message finally reached Cienfuegos and was relayed to Havana, Castro's calmness was converted to volatile anger. Navarro seemed to be correct. He was convinced that they should recall the remaining units of the small Cuban navy. Castro's only recourse was then to radio Khasan and explain that there would be no show of force off Colón that night. After all, where had the protection from the *Kharkov* been?

The Pedro Miguel Locks

James Grambling moved about uneasily in the pilothouse, uncomfortable with the physical limitations of being confined there. His was a world of motion, of fast, hard-hitting guerilla warfare, of high-speed boats. What was the reason and who had given the orders that he end up on an old relic of a destroyer anchored before the Pedro Miguel Locks? Four times in the past hour he had been down on the main deck, checking and rechecking the defenses he had established on the ship.

Though Grambling could grudgingly understand what Paul Voronov wanted him for, he could not imagine defending the ship for a great length of time. Guerilla-style warfare, hit and run, covert action—whatever one called it, the unit was never stuck in one place—was always mobile, always confusing the enemy. If there was anyone more confused by all of this than he was, James Grambling would be surprised.

If someone tried to capture the ship, he reasoned they would have to come aboard at the stern. The bow was too high. But who would be crazy enough to climb over the fantail and present themselves as a target? And who would be dumb enough to do it in the daylight in the first place? If he were going to attack this ship, and he acknowledged Voronov's belief that they would hesitate to sink it unless that became the last resort, he would come by air.

It was at that moment—he was sure the idea and the sound struck him at the same time—he recognized the familiar beat of rotors. Helicopters! That would have to be it—helicopter gunships! But Voronov had been wise. They had dismantled many sections of the ship in the past few days, placing splinter shields to protect the pilothouse and critical work areas, welding metal on top of metal to reinforce weak spots against anything but armor-piercing rockets—in other words, creating an old-fashioned pillbox out of a ship.

"Hey, Jaimé, you hear a familiar noise?" Voronov was practically bubbling over at the sound of the approaching helos.

Grambling nodded, saying nothing. He listened instead. He'd heard that sound before from exercises in the Zone, or when they were allowed out to scour the distant hills where Grambling and his followers lived. They were called Apaches and the U.S. Army used them as a potent weapon. Would they make a pass right now?

Voronov leaned around the splinter shield with his binoculars. "Apaches! Half a dozen of them." He peered back over his shoulder. "I bet they're just investigating this crazy monster we're on."

Grambling wondered at the tenor of Voronov's voice. Voronov seemed positively overjoyed that the gunships were moving toward them. But Grambling, remaining silent, shuddered as a cold chill traced slowly down his back. They wouldn't shoot. He was pretty sure of that. They would come in close to look them over. But they wouldn't fire unless they were fired upon. It would be a wait-and-see game, cat-and-mouse, and Voronov was already at the ship's PA system, warning the crew to remain out of sight.

They would all sit tight right there, and wait and see if Esteban Alvarez was able to convince President Ramos that it was all over. And they would also continue to await confirmation from deep inside the locks' chambers that the explosives were set. Up to now, that was still a bluff . . . and time was short. . . .

Grambling was aware of the incessant throb of rotors, like a heartbeat, as if they were on the pilothouse roof. The steady pulsing hurt his ears, as all other sound was drowned out. They must be hovering right off the wing of the bridge! Dust rose from the gratings, filling his nostrils. Voronov was pulling at his shirt, urging him to come near the open door of the pilothouse. The Russian pointed, and Grambling leaned out the door to look directly back toward the stern through a gap in the splinter shield. They were circling the ship, six of them, staying as close as possible to bridge level in a continuous circle about the superstructure.

Grambling stared curiously at Voronov. He could understand neither why the Russian had dragged him over there nor why he was repeatedly jabbing his index finger toward the stern. But he looked once again and recognized what concerned the other. Through breaks in circling helos he could see another flight maybe a mile astern, hovering just beyond a bend in the Canal. He could see one after another disappearing from sight, dropping down to an unseen landing place, then rising quickly. They were inserting something—someone.

That was the purpose for this race around the destroyer—distract those on the ship from recognizing what was happening farther back. Grambling understood, just as Voronov, without exchanging a word between them, that they could expect some sort of greeting in the next few hours. Grambling looked at the bridge clock. A few more hours until dusk. That's when it would come.

What neither man saw, nor did any of the PRA forces protecting the hill around them as the gunships put on their display, was an encounter at the south end of the locks. That was the real purpose in distracting the ship. There was never any fighting. No one was seen. It was simply that one by one the guards at the south end disappeared momentarily. But one by one they also reappeared, or seemed to do so.

Henry Cobb's men efficiently replaced the PRA guards. They also took over the single radio command post after listening to the PRA radioman report in twice. The entire PRA seemed mesmerized by the action of the gunships circling the destroyer.

Ryng and Cobb had succeeded in moving into position.

The Waters North of the Anegada Passage

The Anegada Passage is a wide stretch of water between the Virgin Islands of St. Thomas, Tortola, and St. Croix to the west, and the northernmost Leeward Islands of St. Martin and St. Kitts to the east. The passage is deep enough for submarines to maneuver, but it is also quite narrow for high-speed combat. Therefore, the blockading Soviet submarine had remained well to the north, above the Sombrero shallows, until orders were received to move into the choke point.

Admiral Khasan had assigned one of his fastest nuclear submarines to that station. She could make over forty knots submerged, and proudly carried the name of the famous *Admiral Lazarev*. On receipt of the last message from Khasan, her captain called the crew's attention to her mission. Now, not only were they responsible for patrolling the Anegada Passage, they had the opportunity to strike. They would commence tracking the two guided missile frigates hovering to the north of the passage in preparation for an attack some time that night.

The frigates *Vandegrift* and *Reuben James* were both newly constructed. Their computer analysis of submarine screw beats in the vicinity of the Anegada Passage had identified *Admiral Lazarev*, a submarine that could outrace them by at least twelve knots. Therefore, their initial strategy was based on one objective—driving the submarine back into the shallower waters.

The day was ending like so many in that lazy part of the world—with a bit of warm rain. Clouds could be seen scurrying across the water, dark cloaks of rain underneath blotting out the horizon. They could also be tracked on radar. A captain could avoid them if he was steaming independently and preferred to luxuriate in warm sunshine.

As the last visible cloudburst approached, Captain Rand decided his *Vandegrift* deserved a bath. He called to his OOD, "Come around until you're heading right for the middle, Johnnie. I guess we could use a fresh water washdown." His ship couldn't possibly produce enough fresh water in that climate to satisfy every need, and water became a luxury. Washing down the grime and accumulated salt and dirt that gathered on a ship at sea for an extended period was limited, and sailors also suffered. Showers were in great demand among men living in close quarters in the tropical climate. "Pass the word that we're going to take a bath in a few minutes. Anyone not on watch can get a free washdown for themselves." There were times at sea when rain was a problem, and others when it was a welcome relief.

Captain Rand moved back to the chart table. They were on a westerly course about twenty miles north of Sombrero. *Reuben James*, the junior ship, was three miles distant on the port beam. Perhaps she could use a shower too. Rand called on the secondary tactical frequency, "We're going to take a bath up ahead there. If you care to join us, you're free to maneuver independently astern. After we shake ourselves off, I'm going to reverse course due north of Anegada Island and we'll make a sweep east, then straight down the passage with our helos. Over."

"Roger, we could use a bath too. Thank you for the thoughtfulness." There was a pause, then, "By the way, my sonar operator might have picked up some faint screw beats a few minutes ago. It's hard to be sure, but perhaps that submarine may be coming our way . . . still a long way off though. Over."

"What bearing do you read him? Over."

"We don't have anything solid. Too much civilian traffic. It's a hell of a mishmash, but we located it down where you figured—southwest generally—in the passage. I think I agree with you that he's been doing a lot of sitting and waiting. Maybe now we're close enough that he's going to come out and play. Over."

"Roger. I think we can spare a few minutes. We'll initiate a search plan after our bath and go take a look. Out."

Vandegrift ducked into the shower. It was a wall of water. The men on *Reuben James* saw the other outlined against the cloudburst, stark gray against inky black. Then she passed through the wall, disappearing as if she had stepped through a mirror. There was no longer any trace of *Vandegrift* on radar. She had disappeared into an impenetrable shield of water. Only the familiar sound of her single propellor was identifiable in sonar.

Aboard *Vandegrift* naked men pranced about her decks, passing cakes of soap from one to the other. It became an indescribable luxury for men limited to "navy" showers. There was no need to get wet, then turn off the water before soaping. This deluge was heavier than anything they could possibly experience in the ship's showers. As fast as the soap foamed on their bodies, the warm rain beat it down the deck and through the scuppers into the ocean. It was a refreshing interlude for both men and ship.

Ten minutes later *Vandegrift* emerged into a golden setting sun, her hot decks steaming. Invisible astern, *Reuben James* was now enveloped in the torrent, enjoying the same momentary lull.

Captain Rand reveled in the heavy smell of clean dampness as he and his executive officer laid out a sweep plan down through Anegada Passage. They would steam back east for fifteen miles, then turn due south. Helicopters would be spotted as soon as optimum sonar conditions were determined. If the submarine was indeed blockading the passage at this moment, there was almost no way she could escape them.

• • •

Aboard *Admiral Lazarev*, Captain Loshki was indeed moving toward the frigates. Much of the past twenty-four hours he had been biding his time, hovering near the bottom, barely moving. There was no point in giving his position away. Unlike other commanding officers, Loshki was not aggressive until he was sure of his quarry. He was not a tracker or trickster. He preferred to wait for his prey—let them come to him. His tactics had been so successful in past exercises that his next orders were to a senior strategic billet.

Loshki knew the frigates were prying about the waters to the north of the islands, searching for *Lazarev*, awaiting orders to attack. He spent much time with his sonar operators, listening over the hydrophones, puzzling over the melange of sounds overflowing the Anegada Passage. The computer could sometimes single out the American warships to the north. Though the computer was unable to identify the individual signature of either ship, Loshki did know they were prowling that area for only one purpose. He also knew, among other things, the maximum speed of the ships, the range of their radar and sonar, the weapons carried aboard, and the range of those weapons. The only aspect that bothered Loshki was the LAMPS helos flown from both ships. From beneath the surface of the ocean Loshki felt confident that he could do just about anything he wanted to the two surface ships, but he realized that there was no way of telling where those damned helos were until they dipped their sonars and began pinging. It could be at a great range, or it could be right on top of him, and he knew when the latter occurred that the next sound he would hear would be the ominous splash of the torpedoes.

Loshki knew by his watch that the sun was setting above him. That meant most pleasure craft would be entering harbor and the ocean would be free of all but occasional fishermen. As usual he would proceed quietly near the surface, antenna extended for any messages directed specifically to *Lazarev*, but this time he would have a goal in mind and he would be heading to the north. He was going out to meet those frigates. He called his weapons officer to his cabin for a moment and explained that the usual check of the weapons systems this evening would be a double check. He intended to utilize both his torpedoes and his anti-ship missiles.

When the destroyers turned south simultaneously, *Vandegrift* held *Reuben James* three miles abeam. The afternoon clouds had vanished and the frigate to the west was outlined against a multi-hued sky. Captain Rand was forever reassured of why he loved the sea when he saw a sight like that! It could be any ship—a boat in full sail, a liner, even a freighter. The silhouette, the ever-changing colors, the gentle ocean—all combined to literally hypnotize him.

But they were now going after a target—committed. No more endless patrolling. They were hunting—possibly being hunted—and the mission had now evolved into a deadly game. Admiral Pratt had charged them to seek out targets of opportunity, to insure that each passage into the Caribbean was once again open to American warships. He understood the tremendous power of the nuclear submarine that was out there, and he granted the sub the initial advantage.

The ASW officer reported the sonar conditions at that moment, and Rand knew that not everything benefited the enemy. Though water temperatures were perfect, shallow water would be a real problem. It would create bottom return interference on the sonar. With depths ahead no more than five hundred feet, that was of greater concern to the deep-diving submarine. There was no temperature gradient to slip under, no abyss to slip into and hide, and best of all, limited space under his hull to maneuver. Five hundred feet definitely gave the submarine something to be concerned with.

Captain Rand would pass down the middle of the Anegada Passage with *Vandegrift* slightly to the east of center and *Reuben James* to the west. Their helos would initially cover the shallows to either side of them. If the sub was tracking too close to the frigates, she would likely change course to either side. If the helos located it close to the islands, the sub would be forced into the center of the channel. That was where Rand expected the two frigates would take on the submarine.

Reuben James again picked up a specific underwater sound whose signature was remarkably similar to the earlier ones. It increased in intensity as they moved south. Anxiety, an emotion integral to the search for a submarine, increased among Rand's men at their action stations. As the darkness spread silently from east to west, each man seemed to be counting the passing minutes.

Reuben James's helo established the first solid reading east of Tortola, and immediately the contact tracked toward the middle of the channel, into deeper water. Moments later the sonar operator on the helo classified his contact as a definite submarine. Captain Rand was in the process of ordering a torpedo attack by the helo when its dipping sonar went dead. As quickly as a live target had been located, an electronic casualty allowed it to escape. Captain Rand silently acknowledged that any advantage had already been lost. Just by simple calculations, the sub could determine their approximate location.

Captain Loshki was somewhat at odds with himself. He had fallen into the exact trap that he feared most—a helicopter. He should have known that the helos would be vectored to the shallower waters, forcing him into the middle for the frigates! But what a stroke of luck—for some reason they were no longer pinging on him. Perhaps the advantage would fall back to him. Now that they knew where he was, it made sense to increase speed and move into position as rapidly as possible. There was no longer any purpose in maintaining silence.

As his executive officer conned *Lazarev* into deeper waters, Loshki mulled over his chart. Two ships, sonar ranges out to . . . well, they should be able to cover the entire Anegada Passage at peak power, but bottom return would probably limit them . . . so they would proceed right about here—he laid out an optimum track for the surface ships—and they would each fly helos, probably one each, here and here, to either side of the passage. Loshki's sonar operator had the frigates' bearing on his set but had yet to determine the precise range. One thing Loshki was sure of in this situation—he would have the first target solution unless he was picked up by a helo again.

He doubted that, even if the frigate's sonars found him, they could develop a solution that quickly.

With an initial contact Captain Rand no longer required his own helo on the east side of the passage. He ordered CIC to vector it on an intercept path directly ahead of them. The frigates would be perfect targets for *Lazarev*'s missiles. At this close range the sub could fire from underwater and a missile could home right down the frigate's approach path.

Within seconds of each other the sonar operators on both frigates confirmed dual screw beats. They were much higher speed than before, from the location projected by the computer, and they were closing. Nothing else had been reported in the vicinity that could match a submarine's signature. Their lines of bearing on the sound covered too large an area to pinpoint the target, but it seemed about eight to ten miles distant.

"Captain . . ." came the ASW officer's voice from sonar. "We have something in the water . . . almost like a noisemaker . . . no, an explosion . . . now it's gone. . . ." The same report came over the radio from *Reuben James*.

Rand understood what it was even before he could speak—a missile. He had not been a part of the Battle of the Mediterranean, but he had listened to stories of that telltale sound as an anti-ship missile ejected from a submarine, followed by the burst as it was powered free of the water.

"Missile!" Rand's voice boomed out. His mind raced through the fact sheet on Charlie-class submarines—SS-N-9 anti-ship missiles . . . supersonic . . . infrared and active radar homing . . . require mid-course guidance for long range . . . not a chance for that here . . . had to be a shot in the dark by the sub!

The frigates' only anti-missile protection was chaff—or with luck, their Phalanx guns—but that was last ditch! No time! "Take evasive action," he called instinctively over the radio to *Reuben James*. Then he felt *Vandegrift* heeling as her rudder bit sharply into the water. Fine move by his OOD, he thought. The missile would be coming directly at them . . . open up the Phalanx, which was blanked by the bridge. . . .

Seconds ticked by. A radar operator reported painting the

missile on his screen. Then he noticed *Vandegrift*'s helo seemingly converging with the faint dot of the missile. "The helo . . . it's going to . . ."

Rand understood. His LAMPS helicopter had been vectored toward the contact area. He could visualize that it had passed in front of both ships. He could almost sense the infrared cone in the missile's nose homing in on the heat from the helo's engines.

"It did . . ." There was a deep sigh from the radarman as he saw the two blips on his screen merge. An explosion, audible even within the confines of the Combat Information Center, shook the darkness outside. Captain Rand knew there would be nothing to search for. The warhead, designed with the capability to break a ship like his own in half, would have blown the helo into incalculably small pieces.

Now they had a datum, an exact spot where the missile had emerged seconds before, marking the position of the submarine. But the single remaining helo's sonar was inoperable. There was no time to launch the others. Half of their offensive punch was gone. All that remained was for Rand to give orders to close the submarine at high speed for torpedo attack.

Captain Loshki could tell as well as any other man on the ship that his missile had failed to hit the intended target. Both ships were now closing him at high speed. Whatever had gone wrong with the first missile certainly wouldn't effect the second one. His range and bearing to the closest ship were accurate now.

Once again he felt the familiar shudder of the missile ejecting. There would be minimal delay between the weapon breaking surface and impact. Loshki felt it was more a matter of missile ignition, instant lock-on, a short high-speed trip to the target, and literally no time for the ship to put up any type of defense.

Now he must concentrate on the second ship. He saw that its speed remained steady, almost twenty-eight knots, its course erratic, with no discernible pattern. It was most certainly a contest of wills at this point. Both he and the captain of the second frigate would make attacks. There could be only one survivor.

As Loshki prepared, checking the computer against his own intuition, there was a report that the closest vessel had apparently lost power.

The ignition of the second missile was still vivid in Captain Rand's mind as he ran onto the bridge. A bright flash followed by a frighteningly beautiful glow set against the cloud of spray and steam and smoke. Reports of a missile in the air echoed his own horror as he watched it race directly into *Reuben James*.

There had been no time for the other ship to react. Perhaps, Rand thought, the Phalanx began firing just before detonation. He couldn't be sure whether that had simply been a hopeful image recorded in his mind. There had been a tremendous explosion.

Could the Phalanx have exploded the warhead just before it struck? If so, *Reuben James* might just be damaged by the blast. But the climbing tower of flame where her bridge was seemed to indicate otherwise. The flaming pyre illuminated the bow and stern of the frigate, and Rand was surprised to see that neither end was burning. Then, peering more closely through his binoculars, he realized that the bow and stern were separate from what he had thought was *Reuben James*. What he actually was viewing was a molten mass that had been her midships section. While he tried to assimilate what had taken place, the flame was dying, replaced by bubbles and steam as the midsection of *Reuben James* settled, slowly at first, then quite rapidly.

A voice repeating his name—at first a distant echo, then a shout beside him—brought him back to reality. "Captain Rand, we have a solution . . . we're ready to fire torpedoes."

Rand reacted involuntarily. "Fire!" He had been trained to work directly on an attack, checking ranges, course, speed, depth settings, solutions—but none of that seemed necessary as he gave the order. His men had been trained for their job. His responsibility was to insure that they knew it thoroughly, and his order was instinctive rather than rational.

He leaned out over the starboard wing to watch the torpedo leap out from the side of the ship. But it had already gone. All that remained was a brilliant, phosphorescent spot where it had hit the water, and that was barely visible as the ship hurtled along at maximum speed.

"Right full rudder," he bellowed back into the pilothouse. They had to be under attack! There had to be at least two torpedoes heading toward *Vandegrift* right at this moment! It seemed logical to turn to the left, away from the submarine, after firing with the starboard tubes. But strangely enough, once again his reaction was instinctive—turn right—yet he was vaguely aware why he was doing it. . . .

Loshki had fired torpedoes just seconds before the frigate, expecting the surface ship to turn toward its sinking sister. It had not done so. As it became evident that the American had done exactly the opposite, Loshki prepared to fire two more torpedoes. There was still a respectable chance that the homing torpedoes would be able to pick up a surface ship in a stern chase at that speed. As he cautiously checked his solution, he was startled by the cry from sonar—two torpedoes!

Loshki immediately forgot his firing plan. He reversed course at maximum speed. Unsure whether the torpedoes were faster than his own boat, he now found himself the victim of a stern chase. He increased his depth as rapidly as possible, releasing noisemakers at the same time. The waters should be shallow enough to confuse a torpedo homing device—speed, decoys, bottom echo, a catch up run—

WHAM! The Russian submarine seemed to leap upward. Captain Loshki heard the explosion of the torpedo warhead, felt himself hurled through the air, sensed contact with something solid that tore at his soft body and smashed bones, was aware briefly as the lights blinked out . . . that the sea roared into the torn submarine. As the water cloaked him with a relaxing softness, Loshki had no idea whether he rested on the deck or the overhead of the submarine.

•   •   •

Rand raced into sonar to hear for himself the sound of the submarine breaking up ahead of them. He desperately wanted to pass through the area to search for anything that might identify the submarine they had just sunk, for he had a sudden feeling of kinship with the captain whose torpedoes had been fired just seconds too soon. But just as desperately, he must return to the spot where *Reuben James* had vanished. He had overheard the reports from the bridge that *Reuben James* was completely gone, bow and stern quickly following the midsection. Perhaps there would be some survivors.

The Atlantic Ocean East of Galleons Passage

By far the largest contingent of Soviet warships was confidently steaming toward the Galleons Passage, which cut directly between Grenada and the islands to its south, Trinidad and Tobago. Although the most navigable of the West Indies passages, there was no more than seventy-five miles between those islands. No other passage meant more to the United States; more than sixty-five percent of the oil used on the eastern seaboard passed within a few hundred miles of Grenada. As a SLOC—a sea line of communication— Galleons was as critical as Gibraltar, Hormuz, Malacca. It was common sense, then, that the Russians sent their largest force to this vital point. It was intended as a display to the rest of the world of the weakness of the Americans.

It was also the reason that Admiral Pratt sent a powerful surface action group. The mighty battleship *Iowa* now added long range Tomahawk cruise missiles to her powerful sixteen-inch guns. She was joined by the Aegis guided missile cruiser *Valley Forge* and six multi-purpose destroyers. The force was quite able to protect itself from air attack by long range Soviet bombers, but its main mission was to deny the Russian ships access to the Caribbean. *Valley Forge* was the cornerstone of the group, a floating, high-speed computer capable of coordinating the weapons of the entire surface action group. She was designed to acquire air, surface, and subsurface targets, track them, and finally designate the ship and/or weapon to counter the anticipated attack. This particular group, in effect, was not only a formidable offensive threat, but it literally provided itself with a shield against all but a suicide attack.

The Soviet force that merged near Galleons in the final forty-eight hours possessed a competitive offense. It was tracked earlier by satellite intelligence; long range patrol planes later reported as each element joined up with the flagship *Rostov*. This Slava-class cruiser was potent, with her long range SS-N-12 missile tubes, and the older cruisers and destroyers in company were equal in throw weight to the American ships. The only item that continued to confound Admiral Pratt's intelligence experts was the inclusion in the force of one of the Soviet Union's largest amphibious ships. She'd emerged from the Mediterranean weeks before and set course toward the South American coast with her two escorting destroyers, seemingly on a mission separate from the powerful warship. Now, as an element of a striking force, her mission remained unknown.

The path of advance of the two forces was obvious to both countries. The American ships had assembled south of Bermuda a few days before. The Soviet vessels, meandering about the Atlantic like water bugs, converged at a point two hundred miles southeast of Barbados. The Russian objective was to insert the powerful surface group into the Caribbean, via the Galleons Passage, upon signal from Admiral Khasan. The mission of Pratt's surface action group was to interpose itself in that choke point, denying the Russians access. It became a matter of timing and wills and nerves as they approached each other. At three hundred miles the Soviet force had the initial advantage of missile range, but Khasan had yet to receive confirmation from Paul Voronov on securing the Panama Canal.

The speed of advance of the two groups, each at almost twenty-five knots, brought them about one hundred miles closer every two hours. At a range of two hundred miles, when the American Tomahawk missiles could strike, Paul Voronov had reported only that his destroyer was in position and that the Panamanian insurgents were in control of the area around the Pedro Miguel Locks; but he still had not heard from his demolition teams within the chambers of the locks.

Admiral Khasan wanted to order his surface force to circle in position, maintaining a slight missile advantage over their American counterparts at that range, but that would allow the Americans to position themselves directly across Galleons Passage.

Admiral Pratt paced tensely in his flag plot aboard *America*, waiting apprehensively for the first report that the Russians were launching their longer range missiles; but it never came. He could see the dilemma facing Khasan, and he silently concurred that he would have continued to advance himself. Whether or not he received a report that Pedro Miguel was under attack by Ryng's SEAL team, he would allow his ships to open fire.

At a range of ninety miles Khasan was informed that Paul Voronov's men had reported the placing of some of the explosives and timing devices within the locks. He ordered his surface force to close Galleons at maximum speed, firing at will. The amphibious ship that remained at the tail of the surface force now dropped farther back, as had been previously planned. The destroyers prepared to open fire with their missiles, wishing desperately that they carried the longer range weapons already airborne from the cruiser.

Iowa's Tomahawk missiles, virtually untried in surface warfare, also fired. The escort ships charged ahead, preparing to fire as they approached maximum range.

Dave Pratt, heedful of the missiles already in the air, carefully concentrated his intelligence gathering devices on the amphibious ship now almost dead in the water. He hated secrets.

The Panama Canal—Just North of the Pedro Miguel Locks

Bernie Ryng observed the gunships circling the destroyer like a swarm of mosquitoes buzzing about a sleeping camper's head, searching for the softest skin. There was nothing the sailors on that ship could do. The helos moved too fast, doing nothing more than creating an irritant. Perhaps we should order them to fire, he thought. But on the other hand, there was no telling what that might bring on. It still was necessary to get aboard and gain control. There was no logic in taking chances.

Dusk was approaching when he gave the signal. Though there was no need for silence, the men conversed in whispers —a habit, an unwritten custom before a mission began. There was a common bond established by the rigor of their training and the respect for each man who survived it, and that was strengthened by the covert action the majority of them had taken part in during their careers. They were a rock-hard team united by a dependency on each other. As individuals they could survive almost anything ever designed to kill a man; as a team, they could destroy almost anything ever devised by man.

They slipped into the warm, always muddy water at the Gaillard Cut, descending to thirty feet. Bernie Ryng was the leader of the forward line, four men strung out to his right, gauging the distance between the others by the tiny lamps attached to their wrists. Each man in the forward line was assisted by a tiny but powerful electric motor that silently pulled them through the dark waters. A thin nylon cord attached to their waists went back to the second line of four. Two of these men carried the torches that would be used to cut through the hull near the ship's generators. The other two carried satchels of high explosives. Behind them were three more lines of swimmers, each attached to the trailing cords, each weighted down with waterproof bags containing small arms, automatic weapons, grenades, and ammunition. At that depth there was absolutely no way they could be seen from the surface. Each understood his part in the plan. They knew where they would slip aboard ship and exactly how the weapons would be distributed. SEALs adapted to a situation and each other instinctively.

As they neared the ship, machinery noises became clearer, until it seemed they were almost on top of it. At a distance of twenty-five yards Ryng gave the signal to stop. The two men with the cutting equipment were sent on alone.

Unhooking their safety lines, Wright and Ryng swam to either side of the ship. They surfaced quietly, barely moving or breathing as they studied the vessel. Dusk had turned into night. Though a very dim glow remained in the western sky, a few bright stars already twinkled through the humid night air. The guards on the main deck were in the same positions as they had been during the day—two on the stern, two amidships and two forward of the main deckhouse. And they were bored, their automatic weapons propped beside them as they chatted and smoked. It was exactly as intelligence reported a few hours before, once the excitement of the buzzing helos wore off. The PRA controlled the shore, or so they thought. The ship seemed secure.

At a signal from Ryng, Wright slipped below the surface and joined him near the other waiting SEALs. Safety lines were unhooked. Silently, one by one, the men bobbed to the surface near the destroyer's hull. Slipping out of their breathing gear, they quietly awaited their leader's next move.

Ryng reached up, grasping the rudder guard on the starboard side, and slowly heaved himself up until he was balanced in a squatting position. Rising tentatively, he peered across the deck. Directly opposite, Wright's eyes met his own.

Both guards were leaning against the after gun mount, smoking. At Ryng's hand signal one of his men splashed a few times off the stern. The guards ambled back to peer into the night. Very quickly Ryng and Wright were over the lifelines. There was never a sound. Moving with the speed and silence of cats, they dropped garrote wires over the guards' necks, yanking them taut before either man could utter a sound. The limp bodies were lowered over the side.

Ryng and Wright reconnoitered the after section of the ship. Everything was sealed. Ryng moved up the starboard side to check the nearest hatch leading down to the engineering spaces. It was welded shut, and as he was moving his hand about feeling for any weakness, the midships guard called to him. He was out of matches—he wanted a light! Ryng answered back that he had no matches, but the man persisted in coming over to him anyway. Ryng eased back into the shadow. Though it was dark, enough of a glow was cast by the lamp near the midships passageway that five feet away the approaching guard recognized that Ryng was not the man he was supposed to be, nor was he wearing the right uniform.

He let out one shout, a brief one, but with enough fear and

surprise that it would bring others. In an instant he was dead and over the side. Ryng retreated back to the stern. "No choice," he said quietly to Wright. "He could have made more noise, but that was enough. The hatch on this side's sealed. How about you?"

"Same on the other side. And the main deck appears to be permanently sealed off on both sides before you get to the midships passageway. They've also cut the ladders up to the next level."

"Same for me. It looks like you might get into the midships passageway, but there must be a trap of some kind. The exterior hatches down to the engineering spaces are sealed tight as a drum." He shook his head unhappily. "Looks like there's no choice but to get inside from the level above if we want to get down to those spaces."

On the stern the team had already distributed firearms. Each man had the weapons he was best trained with. They were prepared to move, each attired in black, their faces smeared with soot.

Two guards appeared on the edge of the helicopter deck above, peering down through the darkness, their guns pointed over the edge. They could make out shadows on the stern, too many of them. One of the guards shouted with surprise before an automatic rifle burst silenced them both.

The shots brought startled attention from the hangar on the level above. Two SEALs, crawling into position on top of the after mount, picked off three of Grambling's men before the others scattered back to the safety of the hangar. Within moments, two more SEALs vaulted like acrobats from partners' shoulders onto the hangar deck. Then they started the perpetual motion chain of men and equipment to that deck. It was only a matter of seconds.

Grambling's men, momentarily stunned, opened fire on the figures climbing up to the hangar deck. The two SEALs on the mount lay down a suppressing fire with automatic weapons. Ryng shouted for a grenade launcher on the mount. As if they were anticipated, three antipersonnel grenades arched into the tight confines of the hangar. Four SEALs closely followed the blasts into the hangar bay. Six bodies greeted them.

The two men on the mount remained to guard their rear. In-

side the hangar Ryng said, "We can go through there," pointing at the exit onto the same level forward, "or we can drop
down to the main deck through that hatch."

"I think both," answered Wright. "No choice!"

Ryng nodded. There wasn't a choice. They would be hit
from behind if they didn't clear resistance above and below
immediately.

Wright would move forward and take the bridge; Ryng
would silence the five-inch guns from below. "You take this
level," he told Wright. "There's forty feet of open space to
cover and they're going to have a field of fire from above you
. . . maybe on the roof of the hangar, behind you as you go out
. . . maybe up forward from the signal bridge. I'll go down to
the main deck, move up through the midships passageway,
and neutralize the interior spaces . . . meet you at the forward
ladder."

Wright and three SEALs gingerly pushed open the hatch to
the space outside. They were greeted with automatic weapons
fire from forward. Ducking back inside, shaking his head,
Wright said, "Machine guns near the signal bridge. The only
way to hit them is from the top of the hangar," he concluded,
pointing above.

Ryng went to the rear of the hangar, shouting back to
the men on the mount, "Can you see anyone up there?" He
jerked his finger toward the roof of the hangar. There was a
pause, then a shrug from one of the men. They couldn't tell.
He called Wright over. "Could be whoever is up there is smart
enough to wait. Those photos we had showed it was clean at
the time, but that doesn't mean there's no one there now.
Come on. One apiece up top . . . like basketball," he added,
cradling a grenade in his hand.

Ryng motioned two others over to the ladders that led to the
top of one hangar. He and Wright slipped the pins from antipersonnel grenades, waited to the count of three, and lofted
them in a hook shot onto the hangar's roof, one on either side
of the electronics mast. Two SEALs scurried up the ladders,
peering cautiously over the edge as the smoke lifted.

"Damn good thing, Mr. Ryng," one of them called down.
"They had two men with rapid fire." The SEALs crept forward on the roof of the hangar and were just beyond the elec-

tronics mast when the area was raked with machine guns. One of them staggered backward over the edge, crumpling on the hangar deck. Two more SEALs scampered up to back up the remaining man. Wright, waiting by the hangar's forward hatch, was ready to move out onto the open level. He looked back to Ryng. The latter shook his head.

Inching up the ladder, Ryng saw his three men firing across the open space toward the signal bridge. It was return fire from that same area that had kept Wright from getting to the open deck. The SEALs were inching their way forward on their bellies toward the safety of the after stack. But it was through a hail of bullets. Another of them stopped moving, sprawling facedown on the deck, a pool of blood spreading under him.

There was no way they could get into a position to silence the machine guns. No one could leave the hangar, nor could the men above get off the roof now. Ryng dropped back down into the hangar. "No way," he told Wright. "We need all the men we've got to capture this thing. We'll just lose them one by one this way. I'm calling in gunships to spray the signal bridge. That'll drive them back . . . or with some of their heavier stuff, they might just wipe out everything for you. Then you can get across that deck." He spoke into his radio for a moment, then handed it to Wright. "I'm going below, see if I can clean out those spaces. When the birds show in a few minutes, have them blast until you can get your men in place, then move the helos back again. Can't afford to have one of them crash this ship, but I want to keep them busy enough up there so I can get to the handling room."

Ryng gave a sign to the two men joining him. One lifted the hatch to the space below just enough for the second to drop two grenades down. The first slammed the hatch, which lifted slightly against the blast, then pulled it open quickly. Ryng dropped through, never touching the ladder. He hit the deck in a darkened room, the smell of cordite and blood pervasive. The blackness was sliced by the thin beam of a light at his waist as the other two landed beside him. There was no one alive in the room. The two mangled corpses had been waiting patiently for them.

There were shouts outside in the passageway, then the door

swung in toward them. The SEAL beside Ryng fired a burst before it ever opened fully. The second stretched through the doorway, tossing grenades in either direction down the passageway.

Simultaneous blasts were echoed by piercing screams. One of the SEALs peered out the door. Two men lay dead to their left. A third had been right outside the door.

They moved forward and Ryng indicated the next doorway down the passage. One man moved ahead, positioning himself against the bulkhead on the far side, his hand poised above the doorhandle. Ryng pulled the pin of the next grenade, waited momentarily, then nodded. He leaped past the open door, tossing the grenade, then flattening himself as the door was slammed tight. They were greeted by screams of pain as it exploded. The third SEAL sprayed the interior with his automatic weapon. When the echo of the gun died, they were met with only silence.

They did the same for the next space. There was no one there. In the third compartment, following the same method, they were greeted by one dead, unarmed sailor. The following compartment was also empty. If there were others in that section of the ship, they remained in front of the SEALs.

Ahead, beyond a bend in the corridor, was the hatchway that led to the main deck. They should be able to exit onto the deck in front of the protective shields that denied any movement forward from the stern. That should also allow them access to the ladders to both the open deck above and to the forward part of the ship, and they would also be able to get to the hatches that led to the handling rooms three decks below.

The first SEAL rounded the corner leading to the open midships area and was blown back by a machine gun burst that dropped him at Ryng's feet. Three feet ahead there was a no-man's-land, an area that had to be secured before they could work again with Wright or gain access to the lower decks.

Ryng considered his choices. There were just two of them now. He had no idea how many were ahead, waiting for them to come through that hatch. They had automatic weapons, and probably much more. He could think of nothing other than to wait until the gunships opened up above. That would have to attract their attention. He tried his walkie-talkie—but

got nothing but static. He waited, listening, thinking he could
hear the sound of rotors. But if there were any, they were
drowned out by the sound of bullets richocheting off the
bulkheads as someone inched into the passageway ahead
under covering fire. If it was Ryng, he would use that sort of a
ploy to get close enough to roll a grenade around the corner.
Looking at the man beside him, he realized that all they could
do was let loose with their own guns.

Havana

Commodore Navarro was amazed by his own quiescence. The one task force he had ever assembled, even at the behest of another power, had been a personal source of pride. And now, in a few short minutes, it had ceased to exist. His shock at the outset made rational thought impossible. He had gone to Castro in a rage, understanding what he had not cared to admit earlier—that Admiral Khasan had sacrificed those ships and sailors to determine how far the Americans could be pushed.

Navarro would never recall every word he had used when he barged into Castro's office—he knew there were things he never would have said at any other time, and he would remember the Premier allowed him that privilege, considering the debacle that had just taken place, before he retreated to compose himself. Navarro was not a brilliant man and he was well aware of that fact. But he could sense a trap and he could even sense the bait, Navarro, his navy, his sailors, Cuban troops, Fidel Castro, all of them—they were the bait. Even with their failure, the Russians remained in a perfect position to pull back. At that moment Navarro had no idea of Admiral Pratt's forces in or out of the Caribbean, nor did he have the least suspicion that the entire strategy had been anticipated days before in Washington.

Commodore Navarro knew only that he had lost the heart

of his tiny fleet and he felt that the remainder, those ships that were right now moving into the Florida Straits as a pincer group to the American's rear, would meet the fate of their sister ships off Colón. He had no intention of allowing his remaining men to fall into that trap. What he also intended to accomplish was to save the Cuban brigade intended to land on Panama's north coast. If they were challenged by American air and ground forces, he saw a slaughter in the making. By the time he finished talking to the Premier he decided, with a wry smile to himself, he would either be considered a patriot or a traitor.

Castro looked up as Commodore Navarro returned, striding purposefully through the door. He had been thinking about that brigade and he had never before experienced such hesitancy about committing his forces in a revolution. Now, here was Navarro coming to cry on his shoulder. "Unless you have something of value to tell me concerning the next few hours," he stated coolly, "I am very busy."

"It will take but a minute," Navarro said, then drew a deep breath. "I cannot, without speaking to you, in good faith allow our brigade, or my ships in the Florida Straits, to continue on their missions."

Castro's eyes opened wide. It was eerie, disquietingly so, that Navarro was expressing the same fear that had just come over him.

Aboard U.S.S. *America*

"I have Admiral Bechtel patched into line two, sir," the communications officer repeated. When there was no answer the first time, he'd turned to see Pratt pull open the hatch and gaze across an endless expanse of Atlantic. Thank God I don't have his responsibilities the communications officer thought. This is the second time in his life he's run up against them—more than any man should have to accept.

"Oh, thanks . . . sorry . . . he's on the scrambler?" Pratt inquired as he turned from his distraction.

"Yes, sir. And he's anxious to talk to you."

Pratt picked up the phone, keying the button tentatively. "You there, Tommy?"

"Right where you'd expect me to be—up to my ass in politicians. . . ." There was a silent hesitation on the other end. "They've got some reports of our losses. Dave, you've got a war going on down there, but Moscow's strangely silent. Nothing from Havana. Not a word from Panama City."

Pratt considered Bechtel's statement. The main combatants were keeping their mouths shut. "Have you checked with the White House on that?" Pratt asked.

"The only thing the President's aides have mentioned is a Colombian ambassador who seems to be hopping mad about some goddamn destroyer of theirs that disappeared."

"You don't have to look any further, Tommy. It's sitting right beside the Pedro Miguel Locks in the Canal, a floating time bomb."

"That was the kicker you couldn't figure out?"

Pratt explained what he'd heard up to a few moments ago from Henry Cobb. "I took a chance, Tommy. The President's either going to love me or hang me—I sent a bunch of Air force F-4s out and erased that little Cuban task force off Colón."

Again there was silence on the other end. "Ahh . . . since we haven't heard anything official from Havana yet, I'm going to ask permission to send some jets out to scare off a small Cuban landing team threatening Colón . . . and I'll ask for permission to fire only if fired upon. Consider it done."

"Thanks, Tommy, that's the easy part. What are you going to do about those bombers closing me from the northeast?"

"We've been tracking them for some time, Dave. They want *America*, I'm sure. How far to max missile deployment?"

"Fifteen . . . twenty minutes at most. I doubt they'll fire from there, not unless it's a coordinated attack with their submarines."

"Have your Hawkeyes got them now?" The Hawkeyes were long range patrol planes sent out on perimeter shield as a carrier's first line of defense against missile attack.

"Sure do."

"Let me know the minute there's any sign they're going to

use missiles. I've got a man at the White House right now who's tagging along with the President's military aide. How's *Iowa* doing?'' Tommy Bechtel had been a young ensign aboard the old battleship during the Korean War.

"Wait one, Tommy." Pratt's operation officer was interrupting with the latest satellite photos—the Russians had just initiated a missile launch off the Galleons Passage. The last photo was even more interesting. Soviet ingenuity at its best!

"Tommy, *Iowa*'s under fire. I've got a photo here of missile boats deploying from the back end of that Russian amphib— right in the middle of the damn ocean! You better get hold of your man at the White House. I'm down to minutes here. Out!"

To Admiral Bechtel the instant cessation of background noise over his receiver indicated that Dave Pratt really was down to minutes. He could picture Pratt covering the short distance from his private office to flag plot.

Inside the Pedro Miguel Locks

The interior of the Pedro Miguel Locks reminded Henry Cobb of an immense wine cellar. At each turn in the corridors descending deeper into the cavernous locks, he expected to find walls lined with dusty bottles in spider-webbed racks. But there was never anything more than the rough cement walls.

The sides of the locks were eighty feet in depth, but it was not a simple matter to get to the bottom. When the cement had been poured more than seventy years before, the base of each lock was twenty solid feet of concrete; then the inner walls were built back in six-foot steps to allow reinforcement for the water-bearing tunnels that snaked through them. The engineers who designed the lock system had sincerely expected these walls and lock gates to last forever, and Henry Cobb was gaining a new respect for those long-dead men's interpretation of *forever*.

The corridors were damp and cool, a dank, fetid smell pervading the air. Lights were placed at intervals so that there was never a dark section. Yet deep within the bowels of the chambers there had never been a man who felt there could be enough light. Concrete steps descended to various levels from which passageways extended to chambers whose intent had long been forgotten. Some were completely empty. There were places where water had inevitably trickled through crevasses to wear away at the concrete. Little piles of crumbled cement indicated where someday in the future an engineer would have to reinforce the thick walls.

As they neared the base of the labyrinth, the hum of machinery grew more evident. Pumps circulating water through the vast tunnels honeycombed the chambers. There was machinery to back up anything man-made that might fail at a critical moment, electrical generators for the lights and pumps, and motors that turned the gigantic bull wheels which opened and closed the immense gates—sixty-five feet wide and seven feet thick! The machinery to operate such a system had been beyond the imagination of all but a few men in 1913. Henry Cobb marveled at it more than seventy years later.

The original plans had been old and cracked with age, so Cobb was using copies made that day which contained blank spots created by age and incessant folding of the originals. But he arrived exactly where he intended—on the bottom level where the critical machinery to supply electrical power to the huge bull wheel motors was located. That was where they came upon their first corpse.

For just an instant Henry Cobb realized this place reminded him of a never-ending crypt—especially when he saw a man, obviously a worker, with his back stitched with bullet holes.

Cobb split the team, six with him working along one wall single file toward the north end of the locks, the other six with Gorham, far enough behind to be safe if Cobb's team was hit. There was no way to muffle the sounds of their approach —any noise at all echoed through the caverns of cement.

How many enemy were down here, Cobb wondered? Four had been seen leaving the destroyer. But there were also men who carried demolition materials for them. They had been told that PRA troops ashore had joined those from the ship when they descended into the chambers. Therefore, there had to be guards of some kind! Even if the PRA anticipated no trouble, they had to dispose of the workers who maintained and ran the machinery. There were fourteen in the SEAL team. Four were demolition experts and were expected to defuse the explosives—if they got that far.

Cobb ducked instinctively as he heard something ahead. The others followed his motion, diving to the floor split seconds before the chatter of automatic weapons fire shattered the air, followed by the sharp echo reverberating off the walls as bullets screamed about them. They were showered by chips of concrete stinging the skin like so many bees, but then the suddenness of gunfire was followed by the equally frightening sound of silence. Only the short, deep gasps of men still thankfully breathing could be heard.

Cobb peered through the dim light straight ahead. As far as he could see there was only a straight tunnel. Forty to fifty feet in front of them the map showed another tunnel off to the left that ran to a storeroom. It had to have come from there. But how many were there? And how could he get to them? He considered the flat walls and ceilings. Everything seemed to be at right angles. The storeroom tunnel ahead cut off at exactly ninety degrees. It would be folly to inch far enough ahead to shoot into it.

The second man behind carried a grenade launcher. Cobb considered moving him forward but thought better of it. No man was a better shot than he. He reached back, exchanging his automatic rifle for the weapon. Slipping a concussion grenade into the launcher, Cobb crawled noiselessly across to the opposite wall.

He waited . . . but there was nothing. He inched forward slowly, a yard at a time, until he was halfway there. Then he raised the launcher to his shoulder. No need to hit anything . . . just bounce the grenade off the far wall of the tunnel that cut off to the left. A concussion grenade near anyone in that tunnel would immobilize them for long enough.

He fired and held his breath. The grenade hit within inches of where he aimed, bouncing off that far wall, then rattling back and forth into the side tunnel. There was a frantic scurrying of men falling over each other to escape, and one actually dove out into the main tunnel just as the grenade went off. Though he escaped the full force of the blast, he had little time to appreciate his luck. A SEAL put a bullet through his head before he could look up.

Cobb was on his feet, dashing for the side tunnel as smoke billowed out into the main passage. With the others right behind him, he rolled across the opening. On his stomach, peering through the smoke, the dim light outlined three men spread in bizarre positions across the floor. Cobb's team collected four automatic rifles before they moved on. The persistently increasing hum of machinery brought them closer to their goal.

Two single rifle shots echoed through the tunnel as the group emerged into a cavernous, high-ceilinged chamber. Cobb's first reaction—that the shots came from a marksman—was the correct one. There were no ricochets this time. Two of the SEALs, one behind the other on the opposite side of the passage from Cobb, were knocked backward by the impact of the bullets as they struck their foreheads. No one doubted they were dead before they ever hit the concrete.

Who would be next? Cobb thought. They waited expectantly, once again on their bellies. Why didn't he fire again? It was simple, Cobb realized. Now that they were waiting, the next shot would reveal his position. He was waiting for them to move again . . . or perhaps the marksman was moving, finding another safe spot before they figured out where he was hiding.

There was really only one solution. There wasn't a man in the team who doubted how it had to be done, and they waited silently for their leader to make the decision. Cobb looked at the men behind him, then across from him. Gorham had only four men left. Cobb reached behind to tap the next man on the shoulder, but hesitated. Only one target made it too easy. He pointed across to the man behind Gorham, indicating that he should move with the man behind Cobb on signal. Slowly, so slowly that only those near them could recognize the movement, the two men rose from flat on their bellies to a crouch. The one on Cobb's side would move diagonally across the passageway, well in front of Gorham; the other would do the same in the opposite direction. They would draw fire, and it was only a question of who would be the target. Before, unsuspecting, it was easy for the sniper to take two men out.

This time, with both moving, one would likely be home free; the other might have a fifty-fifty chance.

Cobb snapped his fingers and they were moving, but not in a straight line. Survival motivated the direction of their feet. There was a shot, a rebounding echo, the sigh of a ricochet, a second shot, and a cry from the man who had been behind Cobb. He went down in a heap, bouncing off the wall, rolling almost to the center of the passageway, then scrambling frantically away from the certain death in the open but never making it. A third shot snapped out. There was no ricochet. Nor was there any further movement from him.

Gorham had rolled into a kneeling position, his gun already firing before the sound of the last shot died out. One of the men on Cobb's team had also seen the origin of those last shots. Their gun barrels were elevated. Cobb looked up. A man was running for cover on a catwalk ahead and above them. Two others appeared from the end he was racing for, firing wildly to cover the SEAL's fire.

One man, then a second, lurched off the top of the catwalk. They were replaced by others before their bodies hit the floor. SEALs were in motion now, firing their own weapons, ducking behind anything that offered momentary protection, but constantly moving. The bullets whining off the concrete were as dangerous as any that were aimed. The SEALs were simply following the old theory that he who keeps moving becomes less of a target.

In the moments that followed, Cobb saw two more of his men hit. There was no time to stop. There had never been any intention of stopping, only pushing forward until they reached the main machinery area. As they passed beneath the catwalk, firing up at two remaining men, grenades dropped down from above. They had been held for a moment after the pins were pulled, exploding just before they hit the floor. Two more of his men went down.

Cobb ducked around a corner and found himself entering an even larger chamber. This was where the main generators were located, along with the machinery that controlled the bull wheels and the largest water pumps. This had to be the space in the Pedro Miguel Locks selected for demolition! And seven members of his team, including one explosives expert, died to find it.

One of the first things Cobb spotted as he eased into the room was a man racing toward stairs at the far end, a large bag of some kind hanging over his shoulder. Cobb brought his rifle up, aimed quickly and squeezed off two very accurate shots, the body landed with a thud.

Cobb knew he was right as he ripped open the bag to find explosives. That would help—anything would help—to know what was being used, perhaps where to search for the charges and how to disarm them.

The chamber they were in was cavernous, and it smelled of oil and grease and metal, mixed with the familiar, dank aroma of dampness and mold. The charges might be set now, or most of them—the man he'd just shot could have been setting the last one when they broke through. There were two entrances to the huge room—one they'd just come through, the other at the far end where the man had tried to escape.

It would have been better defended, Cobb was sure, if they'd had a notion that his SEAL team was nearby. He was certain that the timers were set for a long enough delay to allow the PRA to return and defuse them if the threat was successful. But Bernie Ryng, on top, would negate that threat and no one would be back down there—they would make good their threat even though they ultimately would lose, unless his men could succeed. He set up one man to cover the tunnel they'd just come from; a second guarded the exit on the far end.

He found the first device himself. It wasn't hidden and, he reflected, there probably had been no thought of hiding the explosives. Who, after all, was going to look for them at this stage? Then other devices were discovered, out in the open—in what were perfect locations to cause the most damage. That had been the goal, and it still could be successful if time ran out.

Suddenly rapid fire from the rear tunnel brought Cobb back to the here and now. Though his man on that end was well covered, the fire was intense and Cobb knew backup would be needed quickly. Three of the enemy burst into the chamber, vaulting over the bodies of their comrades, wildly scattering grenades. They were cut down efficiently by Cobb's man as shrapnel and bullets sang through the air. But that was a suicide attack, and Cobb knew more had to follow. Shots now came from the other end of the chamber as his men worked cautiously on the explosives. They were being assaulted from both ends. . . .

Above the Pedro Miguel Locks

Kitty Alvarez leaned back in exhaustion against the hard, inner wall of the helo. She'd flown in a variety of them before but she had never in the past considered that you could fall asleep in one.

Jolted awake by the chatter of guns, she got up and moved forward behind the pilot, who was banking away from the action. Ahead she could see Apache helicopters swooping down on the hillside above Pedro Miguel, rockets and machine gun fire tearing at the PRA defenders. She couldn't believe it would last long—the Apaches' firepower was so much stronger. Yet she saw two of them fall to wire-guided missiles.

Outside of realistic training missions many years before, Kitty Alvarez had never been involved in actual combat. Her assignments had been mostly intelligence gathering, and in those days the CIA always sent in the men whenever they expected things might get rough. She had been recruited in her college days, trained right afterward, and worked sporadically for them in her own country until the agreements were signed to turn the Canal over to the government. At that point she acknowledged that assisting her developing country meant more to her than the excitement of occasional undercover missions. It had been three months now since she had been introduced to Admiral Pratt during a trip to Washington. She agreed to cooperate only because she knew her country was now threatened from the outside.

This was the last time—the only time, she now promised herself—she would ever do this. She had something vital to live for, something beyond anything she could ever imagine. She had once been in love with James Grambling, but that was years ago. They had been students, and they loved passionately and quickly in those exciting years. But they also found that they were as emotionally involved in opposing causes as in each other. Neither would meet the other halfway, and in the end, they erected an insurmountable wall between themselves. Kitty did think of James at times, often affectionately, but about more pleasant, youthful memories than of a lost love. With Bernie Ryng she had found something else, something more mature. Though he could be as aggressive and violent as Grambling, Ryng had also found a void within himself that Kitty filled. He'd expressed that in a few simple, awkward words as he pulled her from the pool amidst the rubble of Casa Rejean, grateful that she was alive as he tenderly wrapped the robe around her shoulders. All of this came back to her as she knelt silently, watching over the pilot's shoulder as the Apaches raked the hillside above Pedro Miguel.

Now, after Horacio Ramos had convinced her to make this one last effort—for her country, for him—she could not refuse. Only she could bargain for Ramos, who wanted the traitor, James Grambling, alive.

Aboard the U.S.S. *America*

Dave Pratt's aide lost count after twenty-six. He had been counting the number of times the Admiral removed his baseball cap to smooth back his hair. It was his only visible physical reaction to the events unfolding in Panama, in the Caribbean, along the islands of the West Indian chain, in the Florida Straits, and off Galleons Passage.

The Cuban threat seemed to have been negated. There would be no task force steaming off Colón. The Cuban missile boats and a single frigate had reversed course in the Florida Straits; and for some unknown reason the transport carrying the Cuban brigade had turned north fifty miles from the Panama coast.

On the other hand, *Kharkov* had launched another flight,

now clearly destined for Panama. Would they attack or would they, too, reverse course? They would soon be aware, if they did not already hold them on radar, that a flight of American attack planes escorted by fighters had been launched toward the Russian carrier from the Canal Zone. A second flight was on its way to Bluefields in Nicaragua, ordered to neutralize Soviet aircraft there.

Dave Pratt was still unsure at the moment who was actually affecting the blockade of island choke points. Reports were streaming in of individual battles between American and Russian submarines and surface ships. Losses on both sides appeared consistent. Neither yet retained the advantage.

And in Galleons Passage it was might against might. The combatants had yet to hold each other visually, but the missile exchange had commenced.

As Dave Pratt searched the displays in flag plot for an answer, for any clue to something more that he might do at this stage, he noted that some of the long range Soviet bombers had broken through the perimeter defense and were converging on *America*. The carrier was built to sustain a number of hits, but past experience reminded him that aircraft carriers were eventually as susceptible as the tiny frigates. It simply required a greater effort—the more missiles fired at the carrier, the better the odds of inflicting fatal damage.

Aboard *Kharkov*

Admiral Khasan no longer marveled at the power of *Kharkov*, nor did he yearn to take one more tour of her decks. The resistance in Panama was more than had been anticipated . . . or was that really the answer? Those people were said to have so little to defend themselves with. Much of the leadership of their Guardia supposedly supported the rebel PRA, yet the troops had not risen up behind their officers, nor had the people come out to support the PRA. That professor, Alvarez, who had been so positive, and claimed to have the ear of President Ramos, had apparently been unsuccessful in convincing Ramos to step down. Early reports indicated that the Cuban navy was unable to defend itself without the air support he had hoped to offer them, and Havana was surprisingly quiet, except for the outraged messages from Castro. Khasan wondered what the hell Castro really expected when outside interests supported a *golpé*. Had he really forgotten the casualties of a revolutionary war? This was more than twenty-five years after his own *golpé*, and he should understand that it would be that much more deadly.

Khasan had given orders that he hoped he would not regret later. When Paul Voronov reported that the destroyer was in command of the Pedro Miguel Locks and that his men had entered the chambers to set their explosives, Khasan had considered the job as good as done. He had given his ships on the island chain permission to attack, logically assuming that such firepower combined with the Canal becoming a hostage would settle matters more quickly. On the contrary, the Americans had seemingly anticipated the push from the Atlantic and were meeting force with force. And for some unknown reason, the key to the entire plot, the Pedro Miguel, had yet to be secured. It was beyond Khasan's comprehension that anyone could possibly figure out Voronov's intent, if not actually mount an effort to neutralize an almost perfect scheme. His thoughts wandered back to that elusive student, Lieutenant Corazon, who had so mysteriously vanished from Havana. Khasan refused to believe that one man might be the key.

He was jolted from his reverie by the missile alarm. It couldn't be! They were supposed to be secure against any possibility. The Americans were supposed to remain on the ground in Panama when Ramos stepped down . . . but now *Kharkov* was the target of a missile attack!

The Atlantic Ocean, East of Galleons Passage

The surface action group's final orders from Admiral Pratt were a lesson in simplicity. They were to defend themselves against close-in submarine attack, but they were not to search out and destroy. The prime responsibility was to halt the Soviet surface group intent on entering the Caribbean via

Galleons Passage. Pratt's goal was to stop them, make them think, turn them around and send them on their way "sadder but wiser." Those last words had been Pratt's, added at the last moment to inject a personal flavor to an order that frightened him. To say this little touch had been appreciated by the men of the surface action group would have been an understatement. Every sailor in the fleet identified with Pratt, though he was unaware that his personal touches were taken so seriously. To send the Russians away "sadder but wiser" became the personal credo of every man in the group.

Missile battles occur over a very short time span—minutes! Because of this, helicopters were placed well beyond the American group as an anti-submarine barrier. Closer in, frigates established a second line of defense. *Valley Forge*, the Aegis-equipped cruiser, shared a central position in the force with *Iowa*; the former coordinated the group's defenses, the latter carried the first line of offense, the Tomahawk missiles. Spread in a half-moon ahead of them were the destroyers, their missiles poised.

Vladivostok and her sister ships were a fine example of Soviet doctrine—the air was filled with missiles. The objective in any sea battle is always to seek out and destroy the largest and most dangerous ships; but in a force action over the horizon, initially they are indistinguishable to the unseeing eye of a homing device. Some missiles are intended to fly by themselves to the target while others can be taken under control during flight by a helicopter and directed to the target. The Soviet helicopters on exactly that mission had come in low over the ocean to avoid radar detection. American LAMPS helicopters spotted them but had no guns and could only warn of their approach.

Aegis electronically detected each approaching object, assigning weapons according to the threat factor. Incoming missiles were decoyed by clouds of aluminum chaff fired skyward to distract their homing radar and by electronic devices sending out false signals of targets where there was nothing but open sea. A number of missiles were decoyed and exploded harmlessly. Others were knocked out of the air before they became a factor by Sea Sparrow missiles. Those that broke through to lock on a ship then had to fly through an almost impenetrable shower of bullets from Phalanx gatling guns to their target.

To the few men on the American ships who actually saw the effects of the attack, it was a surreal experience. There were no enemy ships on the horizon, no flash of big guns or smoke, no splash of shells in the sea, no diving aircraft. Rather, it was a blast here, an explosion there, as the Sea Sparrows hit one missile after another. There was also the explosive roar as Phalanx mounts activated their six barrels, spraying 3000 rounds per minute of depleted uranium bullets at missiles now diving on their targets.

Statistics in an electronic/missile environment are as much a factor in such a battle as men. Aegis could not possibly bring down every weapon fired at the force. It was particularly difficult to detect and track the huge missiles screaming in just above the surface. The first missile to hit *Iowa* roared in three feet off the water and exploded into the heavy armor belt surrounding the hull. The entire ship vibrated with the blast, a column of smoke and water rising well above the bridge. When it cleared, the immense ship steamed on with minor surface damage on the decks directly above. A second missile hit well forward, tearing a gaping hole in the bow, and fires erupted in the decks below. Yet there was no decrease in speed as *Iowa* plodded onward. The well-armored mount closest to the blast revolved on its barbette to insure there was no damage.

Valley Forge seemed blessed with its Aegis defense system, but the outer perimeter of destroyers was not as lucky. Being closer to the Soviet helicopters, they became the targets of redirected missiles. The bridge of *Coontz* was wiped out by a direct hit, the inward force of the blast wrecking her CIC. She wheeled erratically out of station, careening blindly through the screen of sister ships until her executive officer could assume command. Unable to see, she dropped astern until her fires could be controlled.

The Soviets attempted to knock the center out of the screen. *Tattnall*, a mile abeam of *Coontz* was first hit aft, knocking out both her five-inch gun and missile launcher. The missile penetrated the main deck before exploding, starting fires in the engineering spaces. A second missile dove into her bow, exploding in the forward magazine. Flames swept back over her bridge. Water rushing into her bow enlarged the already gaping hole, and the forward part of the ship eased visibly into the trough, each swell seeming to drag her lower.

On the Soviet side the first hit was on a new Udaloy destroyer racing ahead of the huge cruiser at thirty-five knots. A Tomahawk missile impacted directly into the SS-N-14 missile tubes. Three warheads detonated at the same time. The blast knocked the ship sideways, ripping away most of the bow section. Her bridge was blown up and off the deckhouse. Before another ship could close to remove survivors, she pitched headfirst into the ocean, her dual propellors thrashing the air. She had disappeared in less than sixty seconds.

Vladivostok was hit astern, one of her launchers disabled and her after engine room set afire. Able to make only fifteen knots, she gradually dropped out of the formation, only to become a perfect target. Ten minutes later, one of *Iowa*'s Tomahawks hit almost in the same location as the first. Fires that had been under control were rekindled and fuel ignited. Water pressure in the stern section disappeared with the second blast. Within moments the flames set off one of the after magazines. Now almost dead in the water, two more missiles slammed into her, one knocking out her anti-submarine launchers and a forward gun, the second destroying her bridge. Fires raged out of control fore and aft. There was no choice other than to abandon her.

As other ships were hit, some disabled, some in danger of sinking, the secondary strategy of the Russian force became dangerously clear. Half a dozen high-speed missile boats, their identification undetermined when they first appeared from the back of the amphibious ship, now raced line abreast at maximum speed toward the hole blasted out of the center of the American formation.

Hugging the water at high speed, still undetectable by radar, they would be on top of the American ships before they could be targeted. Their Styx missiles had a possible range of more than thirty miles, though Soviet doctrine normally waited for a more reliable twelve-mile shot. As Dave Pratt analyzed the pictures from the satellite, he realized they might have fired almost at the moment they deployed from the mother ship. It seemed that only missiles could stop them, yet they were a useless weapon until the approaching boats could be tracked by radar.

At that moment Pratt experienced a sense of omniscience. Here, twelve hundred miles from the source of the battle, yet able to survey the proceedings, he was capable of warning the participants before they were aware of their own danger. Over the long range radio net he contacted the commander of the surface action group and explained in as few words as possible the threat bearing down on them. There seemed only one defense, and that was a weapon from the past.

Traces of smoke were still curling around *Iowa*'s gun barrels as her sixteen inch mounts rotated in the direction of the approaching boats. A single gun fired the first one-ton shell. The maximum range was about twenty miles. The only available method for spotting the fall of the shell was via one of the LAMPS helicopters. It moved into the area with no defense at all against the well-armed boats.

The first shell dropped five miles ahead of the line of Osa missile boats. *Iowa* readjusted and waited another two minutes as the helicopters hovered just above the water, desperately hoping to remain unseen by the boats. The next shell landed two miles ahead of them. They still could not be seen visually from *Iowa*, nor had any radar acquired them. Yet somehow the boats found themselves racing full speed into some unknown and powerful menace. The second mount fired a broadside, three guns at once.

The two crewmen in the helo watched the line of boats approaching, white foam curling back from their bows. At any moment now they could fire missiles with a good chance of hitting their intended target.

Then the ocean seemed to erupt directly in front of the two boats on the far side. One of them veered away from the geyser, the second had no chance. Too close, the boat lifted into the air as the ocean rose in front of it, climbing skyward, then tilting back in a graceful arc. It had turned completely over before landing in the water, hull briefly visible before it disappeared.

Iowa's gunnery computer had accurately calculated the line of advance against the speed of the boats. With a slight adjustment to one side to compensate for the loss of the farthest Osa, the next broadside landed in the middle of the line. One boat simply disappeared when the cloud of water settled. A second had been ripped apart by shrapnel from the blast and lay over on its side. Three now remained, charging at the same speed but in a ragged line.

The next broadside was a bit shorter, landing a few hundred yards ahead. But it had the desired effect, as each of the remaining boats maneuvered now on their own, desperately trying to outthink the computer controlling the guns. As concerned about avoiding the immense shells as they were about firing their missiles, they had no chance to fire. Now, at twelve miles, one of the boats fired two missiles, one closely following the other. But Aegis, anticipating the missile boats, easily tracked and brought down the missiles before they endangered any of the ships.

The remainder of the attack was futile. The Osas bravely attempted to close. They could be hit as easily trying to escape as to attack, so they came on. But now the closest destroyers were able to acquire them on radar and the threat was all but ended. Not one of the Styx missiles had found a target. They had been defeated by a man more than twelve hundred miles away.

The American surface action group was still moving directly into their path when it was determined that the Soviet Force appeared to be reversing their course. As much as he wanted to follow them, Dave Pratt ordered his ships back into the Galleons Passage. He could not leave a choke point undefended. He was more concerned about Soviet submarines moving into the gap, which would have made the defense of Galleons Passage futile.

With cruise missile bombers still closing *America*, concern remained high over both the Pedro Miguel Locks and *Kharkov*, the Russian carrier that posed so great a threat to Panama.

Aboard the Destroyer—
Pedro Miguel Locks

Bernie Ryng found himself in a quandary, a situation he rarely encountered. But he also had never found himself enclosed in what was becoming an iron coffin. The air stunk of burnt powder and blood. Sand-colored metal bulkheads seemed to be closing in on them. Ryng glanced at the other SEAL and found that he was staring back with the same quizzical expression. At precisely the same moment they shrugged their shoulders, grinning foolishly at each other, and inched backward.

The machine gun bursts from beyond the bend in the corridor ceased, though that meant little. It indicated their enemy had tentatively stopped firing, most likely to listen for signs of life or for any sound that might indicate what lay ahead of them when they rounded that bend in the corridor. They had to be just as worried, Ryng concluded. No man welcomes what lies around the next bend if bullets have been coming from that direction.

Retreat would allow time, precious seconds, perhaps minutes, depending on who was the hunter and who the hunted. As Ryng inched backward, a parade of incidents galloped before his eyes, situations where he had no longer been able to advance, where he recognized death creeping closer if he failed to react properly. Each time, he had been somewhere he could jump, dive, dodge left or right, or run for cover. Here, there was no cover other than the bend in the corridor, a corridor no more than three feet wide and bounded by metal bulkheads.

Distraction—that seemed the only alternative of the moment—keep those ahead at least beyond that bend. So he pulled the pin from another grenade, held it until the last possible second and tossed it gingerly, bouncing it off the bulkhead so that it would land beyond that bend. Perhaps it would force someone to hesitate for a moment—those precious seconds.

The grenade burst with an ear-shattering explosion, echoing through the narrow corridor. It was followed by a scream of pain, rapid movement, and what he could only assume was the sound of someone being dragged away. He pushed open the door to one of the compartments they had passed. Two corpses were sprawled grotesquely across the floor. There was a thump and rattle, and Ryng saw what he had apparently considered in the back of his mind—the others were using the same ploy. The grenade seemed to increase in size as it bounced toward them.

Both men leaped through the door at the same moment, sprawling in a tangle on top of the bodies as the grenade burst just beyond the door. Ryng grunted as something stabbed into his upper arm. He looked down to see a small piece of jagged metal embedded in his shoulder. It had penetrated the flesh for only half an inch; he pulled it out with his fingers, allowing it to bleed freely. For the moment they seemed secure enough, but security seemed to be measured in seconds.

Waiting, barely breathing, a new sound came to them, muted at first but rapidly increasing in intensity. Then the SEAL beside Ryng recognized the rhythmic beat of rotors over the rumbling engines—Apaches—the helos Wright had called in!

As quickly as the deep growl of engines seemed to invest the vessel, the high-pitched chatter of machine guns drowned out all other sound. It rose to an intensity that threatened to burst eardrums, yet above it all they could also recognize the thump of rockets. The Apaches were showering the superstructure with a tempest of metal so overwhelming that it seemed impossible for any life to survive. Ryng could picture Wright and his men peering out at the devastation. If there was anything left after the Apaches ceased fire, it certainly would be pure luck.

What the hell are we doing here? Ryng inquired silently of himself. He jabbed his partner in the ribs, beckoning with a sweep of his arm as he leaped from the room and ran up the corridor. There was no doubt in his mind, no sane man would calmly advance down that corridor when those Apaches were turning the destroyer into pieces of scrap metal with that firepower. If anything, they should be immobilized by the overwhelming noise. The shock factor was on his side.

Rounding the bend in that corridor had seemed so much like climbing a mountain moments earlier. Now Bernie Ryng kept his rifle on automatic, clutching it tightly. Only one man stood between him and the far door, and that man's back was turned. The impact of the bullets propelled him through the hatch and across the expanse of deck, into the far bulkhead.

Ryng dropped to the deck, reaching for another clip. His partner vaulted over him and dove through the hatch, firing as he rolled. Then Ryng, too, was through the hatch, spraying bullets in the opposite direction; but there wasn't a soul there to stop them.

Looking to his left, Ryng saw two corpses, one grotesquely draped over the lifelines. There wasn't a soul visible on the opposite side. There was nothing blocking their intended path but the two bodies. Conversation was impossible as the Apaches continued to pound the superstructure with vicious fire.

As abruptly as it had begun, the hammering from above ceased. They could tell by the engine sounds that the helicopters were dropping back. That was followed by the sound of running feet above. Ryng eased cautiously out on the deck and saw Wright looking down at him.

Wright shouted matter-of-factly, "There can't be anything left alive up there." They looked up to the three separate levels leading to the bridge. It was now a mass of twisted metal and torn bodies. Not a thing moved.

"Don't count your chickens yet," Ryng shouted. "There may still be holdouts in the forward part of the bridge and—" Suddenly he was interrupted by a loud blast from the bow. The ship shuddered. It was followed by a second.

Wright held the radio to his ear. The voice coming over the radio was the commander of the Apaches, who said, "The bow gun on the destroyer is firing." He was reporting it to anyone who would listen. "They're shooting at the main control station in the middle of the locks."

Ryng slammed his fist against the steel bulkhead. "Goddamn!" That's just what he'd feared most. "Those helos can't penetrate the armor on that mount." He looked up at Wright. "That's their last resort. They didn't want to do that. I bet that's a signal to start blowing the locks. Let me have two of your men. I've got to get to that handling room." There hadn't been enough time for the SEALs to cut through the hull to flood the electrical spaces.

As he turned, another voice came over Wright's radio. "Is there a Commander Ryng down there?" Wright acknowledged, and the voice continued. "We're bringing someone in from the President's office . . . looking for prisoners—" The rest of the transmission was cut off, but there was no doubting the incredulous look in Ryng's eyes. He didn't believe in taking prisoners.

"Get up to the flight deck," Ryng shouted to Wright. "I'm going below." He jumped down a forward hatch, paying no attention to the rungs on the ladder, followed by the SEAL team members. Trying to take the handling room was a last resort.

Aboard *Kharkov*

Admiral Khasan was perplexed. Too long a professional, he was not the type to be afraid, but he realized there were reasons for concern. The persistence of *Kharkov*'s missile alarm confirmed that.

He felt certain that the Cuban element was lost to him. The flight of jets he had sent toward Panama encountered resistance, probably American fighter planes from what he could gather. It had never been intended that Soviet units seek direct combat with the U.S. Strangely enough, he had received no reports from his flight leader for the past fifteen minutes. He also knew his task force east of the islands was encountering heavy and unexpected opposition. Because his orders from Moscow were quite specific concerning heavy casualties, his only fear was being tried for dereliction of duty—for allowing the Americans to inflict severe losses.

He winced as he recognized the familiar sound of the missile launchers releasing their powerful weapons. Opening the hatch to the small weather deck outside his command area, he saw that the escort ships were also firing. Eerie flashes were the benchmarks as rocket engines ignited and hurtled their burden into the night skies.

They couldn't be under attack! It was unthinkable! As that thought repeated itself, he saw a destroyer directly on *Kharkov*'s beam blossom with flame. The smaller ship was outlined in stark detail against the blackness. Then it dimmed for a moment as the sound of the blast roared across the water. But that was only momentary, a prelude, for the destroyer was transformed into a torch and he could clearly see great chunks separating from the ship and hurtling through the air. He could actually feel the force of the second explosion as it rolled across the water.

It was at that very moment that the initial missile struck *Kharkov*.

A mighty blast slightly forward of the bridge area knocked Admiral Khasan to the deck. As he rose shakily to his feet, a second explosion rocked the hangar deck to his rear. The flight deck appeared to open like a flower as a tower of flame leaped into the sky. He understood, too well, that a fuel storage tank had ruptured.

Admiral Khasan still held no fear for his personal safety, but he now felt a wave of gut-wrenching terror for the survival of this great ship. His thoughts drifted back to earlier in the day, when he had wandered her decks, peering over the side at the blue Caribbean sliding by. She had seemed invincible then, too beautiful to sacrifice for anything he could imagine.

He turned and stared back as another blast, and then another, fed the flames. It was exploding ammunition! He felt *Kharkov* shudder and heel slightly to port. He could feel her losing speed. Khasan went back into his command center, where the fearful eyes of his staff met his own. There was no need to fool them. They understood.

He decided it was time to talk to the captain. As he stepped into the pilothouse, the forward section of the ship seemed to rise up in orange flame to meet him. He sensed objects flying through the air toward him before the searing heat incinerated every human being in the bridge area. . . .

Inside the Pedro Miguel Locks

Henry Cobb jammed in a fresh clip and fired toward the tunnel. In concert with the staccato reports of his rifle came the sudden realization that there should be no reason for these people to be attacking with such fury if all the explosives had been planted properly. My God, they must have been working when we made it in here, he thought, or else they may not have seen the need to destroy everything. Now, if they want to complete the job, they have to come to us!

He crawled over to his nearest demolition man. Indicating the satchel charges, Cobb beckoned him to follow. The bodies strewn grotesquely at the rear tunnel entrance seemed to have made an impression. Their enemy appeared to be regrouping. Henry Cobb knew that sooner or later enough of them would find a way to succeed, unless there was no longer an access to the chamber.

Shouting instructions into the other's ear, they inched their way over by the tunnel entrance. Cobb hurled three grenades down the passage to allow his man time to set the charges. The process was difficult enough without the added distraction of ducking bullets. Cobb provided cover until it was set.

As a new wave attacked from the tunnel, a powerful explosion shook the huge chamber, echoing back and forth across the cavern. It was followed by a rumble and clatter as hundreds of tons of concrete, loosened by the satchel charge, shattered down over the tunnel entrance. It seemed to Cobb that it might never stop until the entire room had crumbled and filled itself in.

But it did stop, and through the dust he could see that the tunnel was completely sealed. There was now only a single entrance and exit to the chamber—only one to attack and to defend.

Panama City

Horacio Ramos held Alvarez's arm in a firm grip as they stood by the window looking down on the broad thoroughfare. The street was mostly deserted, though it should have been teeming at that hour of the evening. Armed Guardia patrolled and occasionally one could hear sporadic shooting in the distance. But for a city supposedly in a state of siege, it was remarkably quiet.

"When was the last time you heard aircraft overhead, Esteban. . . . ?" Ramos's voice tailed off dramatically at the end for emphasis.

Alvarez said nothing. There had been no jet planes crisscrossing the skies over the city for almost two hours, since before sunset. At this stage it should have been crowded with them, low fliers swooping over the central plaza and the university area—so many other places had been suggested —broadcasting by their brazen presence that the revolution was in full swing and that now was the time for the people to take to the streets in support. But the people hadn't come out, nor did it seem they would. Ramos's orders to the loyal Guardia had been to politely ask them to return to their homes—show that the government remained in control, he explained—before they were placed in protective custody.

"There are a number of good men—and women, I think—who will be dead tomorrow, Esteban," Ramos continued. "We still have control of the radio—I knew that was critical. The people know about the Cuban force that was sunk north of Colón . . . they know that the Soviet jets have been turned back by the Americans . . . that the Russian carrier is under attack . . . that the Americans are helping us in the Canal . . . and they also know that the Americans are

fighting a great sea battle to the east.'' He released Alvarez's
arm. It was unnecessary to lead his old friend about like a
puppy. Horacio Ramos knew that there was no reason to go
on. Alvarez must understand that this was not to be the PRA's
day. It was time to save lives, to offer conditions of surrender.
''I think only you can make them understand at this point.
You know how to call a halt to this. Please, Esteban . . . if
there is a senseless slaughter, it will be because you failed to
heed my warning.'' Ramos's voice was firm now. ''You
must—''

''For myself, I don't have to do anything.'' Alvarez wheeled
to face the President. ''For the people who have been loyal to
us, I will do what you ask to save lives. But there is something
you *must* do, Horacio.'' He placed great emphasis on the
word *must*. ''You must put in writing exactly the terms you
will offer my people. Then I will ask them to put down their
arms. If I can't say that I have your word in writing,
something that I can show the world, they will not listen to
me.''

Ramos went immediately to his desk. ''We will write it
together. Here, pull up that chair. Sit beside me.'' The two
men, side by side, prepared the instrument that would end the
bloodshed between countrymen. So engrossed were they in
their work that neither one considered that the two superpowers were still engaged in a violent conflict well beyond the
border of their little country.

Aboard the Destroyer—Pedro Miguel Locks

Wright, his weapon resting across his arm, watched curiously
as the figure was lowered from the helicopter toward the
hangar deck of the destroyer. Apaches hovered on either side
in a protective shield. When there appeared to be some activity
near the forward section of the bridge, they sealed the area
with a spray of machine gun and rocket fire.

As the figure swung just above the deck, one of Wright's
men grasped the person tightly while another quickly lifted the

harness away and waved off the helo. To Wright's amazement he was face-to-face with a most attractive woman—Kitty Alvarez, the one who had been involved in their briefing earlier in the day!

"Miss Alvarez . . ." He could think of nothing else to say.

"The leaders . . . Grambling and Voronov . . . have you got them?" she shouted over the howl of the disappearing helo.

Wright shook his head. "Haven't seen either one of them. If they were in the bridge area, they'd be damn lucky to be alive right now." He gestured toward the wreckage of the superstructure.

Her voice was urgent. "I have to find out."

"It's a hell of a mess. I don't think you're going to find—"

"I've been asked by President Ramos to help bring those men out alive—by negotiation, if possible." She was walking forward, through the hangar, but paused as she came onto the open deck and stared up at the tangle of metal that had been the signal bridge area. She stopped in midstride, her eyes wide, riveted on the grim reality of the bodies amidst the wreckage.

"I'm afraid that's the way it's going to look up forward too. Bernie left me to secure the bridge. I'm headed up there now and—"

"Bernie—where is he?" The realization that Ryng had not come out to meet the helo momentarily frightened her. She grabbed Wright's arm tightly.

"He's trying to stop that," Wright replied, indicating the crashing sound of the forward gun, steadily firing one shell after another. "They haven't cut through the hull yet. Must be tough going. Bernie didn't have a choice. He's going into the handling room . . . that's our only other choice—if we can't cut off the power to the mount, cut off the ammunition!" Between blasts from the five-inch guns, there was the hollow rattle of small arms fire below decks. "There's still some resistance down there." His grim expression answered her question.

Kitty Alvarez closed her eyes, squeezing them tightly, as if that would remove her fear for Ryng. But he was involved in something that frightened even Wright. Grambling was aboard, one of Bernie's targets. Yet she was supposed to try to save James, and the Russian, for Horacio Ramos.

Kitty waited back in the hanger as Lieutenant Wright and his men climbed into the wreckage. When Wright called for her, she followed his path up the ladder to the signal bridge. It was impossible to avert her eyes from the gruesome remains left by the Apaches. There didn't appear to be a soul alive as they approached the bridge wing. Then a single automatic weapon opened fire from the door to the pilothouse.

One of his team fell dead at Wright's feet. Two of the others automatically returned a covering fire. There was no answer. Signaling one of his men to circle around to the opposite side, Wright eased up to the open hatch, his back against the bulkhead, and lofted a grenade inside. As it exploded, the two of them dove into the pilothouse from either side. But there was no need for weapons. It seemed impossible to tell which of the bodies sprawled in the pilothouse had fired on them.

Wright waved out to the others. The upper levels of the ship were secure. They checked the bodies one by one, kicking, prodding with rifle barrels. They were taking no chances. A pained groan issued from the far side of the wrecked pilothouse. Paul Voronov opened his eyes to stare unsteadily up at them. He appeared relatively unscathed. "You are the Russian, Voronov," Kitty said, staring down at him dispassionately. Her only concern was Bernie Ryng.

He gazed at her, surprised to hear the voice of a woman. There was no response. He blinked once, then a second time, turning his head as if unsure of where he was. Flexing his arms, then his legs, he appeared to be checking himself thoroughly. Apparently satisfied, he eased himself into a sitting position, eyeing the weapons trained on him. Then his gaze returned to Kitty. "You know who I am?"

"You have been working with James Grambling," she replied matter-of-factly.

"Ah, Jaimé . . . you know my friend, Jaimé, eh?"

"Where is he? Alive?"

Voronov gestured toward the bow of the ship, where the five-inch gun continued to pump shells at the control station. "As long as that keeps shooting, Jaimé is alive," he said with finality.

"He's in the gun?"

Voronov shrugged. "He's down below . . . but what does it matter? He wanted to hold the ammunition spaces just long enough for his people to blow the locks. Then it doesn't matter. The government will surrender to save the rest of it."

Kitty turned to Wright. "Please, I must get down there. Maybe there's a chance to take him alive. He's a symbol to the people . . . just like the Canal."

Wright led her down the twisted ladders. They followed Ryng's path cautiously, wending their way down through bullet-pocked spaces, stepping around bodies that littered their path. On the forward side of the mess decks, where another ladder led down to the handling area, they could hear sporadic gunfire, then silence.

Wright eased over to the ladder, cautiously peering down before lowering himself to the space where Ryng and his men huddled. "The bridge is secure. Voronov was up there. He told me and the girl that Grambling is the one holed up in there."

"What girl?" Ryng asked. "Not . . . ?" but he already understood . . . too well.

"The one that was with us during the briefing . . . the one from the President's office, Miss Alvarez—"

"You mean Kitty's here . . . on this goddamn ship?" He should have known they'd use her this way.

Wright gestured with his thumb to the level above them. "She's the one that came in on that helo. The President, Ramos, sent her here to try to get their leaders out alive, she said."

Ryng glared angrily as Kitty dropped down from above. "I've been—" she started, touching his arm.

Ryng shook her away. To Wright he said, "Get her out of here! That son of a bitch in there is mine." After the men Ryng had lost, they couldn't deny him this satisfaction.

Kitty persisted. "President Ramos insisted that I try to get him back alive." Even that didn't sound right to her now.

"There's nothing you can do," Ryng answered.

"I can talk to him," she interrupted. "He might still listen to me."

Ryng looked back at her incredulously. Before he could

control himself, his anger rose to the surface. "You think you were so good, then, that you can save your country now?" he blurted out.

There was no purpose in responding. She continued, "I knew him very well . . . long ago, very long ago . . . well before I'd ever heard of a Bernie Ryng, as I once told you. . . ." She paused, then asked, "And how would you do this?" She smiled sadly through the tears that threatened to erupt.

Ryng indicated one of his men who had just finished inserting the detonator in an explosive device. "Simple. Blow the hatch and then . . ." His voice tailed off. "Perhaps the blast will get him. If not, I will. . . ."

The lights flickered, then there was darkness. Emergency battle lanterns snapped on automatically, their beams cutting through the dust and smoke. "That's it," Ryng exclaimed with finality. "They're through the hull. There goes the power to the mount."

Kitty broke the sudden silence. "Is there any way now I can speak to him?" The expression on Ryng's face had softened as the gun ceased firing. It was a moment of triumph—a personal one.

Ryng nodded at the intercom on the bulkhead. He pushed down one of the buttons. "If you want to say something, just depress that switch," he replied gruffly. Quite suddenly the pressure was gone. He felt twinges of regret.

Tentatively she stepped forward. She held the switch down for a moment, but the words would not come. Eventually she found her voice and stuttered, "James . . . James, can you hear me?"

There was silence. Then a hollow static broke the hush as the lever was depressed on the other end. A voice demanded, "Who's that?"

"This is Kitty, James . . . Kitty Alvarez. . . ."

Again there was a prolonged silence. "Kitty, where are you?"

"Right outside."

"Why?"

"Because Ramos asked me to come."

"You can go now."

"He was sure I was the one who could convince you to surrender. . . ."

"Not you . . . not anyone . . ." The words were measured, the tone dull.

"Please. Let me at least talk to you . . . in there . . . out here . . . wherever you want."

"Who's out there with you?"

"Americans."

"That's what I thought." The bitterness seemed to drip through the speaker. "Remember, Kitty? That's what I told you long ago—that when it came down to a people's revolution, the Americans wouldn't let us have it. I told you they'd come in—just like they've done for a hundred years."

"It isn't like you think this time. President Ramos asked them to. James, please, let me talk to you."

"Ramos asked them to, Kitty—not me, not your father, not anyone in the revolution. Remember? Our *golpé* was for the people—"

Kitty interrupted. "The people didn't come out, James. They knew what was happening and they didn't come out . . . they didn't support you. There were too many Cubans, too many Russians—"

"Russians! Where's Voronov?" he snapped.

"He's alive, James. We have him. Please let me explain what Ramos is willing to do." She looked toward Ryng, but he wouldn't look back. There was so much he couldn't understand.

"No, Kitty. Remember—you were the one who turned against me. I loved you and you left. There's no reason to talk now." There was a pause while the lever remained depressed. "You know, my people are going to blow the Pedro Miguel shortly. Then we'll have something to talk about."

"It hasn't been blown yet, James, and I don't think it will. We have people down inside there. If it hasn't been blown yet, I don't think it will go."

"I have my best men down there, Kitty. They were ordered to set everything off if this ship started shooting, no questions asked."

"There are Americans down inside the locks, James, just

like the ones that took this ship. . . ."

There was a dull thud against the hatch from the inside. It was followed by a muted cry of pain and anger. Kitty understood. She'd seen it more than once. Even after all these years Grambling's temper could still get the better of him. She could picture him now massaging the fist he'd slammed against the metal door. "Are you all right, James?" There was no answer. "James?"

"You don't need your Ramos, Kitty. He's just a figurehead. Why don't you just install one of your American friends in the Presidential Palace? That's what they want . . . and they always get what they want . . . and this time"—there was again the sound of his fist slamming against the door—"they've even got you!"

"Come on, Kitty, we've waited too long," said Ryng contemptuously. "We're set now. We'll just blow off the hatch and sweep up whatever's left inside." Bernie Ryng's voice was ugly and unnatural, a part of him she'd never seen. His remark seemed made to no one in particular, although he'd used her name. His eyes saw what was happening around him, but they failed to acknowledge people. He stared right through her. He was jealous, he hated, he understood now there was much more he hadn't been told. This was the Bernie Ryng she had been warned about, by another Bernie Ryng residing within that same human shell, one aware of the man lurking below the surface who now killed as he had been trained, with great skill and no remorse.

She touched Ryng's arm. "It means a great deal to us . . . to President Ramos, who was more of a father to me than my own father . . . but mostly to me, because I once loved James Grambling. That was when I was still a girl. Now I am a woman and I love Bernie Ryng. Do you understand what I'm saying?"

He looked down at the hand resting on his arm. For a moment his eyes softened as he studied her face. She could sense the old Bernie Ryng trying to come back to her. But the memories of all the fine friends who had died in the last hour crowded back, blotting out the lovely, concerned face before him. "One more minute, Kitty, and then I do it my way. I don't intend to lose anyone else." His voice was raw, commanding, anxious for revenge. He wanted to hold her, to explain that the Bernie Ryng she knew really hadn't disappeared. But he couldn't. It would come later.

"James," she called over the intercom. "Please, let me explain, just for a minute. Nothing is what you think it is. Please," her voice pleaded. "Ryng . . . he'll get you out his way—"

"Ryng? Who's that, Kitty? A boyfriend . . . a lover?"

"It makes no difference."

"Thirty seconds," Ryng interrupted.

"So you're sleeping with the Americans now, Kitty," Grambling remarked sarcastically, his tone changing. It remained bitter, but there seemed also a note of finality. "All right, Kitty. You can come in to talk if you want. I'll release the hatch, but everyone out there back against the wall or it's no good. No matter what they try, I'd get some of them. Does everyone understand?"

She looked at Ryng. "I have to . . . please." She saw that he understood, even if he couldn't accept it.

"Only if he keeps the door open," Ryng responded. "It can be hooked back there. If he lets you do that, okay," he added with resignation.

"We want to leave the door hooked open, James. I'll do it. They'll all be back against the wall. Is that all right?"

"That's fine, Kitty," Grambling said. There was now almost a boisterous tone to his voice, as if he'd made up his mind about something and was now pleased with his decision. "Just tell your American friend that I can cause a lot of damage to them before they get me, if they try anything."

"There's no problem, James. Just release the hatch and I'll hook the door open and we can talk." There had been an almost mystical aura to the entire conversation over the intercom, as if two people were talking formally across a desk. They were detached from the real world of the destroyer.

One by one the dogs on the hatch were undone. It swung open, but nothing could be seen inside. Kitty swung the heavy door back and hooked it open. Ryng and his men were in view, their weapons centered on the opening. Kitty was aware they would have fired if Grambling had shown himself. Gingerly, peering inside the handling room, she found

Grambling back against the inner wall, looking directly at her. His arms were folded, a look of benign amusement across his face. He inclined his head slightly, nodding recognition. She climbed slowly over the high coaming, stepping into the middle of the room, remaining in view of the men outside.

Grambling crossed over, looking first down at her, then through the hatch at the people outside. "Which one is Ryng?"

She extended her arm, pointing at Ryng, his back against the bulkhead, automatic rifle under his arm. The men held each others' eyes for a second, each recognizing the hatred within the other. "He is your lover?"

Kitty looked up at Grambling, then out at Ryng. Everything seemed to be in slow motion. Nothing was as it should have been. She could see that each was waiting for the other to make the slightest move. She looked down without saying a word.

Grambling called through the open door. "Were you in that boat off Colón that night?"

Ryng's eyebrows rose, remembering, and he nodded his head. "Yes. You almost killed me."

"We both lost," Grambling said, considering Ryng for a moment. "That was the only time I have ever lost."

"Until now," Ryng responded in a monotone.

"We both do, American. But if I have to lose my country, you have to lose something you love too." His hands fell to his side, exposing the apple-green grenade in his right hand. The pin had already been removed; the handle clanked to the deck as Grambling held it out in his palm. "I have known your Kitty . . . my Kitty . . . for a long time, American. I knew all about you the moment she mentioned your name."

The only movement was from Grambling as he took one more step. Now he stood within inches of Kitty, cradling the grenade in his hand so all could see it clearly. His other hand firmly held Kitty by him. They were transfixed, immobilized by the weapon. Seconds ticked by as eternities until the inevitable became a reality.

Bernie Ryng would always remember the changing expressions of Kitty Alvarez and James Grambling staring at each other before the metal shards ripped their bodies apart. The actual explosion never registered with Ryng. All that he heard was the sound of his own agonized screaming before the candy-colored grenade exploded. The inhuman howl continued even after he had hurled himself through the hatch, not stopping until two of his men succeeded in dragging him off James Grambling. He had been pounding the lifeless bloody head against the deck.

They refused to leave him until he came to his senses. When Ryng explained that he needed to be by himself with the girl, Wright understood. They left him alone until he came out on his own accord.

Inside the Pedro Miguel Locks

Henry Cobb was unable to concentrate on the single, remaining entrance to the chamber. Chunks of concrete would break away behind him, tumbling down the slope of rubble with an unnerving clatter. Resistance seemed lighter now, almost nonexistent. He couldn't be sure at first whether it was due to attrition or simply that the opposition was resigned to the fact that control of the chamber had been taken from them. Cobb had two men furiously disarming the explosives set around the machinery; he and two others were the only men capable of defending the room.

Cobb watched one of his men carefully deactivating a detonator, waiting patiently before he whispered, "How many more?" as if a louder voice would set off the explosive.

The man continued to work cautiously. "Maybe half a dozen," he replied in a normal voice. "Can't tell for sure. Some of these have been armed, and others seem to have been left for later, as if they never really expected or wanted them to go off."

"Any consistency in it?"

"Yeah, there is. The smaller stuff . . . lighter explosive . . . the ones set around the secondary gear were ready to blow on timers. None of the big ones were activated, like they didn't want to take a chance destroying the critical equipment. I think these guys were so sure of themselves that if it came to blowing anything, they'd just damage the insignificant stuff."

Cobb considered that idea. "Perhaps they figured if a couple of bombs went off like that, the government would give in."

The man went back to his work. "Like this one . . . this little generator. It doesn't mean a hell of a lot. And it's set to blow soon. But the heavy stuff, around the bull wheels and the engines that make them turn—those bombs were never set. Hell, they may be just like us. It's easy to make one and set it off. But it's hell to try to disarm. Maybe these guys were so sure of themselves that they didn't want to take the chance of blowing themselves up when they deactivated the big boomers."

It made sense. That may have been why they were so fanatical about getting back in. Cobb didn't know what was happening above, but it appeared the PRA was losing. Since there would always be enough fanatics willing to go back down into this chamber and blow everything apart along with themselves, it all had to be disarmed.

The final attack was made by only three men. They dashed through the entrance behind a barrage of grenades and automatic weapons fire. But by then Cobb and his men had found more than enough time to throw up barriers, and none of them were hit. The last of the three attackers never advanced more than ten yards. Two of the bodies were Russian, Cobb found, and they were each carrying instant detonators. Their objective was to set off as much as they could in a short time. If that had ever happened, the threat would have become a reality.

There was no opposition as Cobb and his four remaining team members mounted the long concrete stairs to the surface at the north end of the Pedro Miguel Locks. When Henry Cobb cautiously pushed open the door that led out onto the Canal wall, he was surprised first that it was so dark. The destroyer was fully illuminated by spotlights set on the eastern side. He saw Wright on the bow with other team members. As his eyes grew more accustomed to the bright lights, Cobb stared in astonishment at the ship's torn superstructure. Ragged shards of metal projected at impossible angles. Sections of

he upper areas, especially the signal bridge, had been battered
›eyond recognition.

What Cobb could not see was a man in a tattered black
ıniform perched on an empty gun case on the far side of the
hip. To the SEAL who guarded him, Paul Voronov appeared
ınconcerned with the activities around him. Moments before,
n almost perfect English, he'd politely requested a cigarette
'rom his guard. His cautious smile, combined with the in-
ıerent politeness of the vanquished, had been carefully prac-
.iced. The SEAL picked a cigarette from his own breast pocket
vith one hand, the other still holding the gun on Voronov's
:hest, and tossed it to the Russian. Then he extracted a pack of
natches and flipped them at the other's feet. When Voronov
ndicated he would toss the matches back, the SEAL shook his
ıead. There was no way he would take that chance.

Paul Voronov smoked dramatically, dragging deeply on the
:igarette, then sucking the smoke down in his lungs in a gesture that would raise his head into the air as he threw his chest
out. With each puff he gauged the distance between himself
and his guard, contemplating the options that remained to
him, if any, and the odds of surviving if he chose one of them.
Time was increasingly against him.

No more than twenty yards away, Wright was hollering to
someone on shore about another light. Voronov monitored
the conversation cautiously, offering no hint that he was at all
involved in what was being said. But he heard the shout from
shore when another spotlight was about to be turned up.
When he saw the first glow of increased light on the guard's
face, followed by the reflection in the man's eyes as the light
came up to full power, he sprang with incredible speed.

The brightness from the shore had indeed drawn the
SEAL's attention, momentarily catching his eye. It was all
Paul Voronov required. There was no plan to do anything
other than escape, no reason to fight with his guard, no need
to wrest the gun away, no purpose in any unnecessary motion.
He hit the SEAL full on, sensing pain in his forearm as he
warded off the butt of the rifle aimed at his head. His other
elbow slammed into the guard's face, knocking him backward. Together they fell against the lifelines. In the dim light
Voronov smashed the guard's head against a stanchion. He

felt the man's grip on his arm relax momentarily. Rather than strike out, Voronov wrenched himself free. He could hear the shouts as he propelled himself over the edge into the blackness. There was no sign of water on the dark side of the ship, no sense of impending security until he hit the surface and felt the warmth of escape surge through his veins.

Voronov dove deep. He thought he heard shots before he hit the water. It was probable that they were firing while he was still in the air. Yet there was no sensation of pain as he stroked deeper, then in the direction of what he was sure was the dark side of the Canal. His lungs ached with the desire for oxygen and he fought with himself to avoid rising to the surface.

All of this had taken place as Henry Cobb peered out at the ship. He called back to the four men waiting just inside and motioned them out. He turned back to the destroyer to see a man in a strange, tattered uniform leaping over the far side of the ship. It was as black on that side as it was bright on this one. He saw Wright run to the opposite side with the others. There was shouting and firing into the night. For a moment Cobb even considered the possibility of pursuit, but he could have cared less at that stage. Their battle was over. Hooking up with Bernie Ryng was foremost in his mind.

On the far side of the Canal, Paul Voronov scrambled up the bank and disappeared into the safety of the jungle. He had never been a prisoner before and he had no intention of remaining one now. Like a cat he was a survivor, and he had many more lives to go.

Havana

Commodore Navarro stood at attention on the pier, a forlorn figure, saluting the flag as each of his ships moved past to their docking space. There were six missile boats, one frigate, and two old submarines; another submarine would tie up in Cienfuegos, and that would represent the remains of his Cuban navy. It had never been an imposing force, but it was capable of protecting the maritime interests of his country—that had been his goal. Navarro had never intended that his ships participate in a war.

He turned disconsolately and ambled slowly up the pier. He must go back to his office and continue the letters he was writing to the families of his fine dead sailors. To his surprise he noticed a familiar black limousine at the head of the pier. Fidel Castro leaned out the window and waved to him to come over.

Navarro's gait had become slower and more labored over the last few days. Castro got out of the car and stood waiting patiently. He understood. When the Commodore approached with a tired salute, the Premier put a comforting arm around his shoulders. "I've been watching too. It's a sad sight . . . very sad." He turned and placed both hands on Navarro's shoulders. "I need you to do me a favor. There is a plane arriving at the airport in an hour from Panama. I want you to meet it. Esteban Alvarez will be aboard. I know nothing of the details, but we have received a cable that he is coming to us. . . ." Castro paused, searching for the proper words. "He was the one who guaranteed so much . . . his people would rise up alongside the PRA. . . ." Castro's voice dropped off almost to a whisper. "I think, for some reason, Ramos has allowed Alvarez to leave and he is sending him to us. Would you meet him at the plane?"

Commodore Navarro nodded wordlessly.

Esteban Alvarez watched the hot cement of José Marti Airport leap up to meet the wheels, relaxing as the plane bounced once before rolling down the runway. A million thoughts had run through his mind on the flight across the Caribbean. He knew Ramos was right—that he would never be allowed to live in his own country. Horacio had guaranteed his life only if he departed immediately for the airport, after insuring that the PRA would put down their arms. It had been a black moment in his life . . . in his country's short life.

Though it was night when he'd left, he had been unable to sleep. The sun shone brightly in Havana now, and he blinked against the glare as he slowly descended the steps from the plane. He would have to find some new clothes soon. He'd left with what was on his back, lucky to be alive.

He saw Commodore Navarro waiting at the foot of the steps. The man looked exhausted, beaten. Alvarez couldn't imagine why anyone was waiting for him. Perhaps Horacio had sent a message ahead, notifying them of his arrival. After what had taken place the past few days, it seemed unlikely that Ramos would have anything to do with the Cubans.

Alvarez extended his hand in greeting as he stepped onto the runway, but he had no time to say the words that he had rehearsed as he came down the steps. There was the initial shock of seeing the gun in Navarro's hand, but that changed to complete understanding as the sound of the first shot registered. Alvarez was hurled backward by the impact. He also sensed the second and the third bullets enter his body. But the final three were never heard or felt.

A muscle began to twitch uncontrollably under his right eye as Commodore Navarro's hand fell to his side. He was unaware of the gun dropping to the ground or of the startled shouts from the people around them. Looking down at Alvarez's body with satisfaction, his lips began to move in a prayer he had learned as a boy. The words were not for himself or the man who lay dead before him. They were for his country, which now faced an entirely different world. He felt no fear of either the Americans or the Russians. His one and only concern was for the defense of his country, a responsibility that he had been trained for longer than he could now remember. In a very short time, this man—Esteban Alvarez— had drawn Cuba, drawn Navarro, into a situation that required that Alvarez's people rise up against their government. But they had not. Now, much of Commodore Navarro's navy lay at the bottom of the Caribbean. The man who was responsible for that lay at his feet.

The Naval Air Station, Oceana, Virginia

Long before Dave Pratt's plane from *America* landed, Tommy Bechtel made sure that he kept his promise. He relayed through the President's military aide that the Admiral needed some time to himself. He would have preferred to ride the carrier into Norfolk but the trip would have been too long.

America had taken two cruise missiles, and one of them had badly damaged her after engine room. When Bechtel learned of the seriousness of the fires, he'd even considered ordering Pratt to shift his flag. But Pratt would have none of that. As long as there was a threat, it was his duty to remain in his flagship. That must have been about the same moment, Bechtel realized later, that Moscow recalled all her bombers. There was no longer a reason to continue. The Canal would remain in Panamanian hands.

As Pratt's plane taxied up the runway at the Oceana Naval Air Station, sailors streamed from the hangars. The pilot followed his orders, parking the plane in the spot designated by ground control. As he surveyed the scene from the plane window, Dave Pratt was satisfied to see that the brass had remained in the background—the greeting party was composed only of sailors in their work uniforms. There were some in dungarees, some in T-shirts covered with grease—mess cooks in aprons, just the way Pratt liked his sailors—nothing fancy at all.

There were no bands, no officers with scrambled eggs on their caps, no civilian officials basking in someone else's glory. Tommy Bechtel had seen to it. A loud cheer reverberated across the runway as the door opened and Pratt stepped out. Until then it had only been a rumor that Admiral Pratt could walk again. The sailor's admiral—the one who belonged to the fleet—was back among them, and they cheered themselves hoarse. Pratt waded into the crowd with a broad smile, shaking every hand he could grasp. Finally a chief petty officer pushed his way through the crowd, shouting an order that only the nearest men could hear. But it was what they were hoping. Pratt had heard it, too, and nodded his assent.

Pratt let them hoist him onto their shoulders. He was escorted by a wave of cheering sailors to the front of the hangar, where he was deposited before a smiling Tommy Bechtel. The enlisted men stepped back, forming a half-moon around the two admirals, and silence followed. Only when Bechtel, his emotions overwhelming him, threw his arms around Pratt in a bear hug, did the cheering start again.

As the two older men moved into the hangar, Henry Cobb stepped out of the shadows. His face was grim, his mouth set in a hard line, but he extended his hand to Pratt.

"Thank God, you're back," said Pratt. He looked about curiously, then back to Cobb. "Bernie—is he all right? I was told he was okay."

"He is. Hardly a scratch. I tried to get him to come back with me." Cobb paused for an instant, searching for the right words. "No . . . no, come to think of it, he's not really all right." Cobb touched a spot over his heart. "He got hurt in a way he's never been hurt before," he added, looking closely at Pratt. "Dave, did Kitty Alvarez work for you?"

"Yes . . . she did," Pratt replied slowly. *So that's what it was!*

"I guess Bernie'll come home when he's ready."